Dark Fire

Julia Bell

Published by Julia Bell, 2024.

DARK FIRE

First edition. November 7, 2024.

ISBN: 979-8227701862

Written by Julia Bell.

Chapter 1: A Dance in the Ashes

The heat from the flames washes over me, a cruel reminder of the chaos that once defined this place. The air is thick, clinging to my skin like a second layer, oppressive and stifling. I glance around, the remnants of what was once a thriving neighborhood standing as silent witnesses to our desperation. A child's shoe, a cracked picture frame, and a half-burnt teddy bear lie scattered amidst the debris—a tragic collage of innocence lost. Each step I take crunches underfoot, a symphony of broken glass and splintered wood that harmonizes with the crackling fire in the distance.

Vincent's grip is surprisingly warm, grounding me in this hellscape. My heart thrums in my chest, not just from fear, but from an unsettling excitement. I can't help but wonder how we arrived at this moment, standing together in the wreckage of our own lives, poised on the edge of a choice that could change everything. The shadows of the buildings loom around us, silent sentinels watching this fragile alliance unfold, their jagged edges illuminated by the flickering flames.

"What are you waiting for?" His voice cuts through the haze, sharp and laden with an urgency that pulls me back to the present. "We don't have time for games, Arielle."

Games. That's rich coming from him. Our encounters have always felt like a battlefield—a twisted chess match where each of us played for keeps. "I'm not the one playing games here, Vincent." I try to inject a note of defiance, but it falters, lost in the din of my racing thoughts. Why had I let my guard down? Why had I taken his hand?

"Then let's not waste any more time." He releases me, moving with a fluid grace that belies the tension radiating from his body. "We need to get to the rendezvous before they realize what's happening."

A surge of adrenaline propels me forward as I follow him, my instincts battling with my trepidation. I know the stakes; this isn't just a simple mission. If we fail, we lose more than our lives—we lose the last shreds of hope for those who remain. The enemy is closing in, and the city, with its crumbling facade and lingering ghosts, feels like a living thing, breathing chaos and despair into our every step.

We weave through the wreckage, navigating the treacherous landscape of ash and sorrow. Each building we pass tells a story, a reminder of the lives that once thrived here, now reduced to whispers carried away by the wind. I catch a glimpse of a child's drawing stuck to a blackened wall, a sun shining brightly above stick figures. I shudder, a lump forming in my throat. It was just yesterday that this neighborhood was filled with laughter, with life. Now, it feels like we are the last two people in a world that has forgotten joy.

"Stay close," Vincent calls over his shoulder, his tone both commanding and oddly protective. Despite my resolve to remain detached, the warmth in his voice ignites a flicker of something within me. I hate that I can feel it—a dangerous thrill that unravels in my stomach. Our history is fraught with conflict, our motives tangled in a web of mistrust. Yet here I am, drawn to him like a moth to flame, knowing full well the risks.

"Are you worried I'll get lost?" I retort, injecting a playful bite into my words, a feeble attempt to lighten the heavy air between us.

His lips curve into a smirk, a brief flash of something unguarded. "No, I'm more worried you'll decide to pick a fight in the middle of an inferno."

Before I can reply, a distant explosion rattles the ground beneath us, the force sending a shower of debris into the air. We both instinctively crouch low, hearts pounding in synchrony, the moment stretching out like an elastic band pulled taut. I steal a glance at him, the way his jaw clenches, the flicker of concern in his eyes. It reminds me that beneath the bravado lies a man grappling with the same fears as I am.

"Come on," he urges, urgency threading through his words as he extends his hand once more. The world around us is a whirlwind of smoke and fire, but the contact feels almost normal, grounding me in the chaos. I take it, and we sprint down the street, the heat of our footsteps melding with the scorching ground.

We duck into an alley, the shadows enveloping us like a protective cloak. It's darker here, the faint smell of charred wood and singed paper swirling in the air. The silence feels heavier, thickening the tension that crackles between us. I turn to him, our faces barely inches apart, and for a moment, time seems to stand still.

"Why are you really doing this?" I ask, my voice barely above a whisper, the question spilling out before I can think better of it. I see the flicker of surprise in his eyes, quickly masked by his trademark stoicism.

"Because I have to," he replies, a vague answer that does little to soothe the gnawing curiosity. "And because, like you, I'm tired of watching everything burn."

His honesty catches me off guard. For all our banter, for all the times we've squared off like gladiators in an arena, I never considered what lay beneath his armor.

"Then let's finish this," I say, surprising myself with the conviction in my voice. My heart races, not just with fear, but with an overwhelming desire to see this through. Together.

As we prepare to leave the safety of the shadows, I steal another glance at Vincent, and in that fleeting moment, I recognize a shared resolve. The world may be crumbling around us, but we have a chance to rewrite our stories amidst the ashes.

The alley feels alive, pulsating with the echoes of our hurried breaths and the distant chaos beyond. Each step we take reverberates through the stillness, our footfalls a counterpoint to the roaring flames just a few blocks away. The air is thick with the smell of smoke and burnt rubber, sharp enough to sting my eyes, yet I find myself craving the adrenaline that courses through my veins, heightening every sense and sharpening my focus. Vincent glances back, his expression a mix of urgency and something I can't quite decipher. Is it concern? Or merely the weight of our shared mission pressing down on him?

"Keep moving," he murmurs, breaking the silence, and I can't help but notice the way his voice low and intense stirs something within me. There's a magnetism that I both loathe and long for, a thread that ties us together in this web of destruction. As we push deeper into the shadows, I catch fleeting glimpses of his face—each flicker of the fire illuminating his strong jaw, the way his dark hair falls into his eyes, obscuring his expression, hinting at layers I am only beginning to peel back.

We emerge from the alley into a street partially untouched by the chaos. The coolness of the night air contrasts sharply with the stifling heat of the burning buildings, invigorating me as I inhale deeply, as if drawing strength from the remnants of what was once a vibrant community. A few homes still stand, their windows flickering with a light that's both comforting and eerie, while others lie in heaps of ash and rubble—a testament to the violence that has befallen us.

"Where do we go from here?" I ask, trying to focus on the task at hand. My mind races with scenarios, with all the places this could lead us. I can almost feel the warmth of hope mingling with the cold dread of failure, creating an unsettling cocktail that I know too well.

Vincent scans the area, his sharp gaze assessing every detail with the precision of a predator on the hunt. "We need to reach the warehouse on 5th Street. It's where the exchange is happening." His voice is steady, and yet, I sense the underlying tension, the weight of something unspoken hanging between us like a thick fog.

"Exchange?" I parry, my tone laced with skepticism. "You make it sound so simple. What exactly are we exchanging? Our lives for a chance at survival?"

His lips twist into a smirk, but it doesn't quite reach his eyes. "Something like that. It's a deal to get us both out of this mess. If we play our cards right." He turns back to face me, his expression earnest. "But we can't afford to get caught. Not now."

A wave of determination courses through me. I might be terrified, but I refuse to let fear dictate my actions. "Then let's not waste time."

We push forward, the tension between us palpable, as if we're both acutely aware of the stakes. As we approach a more deserted section of the street, I spot a flickering neon sign in the distance, its glow bathing everything in a surreal palette of colors—a stark contrast to the charred world surrounding us. It's a dive bar, still standing, its door slightly ajar as though inviting us in for one last drink before the end.

"Vincent, wait," I call out, feeling a strange pull toward the place. "We should check it. We might find something useful."

He hesitates, his brow furrowed as he contemplates the risk. "It could be a trap."

"Or it could be an opportunity. We could use anything that might help us." My tone softens, trying to coax him into seeing the potential rather than the peril.

"Fine," he concedes, and I can see the begrudging respect in his eyes. "But we go in fast, grab what we can, and get out."

The bar is dark and claustrophobic, the air heavy with the scent of stale beer and despair. As we step inside, the quiet is oppressive, broken only by the distant crackling of a radio barely audible above the sound of my heartbeat. The dim lighting reveals dusty tables and chairs strewn haphazardly, memories of laughter and camaraderie long extinguished.

"Over there," Vincent whispers, pointing to the far end where the bar's shelves are partially stocked. We make our way across the room, careful to avoid the creaking floorboards that threaten to betray our presence. I can feel the heat of his body close to mine, an intoxicating blend of danger and familiarity that makes my heart race.

"Look," I say, reaching up to a shelf and grabbing a dusty bottle, its label barely legible. "This might not be what we need, but it could keep our spirits up." I hold it up, trying to inject some levity into the moment.

Vincent snorts softly, shaking his head. "As if we have the luxury of drinking ourselves into oblivion right now."

"Hey, you never know when you'll need to celebrate," I retort, winking at him. "Or drown our sorrows in something stronger than smoke."

A grin breaks through his serious demeanor, and for a moment, we both share a laugh, an unexpected relief in the tension that has enveloped us since we stepped into this chaos. But then I catch movement out of the corner of my eye. My heart sinks as I notice a figure lurking at the entrance, silhouetted against the smoky backdrop of the night.

"Vincent, we're not alone," I whisper urgently, and he tenses, instantly shifting into a defensive stance, his eyes narrowed as he scans the room.

"Stay behind me," he orders, and I comply, though a part of me bristles at the command. I want to be strong, to prove that I can handle whatever comes next. But as the figure steps into the bar, a sense of dread washes over me.

It's a woman, tall and slender, with a mane of fiery red hair that falls around her shoulders like flames licking at the night. She wears a leather jacket, the kind that speaks of past battles, and her eyes—piercing and sharp—lock onto ours with a mixture of curiosity and caution.

"Looks like I'm not the only one playing with fire tonight," she quips, her voice laced with a wry humor that defies the dire circumstances.

Vincent straightens, his posture tense as he sizes her up. "Who are you?" he demands, and I can hear the undercurrent of warning in his tone.

"A friend," she replies, a smirk playing on her lips. "For now. But I suggest you lower your weapons, boys. I'm not here to fight. Just trying to survive like you."

In that moment, I can feel the shifting dynamics in the air, a precarious balance of trust and doubt, and I know that our night is about to become far more complicated than I could have ever imagined.

The woman stands in the doorway, framed by the dim light of the street, her vibrant hair glowing like a beacon against the encroaching darkness. The tension in the room thickens, palpable as we size each other up, a quiet battlefield of unspoken words and potential alliances. Vincent's posture remains defensive, but I can see a flicker of curiosity in his eyes, a crack in his steely demeanor that tells me he's intrigued despite himself.

"Who's your friend?" I ask, trying to break the suffocating silence. "And what do you want?"

"Call me Lyra," she replies, stepping further into the bar, her boots crunching on the broken glass strewn across the floor. "I've been watching you two for a while now. I know you're in deep, and I might just have a way to help you get out."

Vincent shifts slightly, his skepticism evident. "Help us? Why would you do that?"

"Because I know what's at stake," she replies, her gaze unwavering. "I lost my family in this mess, just like you. I'm not looking for trouble, just a chance to make things right."

I catch the softness in her voice, a crack that reveals the heart of a warrior turned survivor. "What do you have in mind?" I ask, cautiously intrigued.

"A plan," she says, and the way her lips curl into a half-smile makes me want to trust her, despite every instinct telling me to be wary. "There's a convoy moving through the area tonight. It's packed with supplies and intel, and if we can hijack it, we'll have what we need to turn the tide."

Vincent's brows furrow, his analytical mind clearly at work. "Hijacking a convoy is risky. You know that."

"Risks are part of the game," she shoots back, a fierce glint in her eyes. "And you're not in a position to refuse. We're all in this together now, whether we like it or not."

A silence stretches between us, the weight of our uncertain alliance settling in. I glance at Vincent, gauging his reaction, and I find a flicker of agreement behind his guarded expression.

"Fine," he relents, his voice low but firm. "But if this goes south, we cut our losses and bail. No heroics."

Lyra nods, a fierce determination shining through. "Deal. We'll meet at the old warehouse by the docks in one hour. It's the perfect spot to set up an ambush."

With the plan set, we make our way out of the bar, the adrenaline coursing through my veins as we step back into the smoky streets. The chaotic world outside feels both familiar and alien, each sound amplified in the charged air. I steal a glance at Vincent, whose expression is inscrutable as we navigate the debris-strewn road.

"Are you really okay with this?" I ask, curiosity bubbling beneath my facade of composure. "Working with her? We've never exactly operated on a team before."

He shoots me a sidelong glance, the tension crackling between us. "Trust is a luxury we can't afford right now. We have a common goal, and that's enough for me."

"Common goal," I repeat, my voice barely a whisper. The phrase stirs something in me—an acknowledgment of how far we've come from our antagonistic encounters. It's strange, being thrust together under such dire circumstances, yet feeling an odd sense of camaraderie blooming amidst the chaos.

As we make our way through the wreckage, I try to shake off the weight of impending doom that hangs over us. The shadows cast by the flickering flames seem to reach for us, threatening to pull us back into the chaos. My heart races, not just with fear, but with the intoxicating mix of uncertainty and exhilaration that comes with the unknown.

We finally reach the warehouse, a hulking structure that looms ominously against the star-studded sky. I can hear the distant sounds of machinery and the low hum of voices, the life within contrasting sharply with the death surrounding us.

"Stay low," Vincent instructs, his voice a quiet whisper as we approach the entrance. "We don't want to alert anyone before we're ready."

We slip inside, the cool air a relief from the oppressive heat outside. The interior is dimly lit, shadows clinging to every corner, creating an atmosphere thick with potential danger. My pulse quickens as I scan the space, taking in the rows of crates stacked high, each one holding the promise of survival—or doom.

Lyra is already there, crouched by a stack of crates, her sharp eyes focused on something in the distance. "They'll be here any minute," she murmurs, her expression serious. "We need to position ourselves."

As we move into position, I feel the weight of our combined fears pressing down. I catch Vincent's eye, and for a moment, the world falls away—just the two of us standing in the middle of this chaos, bound by circumstance and something more profound, something that simmers beneath the surface.

"Whatever happens, we stick together," he says, his voice steady, grounding me amidst the storm.

"Together," I echo, a silent vow that solidifies our tenuous alliance. But as we prepare to make our stand, an unshakeable sense of foreboding settles over me, like a dark cloud ready to burst.

The distant roar of engines grows louder, reverberating through the air, each beat of my heart syncing with the impending chaos. My stomach twists with anxiety, and I glance around, feeling the prickling sensation of eyes watching us.

Suddenly, a shout pierces the air, shattering the tension like glass. "They're here!" Lyra yells, her voice filled with urgency as the sound of heavy footsteps echoes closer.

Vincent moves into action, adrenaline fueling every motion as he readies himself for whatever comes next. I follow suit, heart pounding, pulse racing. As we crouch behind the crates, the atmosphere thickens with anticipation, electric with danger.

But just as we brace for impact, the warehouse door bursts open, a flood of figures pouring inside—armed men, their faces obscured by masks, and their intentions clear. The light from outside floods in, revealing our hiding spot, and my breath catches in my throat.

"Get down!" Vincent shouts, pushing me behind him as chaos erupts. I barely have time to process what's happening before gunfire erupts, bullets ricocheting off the metal walls like angry hornets.

In that moment, as the air fills with the acrid smell of gunpowder and the staccato rhythm of chaos unfolds, I realize that our dance in the ashes has only just begun—and that our survival hinges on choices yet to be made. The stakes have risen higher than I could have ever imagined, and as I glance at Vincent, I see the same realization dawning in his eyes.

We're not just fighting for ourselves anymore; we're fighting for a future that hangs in the balance, teetering on the edge of disaster, and I know—whatever happens next will change everything.

Chapter 2: Between Fire and Flesh

The air crackled with heat, the remnants of a once-vibrant city reduced to ash and shadows. I could barely breathe as we stumbled through the debris, my heart pounding not just from fear but from the sheer intensity of Vincent's presence beside me. His grip on my arm was firm, almost possessive, pulling me along as if he feared the ground beneath us would collapse entirely if I faltered. Each stride we took sent a cloud of soot swirling around us, filling my lungs with the gritty taste of despair, but I didn't dare break free. Something deep inside whispered that I was safer by his side, even as every instinct screamed that he was part of the very threat I had sworn to fight.

Vincent was an enigma wrapped in a leather jacket, the Breed's emblem emblazoned on his back—a mark of the very organization I had dedicated my life to dismantling. Yet here he was, dragging me from the fire, his face set in grim determination. The juxtaposition of his chiseled features and the roughness of his demeanor stirred something unexplainable within me. It wasn't just the heat of our surroundings; it was the heat of a thousand questions swirling in my mind, each one igniting a mix of fear and fascination.

"Keep moving," he said, his voice a low rumble, carrying an edge that made my heart skip. There was no room for softness, no time for hesitation. This was survival, stripped to its bare essentials, and somehow, despite everything, I found comfort in his urgency.

I glanced up at him, searching for answers in the depths of his stormy gray eyes. They held secrets, heavy burdens that made me wonder how someone so entwined with the enemy could be my savior at this moment. "Why are you helping me?" I managed to choke out, my voice barely above a whisper, drowned by the crackling of flames not far behind us.

Vincent shot me a sidelong glance, his jaw tightening as if my question had struck a nerve. "Because it's not your time to go," he replied curtly, his gaze flickering toward the horizon, where the sun struggled to break free of the smoke and chaos. There was a truth in his words, a conviction that caught me off guard. He wasn't just saving me out of obligation or guilt; there was a fierce protectiveness there that made my breath hitch.

As we pushed further into the labyrinth of ruin, I could hear the distant sirens wailing—a chilling reminder that the Breed's reach extended beyond our immediate danger. I had fought against them for so long, my spirit hardened by loss and fueled by a desire for revenge. Yet, in this moment, with Vincent's arm brushing against mine and the scent of charred wood and scorched earth swirling around us, the lines between friend and foe blurred into something I couldn't quite grasp.

A sudden explosion rocked the ground beneath us, sending shards of concrete cascading like hail. I stumbled, instinctively reaching for Vincent, and he caught me, his grip a tether that pulled me back from the edge of panic. "We need to find shelter," he urged, his breath warm against my ear, igniting something within me that I dared not explore.

"Why are you doing this?" I pressed again, needing clarity amidst the chaos, needing to understand the man who held my fate in his hands. I had spent years cultivating a shield around my heart, and here he was, cracking it with each fleeting touch.

"Because there's more at stake here than you realize," he said, his voice softer now, as if we were no longer in the eye of a storm. "I know what the Breed is capable of. I've seen the destruction they leave in their wake." His eyes darkened, shadows flickering across his face as if the memories haunted him. "I'm not the monster you think I am."

I wanted to argue, to tell him that his very affiliation painted him with the same brush as the others. Yet, as we found a momentary refuge in the hollow shell of a collapsed building, I saw the truth in his eyes—a depth of pain that mirrored my own. He had lost something, too; I could sense it in the way his shoulders sagged, in the way he exhaled, as if he were releasing the ghosts that clung to him.

We crouched low in the shadows, the world outside a cacophony of destruction. "What do you know about the Breed?" I asked, my voice steadying as the adrenaline began to wear off, leaving room for the weight of our reality to settle in.

"They're planning something big," Vincent said, his tone grave, as if he were sharing state secrets. "They want to cement their power by taking out the rebel factions once and for all. You're part of that resistance, aren't you?"

I nodded, the familiar surge of loyalty filling me. "We're fighting for a chance at freedom. We can't let them win."

Vincent leaned closer, his presence magnetic, and for a moment, the chaos outside faded into the background. "Then we need to work together," he said, his gaze locking onto mine, an intensity that sent shivers racing down my spine. "I can help you—if you let me."

Trust was a fragile thing, and I felt its delicate strands stretch between us, threatening to snap under the weight of history and betrayal. But as I looked into Vincent's eyes, I recognized a flicker of sincerity, a shared determination that ignited a spark of hope. The world outside may be on fire, but perhaps, just perhaps, this unexpected alliance could be the ember that kindled something new.

The dust settled around us like a shroud, muffling the distant sounds of chaos, leaving only the muted roar of the fire licking at the sky. It was an eerie calm in the aftermath of destruction, a moment caught between breaths. Vincent's presence next to me was both a comfort and a curse, a living contradiction that set my heart racing and my mind whirling. I had spent years learning to navigate the treacherous waters of trust, and yet here I was, teetering on the brink of an unsettling alliance with a man who wore the emblem of my enemy.

"Do you always pull people from the flames?" I asked, trying to inject a note of levity into the heavy atmosphere. My attempt at humor hung awkwardly in the air, but I felt the need to break the tension, to dispel the haunting memories of what had just transpired outside.

Vincent shot me a sidelong glance, a smirk tugging at the corner of his lips. "Only the interesting ones," he replied, his tone teasing, but his eyes still shadowed with concern. For a brief moment, I caught a glimpse of the man beneath the hardened exterior, a flicker of warmth that made my heart leap despite the circumstances.

"Interesting? Or reckless?" I countered, my voice light, but my pulse quickened as I felt the weight of his gaze on me. He held secrets, I was sure of it, and I wondered what kind of truths lay buried beneath his rough demeanor. But before I could delve deeper, he shifted, his expression darkening again.

"We need to find a way out of here," he said, the teasing edge of our banter evaporating. "The Breed won't stop until they find us."

I nodded, the gravity of his words grounding me. My playful facade crumbled, revealing the urgency of our situation. "Where do we go?" I asked, glancing around at the debris-laden landscape, the skeletal remains of buildings casting long shadows in the fading light.

Vincent pushed a piece of concrete aside with a boot, revealing a narrow path that led deeper into the wreckage. "Follow me. There's an old subway entrance not far from here. It'll get us below ground, where they're less likely to find us."

The thought of descending into the darkness made my stomach twist with unease, but there was no time to hesitate. I fell into step behind him, our movements synchronized as we navigated the ruins.

With each step, the world above us felt more distant, as if the weight of the chaos and destruction was slowly being left behind.

As we reached the subway entrance, the air turned cooler, carrying the faint scent of mildew and rust. The darkness swallowed us whole, the dim light from my phone barely piercing the shadows that wrapped around us. My heart raced—not just from fear, but from the electric tension that hung between us, a taut line that pulled tighter with every shared glance.

"Stick close," Vincent instructed, his voice barely above a whisper. The flickering light illuminated the sharp angles of his jaw and the rugged planes of his face, making him look more dangerous than ever. I could feel the unspoken words lingering on my lips, the questions that gnawed at my mind, but the seriousness of our situation made it impossible to voice them.

We moved through the tunnel, the sound of our footsteps echoing off the damp walls. The further we went, the more the silence between us grew, charged with anticipation and uncertainty. I wanted to reach out, to bridge the chasm of confusion between us, but I was tethered by my own fear. "What's your angle, Vincent?" I finally blurted out, breaking the heavy stillness.

He paused, turning to face me, and the flicker of something unreadable passed over his features. "My angle?" he repeated, a hint of amusement lacing his words. "You mean besides saving your life?"

I stepped closer, my heart hammering in my chest. "Yes, besides that. You're a member of the Breed. What's in it for you? Why risk everything to help someone like me?"

He took a deep breath, the tension radiating off him palpable. "Because I've seen what the Breed does to people like us. I was once just like you—fighting for a cause I believed in, blinded by loyalty. But loyalty only gets you so far when the people you trust turn on you." His gaze was fierce, filled with a burning intensity that sent a shiver through me.

I hesitated, the weight of his confession sinking in. "You're saying you've defected?"

"I'm saying I've had enough of their lies," he replied, his voice steady. "I'm done playing their games. Helping you is my way of taking back control."

Control. The word hung between us like a challenge, and I felt an undeniable connection forming, a fragile thread woven from shared pain and rebellion. "What do we do next?" I asked, my voice softer now, the urgency tempered by the realization that we were on the same side after all.

"First, we need to reach the old rebel safe house. It's a few miles from here," he said, motioning me to follow him further into the tunnel. "From there, we can regroup, figure out our next move."

As we walked, the darkness began to feel less threatening and more like a cocoon, a place where the outside chaos couldn't reach us. Vincent moved with confidence, and I found myself drawn to him in a way that both terrified and exhilarated me. In this subterranean world, stripped of the noise and destruction above, I felt the stirrings of something I hadn't anticipated—a fragile trust beginning to take root.

"Just so you know," I said, a playful edge creeping into my tone, "I'm not usually in the habit of following dangerous men into dark tunnels."

Vincent shot me a sideways glance, a half-smile tugging at his lips. "Good thing I'm not your average dangerous man then."

"Or maybe I'm just not that smart," I replied, laughter bubbling up despite the heaviness of our situation.

The sound echoed in the tunnel, and for a moment, it felt like we were just two people sharing a secret, two souls connected in the midst of a world gone mad. The path ahead was uncertain, shrouded in darkness, but as long as Vincent walked beside me, I found a flicker of hope to cling to—an ember that might just ignite into something more than survival.

The tunnel stretched before us like a gaping maw, the walls damp and slick with age, casting a foreboding chill that crept into my bones. Vincent led the way, his figure moving confidently through the shadows, a dark silhouette against the flickering light of my phone. Every step echoed in the narrow confines, a rhythmic reminder of our precarious situation. There was a weight in the air, a pulse of uncertainty that thrummed in tandem with the pounding of my heart.

"Is this where you tell me about your tragic backstory?" I quipped, attempting to cut through the tension with a touch of humor, my voice sounding much too loud in the oppressive silence. "You know, the one that explains how a charming guy like you ended up as a rogue in a militant group?"

Vincent glanced back at me, his expression inscrutable for a moment before a hint of amusement danced in his eyes. "What makes you think it's charming? Maybe I'm just here to keep you from tripping over your own feet."

"Charming and witty, then. I'll take it," I shot back, my spirits lifting at the banter. "But seriously, how did you end up with the Breed? You don't seem the type to blindly follow orders."

He paused, and the flickering light illuminated the shadows on his face, revealing the contours of a man burdened by memories. "I was trying to protect someone," he finally admitted, his voice heavy with the weight of the past. "I thought I could change things from the inside. Turns out, I was just a pawn."

"Like all of us," I replied, a shiver of recognition rippling through me. "I joined the rebellion because I wanted to fight back, not just for myself, but for everyone who's suffered."

Vincent's eyes flickered with understanding, the tension between us shifting, becoming a shared burden rather than a chasm.

"And what if fighting back means working with someone you can't trust?" he asked, his tone serious, his gaze piercing.

"Then I guess we'll have to find a way to earn that trust," I replied, the words feeling more like a challenge than a promise. As we continued deeper into the bowels of the earth, I could sense the duality of our mission: two people caught in a conflict larger than either of us, navigating through alliances that felt both fragile and electrifying.

Suddenly, we heard it—a distant sound, a faint scuffling that cut through the stillness like a knife. My heart dropped, adrenaline spiking through my veins. "Did you hear that?" I whispered, instinctively shifting closer to Vincent.

He nodded, his expression tightening. "Stay behind me."

We pressed onward, our footsteps growing more deliberate as the scuffling escalated into a series of echoing thuds. My mind raced with possibilities, each more alarming than the last. Were we being followed? Had the Breed found us already?

Vincent slowed, his body taut with tension, and I could almost see the gears turning in his head as he strategized our next move. "There's an old maintenance room up ahead. We can hide there until we figure out what's going on."

With a determined nod, I followed him, the flickering light casting eerie shadows on the walls, making the dark corners of the tunnel appear alive with menace. Each heartbeat thudded in my ears, a countdown to the unknown.

As we reached the door to the maintenance room, Vincent turned to me, his expression fierce and protective. "No matter what happens, don't make a sound. If it's them—"

"I know," I interrupted, an unspoken agreement passing between us. Whatever was lurking in the darkness, we would face it together.

He pushed the door open just enough for us to slip inside, the dank air hitting us like a wave. The room was small and cluttered, filled with remnants of a bygone era: rusted tools, broken machinery, and cobwebs that draped over everything like a veil of neglect. We huddled in the corner, the door barely closing behind us, our bodies pressed together in the cramped space.

Time seemed to stretch as we waited, each passing second amplifying the sounds from the tunnel outside. The scuffling grew louder, a rapid rhythm that hinted at something—or someone—closing in. I could feel the heat radiating from Vincent's body, a stark contrast to the cold dread settling in my stomach.

And then, the unmistakable sound of boots echoed against the concrete. My breath caught, and I clutched Vincent's arm, an instinctive reaction to the impending threat. "What if it's them?" I murmured, fear tinging my voice.

"Stay quiet," he whispered, his breath brushing against my ear, sending a jolt of awareness through me. "We'll wait for them to pass."

The noise grew louder, and I strained to hear through the pounding of my heart. Shadows danced under the crack of the door, figures moving with a purpose that sent a chill racing down my spine. I held my breath, acutely aware of Vincent beside me, his presence grounding yet electrifying.

Suddenly, the door creaked slightly as a figure pushed against it, testing our makeshift barricade. I froze, my mind racing with all the ways this could go wrong. "If they find us, we need to—"

Before I could finish my thought, the door swung open, revealing a soldier clad in the Breed's uniform, a menacing smile on his lips. "Well, well, what do we have here?"

Vincent reacted in an instant, pushing me back behind him as he stepped forward, an imposing wall of determination. "You shouldn't have come here."

The soldier laughed, a cruel sound that echoed in the small room. "And why not? You think you can hide from us? You're in our territory now."

I felt a rush of panic as Vincent and the soldier squared off, the tension in the air palpable. "We don't want any trouble," I said, my voice rising in defiance, but fear gnawed at my insides.

"Too late for that, sweetheart," the soldier sneered, raising his weapon.

In that instant, time slowed as I saw the glint of metal, my instincts kicking in as I lunged forward. "Vincent!" I shouted, throwing myself at him just as the soldier pulled the trigger. The world erupted into chaos, and in that moment of blind courage, I realized that there was no going back; the path ahead was shrouded in uncertainty, but one thing was clear: everything was about to change.

Chapter 3: Ghosts of Midnight

The air is thick with tension, a tangible force that seems to swell in the space between us, binding me to Vincent as we slip through the narrow alleyway, each footfall muffled against the cobblestone. My heart beats a frantic rhythm, a reminder of the shadows that whisper secrets just beyond the edges of the light. I can almost hear their murmurings, taunting me with the specters of my past—my sister's laughter that echoes like a phantom in the recesses of my mind, the sweet smell of her vanilla-scented hair, a tether to the innocence I lost so long ago. The night wraps around me, a cloak of sorrow and dread, and I can't shake the feeling that I'm being watched, the eyes of the forgotten ghosts boring into my soul.

"Lynn," Vincent's voice breaks through the haze, steady and unyielding. "If you're going to let those shadows consume you, we're going to have a problem." He says it with a casual arrogance, as if we're discussing the weather rather than my very real fears. There's an underlying current in his words, a challenge that ignites a fire in my chest. I refuse to be intimidated, but the truth is, his presence unnerves me, a double-edged sword of attraction and danger. I can feel the heat radiating from him, a warmth that makes me ache to know him beyond the surface.

"It's not the shadows I fear," I retort, keeping my voice low and steady, masking the tremor that betrays my vulnerability. "It's what they hide." I glance at him, searching his inscrutable expression for a flicker of understanding. But his face is a mask, and I'm left wondering if I'm speaking to a man or a myth.

We reach the door, a weathered slab of wood with iron rivets, half-hidden beneath a tangle of ivy. It creaks open, revealing a dimly lit interior that smells of damp earth and something metallic—perhaps the remnants of fear still clinging to the walls. Vincent steps inside, his silhouette cutting a stark figure against the flickering light of a single bulb hanging from the ceiling. The warmth spills over me like a welcome embrace, but the deeper shadows cast by the corners make my pulse quicken anew.

"Welcome to our little sanctuary," he says, his tone shifting, the sardonic edge replaced by something more genuine. "We've had worse places." He gestures toward a rickety table strewn with papers, the chaos a stark contrast to the crisp order I usually prefer. I hesitate, caught between curiosity and caution, wondering if stepping over the threshold will lead me deeper into the darkness or provide the solace I so desperately need.

As I cross the threshold, the door creaks shut behind me, sealing off the night. The atmosphere inside is charged, heavy with unspoken words and unacknowledged fears. There are others here, faces half-hidden in shadow, each one steeped in their own stories of loss and survival. I take a moment to observe, to absorb the palpable sense of camaraderie among them. They exchange glances, wary yet protective, as if each is acutely aware of the fragility of life in this world.

"Lynn, meet the team," Vincent announces, his voice echoing slightly in the small space. "They're not as terrifying as they look, I promise." There's a hint of a smile on his lips, a brief glimpse of the man beneath the bravado, and my heart does a strange flip. I want to believe him, but trust is a luxury I can't afford.

The first to step forward is a woman with bright blue hair, spiked and defiant, her expression fierce yet inviting. "I'm Nova," she declares, her voice a low, melodic hum that contrasts with her sharp appearance. "And if you're here, it means you've made some interesting choices." She raises an eyebrow, as if gauging my worthiness, and I find myself standing a little taller, ready to defend my presence here.

"Choices are all we have left," I reply, my tone steely. "And sometimes they lead to unexpected alliances." The tension in the air shifts, a subtle acknowledgment of the shared burdens we carry.

The others introduce themselves in quick succession—Finn, a tall man with an easy smile that doesn't quite reach his eyes; Zeke, whose silence speaks volumes; and Tessa, the mother figure of the group, her warmth palpable even in the gloom. Each of them wears their scars like badges of honor, tales of survival etched into their very beings.

"Now that we're all friends," Vincent interjects, an amused glint in his eyes, "let's discuss why you're really here." The shift in his tone sends a shiver down my spine. I sense that beneath his light-hearted banter lies an unyielding seriousness, an unspoken understanding that this is not merely a gathering of misfits but a coalition of those who refuse to be broken by the darkness encroaching on our lives.

I take a deep breath, steeling myself for what's to come. "I need to know about the Breeds," I state, my voice steady despite the tremor of fear coiling in my stomach. "Everything you know."

Silence blankets the room, heavy and oppressive. Vincent's expression hardens, and I can see the flicker of something—fear, perhaps—behind his eyes. It's the first crack in his armor, and I can't help but lean closer, drawn to the intensity of his gaze. "That's a dangerous road you're treading, Lynn," he warns, the playful banter replaced by a seriousness that grips my heart. "And once you step on it, there's no turning back."

"Good," I reply, my voice resolute. "I wasn't planning on retreating."

As the shadows close in, I feel the weight of my decision settle over me, binding me to these strangers—these allies. The night is far from over, and with it, the ghosts of our pasts linger in the corners, waiting for the moment we confront them.

The air inside the shelter vibrates with unspoken tension, the kind that clings to your skin and wraps around your throat like a vice. Vincent leans against the doorframe, arms crossed, the way a gatekeeper might look at a potential intruder. His posture is casual, yet there's an edge in his stance that suggests he's ready to spring into action at a moment's notice. As I survey the space, I catch snippets of conversation, the soft murmur of voices that blend into a backdrop of uneasy camaraderie. A flicker of doubt gnaws at me; this place feels too much like a den of secrets, each person here a thread in a tangled web that I might not be ready to unravel.

"Okay, let's get this over with," Vincent says, his tone cutting through the ambient chatter. "You want to know about the Breeds? I hope you're prepared for some uncomfortable truths." There's a gleam in his eyes, a mix of mischief and challenge, and I can't help but feel that he revels in this—testing my resolve as if it were some game.

I square my shoulders, determination stiffening my spine. "I've faced worse," I shoot back, forcing my voice to remain steady. "What's one more monster in a world full of them?"

He chuckles, a low, rumbling sound that reverberates in the quiet space, and it draws a few glances from the others. "That's the spirit. The Breeds are not your typical adversaries. They don't just lurk in the shadows; they thrive in them. They're creatures of instinct, survivalists in a game where the stakes are life and death. Most people think they're just stories—fairy tales to scare children into behaving." He pauses, letting the weight of his words sink in. "But they're real. They're flesh and blood, and they play by their own rules."

"Like you?" I can't resist the quip, my tongue sharper than I intend. But the truth is, I'm probing, trying to gauge how much of Vincent's bravado is a facade and how much of it is genuine.

He smirks, a flash of white teeth against the backdrop of dim light. "Touché. But there's a difference, Lynn. I'm not hunting the innocent, and I don't bite unless provoked." His eyes narrow slightly, challenging me to dissect the truth behind the bravado. I'm not here for a debate, but something about his candor draws me in, and I can't help but lean a little closer, the air between us charged.

"Why do you care?" The question slips out before I can stop it, raw and unfiltered. "Why are you helping me?"

Vincent's expression shifts, the playful facade crumbling to reveal something more complex—a hint of vulnerability, a shadow of his own burdens. "Because," he says quietly, "I see you. You're not just another scared girl in a dark alley. You're fighting, and that's more than most can say. I admire that."

I feel my breath hitch, his words wrapping around me like a warm blanket against the chill of uncertainty. "Admiration can be a dangerous thing," I retort, though my heart races at the compliment. "Especially when it comes from someone like you."

"Someone like me?" He raises an eyebrow, clearly amused. "Or someone like the creatures we fight against?"

Before I can answer, a loud crash from the back room sends a ripple of alarm through the group. Vincent's posture instantly shifts from casual to alert, and he moves towards the source of the noise with a predatory grace that makes me realize just how dangerous he truly is. The others fall silent, their expressions hardening as they prepare for the unknown.

"What was that?" Nova's voice is sharp, and her blue hair seems to crackle with tension.

"Stay here," Vincent orders, his eyes narrowing as he pushes the door further open, disappearing into the shadows. My instinct screams to follow, but the caution in the eyes of the others holds me back.

"What if it's the Breeds?" Finn whispers, his voice low but urgent. "They could have found us."

"Or it could be something far worse," Zeke adds, the gravity of his words thickening the air.

My heart pounds against my ribcage as I exchange glances with the others, each of us grappling with our own fears. But the flicker of danger ignites a spark of resolve within me. I refuse to be sidelined in this battle. "I'm going after him," I declare, voice firm as steel.

Before anyone can protest, I slip past them, following the faint light into the depths of the shelter. The shadows swallow me, and I tread carefully, every step a silent pledge to myself that I will not be paralyzed by fear. Vincent's silhouette comes into view, his form tense, poised for action as he peers into a small room where flickering shadows dance ominously on the walls.

"Lynn," he snaps, his voice low and urgent, a warning that brushes against my skin like a cold wind. "What are you doing here?"

"I'm not hiding," I respond, meeting his gaze with defiance. "And neither should you. What's in there?"

With a slight nod, he pushes the door open wider, and together we step into the dim light, revealing a chaotic scene. Scattered papers flutter like frightened birds, and a metallic scent fills the air, sharper than before. A figure sprawls on the floor, their form obscured in the murky light, and my heart sinks at the sight.

Vincent moves forward, his instincts sharp and alert. "Tessa!" he shouts, his voice cutting through the haze. I rush to his side, and together we kneel beside the fallen figure, dread pooling in my stomach.

Tessa's eyes flutter open, confusion swirling in their depths. "I... I'm fine," she murmurs, but the blood trickling from a gash on her forehead tells a different story. "I was looking for supplies..."

"What happened?" I demand, urgency pricking my skin.

"Ambush," she gasps, gripping my wrist with surprising strength. "They knew we were here."

A cold wave of realization washes over me, the implications hanging heavy in the air. This was no random attack; someone had betrayed us, and the shadows were growing deeper. I glance at Vincent, and for the first time, I see a flicker of fear mirrored in his eyes.

"Get her to safety," he orders, rising to his feet, the tension in his body coiling tight like a spring. "I'll secure the perimeter."

"No," I argue, my voice firm. "I'm not staying behind. If there's danger, I'm in this with you."

He hesitates, and in that moment, I see the conflict etched across his face—an internal struggle that twists my heart. "Lynn—"

"No more arguments. I'm done being afraid. If you're fighting, I'm fighting too."

His gaze pierces mine, searching for something—trust, perhaps—but all I can offer is my resolve. The walls around us seem to close in, the night thickening with the promise of danger. I feel the heat of his frustration, but as he turns to face the unknown together, I know I'm in this for good. We are bound now by the ghosts of our pasts and the uncertain future that waits just beyond the shadows.

The air is electric as Vincent and I prepare to face whatever lies beyond the confines of the shelter. Tessa's injury is a stark reminder that danger is no longer lurking in the shadows; it's at our doorstep, knocking with urgency. I glance at her, gauging her strength as she leans against the wall, her face pale yet fierce.

"We need to get her to safety," I insist, the weight of responsibility pressing on my shoulders.

"Safety?" Vincent echoes, a hint of incredulity in his voice. "There's no safe place when the Breeds are hunting you."

"Well, then let's give them a reason to think twice," I counter, a fire igniting in my belly. "They've already come for us once. I'm not waiting for them to strike again."

His expression flickers between admiration and exasperation. "You're reckless, Lynn. That could get you killed."

"Better reckless than a sitting duck," I shoot back, and I can see the corner of his mouth twitch in reluctant amusement. It's a small victory, a moment of shared understanding amidst the chaos that surrounds us.

Nova approaches, her blue hair a stark contrast against the drab walls, determination radiating from her. "We can't stay here. We have to move, now. If they found Tessa, they'll find us."

Vincent nods, and there's a resoluteness in his demeanor that bolsters my resolve. "Alright. We need to split up. Nova and Tessa will head to the secondary hideout. Zeke, you're with me."

The plan comes together quickly, the urgency of our situation propelling us forward. I watch as Tessa steadies herself, her fierce spirit shining through the pain etched across her features. "You're coming with us, Lynn," she insists, her voice firm despite the tremor.

"I can't," I reply, the weight of the decision heavy on my heart. "I need to know what we're up against. I have to help."

"No one fights alone," Nova interjects, her voice a low growl. "If we're all in this, then we're all in this together."

Before I can protest, Vincent's hand closes around my wrist, grounding me. "You can't save everyone, Lynn. We need to be smart about this."

His grip is firm but not painful, a tether to sanity in the chaos swirling around us. I feel the warmth of his hand, a reminder that even in the darkest moments, there's a flicker of connection. "You're right," I say, the admission tasting bittersweet on my tongue. "But I won't be left behind."

His eyes soften, and for a moment, I think I see a flicker of something in the depths—an acknowledgment of shared pain, perhaps, or maybe just the weight of our choices. "Then let's make it count," he says, his voice low and steady.

We gather our supplies quickly, the atmosphere heavy with anticipation. The air buzzes with a sense of urgency as we slip out the back door, the cool night enveloping us like a shroud. Vincent leads the way, his instincts honed to a razor's edge, and I stay close, hyper-aware of every sound—the rustle of leaves, the distant scuffle of something in the dark.

"Keep your eyes peeled," he murmurs as we navigate the alleyways, his voice barely above a whisper. "The Breeds are clever. They won't attack where we expect."

"Great. Just what I wanted to hear," I mutter, the irony not lost on me.

"What's your plan if we run into them?" Vincent asks, a hint of challenge in his tone.

"Uh, distract them with my dazzling personality?" I shoot back, unable to resist the urge to inject humor into the tension.

He glances back at me, a smile ghosting his lips. "I'm not sure that'll work, but I'm willing to test it."

We round a corner, and I freeze, my heart racing as the shadows seem to shift, coalescing into something more tangible. "Did you see that?" I whisper, pointing toward the darkness ahead.

Vincent nods, his expression hardening. "Stay close."

As we move forward, the shadows deepen, morphing into shapes that pulse with a life of their own. I strain my eyes, trying to discern if it's merely my imagination or if danger truly lurks ahead. The adrenaline surges, propelling me forward despite the fear curling in my stomach.

Then, in an instant, the figures emerge—three Breeds, their eyes glowing like predatory cats in the dark, their forms rippling with muscle and menace. A low growl rumbles from one, and my breath catches, a primal instinct kicking in.

"Run!" Vincent shouts, and before I can react, he's charging toward the nearest one, fists clenched and ready to fight.

"Vincent, no!" I scream, my heart racing as I feel the weight of panic begin to engulf me. But he's already engaged, throwing punches with a speed and precision that takes my breath away.

I glance at the other two Breeds, their attention shifting from Vincent to me. A chill races down my spine as I feel the predatory glint in their eyes, and I know I can't stay. I pivot, taking off in the opposite direction, heart pounding in my ears, adrenaline coursing through my veins.

"Lynn, get back!" Vincent's voice carries over the chaos, a mix of authority and concern that pushes me to move faster.

The alley stretches out before me, a winding maze that threatens to swallow me whole. My thoughts race alongside my feet as I dodge crates and debris, panic fueling my desperation. I can hear the sounds of the fight behind me—the heavy thud of bodies hitting the ground, the visceral growl of the Breeds as they engage with Vincent.

Then I spot a narrow passageway to my left, and without thinking, I dart into it, praying it will lead me to safety. The walls close in around me, shadows dancing ominously, and I can't shake the feeling that I'm being drawn deeper into their trap.

I push forward, heart racing, when suddenly the ground shifts beneath me—a loose cobblestone giving way, and I stumble, barely catching myself on the wall. My breath comes in sharp gasps, the air thickening with dread. As I straighten, I turn to retrace my steps, hoping to find Vincent, but a low growl resonates from the darkness ahead, stopping me in my tracks.

"Lynn," a voice calls, but it's not Vincent's. It's deeper, more guttural, and it sends a shiver down my spine.

"Who's there?" I call out, my voice trembling despite my attempt to sound steady.

A figure emerges from the shadows, taller and broader than Vincent, eyes glinting with an otherworldly light that makes my blood run cold. The air grows heavy with menace, and I realize that I've walked right into the lion's den.

"Welcome to your end, little girl," it snarls, baring teeth that gleam with an unsettling sharpness.

And just like that, as the shadows envelop me, the darkness takes on a life of its own, leaving me suspended between fear and defiance, a cliffhanger I never saw coming.

Chapter 4: Threads of Darkness

The city pulsated beneath us, a living organism teeming with secrets and shadows. Each street corner held whispers of forgotten stories, each alley bore the weight of choices long made, and somewhere in this labyrinth, something stirred—a darkness that promised chaos. Vincent stood across from me, his silhouette sharp against the dim glow of the flickering streetlight, the atmosphere thick with unspoken words. The tension crackled like static in the air, leaving me both unsettled and strangely invigorated.

I glanced down at the map spread across the rickety table, its corners curling with age and neglect. Dotted lines crisscrossed through the heart of the city, leading to locations marked with ominous symbols. My finger traced the most prominent, a jagged mark resembling a broken key. "This is where we start," I declared, my voice steady, masking the flutter of uncertainty within. I refused to let him see how much I relied on the illusion of control.

Vincent leaned closer, the scent of cedar and something deeper—perhaps danger—filling the space between us. "And you really think the Breed will lead us to whatever they're after?" His words dripped with skepticism, but his eyes flickered with something else—curiosity, maybe even desperation. "They're not exactly known for sharing their toys."

"Neither am I," I shot back, unable to keep the edge from my voice. There was a fire in me, a wild spark that fought against the creeping chill of fear. "But if we're going to survive this, we need to play their game."

"Play their game?" he echoed, amusement lacing his tone. "I'd prefer to burn it to the ground." His laughter was low, dangerous, and yet somehow inviting, a reminder that I was standing on the precipice of something thrilling and terrifying.

"Then let's just say we'll set fire to the pieces we don't need," I replied, my own smirk breaking through. The banter felt like a lifeline, a thin thread binding us together in this chaos. I needed him, this enigmatic man with a sharp tongue and an even sharper mind. Beneath that tough exterior lay a darkness that matched my own, and while I couldn't decipher all of his motives, I sensed a shared understanding—a silent agreement that neither of us wanted to voice.

He tilted his head, assessing me with those stormy gray eyes, searching for weaknesses. I held his gaze, the intensity building like a charged storm overhead. "You think you're ready for this?" His challenge hung heavy, but beneath it, I caught a glimmer of respect. "What if the Breed is after more than just some relic? What if they want you?"

I opened my mouth to respond, but the weight of his words crashed into me. It wasn't merely an idle threat; there was truth lurking within, and I felt it settle in the pit of my stomach. "You think they want me? For what?" I barely managed to keep my voice steady, though my heart raced with the possibilities—each one more terrifying than the last.

"Maybe you're the key," he said, his voice dropping to a conspiratorial whisper. "Or maybe you're the bait."

A shiver crept down my spine, not entirely from fear. The idea of being hunted sent an exhilarating thrill through my veins. I wanted to protest, to declare that I was no one's pawn, but deep down, I recognized the truth in his words. "I won't be used," I stated firmly, the conviction in my voice a defiant armor.

"Good," he replied, a hint of a smile dancing on his lips. "Because neither will I. So let's figure this out together."

Together. The word resonated like a promise, laced with uncertainty. I didn't know how far we could trust each other, but the stakes were rising, and the city's heart seemed to pulse in time with my own.

We set to work, our hands moving in tandem as we plotted routes through the city that would take us away from the mundane and toward the extraordinary. As we marked locations, our conversation flowed naturally, punctuated by laughter and the occasional sharp retort that filled the air with a crackling energy. Each laugh forged a bond, an understanding that we were two unwilling partners facing a storm neither of us could escape.

But beneath the playful exchanges lay an undercurrent of tension, an invisible thread that threatened to snap at any moment. Vincent was no ordinary ally. He was a storm wrapped in flesh, and with each passing hour, I felt drawn to him, the magnetic pull of attraction clashing with the pragmatism I fought to maintain.

As dusk settled over the city, wrapping it in a shroud of darkness, our conversation drifted toward deeper matters—the origins of the Breed, the power they sought, and the looming threat they posed. Each revelation ignited a sense of urgency within me, fueling a determination to uncover the truth.

"Tell me, Vincent," I began, keeping my voice steady despite the tempest brewing inside me. "What do you really know about them?"

His expression shifted, the playful mask slipping to reveal a flicker of something darker. "More than I'd like. They're not just a faction; they're a force. And whatever it is they're after, it won't end well for anyone who gets in their way." His gaze bore into mine, intense and fierce. "We need to be careful."

I nodded, absorbing his warning, but the fire within me blazed brighter. "Careful is good, but we can't just wait for them to come to us. We have to go out there, find out what they want, and take it from them first."

"Bravery or recklessness?" he countered, raising an eyebrow.

I smirked, relishing the challenge. "A bit of both. Besides, what's life without a little danger?"

His chuckle echoed in the darkened room, filling the space with warmth amidst the encroaching chill of uncertainty. "You've got a point there, Lynn. But remember, it's not just our lives at stake anymore."

As I leaned over the map, the city stretching before us like a tantalizing puzzle waiting to be solved, I felt the weight of the world upon my shoulders. The darkness was rising, and with it came the thrill of the chase. Together, we would navigate this treacherous landscape, two unlikely allies entwined in a web of intrigue, danger, and unexpected passion. The city's heartbeat synced with my own as I met Vincent's gaze, knowing that whatever lay ahead, I wouldn't face it alone.

The air crackled with anticipation as we poured over the map, tracing the lines that wound through the city like veins carrying blood to a heart that beat too slowly for comfort. Each mark on the parchment was a potential point of conflict, a reminder that every choice could spiral into something monumental. I could feel the weight of our shared mission hanging over us, a tension that was almost palpable, vibrating with unspoken fears and nascent hope.

"Look at this," I said, tapping a spot near the river's edge, where the ink smudged slightly—a remnant of weathered storms that had washed over the city. "If the Breed is as desperate as you say, they'll be drawn to this location. There's a cavern beneath the old mill that's rumored to be connected to the city's water supply. It could be a perfect hiding place for whatever they're after."

Vincent's brow furrowed, and I felt a spark of satisfaction at drawing him in. "You think they'd risk exposing themselves by going there?" He crossed his arms, a gesture that exuded skepticism but also a hint of intrigue. "The mill is crawling with locals, not to mention the police. They'd be signing their own death warrant."

"Or maybe they're banking on the chaos of the crowd," I countered, relishing the debate. "With enough noise, they could slip in and out unnoticed. And if they're after something powerful, they might be willing to take that risk."

His gaze softened for a moment, revealing a flicker of respect, or perhaps admiration. "You've thought this through. I like that." The compliment caught me off guard, sending a warmth radiating through my chest, which I swiftly masked with a playful smirk.

"I'm just trying to keep up with your charm and good looks. It's hard work," I teased, feigning exhaustion as I slumped back into my chair, earning a chuckle from him that filled the room with an unexpected levity.

"Don't let it go to your head. We both know I'm much more than just a pretty face." He leaned forward, a glint of mischief in his eyes. "Besides, if we're doing this right, my looks will be the least of our worries."

The laughter faded, replaced by the weight of reality settling back in. As the shadows lengthened outside the dimly lit room, I could sense the world beyond us pulsing with danger. "So, what's our plan?" I asked, my tone shifting to match the gravity of our situation.

Vincent leaned over the map again, his fingers dancing over the lines as if coaxing the answers to reveal themselves. "We need intel. We can't just walk into a den of wolves without knowing what we're up against. I have a contact, someone who might have eyes on the Breed."

"Great. Let's meet them," I suggested, eager to take action. "What's the worst that could happen? I get devoured by a pack of vampires while you stand there looking pretty?"

He smirked, but there was a flicker of unease beneath it. "I was thinking more along the lines of betrayal, but sure, let's go with your version."

With the plan taking shape, the night took on a life of its own. We gathered our things—an assortment of flashlights, a couple of old pistols Vincent had procured from who-knows-where, and a sense of purpose that electrified the air between us. The thrill of danger twisted my stomach into knots, a heady mix of fear and excitement, each knot tightening with every step we took toward the unknown.

As we stepped outside, the cool night air wrapped around us like a comforting blanket, a stark contrast to the tension simmering within. The streets were quieter now, the city exhaling a sigh of resignation as it settled into slumber. The flickering neon signs overhead cast a kaleidoscope of colors on the pavement, creating a strange juxtaposition of beauty against the darkness looming ahead.

Vincent walked beside me, our strides syncing in an unspoken rhythm. "You know," he said, breaking the silence, "this could end very badly. We're diving headfirst into something far beyond our control."

"Which is exactly why it's exciting," I replied, the words tumbling out before I could catch them. "If I wanted a quiet life, I'd have stayed in the suburbs knitting sweaters for my cats."

"Ah, the joys of a domestic life," he mused, his voice tinged with humor. "But you know, you might make a great cat lady. I can already picture you surrounded by dozens of them, plotting world domination."

"World domination, or at least a nice cozy living room. I can see the appeal," I admitted, smiling at the image. "But for now, I'd much rather take down a clandestine group of supernatural beings. That sounds much more fun, don't you think?"

"Fun is one way to put it." His gaze turned serious as we approached a dimly lit bar tucked away in a side alley, its entrance flanked by flickering bulbs that barely illuminated the wooden door. "Just remember, once we go in, there's no turning back."

I took a breath, feeling the gravity of his words sink in. "I'm ready," I said, hoping the confidence in my voice masked the unease curling in my stomach. We shared a look, a moment suspended in time where the weight of our choices loomed large, and then we pushed through the door.

Inside, the atmosphere was thick with the scent of cheap whiskey and lingering smoke, the low hum of conversation blending with the clink of glasses. A piano in the corner played a haunting melody, the notes wrapping around us like a spell. I scanned the room, taking in the assortment of patrons—shadows huddled in booths, their faces half-lit by the dim overhead lights, eyes darting like trapped animals.

Vincent led me to a table in the back, where a figure sat alone, their face obscured by a wide-brimmed hat. "There he is," he said, his voice a low murmur. "Stay close, and let me do the talking."

As we approached, my heart raced, not just from the thrill of the unknown, but from the undeniable connection sparking between us. The mystery deepened, swirling around us like the smoke that curled from the cigarette held between the figure's fingers. In that moment, I realized that whatever lay ahead, I had stepped into a world far darker and more enchanting than I could have imagined—a world where secrets lay just beneath the surface, waiting for the right moment to emerge. And I was determined to uncover them, no matter the cost.

The figure at the table shifted slightly, revealing a pair of piercing blue eyes that seemed to hold the weight of countless secrets. As I took in the details of our contact—his thin frame draped in a leather jacket that looked like it had seen better days and the cigarette smoldering in the ashtray—I felt the thrill of anticipation mix with the heavy scent of tobacco. This was no ordinary meeting; the stakes were higher than I'd ever faced before.

"Vincent," the man said, his voice low and gravelly, an undertone of familiarity threading through his words. "You've brought a friend."

"More like a partner," I interjected, forcing confidence into my tone. I took a seat across from him, leaning forward slightly. "I'm Lynn. I hear you might have information about the Breed."

He studied me for a moment, the smoke curling around his fingers as if it were alive. "I don't usually share my intel with just anyone, you know." His eyes narrowed, appraising, weighing the truth of my intentions against the backdrop of our dangerous alliance.

"Good thing I'm not just anyone," I shot back, matching his gaze with defiance. I could feel Vincent's presence at my side, a steadying force, but this was my moment. "What do you know?"

He took a slow drag of his cigarette, exhaling a cloud that hung heavy in the air. "The Breed is restless. They've been moving more aggressively lately, which means they're close to finding whatever it is they seek. I heard whispers about a ritual—something tied to the city's underground."

"A ritual?" Vincent leaned in, intrigued. "What kind of ritual?"

"Something dark," the man replied, his expression grave. "It's not just about power; it's about control. They want to harness the city's very essence. If they succeed, it could tip the balance in their favor."

A chill ran through me at his words. The essence of the city? That sounded ominous. "Where can we find them?" I pressed, urgency spurring me forward.

He looked between us, weighing his options. "There's an old church near the outskirts. They've been using it as a meeting place. You might be able to catch them off guard if you move quickly."

Vincent exchanged a glance with me, a silent agreement passing between us. "And what's your stake in all this?" he asked, suspicion lacing his tone.

The man smirked, the flickering light casting shadows across his face. "Let's just say I have my reasons for wanting the Breed to fail. They've crossed me once too often, and I'm not the type to let that go."

"Fair enough," I said, feeling a rush of adrenaline. "We'll do this, but we need a way to make sure we're not walking into a trap."

"Trust me, it's not a trap." He waved his hand dismissively, but the flicker in his eyes told me otherwise. "Just be prepared. The Breed doesn't play nice, and they won't hesitate to eliminate anyone who gets in their way, especially if they think you're a threat."

With a nod of understanding, Vincent stood up, the tension radiating from him palpable as he turned to me. "Are you ready for this? It's going to get dangerous."

"I've been ready," I asserted, fire igniting within me. "Let's stop talking and start moving."

We pushed through the bar's heavy door, the cool night air hitting us like a wave of clarity. The streets were dim, but the moon cast a silver glow that illuminated our path. As we hurried along the cobblestone streets, Vincent kept pace beside me, his presence reassuring amidst the uncertainty.

"Have you ever considered what happens if we fail?" he asked, his voice steady but laced with an edge of vulnerability.

"I refuse to think about failure," I shot back, though doubt crept into the corners of my mind. "The Breed is counting on fear, and if we let that take hold, they win. We can't give them that power."

"Spoken like a true warrior." He flashed a wry smile, and for a fleeting moment, the weight of our situation lightened. "But just remember, the line between bravery and foolishness can be razor-thin."

I chuckled, shaking my head. "Good thing I'm wearing my sturdy shoes tonight. I'll need them for the dance with danger."

He laughed softly, a sound that felt oddly comforting. But as we approached the old church, the air shifted. The oppressive silence enveloped us, wrapping around us like a shroud. We paused at the entrance, the heavy wooden door looming before us like a guardian of the secrets hidden within.

"Are you ready?" Vincent whispered, his voice barely rising above the wind that rustled through the trees nearby.

"Let's do this," I replied, my heart racing with both trepidation and exhilaration. With a firm push, I opened the door, the creak echoing ominously in the stillness.

The interior was dimly lit, candles flickering on the altar, casting dancing shadows that flickered like specters against the stone walls. My senses heightened as I stepped inside, every instinct screaming that we were not alone.

"Stay close," Vincent murmured, his hand brushing mine, a fleeting contact that sent a jolt of energy through me. I could feel his tension, the awareness that we were stepping into the lion's den.

We crept deeper into the church, the air thick with the scent of incense and something else—a metallic tang that made the hair on the back of my neck stand on end. In the flickering light, I caught sight of figures gathered in a circle, their faces obscured by shadows, their voices low and conspiratorial.

"Are they here?" one voice asked, hushed and urgent, sending a wave of dread coursing through me.

"No, but they'll come. They have to," another replied, the tension in the air palpable. "We can't let them interfere with the ritual."

"Then we need to be ready. They won't get the chance." The words hung in the air, a chilling reminder of the threat we faced.

I exchanged a glance with Vincent, my heart racing as the weight of our situation pressed down upon me. This was it—the moment we had been racing toward, the confrontation we could not avoid. I took a breath, feeling the adrenaline spike as we prepared to step into the fray.

But before we could move, a loud crash echoed from the back of the church, the sound reverberating through the space like a gunshot. The gathered figures turned, their attention snapping toward us, eyes gleaming with a predatory intensity.

I felt a surge of panic, adrenaline rushing through me like wildfire. "We're not alone," I whispered, heart pounding in my chest.

Vincent gripped my arm, his voice low and fierce. "We need to get out of here. Now."

But before we could retreat, the air shimmered, and the shadows began to twist and move, revealing themselves as the Breed, their eyes glinting with a hungry anticipation that sent chills racing down my spine. The realization hit me with brutal force—we had walked right into their trap.

"Lynn," Vincent said urgently, but I was already moving, instincts kicking in as I spun to face our attackers, ready to fight against the dark tide closing in on us. The energy in the room shifted, the air thickening with tension as we stood on the precipice of chaos, and I knew then that this was only the beginning. The hunt was on, and we were the prey.

Chapter 5: The Price of Silence

The corridors wound like serpents, each twist and turn a calculated risk that whispered secrets I was not yet ready to confront. The air was thick with the scent of stale metal and something sharper, more acrid, as if the very walls were steeped in the tension of lives lived in the shadows. I could feel Vincent's presence beside me, a steady force that both anchored and unnerved me. He moved with a confidence that made my pulse race, his quiet knowledge of this clandestine world both disarming and exhilarating. I hadn't expected to feel this way—vulnerable, yes, but also inexplicably drawn to him.

As we pressed deeper into the heart of the Breed's base, my senses heightened, every sound amplified, every flicker of movement sending my heart into a frenetic dance. The low hum of machinery throbbed in the background, punctuated by the distant echo of footsteps, a reminder that we were not alone in this metallic labyrinth. With every step, the stakes escalated; my heart beat louder, each thud a reminder of our purpose and the risks we faced. I had trained for this mission, but the reality was far more visceral than any simulation.

"Lynn," Vincent whispered, breaking the silence with a tone that sent shivers down my spine. His breath was warm against my ear, and I struggled to focus on his words rather than the intoxicating closeness between us. "We're approaching the main operations room. I need you to stay alert."

I nodded, though the action felt absurdly inadequate. Alert was a concept that seemed to slip through my fingers like sand. The way he spoke my name—low and urgent—made it impossible to ignore the tension building between us. Each moment we shared in this claustrophobic space felt like a revelation, layers of unspoken feelings intertwining with the adrenaline coursing through my veins.

A sudden noise jolted me from my thoughts, the unmistakable sound of boots striking the ground in a rhythmic march. Vincent's hand shot out, gripping my wrist with a fierce urgency that sent a spark through my skin. He pulled me into the narrow recess of a doorway, the world outside narrowing to a pinprick of light. My heart raced, the thrum of fear laced with an unfamiliar thrill as I found myself pressed against him, our bodies a tangle of limbs and barely restrained breath.

"Just breathe," he murmured, his voice low, almost intimate. His proximity was disarming, the heat radiating from him a stark contrast to the chill of the corridor. I could feel the rapid rise and fall of his chest, and for a heartbeat, the world outside faded away. It was just us, suspended in time, caught in a web of unspoken words and electric tension.

The footsteps grew louder, an unwelcome reminder of the urgency of our mission. I shifted slightly, trying to adjust the precarious balance between us, but his grip tightened, keeping me anchored in place. I looked up, meeting his gaze—an intense blue that flickered with something unreadable. Was it fear? Desire? Both? The question hung in the air, heavy with unvoiced possibility.

"Do you trust me?" he asked suddenly, breaking the spell. The question was simple, yet the weight behind it felt monumental. I opened my mouth, the words swirling in my mind, but before I could speak, the door creaked slightly, and the footsteps stopped just outside.

"Shit," I hissed, instinctively pressing closer to him, as if that could somehow shield us from discovery.

Vincent's eyes flickered with a mix of urgency and determination. "Stay quiet. If they find us here—" His voice trailed off, leaving the implication hanging like a noose.

I nodded, the gravity of the situation crashing down. The danger wasn't just physical; it was emotional, too. I had never expected to find myself in this predicament, feeling so utterly alive yet so perilously close to the edge. If we survived this, would I be able to look him in the eye again without thinking of the warmth of his breath against my skin? Or the way he had held me, not just as a partner in danger, but something deeper—something I couldn't yet articulate?

The door rattled, a key turning in the lock, and the tension in the air crackled like a storm ready to unleash its fury. My heart raced as I bit down on my lower lip, the taste of iron mixing with the adrenaline coursing through my veins. Would they find us here, caught in this fraught moment? I could feel the inevitability of it pressing down on me like a physical weight, and I forced myself to breathe, to remain steady.

Just then, the door swung open, revealing a shadowy figure framed in the harsh light of the corridor beyond. I held my breath, and Vincent's grip on me intensified, a silent reassurance that somehow we would navigate this perilous moment together. The figure stepped inside, scanning the room, and I could feel the air grow thick with uncertainty.

"Anyone in here?" the guard barked, his voice rough and demanding. My heart stuttered as I locked eyes with Vincent, the unsaid words between us swirling like smoke in the dim light. Would we be caught? Would this strange connection we had discovered in the shadows be severed before it had truly begun?

"Not if we can help it," Vincent muttered under his breath, his gaze unwavering as he assessed the threat before us. My pulse raced, caught between the thrill of danger and the undeniable pull of a bond that felt forged in fire. Whatever happened next would change everything, and as I stood there, heart pounding, I realized that I was ready to confront whatever came our way, as long as Vincent was by my side.

The guard stepped into the small room, his posture rigid, eyes scanning every crevice as if he could pluck us from the shadows with a single glance. I held my breath, aware that a single misstep could unravel everything. Vincent's grip tightened around my wrist, an unspoken promise that we would navigate this together, even as the world outside this cramped sanctuary felt poised on the brink of chaos.

"Come on, we're not running a nursery here!" the guard barked, shuffling further into the room, his boots echoing against the cold, hard floor. It was clear he expected to find something—someone—hiding in the corners, and my heart raced with the desperate desire to remain unseen.

"What do we do?" I whispered, my voice barely escaping my lips, trembling with a mixture of fear and exhilaration.

Vincent's eyes locked onto mine, a storm of determination behind them. "We wait," he murmured, the heat of his breath brushing against my cheek, igniting a flicker of courage deep within me. I could feel the pulse of his heartbeat, steady and strong, grounding me in a moment that felt surreal.

"Wait?" I whispered incredulously, unable to mask my disbelief. "You realize waiting in a corner isn't exactly the hallmark of a master plan?"

"Patience, Lynn," he replied, a wry smile tugging at the corners of his mouth, transforming the tension into something almost playful. "I promise, I'll come up with something." His confidence was infectious, a spark that pushed back the shadows looming over us. It reminded me that while fear can paralyze, courage often thrives in the unlikeliest of places.

Just then, the guard's flashlight beam swept across the room, a glowing predator hunting for prey. My breath hitched, and I pressed my back harder against the wall, willing myself to become one with the cold concrete. Vincent's eyes narrowed, calculating as he pulled me a fraction closer, our bodies barely brushing against each other, heightening my awareness of him in a way I had not anticipated. The fleeting contact was a reminder of our proximity, of the delicate balance between safety and danger.

The guard paused, turning slightly, and I felt the urge to hold my breath become almost unbearable. I could see the uncertainty flicker across his face; he sensed something amiss, but our little alcove was shadowed, a refuge hidden from prying eyes.

"Nothing here," he muttered after a moment, exhaling in frustration as he turned to leave. Relief surged through me like a tide, and as he stepped back into the corridor, the space around us felt expansive again.

"We need to move," Vincent urged, his voice a sharp contrast to the stillness that had settled in. "The longer we linger, the more likely we'll be discovered."

I nodded, finally able to draw a breath. The adrenaline was still thrumming in my veins, a wild symphony playing just beneath my skin. I had faced danger before, but this was different; it felt personal, electric, like we were both teetering on the edge of something significant.

As we slipped out of our hiding place and into the dimly lit corridor, the world outside felt disorienting. I hadn't realized how tight that small space had felt until we were free, yet the freedom came with its own set of anxieties.

"Where to now?" I asked, my voice steady despite the chaos swirling inside me.

"Follow me," Vincent replied, his tone clipped as he moved forward, leading the way with a purposeful stride. I could see the tension in his shoulders, the way he carried himself like a soldier ready for battle. But there was also something else, a hint of vulnerability that danced beneath his confident facade. It was a reminder that we were both in over our heads, yet somehow, we had each other.

The corridors twisted and turned, each corner a new maze to navigate, and with every step, the ambient noise of the base swelled around us—the whir of machinery, the distant murmurs of conversations, the occasional burst of laughter that felt so incongruous in this world of shadows.

"What's the endgame here?" I pressed, trying to break through the tension that clung to us. "Are we just going to poke around until we stumble upon something monumental, or do we have a plan?"

Vincent shot me a sideways glance, his lips quirking into a half-smile. "Are you questioning my superior tactics?"

"Is that a joke?" I laughed, a sound that felt foreign yet freeing amidst the weight of our circumstances. "Your tactics include hiding in closets and praying we don't get caught."

"Hey, sometimes you have to embrace the subtleties of stealth," he shot back, grinning now, the camaraderie weaving between us like a thread of warmth in the cold metal of the base.

Our banter felt like a lifeline, a thread that pulled us closer together even as we navigated the chaos around us. Each quip, each teasing remark, was a small reminder that beneath the surface of this mission, beneath the fear and uncertainty, there was a burgeoning connection that neither of us had anticipated.

But then, a distant shout echoed through the corridor, jolting us both to attention. "Hey! Did you hear that?" The alarm in the guard's voice cut through the air like a knife, and in an instant, the atmosphere shifted, the warmth replaced by a frigid clarity of purpose.

"Run!" Vincent commanded, his voice steady and urgent as he grabbed my hand, pulling me into a sprint down the corridor. I stumbled after him, adrenaline coursing through my veins, every instinct shouting at me to escape, to survive. The world around us became a blur of gray and steel, and I focused on the rhythm of our footsteps, the way his hand fit around mine as if it had always belonged there.

We rounded a corner, and the chaos erupted behind us. The sound of footsteps grew louder, urgency echoing through the halls as we fled deeper into the heart of the Breed's base. "Where are we going?" I gasped, struggling to keep pace.

"To the data center," Vincent shouted back. "If we can get in there, we might find something—something that could bring them down." His voice was resolute, but I could sense the weight of fear beneath it, an understanding that we were racing against time and fate itself.

As we hurtled down the corridor, the shadows closed in around us, the air thick with the knowledge that we were teetering on the edge of a precipice, and what lay beyond was unknown. But I felt it then, a fierce determination igniting within me. Whatever happened next, whatever secrets the Breed held, I was ready to face it all—with Vincent by my side.

The metallic clang of a door being flung open behind us sent a jolt of panic through my veins, propelling us forward with an urgency that felt primal. We skidded to a halt at the mouth of another corridor, breathless and desperate. I could hear the voices of guards rising behind us, a cacophony of commands and confusion that hung in the air like a storm about to break. "Where did they go? Search the area!"

"Not exactly a warm welcome," I muttered, my heart pounding as I glanced back. The last thing I wanted was to be the center of attention for a cadre of armed men. I turned to Vincent, whose jaw was set in determination, his eyes scanning the shadows with the precision of a hawk.

"Stick to the plan," he urged, his voice low but steady, a contrast to the chaos echoing behind us. "We need to reach the data center. It's our best chance of getting what we came for."

"And what is that, exactly?" I shot back, trying to inject some humor into the rising tension, but I felt the weight of reality settle over me. "A souvenir from the Breed? I'm starting to think this was a terrible idea."

He flashed a quick grin, the corner of his mouth lifting in a way that sent a ripple of warmth through my chest. "It's a great idea if you ignore the imminent danger. Besides, you'd look fabulous as a trophy."

I rolled my eyes, but I couldn't suppress a laugh. It was a small victory, a reminder that even in the darkest moments, light could still find a way in. We turned a corner, and the corridor opened up, revealing a series of heavy steel doors lined with biometric scanners—our gateway to the secrets lurking within the Breed's lair.

"Here," Vincent said, his fingers deftly moving over the control panel beside one of the doors. "If I can access this, we'll be inside in no time."

I glanced over my shoulder as he worked, the sound of our pursuers growing closer, each footfall echoing like thunder. "Hurry," I urged, my voice edged with urgency. "They're not far behind."

He didn't respond, his focus absolute as he maneuvered through the complex security systems. I leaned against the cold steel wall, straining to hear any signs of movement. The silence stretched, thick with anticipation, until I caught sight of a figure darting around the corner. "Vincent!"

He looked up, just as the door emitted a low beep and slid open with a hiss. "In!" he shouted, shoving me through the opening before slipping in himself, just as the footsteps rounded the bend.

The room beyond was dimly lit, a stark contrast to the sterile corridors we had just traversed. Monitors flickered with data, the soft hum of machinery wrapping around us like a cocoon. I took a moment to catch my breath, the adrenaline coursing through me like wildfire.

"We need to find what we came for," Vincent said, moving to the nearest console, fingers flying over the keyboard. "We're looking for their files on the Breeds—their operations, locations, everything."

I nodded, trying to focus my racing thoughts. This was it; we were inches away from unraveling a network that had caused untold damage. The weight of the moment settled on my shoulders, and I felt both terrified and exhilarated.

"Got it!" Vincent exclaimed, pulling up a screen filled with documents and data logs. My heart raced as I leaned closer, scanning the information flashing before me. Names, locations, detailed plans that laid bare the Breed's sinister ambitions.

"This is unbelievable," I breathed, the magnitude of what we were uncovering hitting me like a wave. "We could take them down with this."

"Not so fast," Vincent cautioned, his expression turning serious. "We still need to get out of here. This information is our lifeline, but we won't have it for long if they catch us."

A sudden alarm blared, red lights flashing as a voice echoed through the intercom. "Intruders detected! All personnel to the data center immediately!"

"Great timing," I muttered, fear gnawing at my insides. "How do we get out?"

Vincent's eyes narrowed as he glanced around the room, scanning for an exit. "There's a maintenance tunnel at the far end," he pointed, urgency fueling his movements. "If we can reach it before they lock down this area, we might just make it."

I didn't need to be told twice. We bolted for the far wall, hearts pounding in rhythm as we navigated through the maze of equipment and machinery. Every step felt precarious, like walking a tightrope strung between danger and escape.

Just as we reached the maintenance door, a group of guards burst into the room, their shouts a whirlwind of confusion and aggression. "Stop right there!"

Vincent cursed under his breath, grabbing the handle and wrenching the door open. "Go!" he yelled, shoving me through before following closely behind.

The tunnel was narrow and dark, the air thick with dust and the smell of oil. I could hear the guards closing in behind us, their footsteps echoing in the confined space. "Keep moving," Vincent urged, his voice a steady anchor amidst the chaos.

We sprinted through the tunnel, the sound of our breathing loud against the silence of the metallic walls. I felt the cold grip of fear tighten around my heart, but I pushed it back, focusing on the flickering light at the end of the passage that promised safety.

"We're almost there!" I shouted, determination surging as we neared the exit. But as we reached the end of the tunnel, a deafening crash echoed behind us, followed by the frantic shouts of the guards.

"Vincent, we have to go!"

"I know!" he replied, urgency lacing his tone. "On three!"

"On three what?"

But before I could register his words, he turned and charged toward the exit, bursting through the door just as the guards rounded the corner.

"Lynn!" he shouted, panic creeping into his voice as he realized I hadn't followed him.

In a flash, the door slammed shut behind him, a barrier between us and the chaos that threatened to consume us. My heart raced as I turned to face the guards, their faces a mask of determination and menace.

"Don't move!" one of them shouted, leveling his weapon at me.

The reality of the situation crashed down around me, a suffocating blanket of fear and uncertainty. I was trapped, with nowhere to go and nowhere to hide. But in that moment of impending doom, something deep within me ignited—a spark of defiance.

"You'll have to catch me first," I shot back, adrenaline fueling my every move as I turned and sprinted down the adjacent corridor, the echo of my footsteps blending with the shouts behind me.

Behind me, I could hear the guards closing in, but I didn't dare look back. I was running not just for my life but for the secrets we had uncovered, for Vincent, for everything that hung in the balance.

As I rounded a corner, I skidded to a halt, staring into a vast chamber filled with machinery and flickering lights. I had no choice but to push forward, to dive deeper into the heart of the Breed's base, where danger lurked in every shadow.

And as I plunged into the unknown, I knew one thing: I would fight tooth and nail to escape this nightmare, to find Vincent again, no matter the cost. The echoes of my own resolve surged within me, but as I navigated the room, I felt the creeping realization that I was not alone. A figure loomed in the shadows, and before I could react, I heard the chilling sound of a voice that chilled me to the core.

"Well, well, what do we have here?"

The last shred of hope seemed to flicker and die as the figure stepped into the light, revealing a face I never thought I would see again. A chilling smile played on their lips, and dread settled over me like a shroud.

Chapter 6: Beneath the Crimson Veil

The air inside the Breed's vault was thick with the musty scent of stone and dust, a testament to the secrets it had buried over the centuries. Shadows danced along the rough-hewn walls, their flickering forms playing tricks on my mind as I stood before the altar, the object of my fascination pulsing softly in the dim light. The blood-red crystal, cradled on a pedestal of ebony wood, seemed almost alive. It was a vivid hue, like the final gasp of sunset bleeding into night, and as I stared at it, I could almost hear a whisper, a seductive promise that tugged at the edges of my consciousness.

Vincent was beside me, his presence a tempest that stirred the stillness around us. His eyes were locked onto the crystal, a tempest of emotions swirling beneath the surface, and for a moment, I dared to imagine what thoughts lurked behind that meticulously crafted mask of indifference he wore. I had seen him in a variety of moods—calm, sardonic, brooding—but now, there was something darker, an undercurrent of anguish that surprised me. I could feel it thrumming in the air, mingling with the hum of the crystal, the resonance of his suppressed turmoil vibrating through the chamber.

"This... this is what they've killed for," he said, his voice a low rasp that echoed off the stone walls. The words fell between us like a heavy stone, stirring the dust of my earlier confidence. I had brushed aside the implications of our mission, the perilous pursuit that had led us to this subterranean lair, but hearing the bitterness in his tone forced me to confront the gravity of our undertaking. Vincent's gaze remained fixed on the crystal, his brow furrowed as if he were reading an ancient script written only for him. I watched him, my heart racing as I absorbed the intensity of his focus.

The weight of his words settled like a shroud over me. "Killed for?" I echoed, my voice trembling slightly as I tried to reconcile the notion that anyone would die for a mere stone. The crystal flickered in response, casting a ruby glow across Vincent's chiseled features, highlighting the sharp angles of his jaw and the deep shadows under his eyes. It was as if the very essence of the artifact was entwined with him, revealing the ghost of a past he would rather forget.

He turned to me then, and I saw it—the flicker of something raw, something vulnerable, buried beneath layers of control and disdain. It was a fleeting glimpse, like the shadow of a bird passing overhead, and just as quickly, it vanished, replaced by the cold mask he wore so effortlessly. I swallowed hard, wrestling with a surge of conflicting emotions. Part of me wanted to pull away, to sever the bond that was forming, but a more rebellious part yearned to reach out, to discover what lay beneath his armor.

"Why does it matter?" I asked, my tone lighter than the dread coiling in my stomach. "It's just a rock, right?" I tried to infuse my words with a casualness that I didn't quite feel, hoping to draw him out of his reverie. But Vincent's gaze darkened, and a flicker of irritation passed across his features, igniting a spark of defiance within me.

"It's not just a rock," he snapped, the raw edge of his voice cutting through the air. "This is a power source, a conduit for energies we can barely comprehend. It's dangerous, and people have died to keep it hidden." The passion in his words sent shivers down my spine, a thrill mingling with fear. He was a tempest, this man beside me, full of fury and fire, yet there was also an undeniable sadness wrapped in his intensity.

"Then why are we here?" I challenged, a boldness igniting within me. "If it's so perilous, why not leave it buried?"

His eyes narrowed, and I could see the gears turning in his mind, the struggle between duty and desire playing out in real time. "Because we don't have a choice," he replied, his voice a low growl, the tension coiling tighter between us. "We're caught in a web that's been spun long before either of us was born."

There was a silence then, thick and pregnant with unspoken truths, and I felt the pull of fate tugging at my heartstrings. How had I found myself here, in this ancient vault, with this enigmatic man whose emotions seemed as chaotic as the storm brewing in the depths of his gaze? The pull of the crystal was intoxicating, a siren's call that made the air shimmer with unfulfilled promises.

I stepped closer to the altar, drawn to the warmth radiating from the crystal, but Vincent's hand shot out, catching my wrist in a grip that was both possessive and protective. "Don't," he warned, his voice low and fierce, sending a ripple of heat racing through my veins. "You don't know what you're dealing with."

The closeness of our bodies ignited a tension that crackled in the air, a charged moment that suspended time itself. My heart pounded against my ribcage, and I felt a strange connection, an unspoken understanding that flared to life in the space between us. In that instant, the world around us faded, leaving just the two of us and the pulsating crystal, the weight of everything we had fought for and everything we stood to lose hanging heavily in the air.

"Then teach me," I whispered, the words tumbling from my lips before I could stop them. A spark of something ignited in his eyes, a flicker of surprise that gave way to intrigue, and I knew in that moment that we were both standing on the precipice of something monumental—something that would change everything.

His grip tightened around my wrist, the heat of his palm igniting a flurry of emotions that collided within me—fear, excitement, and something dangerously akin to desire. I watched as he hesitated, his features softening just enough for me to glimpse the man behind the carefully crafted facade. There was a complexity to him that made my heart race, a tangled web of shadows and light that drew me in even as it warned me to keep my distance.

"Teach me," I repeated, my voice barely above a whisper. The air between us crackled with an electric tension, an uncharted territory we were both hesitantly exploring. Vincent's expression morphed, a flicker of surprise lighting his darkened eyes before it was swiftly extinguished, replaced by his customary stoicism.

"You think this is a game?" he asked, his tone dropping to a husky growl that sent a shiver racing down my spine. "This isn't something you learn over coffee and pastries. This is dangerous. People lose themselves chasing after this kind of power."

"Isn't that why we're here?" I shot back, my confidence blooming even as his intensity threatened to drown me. "To understand it? If we don't confront it, how can we fight against it?" I felt a surge of bravado, a reckless urge to push him, to unravel the enigma that was Vincent.

"Fight?" His lips curled into a wry smile that held no humor. "You're naive if you think you can just fight it. It's not a monster under your bed; it's a part of the world. It's everywhere, and it has a mind of its own."

I met his gaze, unyielding. "So, what? We just stand back and watch? You're the one who dragged me into this, remember? You can't pretend you're some reluctant hero here."

For a heartbeat, he seemed to consider my words, the storm of his thoughts reflected in the depths of his gaze. I could almost see the wheels turning behind those dark eyes, the way he weighed the risks against the potential for discovery. "It's not just about understanding the crystal," he said finally, his voice low and intense. "It's about understanding what it does to people. It feeds on ambition, on greed. It can warp you, twist you until you don't recognize yourself anymore."

"And you? Have you been warped?" I ventured, a teasing lilt in my voice, trying to coax the truth from him. His expression hardened, and I knew I had hit a nerve. The atmosphere shifted, thickening with unspoken emotions as he stepped back, breaking the connection between us.

"I've seen too much," he murmured, almost to himself. "Too many people lose their way."

"And yet here we are," I pressed, "on the brink of something that could change everything. You're telling me you want to keep running from it? Or are you just afraid?"

Vincent's gaze snapped back to mine, a fierce light igniting in his eyes. "I'm not afraid," he shot back, the defiance in his voice sharp enough to cut. "I know what I'm capable of. But you—" He hesitated, the moment stretching taut between us. "You're different. I don't want to see you get hurt."

My heart twisted at the unexpected vulnerability laced in his words. It was like watching the sun break through clouds, illuminating everything around us with a warm glow. I stepped closer again, emboldened by the shift in our dynamic, determined to bridge the gap between us. "You're not the only one who can fight, Vincent. I'm not just some pawn in your game."

"Game?" He scoffed, though I saw the glimmer of amusement in his eyes. "You think this is a game?"

"Maybe it is," I shot back with a smirk, "but if it is, then I intend to be a player, not a spectator."

A chuckle escaped him, low and rumbling, shaking off the tension like a wet dog. "You're infuriating."

"And yet you're still here," I teased, enjoying the banter that crackled between us, a spark of light in the oppressive atmosphere of the vault.

"Fine," he said at last, his tone turning serious. "If you're so determined, then let's begin. But you need to promise me something."

"What's that?"

"Promise me you won't hold back. If this is what you truly want, you have to be ready to face the consequences."

"I promise," I replied without hesitation, the words feeling heavy with the weight of my conviction.

"Good." He stepped toward the pedestal, his hand hovering just above the crystal, its pulsing glow reflecting in his eyes. "The first thing you need to understand is that this isn't just an artifact. It's a doorway, a connection to something beyond our comprehension."

I watched him, fascinated. "So, how do we open it?"

"Carefully." He met my gaze, a mix of seriousness and mischief dancing in his eyes. "There's a reason no one's managed to use it without dire repercussions. But I have a theory."

"Of course you do," I replied, a teasing lilt creeping into my voice. "What's your theory?"

Vincent hesitated, his brow furrowing as he searched for the right words. "I think it requires a balance—a harmony between light and dark, desire and restraint. You can't let one overpower the other."

"So, we have to dance?" I quipped, unable to resist. "Isn't that a bit cliché?"

"More like a waltz," he countered, the corners of his mouth twitching in amusement. "And trust me, I've never been a graceful dancer."

"Then we'll just have to find our rhythm together." I stepped closer, my heart pounding with anticipation, ready to embrace the challenge ahead.

As he lowered his hand toward the crystal, I felt a rush of exhilaration and dread. The air shimmered with potential, a palpable energy coursing through the space, and I knew, with an undeniable certainty, that whatever came next would change everything.

The moment his hand brushed against the crystal, a shudder ran through the air, as if the very walls of the vault breathed in anticipation. The pulsating red light intensified, illuminating the intricate carvings on the pedestal, revealing symbols I had never seen before, twisting and curling like tendrils reaching for something just out of grasp. I held my breath, caught between fear and exhilaration, as Vincent's fingers hovered just above the surface.

"It's like it's alive," I murmured, my voice barely a whisper, captivated by the allure of the artifact. "What does it want?"

Vincent's brow furrowed deeper as he concentrated, a furrow of determination etched across his forehead. "That's the question, isn't it? Power has a way of drawing in those who seek it. It feeds on ambition, on desire."

"I thought we were here to harness that power, not let it consume us," I shot back, the defiance in my tone fueling the tension between us. "You can't just stand there and overthink it. We have to take action."

"Action, yes, but reckless abandon could lead to—"

"To what? A chance to change everything?" I interrupted, frustration boiling over. "Isn't that why we're here? To confront what others fear?"

With a sharp exhale, Vincent's lips pressed into a thin line, his jaw tightening. "You're relentless."

"Or maybe I'm just passionate," I countered, a smirk playing on my lips. "A trait you might want to consider adopting yourself."

He chuckled, the tension easing just a fraction, and I felt a flicker of hope. "Fine, let's try this." His gaze locked onto the crystal, and as he leaned closer, I caught the glint of determination in his eyes. "But you have to promise me that if this goes south, you'll step back."

"Deal," I replied, though my heart thudded with a mix of excitement and trepidation. I would have given anything to step into that moment, to push boundaries and cross lines that had been drawn for far too long.

With one final glance at me, Vincent pressed his palm against the surface of the crystal. The instant contact sent a jolt of energy coursing through the air, a vibrant wave that resonated through my very bones. I staggered back, instinctively clutching the edge of the altar for support. The room brightened, shadows retreating in the wake of a blinding crimson glow that enveloped us like a cocoon.

"Vincent!" I shouted, fear igniting in my chest as the intensity of the light pulsed in time with my racing heart. The vault transformed around us, reality bending and warping as the light expanded, stretching beyond the physical boundaries of the chamber.

"Stay close!" he commanded, his voice firm yet strained, fighting against the power emanating from the crystal. I nodded, grounding myself as I stepped forward, drawn to him like a moth to flame.

In that moment, the air thickened with whispers—fragments of voices from the past, echoes of those who had come before us, seeking the same power. "Power corrupts... desire consumes..." they murmured, weaving a haunting melody that made my skin prickle.

"What are they saying?" I asked, my voice shaking as I glanced around, half-expecting the specters of the past to materialize before us.

"They are warnings," Vincent replied, gritting his teeth as he struggled to maintain his grip on the crystal's energy. "This is what I meant by consequences. We need to—"

Before he could finish, the crystal surged violently, and the ground beneath us trembled. The altar began to crack, splintering like old wood under pressure, and I stumbled, clutching Vincent's arm to steady myself. "We have to do something!"

"Focus," he instructed, his voice steady despite the chaos. "Focus on the energy. Let it guide you."

Closing my eyes, I reached out, extending my hand toward the pulsating light. I could feel it calling to me, urging me to embrace it, to become part of the power that thrummed beneath the surface. Images flooded my mind—visions of vibrant landscapes, shadowy figures, and fleeting glimpses of ancient rituals. It was intoxicating, overwhelming, yet somehow familiar.

"What do you see?" Vincent asked, and I could sense the urgency in his voice.

"It's—" I started, but my words faltered as the visions grew more vivid. I saw a woman, fierce and defiant, standing before a great stone altar much like ours, her eyes blazing with determination as she invoked the power of the crystal. But as she called upon it, the ground beneath her shattered, and darkness poured forth like a tidal wave, swallowing her whole.

"Wait!" I cried out, pulling my hand back as a cold dread settled in my gut. "She was trying to control it, and it—"

"It took her," Vincent finished, his face pale, the reality of the situation settling over us like a lead weight. "That's the consequence of greed. It can devour everything."

The chamber quaked violently, dust raining from the ceiling as the whispers grew louder, a cacophony of warnings that echoed in my ears. I staggered back, clutching my head, desperate to drown out the chaos. "We have to shut it down! We have to—"

But before I could finish, the light exploded, filling the room with a blinding radiance. I shielded my eyes, feeling the force of the energy crashing against me like a wave. My breath caught in my throat as I lost my footing, thrown backward into the wall, and everything went dark.

When I opened my eyes, I found myself sprawled on the cold stone floor, the air thick with smoke and dust. I blinked against the dim light, struggling to piece together what had just happened. Vincent was beside me, his body tense and his expression strained, and I could sense a shift in the air—a heaviness that whispered of danger lurking just beyond our reach.

"Are you okay?" he asked, his voice low and urgent.

"Yeah," I managed to say, though I could feel the remnants of power pulsing beneath my skin, a lingering reminder of the chaos that had just unfolded.

Vincent helped me to my feet, and as we steadied ourselves, I glanced toward the altar. The crystal lay shattered, fragments sparkling like fallen stars across the stone. A chill ran down my spine as I realized the whispers had faded, replaced by an eerie silence that hung thick in the air.

"We did it," I breathed, relief washing over me, but there was something unsettling in the atmosphere, a tension that made the hairs on the back of my neck stand on end.

Vincent's expression darkened, his eyes scanning the room. "No... this isn't over."

And just as the words left his mouth, a low rumble echoed from the shadows beyond the vault, followed by a chilling laugh that sent ice racing through my veins. The sound was unmistakable, resonating with malevolence, and I knew in that instant that our encounter with the crystal had awakened something far worse than we had ever imagined.

I turned to Vincent, my heart pounding in my chest as the reality of our predicament sank in. "What did we unleash?"

Before he could answer, the vault doors creaked ominously, swinging open with a slow, deliberate groan, revealing a darkness that seemed to pulse with a life of its own. The laughter grew louder, a haunting melody that echoed off the stone walls, beckoning us into the abyss.

"We need to get out of here," Vincent said, urgency lacing his tone as he grasped my hand, pulling me toward the exit. But as we moved, I couldn't shake the feeling that something was watching us, lurking in the shadows, waiting for its moment to strike.

The vault trembled once more, and I glanced back just in time to see the shadows coalescing, swirling together to form a figure cloaked in darkness, its eyes glinting with a predatory hunger.

"Vincent!" I screamed, the panic surging within me as I realized we were not alone. The chase was just beginning.

Chapter 7: Shattered Bonds

The safehouse was a cacophony of destruction, a fragile sanctuary that had once felt like a fortress. I stumbled through the haze of dust and smoke, my heart racing with the remnants of an adrenaline high that left me trembling. It was a stark contrast to the warmth I had felt just hours before, wrapped in the comfort of mundane conversation and shared stories. Now, everything was shattered—both the building and the fragile illusions we had built around ourselves. My eyes darted around, searching for Vincent, though a part of me dreaded the moment our gazes would meet again.

The walls, once lined with the makeshift art of our collective fears and hopes, were now marred by cracks that spidered across the plaster like the frayed edges of our camaraderie. I could smell smoke, acrid and sharp, mingling with the stale air that had grown heavy with desperation. Each breath I took tasted of ash and bitter resolve, a reminder that nothing would ever be the same. I stepped carefully over a fallen beam, the weight of it symbolic of the burden we all carried—an unwelcome reminder of the Breed's relentless pursuit.

"Lena!" The voice pulled me from my daze, and I turned to find Claire, her face streaked with soot, eyes wide with fear. She was clutching a tattered blanket, her only shield against the chaos, and my heart ached at the sight of her. We had become like family through this madness, bound by a shared struggle that had forged an unbreakable bond between us. "We need to get out! They'll be back any minute."

I nodded, my throat tight. "Where's Vincent?"

Claire's expression shifted, a flicker of uncertainty passing over her features. "He went—" The words caught in her throat as the walls seemed to groan under the weight of impending disaster.

A rumble echoed through the safehouse, a sound so low and primal it felt like a warning. The Breed was closing in, and we were trapped like animals in a cage. I could feel the pulse of fear quicken my blood, but it wasn't my own safety that worried me. My thoughts were consumed by Vincent, the man who had become both a puzzle and an anchor in this tumultuous sea of betrayal. What if he was hurt? What if he didn't make it out?

Before I could voice my concern, the door burst open, a whirlwind of chaos and violence pouring into our sanctuary. Shadows danced in the dim light, and I caught sight of dark figures moving with purpose, their faces obscured by the shadows. Instinct kicked in, and I grabbed Claire's hand, pulling her away from the incoming onslaught.

"Follow me!" I shouted, my voice rising above the noise, a beacon of resolve amidst the clamor. We dashed through the remnants of our refuge, my heart pounding in rhythm with the urgency of our escape. Each step felt like a desperate prayer that we would find safety, that Vincent would be there, waiting, ready to fight.

But as we rounded the corner into what had once been the living room, I skidded to a halt, the sight before me stealing the breath from my lungs. There he stood, framed by the broken doorway, a lone sentinel amidst the storm of our world unraveling. His jaw was set, eyes fierce with determination, yet there was something deeper—an undercurrent of sorrow that tugged at my heart. He was battling more than just the external threat; he was fighting the demons that had haunted him long before we had ever crossed paths.

"Lena," he said, voice low and steady, cutting through the chaos like a knife. "You shouldn't be here. Get Claire and go."

"Like hell," I shot back, defiance sparking within me. "I'm not leaving you."

The tension between us crackled like electricity, a fierce bond forged in the fires of our shared struggle. In that moment, as the Breed surged forward, I felt an undeniable pull toward him, a connection that transcended our circumstances. He wasn't just a warrior of the Breed; he was a man caught in a storm, and I was determined to weather it alongside him.

As the first blows landed, the air filled with the sounds of violence and chaos, I leaped into the fray. It was instinct, a surge of adrenaline that pushed me to fight, to protect what little we had left. I ducked beneath a flailing arm, feeling the rush of air as it passed over my head, and I could hear Claire behind me, shouting, her voice laced with a mix of fear and bravery. We were a makeshift unit now, a small force against the encroaching darkness.

Vincent moved with a grace that was almost mesmerizing, the way he fought was like a dance—fluid, powerful, and wholly in control. I couldn't help but admire him even as we faced this dire situation. It was an odd juxtaposition of terror and admiration that sent a thrill through me. In this moment, I understood what it meant to be vulnerable, to truly care for someone when the world threatened to pull you apart.

Suddenly, a figure lunged at Vincent from the shadows, and instinct took over. I grabbed a broken chair leg, swinging it with all my might, catching the attacker off guard. The sound of wood meeting flesh echoed in the air, and for a brief moment, I felt a surge of triumph. But the victory was short-lived, as more figures flooded in, and the tide of battle turned against us.

In the midst of the chaos, I caught Vincent's gaze—an unspoken promise passed between us, a commitment to survive together, no matter the cost. My heart raced as I realized the depth of my feelings for him, a tempest of emotions that could no longer be ignored. He was a part of my world now, and I would fight for him with every ounce of strength I possessed.

With renewed resolve, we fought side by side, each blow and parry igniting a fire within me, the thrill of the fight amplifying the bond that was forming between us. But beneath the adrenaline-fueled haze, I sensed something deeper—an understanding that we were both damaged, both fighting our own battles within the larger war that had ensnared us. And in that shared struggle, something beautiful began to bloom amid the wreckage of our lives.

The dust swirled in the dim light like ghostly dancers, remnants of our sanctuary cloaked in a somber shroud. My pulse pounded in my ears, a relentless drumbeat that drowned out the world around us. I could hardly believe we had come through the storm of chaos that had enveloped us moments ago, yet here we stood—battered but alive. The remnants of our safehouse loomed like a skeletal memory of what had once been, the walls whispering tales of laughter and hope now reduced to echoes of our desperation.

Vincent leaned against the charred remnants of what had once been a doorway, his silhouette stark against the flickering light. His eyes, those deep wells of emotion, shifted toward me, and I felt a pang in my chest. Was it fear? Concern? Maybe a blend of both. I took a step closer, ready to reach out, to bridge the gap that loomed between us like an unspoken chasm.

"Are you hurt?" The question fell from my lips, raw and instinctual. It was ridiculous how much I needed him to be alright, how my heart twisted at the thought of any pain he might endure.

He shook his head slowly, his voice steady but edged with an emotion I couldn't quite decipher. "Just a scratch. I've had worse." The bravado felt thin, a veneer over the deeper wounds he carried—wounds that had been laid bare in the heat of battle.

"Right. Well, the walls look worse for wear than you do," I quipped, trying to lighten the mood, but even I could hear the tremor in my voice. "What's next? Rebuilding a fortress out of charred beams and broken dreams?"

Vincent's lips quirked up in the ghost of a smile, a fleeting flicker that illuminated the shadows lurking behind his eyes. "I think it might take more than a weekend project on Pinterest to fix this place."

Despite the absurdity of the moment, a wave of relief washed over me. We were still standing, still able to share a joke, even amidst the ruins of our world. It felt like a small victory, one I was desperate to cling to. The air crackled with an electricity that had nothing to do with the danger we had just escaped.

"Where do we go from here?" I asked, more serious now. The weight of our situation pressed down, demanding clarity in the chaos.

He glanced around the wreckage, then back at me, his expression shifting into something more contemplative. "We regroup. We find the others." His gaze hardened, determination etching deeper lines on his face. "And we don't let the Breed take us again."

As if on cue, a distant rumble reverberated through the ground beneath our feet, sending a shiver racing up my spine. My mind flashed to the last moments of our fight—shadows darting in and out, the glint of weapons catching the light like menacing stars. The Breed would not rest, and neither would I.

"Right. Regroup," I echoed, my heart pounding with a mix of fear and adrenaline. "But what about Claire? And the others?"

Vincent pushed himself away from the debris, the faintest trace of a grimace passing over his features as he straightened. "We find them first. I can't—" His voice faltered, and for a moment, the walls between us felt insurmountable. "I can't lose anyone else."

The weight of his words hung heavy in the air, and I felt a surge of empathy rush through me. I had seen loss, felt it wrap its cold fingers around my heart. "Then we'll do it together," I said firmly, a promise woven into my tone. "We'll find them. No one gets left behind."

The resolve in my voice seemed to steady him, and he nodded, his eyes locking onto mine with an intensity that sent a thrill coursing through me. I wasn't just fighting for survival anymore; I was fighting for him, for us, for the tenuous thread of hope we clung to amid the darkness.

We turned to move through the wreckage, navigating the labyrinth of destruction with a mix of urgency and caution. Each step brought with it the crushing reality of what had been lost, but there was also a spark of something more—determination, perhaps, or maybe the first stirrings of hope.

As we stepped into what had once been the kitchen, I noticed the remnants of our lives strewn about: a cracked mug, the tattered edges of a map we had studied in secret, the half-finished drawings Claire had sketched while we shared stories to distract ourselves from the looming dread. The kitchen had been our heart, the place where laughter mingled with shared fears over lukewarm coffee and stolen moments of peace.

"It's all gone," I murmured, more to myself than to Vincent. The realization washed over me like cold water, shocking and numbing.

"It's not gone," he replied, his voice low but firm. "We're still here."

His words settled into my chest, a balm against the ache of loss. I turned to face him, and in that moment, I saw not just the warrior but the man—the one who bore scars that told stories of survival and strength, of battles fought and sacrifices made.

A sudden thought struck me, like a bolt of lightning illuminating the darkness. "The artifact!" I exclaimed, the memory flooding back. "It must have been what they were after. It could be a key, a way to understand what they want from us."

Vincent frowned, the shadow of concern flickering across his face. "It could also be a trap. We need to be cautious. We can't let our guard down."

I nodded, understanding the gravity of his words. The artifact was a symbol of everything that had brought us to this point—a connection to the past that was both a blessing and a curse. It had the potential to unlock answers, but it also held the risk of deeper danger.

As we moved through the remains of our sanctuary, each step became a declaration of our intent to reclaim what was lost. With every broken beam we sidestepped, every shard of glass we navigated, I felt the bond between us grow stronger. We were not just survivors; we were partners in this struggle, two souls intertwined in a dance of fate and choice.

With determination lighting my path, I glanced at Vincent, the warmth of his presence a steady flame against the cold reality of our situation. "Whatever happens next, I'm with you," I said, my voice unwavering.

He looked back at me, and for a fleeting moment, the world outside faded, leaving just the two of us suspended in the uncertainty of our shared fate. "Together," he affirmed, a promise that resonated deep within me, wrapping around my heart like a protective shield.

And as we moved forward, ready to face whatever lay ahead, I knew one thing for certain: we would fight, not just for survival but for each other, weaving our fates into a tapestry of resilience and hope amidst the looming shadows.

The echoes of our previous struggle reverberated in my mind, a reminder that the battle was far from over. With Vincent by my side, I felt a strange mix of courage and trepidation as we surveyed the remnants of our safehouse. The shadows seemed to breathe around us, a living entity that whispered of loss and longing, yet also of determination and hope.

"Let's see if we can salvage anything useful," Vincent suggested, his voice steady despite the chaos surrounding us. He stepped carefully over a fallen beam, moving with a grace that belied the turmoil etched into his features. It struck me how resilient he was, yet the haunted look in his eyes betrayed the turmoil within.

"Salvage? In this wreckage? I think we might need a miracle," I replied, half-seriously, as I rummaged through the debris. "Or a very generous contractor."

He chuckled softly, the sound a balm against the tension. "I hear miracles are on backorder these days."

As we sifted through the debris, I unearthed a few remnants of our lives: a half-burned journal, Claire's favorite mug, a twisted piece of metal that had once been a part of our kitchen table. Each item carried with it a memory, a fragment of laughter or a moment of vulnerability that made my heart ache.

"Do you remember the night we tried to make dinner?" I asked, holding up the scorched journal. "You almost set fire to the spaghetti."

Vincent's laughter rang out, rich and genuine. "That wasn't spaghetti; that was an explosion of tomato sauce and regret." His smile faded slightly, replaced by a flicker of nostalgia. "I never thought I could miss a terrible meal so much."

As we reminisced, the oppressive weight of our reality dulled, if only for a moment. It was easy to forget the looming threat when we were wrapped in the warmth of shared memories. But soon, the laughter faded as I became aware of the looming urgency pressing against us like the thick walls that surrounded our wreckage.

"Do you think they'll come back?" I asked, my voice barely above a whisper, the question hanging in the air like a storm cloud.

Vincent's expression turned serious, the playful glint in his eyes replaced by the steely resolve I had come to recognize. "They'll come back. They always do. The Breed doesn't give up easily."

A shiver coursed through me at the thought, my mind racing with the implications. What if they did come back? What if we weren't ready? "Then we need a plan. We can't just sit here and wait to be found."

"Agreed," he replied, and the tension between us shifted, settling into a focused energy that propelled us forward. "We need to find the others first. They could be hiding nearby, but we also need to consider the artifact."

"The artifact," I repeated, the weight of the word sinking into my chest. "What if it's the key to everything? What if it can help us understand the Breed's motives?"

Vincent nodded, his brow furrowing. "It's possible, but it could also draw them to us. We need to be careful. There's too much at stake."

My heart raced at the thought. What if the artifact held secrets that could change the course of our fight? "Then we'll have to be strategic. We'll use it as bait."

He shot me a quizzical glance, a mix of admiration and concern swirling in his expression. "You're suggesting we risk ourselves to lure the Breed out?"

"Only if we have a backup plan. If we can lead them away from the others, we might give them a chance to escape," I insisted, my resolve hardening.

"And what about us?" he countered, the intensity of his gaze piercing through me. "What if we can't get away?"

"We'll get away," I declared, though uncertainty tinged my voice. "We have to believe we will."

The determination that had sparked between us ignited a fire deep within me, fueling my conviction that we could turn the tide. "We can do this, Vincent. We just need to trust each other."

His eyes softened, and for a fleeting moment, the world outside faded away. "I do trust you, Lena. It's just... complicated."

"Complicated is my middle name," I joked, trying to lighten the heavy atmosphere. "Or it should be. Besides, if we keep surviving this, we'll have plenty of time to untangle our mess of emotions."

He smirked, the corners of his lips lifting. “Oh, great. Because nothing says romance like a post-apocalyptic therapy session.”

“Exactly! I can see it now: ‘And how did that make you feel, Vincent?’” I laughed, the sound mingling with the dust motes dancing in the sunlight streaming through the broken windows.

The levity broke through the tension, if only for a moment, and we both knew we had to act quickly. We gathered what we could find—whatever supplies remained intact—and steeled ourselves for what lay ahead.

As we stepped outside into the fading light, the air felt charged, thick with possibility. The sun dipped low on the horizon, casting a warm golden hue over the destruction, a stark contrast to the heaviness in my chest. It was beautiful, and it felt wrong.

“We need to head towards the old factory,” Vincent said, pointing down the overgrown path that led into the encroaching twilight. “It’s where we last saw Claire and the others.”

“Right. And if we run into any Breed members along the way?”

“Then we’ll run faster.” He grinned, a spark of mischief lighting up his expression.

“Excellent plan. I always preferred a good sprint to a slow demise,” I shot back, adrenaline coursing through my veins as we started down the path.

With every step, I felt the weight of our shared burden pushing us forward. The forest loomed like a silent witness, the branches whispering secrets of both danger and sanctuary. The quiet was deceptive, each rustle of leaves echoing like a heartbeat, a reminder of our vulnerability in this vast wilderness.

As we moved deeper into the woods, an uneasy silence enveloped us, broken only by the crunch of leaves beneath our feet. I could feel Vincent’s presence beside me, a constant reassurance in the face of the unknown, yet the tension in the air was palpable. Something felt off, like the calm before a storm, and the hair on the back of my neck prickled with unease.

Then, without warning, a snap echoed through the stillness—a twig breaking underfoot, a sound so mundane yet so ominous in the heavy silence. I froze, instincts flaring to life as I turned to Vincent. His expression mirrored mine, the humor gone, replaced by a sharp focus.

"Did you hear that?" I whispered, barely able to control the tremor in my voice.

He nodded slowly, his gaze scanning the shadows that stretched around us. "Stay close."

With bated breath, we moved forward cautiously, every sense heightened, the world narrowing down to the whisper of leaves and the pounding of our hearts. The shadows deepened as the sun dipped below the horizon, wrapping the forest in an eerie twilight.

Suddenly, from the corner of my eye, I caught movement—figures darting through the trees, cloaked in darkness, as silent as the night itself. My breath hitched in my throat as panic gripped my heart. "Vincent!" I gasped, urgency clawing at my voice.

In that split second, I realized we were not alone, and the impending danger lurked just out of sight, poised to strike. The shadows converged, drawing closer, and in a heartbeat, the world exploded into chaos once more.

"Run!" Vincent shouted, his voice slicing through the thick air as we broke into a sprint. The dark figures emerged, rushing toward us with relentless speed, and my pulse quickened with the thrill of fear.

We dashed through the underbrush, branches clawing at our clothes, the sounds of pursuit echoing behind us. I could feel the darkness closing in, wrapping around us like a shroud, and as I glanced back, dread surged through me.

But the danger was not the only thing closing in. Just ahead, a figure loomed in the fading light, an apparition whose identity sent a chill racing down my spine. I skidded to a halt, panic seizing me as recognition dawned.

"Lena!" Vincent yelled, desperation threading through his voice as he reached for me, but it was too late. The darkness engulfed us, and everything spiraled into chaos.

Chapter 8: Chains of Obligation

The sun rose reluctantly, its pale rays filtering through the dusty window of the makeshift safehouse, illuminating the remnants of our shattered refuge. My heart felt as heavy as the morning air, thick with unspoken words and unresolved tension. I glanced at Vincent, who sat in the corner, a silhouette of muscle and brooding intensity, his dark hair tousled as if he'd wrestled with the night's demons. His silence was a wall, impenetrable and unyielding, and each passing minute intensified the feeling that the connection we once shared was fraying at the edges.

He hadn't spoken much since the attack, and his humor, that sharp, biting wit that had once sparked so much life in our conversations, had faded into the background like the remnants of a dream. I could still hear echoes of his laughter, ringing out like a melody from a time when hope seemed possible, but now those memories felt like shards of glass, sharp and painful. Today, however, there was a tension in the air, a crackle that suggested a storm was brewing, and I was determined to confront it.

"Vincent," I said softly, testing the waters. He didn't look up, his gaze fixed on a point beyond the horizon, as if he could will himself away from the chaos that had become our lives. "We need to talk."

"Talk?" His voice was a low growl, laced with irritation, as if the very word were an affront to his guarded nature. "What is there to talk about? The safehouse is gone. We're stuck here. I'm busy."

"Busy doing what?" I challenged, crossing the room to stand before him. "Sitting in silence and brooding? You're pushing me away, and for what? I need you right now, Vincent." The last words slipped from my lips, filled with an urgency that surprised even me.

"Need?" he scoffed, finally meeting my gaze with those stormy blue eyes that held the weight of a thousand unspoken fears. "Need is a luxury we can't afford. You should know that better than anyone."

His words cut deeper than I'd anticipated. I felt the heat of indignation rise within me, a fiery response to his refusal to let me in. "And what about you, Vincent? What do you need? You're acting like this doesn't affect you, but I can see it. You're not just a shield for me; you're—"

"A prisoner," he interrupted, his voice like ice, and for a moment, I thought I could see the façade cracking. "Just like you. Bound by loyalty, obligation, and the weight of choices I can't change."

The vulnerability in his eyes flared and then flickered out like a candle caught in a draft. It was maddening to watch him slip back behind his walls, but in that instant, I understood: his distance was his armor, protecting him from the emotional wreckage that loomed like a storm cloud over both of us.

"Obligation? Is that all we are to each other now?" I pressed, my heart pounding in my chest. "Just two people shackled to a life we never wanted?"

"You don't understand," he snapped, his voice rising, echoing off the barren walls. "You don't know what it's like to live in the shadows, to owe a debt to a past you can't escape. I have responsibilities, commitments—"

"Responsibilities?" I interrupted, my voice barely above a whisper now, feeling the weight of our reality settle heavily between us. "You mean the kind that keep you locked away? The kind that keep you from being who you really are?"

The air was thick with tension, each word hanging heavily like a suspended chord, waiting for resolution. I could see it then—the tightness in his jaw, the way his hands clenched into fists at his sides. He was a man caught between duty and desire, torn apart by chains of obligation that seemed inescapable. And for the first time, I saw the fear lurking in his eyes, the fear of losing himself to a life he'd never chosen.

"I'm not strong enough for this," he murmured, almost to himself. "Not anymore."

I stepped closer, my heart racing. "You are strong, Vincent. Stronger than you know. But you can't do this alone. You don't have to carry this burden by yourself."

He looked up, and in that fleeting moment, I thought I glimpsed the man he once was—the man who held me close when the world turned dark, who whispered promises amidst the chaos. But the flicker faded, extinguished by the weight of reality, and I felt a pang of desperation clawing at my chest.

"I don't even know who I am anymore," he confessed, his voice barely audible, each word a small surrender.

"Then let's figure it out together," I urged, reaching out to touch his arm, my fingers brushing against the fabric of his worn shirt. "We can't change the past, but we can shape our future."

Vincent's gaze dropped to my hand, the connection electric and undeniable, and for a heartbeat, it felt like the world had shifted. But just as quickly, he pulled away, retreating into himself, and I felt the chill of rejection pierce my resolve.

"Don't," he said, the word laced with a quiet desperation. "You don't understand the dangers. This life... it's not meant for someone like you."

"Someone like me?" I echoed, incredulous. "What does that even mean? Because I'm not shackled by the same chains you are? Because I refuse to let fear dictate my life?"

Vincent's eyes darkened, and a flicker of something—anger, pain, regret—crossed his face. "You don't know what you're asking. To be with me is to invite darkness into your life. You think this is a choice? It's a burden, one that I've carried far too long."

A chill ran down my spine, the weight of his words settling over me like a shroud. I didn't want to admit it, but I could feel the truth in his tone, the specter of danger lurking just beneath the surface. Yet,

I refused to back down. I had faced too much already to turn away now.

"Maybe it is a burden, Vincent, but it's one I'm willing to share. You're not alone in this, no matter how much you try to convince yourself otherwise."

As silence enveloped us, I could almost hear the walls between us crumbling, the air charged with a tension that hinted at possibility. But Vincent remained resolute, locked away behind a fortress built on obligation, and I was left standing in the ruins of our once vibrant connection, yearning for him to take a step toward me, to break the chains that bound him as fiercely as they held me captive in my own sorrow.

The air crackled with unspoken words, a palpable tension threading through the small space as I stood there, my heart pounding with frustration and worry. Vincent's avoidance felt like a personal betrayal, a silent rejection that gnawed at the edges of my resolve. I had wanted to reach him, to remind him that we were still in this together, yet his cold distance was a stark reminder of the barriers he had erected.

I paced the room, my thoughts swirling like autumn leaves caught in a gust of wind. Outside, the world carried on, indifferent to the turmoil inside. The remnants of the safehouse lay scattered in the corners of my mind—fragments of laughter and warmth overshadowed by the looming specter of what had been lost. I turned back to Vincent, my eyes narrowing as I tried to read the turmoil that flickered behind his stoic façade.

"Are you planning to sulk all day?" I asked, my tone sharper than intended, and his eyes snapped to mine, icy and unfathomable.

"I'm not sulking," he retorted, the edge in his voice betraying the frustration bubbling just beneath the surface. "I'm assessing our situation. There's a difference."

"Assessing, or avoiding?" I shot back, unwilling to let him hide behind his bravado. "If you think I'm going to stand by while you wallow in self-pity, you're mistaken."

He laughed, a hollow sound that reverberated through the silence, and I felt a twinge of triumph at breaking through the steel exterior, if only for a moment. "Self-pity? Is that what you think this is? Spare me the lecture, Claire. You don't know what it's like to bear the weight of my world."

"Then let me in," I pleaded, my voice softer now, each word laced with sincerity. "You think I want to be a bystander in my own life? I want to help you, but you're shutting me out. That's not strength; that's isolation."

His expression shifted, a flicker of something unnameable passing over his features before he regained his composure. "Isolation is necessary. I've made choices for a reason. It's safer this way."

"Safer? Or easier?" I pressed, refusing to back down. "Running from your demons won't keep them at bay. They'll catch up with you, and I won't let you face them alone. You might think you're protecting me, but all you're doing is pushing me away."

Vincent's eyes darkened, and for a heartbeat, I saw the weight of his burdens in the creases of his brow, the tight line of his mouth. The man who was so often a bastion of strength now appeared fragile, as though the slightest breeze could shatter him. "I don't want you to see me like this," he admitted, almost a whisper.

"I want to see you. All of you, even the messy bits," I countered gently, feeling the crack in his armor widen just a bit more. "That's how we survive this—together."

For a moment, the room was suspended in silence, our breaths the only sound as we gauged one another, searching for sincerity beneath layers of pain and pride. Vincent's walls seemed to waver, and I felt a rush of hope blooming in my chest.

"Together," he echoed, almost incredulously, as if the word tasted foreign on his tongue. "You really think it's that simple?"

"No, I don't think it's simple," I said, my voice firm. "But I know that if we don't face this head-on, we'll drown in it. So, what's it going to be, Vincent? Are you going to let the darkness consume you?"

His shoulders sagged, and for the first time, I saw the flicker of surrender in his eyes. "I don't know how to let anyone in anymore. I've been fighting for so long."

"Fighting is exhausting," I replied, stepping closer, feeling the gravity of our shared burden. "And it's okay to be tired. It's okay to ask for help."

Vincent's gaze softened, and for the first time in days, I felt the air shift, a subtle easing of the tension that had suffocated us. "You make it sound so easy," he murmured, a hint of vulnerability creeping into his voice.

"Easy? Oh, honey, it's anything but. But if you keep pretending everything's fine, it'll only get harder. You deserve to be free of this weight."

He swallowed hard, the storm in his eyes quieting just a bit. "And what if freeing myself means putting you in danger?"

"Then I'll deal with it. I'm not made of glass, Vincent. I can handle more than you think."

"Handling things has never been my strong suit," he admitted, his voice a blend of sarcasm and sincerity.

"Well, maybe it's time to redefine what strong means," I replied with a playful smile, the tension breaking as a flicker of mischief danced in my eyes. "Besides, I have faith in your ability to bumble your way through this. You've done it before."

The corners of his mouth twitched, a hint of a smile breaking through the shadows. "You really think I'm a bumbler?"

“I’m convinced you could trip over a thought if it were on a sticky note,” I laughed, and the warmth between us began to thaw the icy silence that had defined our recent days.

He chuckled, the sound rich and genuine, and for that moment, the weight of our circumstances faded, replaced by the fragile light of connection. “You’re impossible,” he said, the warmth in his voice revealing a tenderness that had been buried for too long.

“And yet here you are, stuck with me,” I shot back, feeling emboldened by the shift in our dynamic. “What’s your plan? To stare moody into the distance until I lose my patience?”

“Maybe,” he said, the ghost of a grin lingering at the edges of his lips. “But I think you’ve got me figured out. I’m just a bit more complicated than I let on.”

“Complicated is just code for interesting,” I replied with a wink, the atmosphere growing lighter with each shared glance. “And trust me, I like interesting.”

In that moment, the distance that had grown between us began to dissipate, leaving behind an unsteady foundation upon which we could rebuild. The chains of obligation still bound us, but I could sense the potential for freedom lingering just beyond our reach.

“Alright,” he said finally, a new resolve settling into his posture. “Let’s face this together. But I’m warning you, it won’t be pretty.”

I grinned, a rush of warmth flooding my chest. “Pretty isn’t on my agenda. Let’s make it messy and see what we find beneath the surface.”

Vincent met my gaze, the barriers around his heart beginning to dissolve, and in that moment, we stood on the precipice of something new. The weight of obligation was still there, but now it was woven with the threads of shared strength, an unspoken agreement that we would navigate the darkness together, no matter how tangled the path ahead might be.

With an unspoken agreement hanging in the air between us, the heaviness of the past still loomed, but the possibility of hope glimmered faintly in the distance. As the days stretched on, Vincent and I navigated our fragile truce, the silence between us punctuated only by the occasional soft exchange or shared laughter, each moment a tentative step toward healing. It felt like a delicate dance on a precipice, where one misstep could send us tumbling back into the depths of despair.

One evening, as the sun dipped below the horizon, casting a warm golden hue across the makeshift room, I watched Vincent as he absently cleaned the few weapons we had salvaged from the wreckage. His hands moved with a deft precision, yet the furrow in his brow revealed that his thoughts were elsewhere, lost in the labyrinth of his mind. I took a breath, summoning the courage to push a little further into the depths of his guarded heart.

"Why do you really stay?" I asked, breaking the comfortable silence that had settled between us like a soft blanket. "You're not just a soldier bound to a cause; there's something deeper at play here, isn't there?"

He paused, the weight of my question hanging in the air. For a fleeting moment, I thought he might actually share the truth, but he merely resumed his task, his jaw tightening. "I have obligations. You wouldn't understand."

"Try me," I urged, crossing my arms. "I may not know your world, but I'm not blind to the shadows that dance in your eyes when you think no one is watching."

Vincent's laughter was bitter, devoid of humor. "Obligations are a heavy cloak to wear, Claire. One I've been draped in since I was young."

"And do you like it?" I shot back, unwilling to let him deflect. "Because it sounds like a gilded cage to me."

"It's not that simple," he replied, his voice low and strained. "I owe everything to the Breed. My family—my choices—it's all intertwined. You think breaking free is as easy as cutting the strings?"

"Maybe not easy, but necessary," I countered, frustration bubbling to the surface. "You're living a life that's not yours to claim. It's suffocating you."

"Enough!" he snapped, slamming the weapon down on the table, the sound echoing through the room. "You don't get to decide what's suffocating me. You don't know what I've sacrificed."

I took a step back, stunned by the sudden intensity in his voice. "And you don't know what I've been through either, Vincent. We're both trapped, but you're the one holding the keys and refusing to use them."

His eyes softened for a moment, and I saw a flicker of the man I had come to admire and care for. "You really want to understand?"

"Yes," I breathed, my heart racing. "I want to know you—every part of you."

He studied me for what felt like an eternity, and just when I thought he might finally open up, a loud crash erupted from outside, shattering the fragile moment we'd built.

We both turned toward the noise, instincts kicking in as adrenaline surged through my veins. Vincent's expression shifted, a mixture of wariness and alertness clouding his features. "Stay behind me," he commanded, his voice low and steady as he reached for his weapon.

I nodded, every ounce of defiance in me momentarily quelled by the seriousness of the situation. I could feel the tension curling around us like smoke, thick and ominous. "What was that?"

"Something we didn't plan for," he replied tersely, glancing toward the door. "I'll check it out. Just wait here."

"Wait here?" I echoed, incredulous. "You know I'm not going to sit back and let you go off into danger alone."

"Claire—" he started, but I cut him off, stepping closer and fixing him with a determined gaze.

"No, Vincent. I'm not a damsel in distress, and you don't get to make that choice for me. We face this together, remember?"

He hesitated, his grip tightening on his weapon as he weighed his options. "Fine. But stay close and listen to me. We have to move quietly."

With a shared understanding, we stepped cautiously toward the door, the tension thickening the air around us. The remnants of the safehouse whispered memories of laughter and light, now tainted by the encroaching threat. I felt my heart racing, a wild drumbeat against the silence as we edged closer to the source of the sound.

As we reached the door, I glanced at Vincent, searching for reassurance in his eyes. Instead, I found resolve and a hint of fear—fear not just for himself but for me. It struck me then that he wasn't just a protector; he was a man grappling with the weight of everything he cared for.

He pushed the door open slowly, and the hinges creaked ominously, the sound slicing through the tension like a knife. We stepped out into the fading light, the world outside cloaked in shadows, each flicker of movement sending adrenaline surging through me.

"What do you see?" I whispered, my breath hitching as I squinted into the dimness.

Vincent's eyes scanned the area, his body coiling with tension. "Nothing yet, but that noise came from the north. We need to move."

We slipped out, the cool air wrapping around us like a shroud, each step drawing us closer to the unknown. My senses were heightened, every rustle and whisper heightening the anticipation. The forest loomed around us, branches twisting like fingers reaching out, and I could feel the pull of something sinister lurking just beyond our sight.

As we crept along the path, the hairs on the back of my neck prickled, a primal instinct warning me that we were not alone. I turned to Vincent, who was now tense and alert, scanning the darkened trees as if they might spring to life at any moment.

"Vincent," I said, my voice trembling slightly, "do you hear that?"

He stilled, his face hardening. "What do you mean?"

"Listen."

A low growl reverberated through the trees, deep and menacing, like thunder rolling in from a distance. My heart raced, and I instinctively took a step back, but Vincent remained rooted in place, his eyes narrowing.

"That's not good," he murmured, his tone a mix of fear and determination.

Before I could respond, the underbrush erupted with movement, and something dark and massive burst forth, barreling toward us. Vincent reacted in an instant, shoving me back behind him as he raised his weapon, eyes blazing with adrenaline and resolve.

"Run!" he shouted, and the urgency in his voice ignited a fire within me.

I didn't need to be told twice. I sprinted past him, adrenaline fueling my legs as I dashed down the narrow path. Behind me, I could hear Vincent's footsteps, steady and powerful, a protective force racing to keep me safe.

But just as I thought we might escape, a figure loomed in front of us, blocking our path. A figure shrouded in darkness, eyes glinting with a predatory gleam, and an unsettling smile creeping across its face.

"Going somewhere?" it hissed, the voice slithering into my ears like a serpent's whisper.

My heart sank as I skidded to a halt, the chilling realization washing over me: we had been led into a trap.

Chapter 9: Fractured Loyalties

The storm rattled the windows, each gust of wind howling like a banshee desperate to be let in. I sat on the edge of my bed, the frigid air swirling around me, and tried to shake off the lingering chill that crept beneath my skin. Vincent stood in the center of my dimly lit room, his silhouette barely illuminated by the flickering candlelight. Shadows danced across his face, accentuating the deep lines etched into his brow and the scar that ran jagged across his cheek—a reminder of a past he had yet to fully unveil.

"Why do you even care?" he asked, his voice low and gravelly, the weight of his words heavy in the air. He had come to me in the dead of night, as if afraid the world might collapse if he waited until morning. "This isn't your fight."

I leaned back, arms crossed, defiance curling my lips. "Maybe I want it to be. Maybe I don't want to just stand by and watch you drown in whatever this mess is."

His gaze darkened, but I could see the glimmer of something else beneath the stormy surface—vulnerability, perhaps. I tilted my head, trying to read him like a book with torn pages, desperately searching for the story hidden within. The air crackled with tension, a silent plea hanging between us, urging him to share the truth that lay buried beneath layers of bravado.

He sighed, the sound escaping him like a wounded animal's last breath. "You think you want to know. But trust me, you don't. The truth is twisted, tangled in betrayal and loss. It's not a fairy tale."

"I've lived my own twisted fairy tale," I shot back, the bitterness lacing my words sharper than I intended. "Believe me, I can handle a little darkness."

With that, he seemed to shatter, the facade falling away to reveal a raw vulnerability. He ran a hand through his tousled hair, frustration crackling in the air. "Fine," he relented, his voice a mere whisper now. "But don't say I didn't warn you."

As he began to speak, the storm outside raged on, but inside, the world fell silent, holding its breath in anticipation. "I was born into the Breed—a family shrouded in blood and secrets. They didn't tell me everything, of course. You don't get those details until you've proven your loyalty. But I knew enough to understand the gravity of their power. We weren't just a gang; we were a cult, woven together by fear and obligation."

I sat forward, drawn into the web of his story. "A cult? Like a religious group?"

He scoffed, a mirthless sound that echoed in the small room. "Not in the traditional sense. More like a family that consumes itself from the inside out. They taught us that loyalty was everything, that to betray one of our own was to invite death. But I was young, naive. I thought it was about protection. I didn't know it was a cage."

His voice cracked, the weight of memories evident in his tone. "When I was sixteen, my sister was taken. Eliza was everything to me—my light in that darkness. She was spirited and fearless, and she defied them. She had dreams of escape, of breaking free from the chains that bound us. But the Breed doesn't tolerate dissent. I watched helplessly as they took her, their cold eyes locking onto mine, and I knew I was powerless to stop it. The price of loyalty, they told me."

A chill swept through the room, but it wasn't the storm that sent shivers down my spine; it was the anguish etched into his features. "You don't understand what it means to be forced into silence," he continued, his voice shaking. "I promised I would protect her, and I failed. Every day since then, that promise has haunted me. It's a ghost that won't let me sleep at night."

The anger and sorrow in his voice were palpable, wrapping around me like a shroud. I felt my own heart constrict, empathy swelling within me. This was no longer a tale of a villain; this was a man grappling with the weight of his choices, his loyalties fractured by guilt and regret. "Vincent, you're not responsible for their actions," I said softly, trying to reach the part of him that still flickered with hope.

He shook his head, the anger bubbling beneath the surface. "You don't know them. You don't know what they're capable of. They will destroy anyone who stands against them, and I am bound to them, bound by blood. My loyalty is my prison."

I stood up, compelled by a surge of fierce determination. "Then let's break those chains together. You don't have to fight this war alone. I refuse to let you carry this burden by yourself."

His eyes widened, surprise flickering across his face. "You think this is a game? It's not just me at stake here. The Breed is ruthless. They won't hesitate to come after you."

I stepped closer, the distance between us shrinking, my heart pounding like a drum. "Then I'll fight them too. I'm tired of hiding, tired of letting fear dictate my choices. Let's take them down together."

For a moment, silence enveloped us, the storm outside a distant echo to the tempest brewing in his heart. He searched my gaze, uncertainty warring with a flicker of something I dared to hope was trust. "You're brave," he murmured, a reluctant admiration creeping into his voice.

"And you're more than just the scars you bear," I replied, a fierce determination lighting a fire in my chest. "We can't change the past, but we can fight for our future."

Vincent studied me, and for the first time, I saw a glimmer of hope in his eyes—a light that had been long extinguished, reigniting slowly in the face of an uncertain alliance. The storm continued to howl outside, but within that small room, a fragile bond was beginning to form, one that might just break the chains of loyalty and fear that had bound us both for too long.

The candlelight flickered, casting erratic shadows across the walls as we stood there, two souls entwined by shared pain, yet worlds apart in experience. I could feel the weight of Vincent's history pressing against me, almost tangible in the air between us. The echoes of his sister's name reverberated in my mind like a haunting melody—Eliza, the ghost of his past that refused to fade. As he looked at me, I sensed a shift, a silent agreement that perhaps we could stand against the tempest together.

"Let's say we do this," he said, his voice steadying as he squared his shoulders, the flicker of hope now mingling with doubt. "How do you plan to take on the Breed? They're not just some petty criminals. They are a network, a family that thrives on secrecy and violence. You have no idea what you're asking for."

"Then teach me," I replied, the resolve hardening in my voice. "You know them better than anyone. I'm not afraid of the dark if it means bringing some light into it. We need a plan, something concrete."

Vincent regarded me with a mix of surprise and admiration, his eyes reflecting a storm of emotions. "You really mean that, don't you?" he said, the corners of his mouth twitching upward, as if amused by my audacity. "Most people would run at the first sign of danger."

"Maybe I'm not most people," I shot back, a playful spark igniting in my heart. "Or maybe I've just always been drawn to the chaos. It keeps life interesting."

A low chuckle escaped him, breaking the tension, and for a fleeting moment, the burden on his shoulders seemed a little lighter. "Interesting is one way to put it. You have no idea what you're getting into. But fine, if you're serious, I'll help you."

His agreement felt like the first crack in the wall he had built around himself. I could sense the vulnerability beneath his bravado, a part of him that longed for connection yet feared the implications of it. "We need to find a way to gather information, to understand how the Breed operates. If we can disrupt their network from the inside, we might have a fighting chance."

He nodded, a contemplative look crossing his features. "There's a gathering tomorrow night—an initiation for the new recruits. If you want to learn about them, that's the perfect place. It's a chance to see the Breed in action, but it'll be dangerous. You'll have to keep your head down and act like you belong."

"Undercover is my middle name," I said, a grin spreading across my face. "Okay, maybe it's not, but I can pretend like it is. How hard can it be to blend in with a bunch of wannabe thugs?"

Vincent raised an eyebrow, half-smirking. "I can already see the 'pretend thug' persona oozing off you. You might want to work on that."

"Hey, I'm a natural at pretending! Watch and learn, Vincent." I straightened my back, adopting a mock-serious expression. "I'll just be the life of the party. 'Look at me, I'm super tough and definitely not terrified at all.'"

He laughed, a genuine sound that warmed the chill in the room. "You might need a little more than bravado. The Breed can smell fear a mile away."

"Then I guess I'll just have to wear my bravest face," I shot back, feeling a rush of adrenaline. The thrill of the plan fueled my resolve, driving away any remnants of doubt. "What's the plan for tomorrow night?"

"Meet me at the old warehouse on the east side around eight. We'll go in together, but you need to stick close to me. No heroics. We get in, we observe, and if it gets too hot, we get out. Understood?"

"Understood," I said, trying to suppress a grin at the prospect of this adventure. "I'll even wear my best 'I belong here' outfit. What do you think—leather jacket and combat boots? A classic."

"Just try not to attract too much attention," he replied, his tone shifting to serious. "This isn't a game. The Breed won't hesitate to eliminate anyone they see as a threat."

I nodded, the gravity of his words sinking in. "I get it. But I've spent too long being scared. This time, I'm not holding back."

Vincent's expression softened, his protective instincts flickering to life. "Just promise me you'll be careful. I can't lose you too."

Those words settled in my heart, stirring something deeper. "You won't lose me," I assured him, the sincerity evident in my tone. "We're in this together now. Besides, I don't go down without a fight."

As we prepared to part ways, the tension in the air shifted, taking on a new hue. There was a bond forming between us—one forged in shared secrets and a desire for freedom. The flickering candlelight illuminated his face, and for the first time, I saw more than just the troubled man before me. I saw a warrior, and I was ready to fight alongside him.

The night stretched before us, cloaked in uncertainty yet brimming with possibility. As I slipped into my bed, adrenaline coursing through my veins, I couldn't help but feel exhilarated. Tomorrow would be the first step in unraveling the twisted tapestry of the Breed, and no amount of darkness could extinguish the light sparking in my heart. The storm outside continued to rage, but I felt something shift within me—a readiness to confront the chaos head-on, to uncover the truth behind Vincent's past, and perhaps, in the process, discover my own strength.

Sleep came slowly, my mind whirling with plans and possibilities, the images of what lay ahead dancing tantalizingly on the edge of my consciousness. I was no longer just a bystander in my own life. I was about to become a player in a game far more dangerous than I ever imagined, but for the first time in a long time, I felt alive.

The night air was thick with anticipation, the kind that wraps around you like a velvet cloak, weighing heavy with secrets yet to be unearthed. As I stood in front of my mirror, the reflection staring back at me was both familiar and foreign. I had donned a black leather jacket that hugged my shoulders, giving me a fierce edge I desperately hoped would shield my nerves. The combat boots completed the look, scuffed and sturdy, perfect for the chaos I was about to dive into. I could feel the butterflies in my stomach fluttering to a beat that echoed the urgency of my mission.

At the appointed hour, I met Vincent at the warehouse, his presence a shadow in the night. The chill of the air seemed to dissipate in the heat of his intensity, his eyes scanning the surroundings with a predatory focus. "You made it," he said, a hint of surprise threading through his voice as he assessed my outfit. "And here I thought you'd chicken out."

"Not a chance," I replied, my tone playful, even as my heart raced. "I wouldn't miss this for the world. Besides, you think I'd let you have all the fun?"

He smirked, the tension easing a fraction. "Fun, right. Just remember, if things go sideways, we bail. Fast."

"Got it. No heroics," I affirmed, though the thrill coursing through my veins begged to differ. We slipped into the shadows of the warehouse, the stale scent of concrete and rust clinging to the air like a shroud. The space was alive with energy; muffled voices and the occasional clank of metal drifted through the cavernous expanse, hinting at the gathering just beyond.

As we crept further in, I felt the weight of the atmosphere shift. It was like stepping into a den of wolves, the air charged with unspoken power and a sense of impending danger. Vincent guided me to a vantage point, hidden behind a stack of crates, where we could observe without being seen. The flickering fluorescent lights illuminated a circle of figures clad in dark attire, their faces obscured, but their intentions unmistakably clear.

"Welcome, new recruits," a voice boomed from the center of the circle, authoritative and chilling. "Tonight, you take your first step into a family that protects its own. But make no mistake—betrayal will not be tolerated." The crowd murmured in response, nodding in unison, their eyes gleaming with a fervor that sent a shiver down my spine.

I turned to Vincent, a question simmering on my tongue. "Is it always like this? The indoctrination?"

"Pretty much," he muttered, eyes narrowed as he focused on the scene unfolding before us. "They thrive on fear and loyalty. They will use anything to bind you to them. If you're not careful, you could find yourself just like them."

"What does that say about you?" I teased lightly, trying to pierce through the gravity of the situation. But even I could hear the tremor in my voice, the underlying fear that clung to every word.

"Let's just say I've been on the other side of this equation," he replied, his tone somber. "But tonight isn't about me. It's about them."

As the initiator continued, outlining the brutal code of conduct, I felt my resolve harden. This wasn't just about gathering information. This was about dismantling a system built on fear, reclaiming lives stolen by the Breed's twisted ideology. A sudden noise broke my reverie—a scuffle at the edge of the gathering caught my attention, sending a spike of adrenaline racing through me.

"What was that?" I hissed, nudging Vincent with urgency.

He leaned forward, his body tense as he tried to peer around the crates. "Something's off. We need to be ready."

The murmurs grew louder, more aggressive, and the mood shifted palpably. A figure emerged from the darkness, a young woman, her face flushed with panic. “You don’t understand!” she cried out, her voice trembling with fear. “I didn’t want this! I—”

Before she could finish, the initiator stepped forward, a cold smile playing on his lips. “You think you can just walk away? This is a family. You are bound by blood now.” He raised a hand, and with a single motion, the atmosphere thickened with a chilling finality.

Vincent turned to me, his eyes fierce. “We can’t just stand by. We have to help her.”

“What? Are you crazy?” I exclaimed, the weight of his words settling heavily. “This isn’t some hero movie, Vincent! They’ll kill us!”

“I’m not asking,” he snapped, determination blazing in his gaze. “We have to do something. Now.”

Before I could protest, he moved forward, pushing through the shadows, an unstoppable force fueled by the ghosts of his past. My heart raced, a mix of fear and exhilaration propelling me after him. “Vincent! Wait!” I called, but he was already too far gone, too driven by the need to protect.

The commotion escalated. I watched as Vincent confronted the initiator, his voice raised, full of conviction. “Let her go! She deserves a choice!”

“Choice?” the man laughed, a sound devoid of humor. “You think she has a choice? You don’t belong here, Vincent. You should have stayed in your cage.”

My stomach twisted as I realized the danger we were in, the very thing we had come to disrupt now coiling around us like a snake ready to strike. I could hear the sound of footsteps closing in, the crowd’s energy shifting from curiosity to hostility. The recruit—a desperate glimmer of hope—stood frozen, caught between the menace of the Breed and our plea for freedom.

"Vincent, we need to go!" I shouted, panic threading through my voice as I felt the tide turning against us. But he wouldn't relent, standing his ground, the scar on his cheek a stark reminder of the battles he had fought.

Suddenly, chaos erupted. The crowd surged forward, anger palpable in the air, and the initiator's laughter morphed into a roar of fury. "You want her? You'll have to pay the price!"

In that instant, the world narrowed down to the chaos before me, and I felt a surge of adrenaline as I realized we were standing on the edge of a precipice, teetering between salvation and destruction. The warehouse, once just a shadowy place of secrets, became a battleground, and I had to make a choice.

"Vincent!" I yelled, reaching for him just as the crowd lunged forward, fists raised, the chaos swirling like a tempest around us. As I grabbed his arm, a deafening crash echoed through the air, and the world erupted into chaos, plunging us into a darkness where only one thing was certain: the line between freedom and captivity was about to be violently tested, and the stakes had never been higher.

Chapter 10: Shadows of Betrayal

The world unfurls in shades of gray as dawn peeks over the horizon, the remnants of our safehouse dissolving into the mist. I steal a glance at Vincent, his features carved in stone, eyes narrowed against the morning light that struggles to penetrate the heavy fog. There's a tempest brewing within him, a roiling sea of emotions that I can almost taste in the damp air. I've learned to read the signs: a tightening of his jaw, the way his hands curl into fists at his sides. Anger, I suspect, but it is laced with something deeper, something that pulls at the corners of my own heart. I want to reach out, to bridge the chasm between us with words, but I hold back, knowing that to press him now would only deepen the silence.

Instead, I draw my focus inward, mentally charting our course through the twisting alleys of this fractured world. The urgency of survival sharpens my thoughts like a blade, but even as I strategize our next steps, my mind drifts, spiraling into the stories Vincent has shared—fragments of a life that feels both distant and achingly close. He speaks of shadows and betrayals, of loyalty traded for survival, and I can't help but feel the weight of his past pressing down on my chest. It confuses me, this sense of empathy toward a man who embodies everything I was raised to fear. Each revelation pricks at my resolve, twisting it into knots, pulling me further into a whirlpool of conflicting emotions. How is it that I can feel drawn to him, even as he stands for all that I despise?

But before I can untangle that web, a sudden rustle shatters the stillness around us. I barely have time to register the sound before figures emerge from the gloom, their silhouettes outlined against the dawn—a squad of the Breed's scouts, moving with the precision of predators. My heart lurches, a wild animal caught in a trap, and panic spikes through me. I want to shout, to warn Vincent, but my voice fails me, lodged somewhere between disbelief and terror.

Their black uniforms blend seamlessly with the shadows, and the cold, calculating glint in their eyes sends a shiver down my spine. We're outnumbered, trapped in a corner of the world that offers no sanctuary.

Vincent's instincts kick in, and he shifts into a protective stance, his body instinctively positioning itself between me and the encroaching danger. There's something primal about the way he moves, fluid and fierce, as if he's a part of the very shadows that are closing in. The first scout lunges, and Vincent responds with a speed that astonishes me. It's like watching a storm break—a force of nature unleashed. The crack of fists meeting flesh fills the air, punctuated by grunts of exertion and the thud of bodies hitting the ground. I stand frozen, my heart racing in tandem with the chaos unfolding before me.

"Get back!" he shouts, voice hoarse and urgent, slicing through my paralysis. It snaps me into action, and I dart to the side, narrowly avoiding a grappling pair of hands that reach for me. The adrenaline coursing through my veins feels electric, sharp, as I try to find my footing amidst the fray. Every instinct screams at me to run, to escape this nightmare, yet I find myself rooted to the spot, torn between the instinct to flee and the bewildering urge to stay close to Vincent, the man I'm supposed to despise.

He fights with a ferocity that takes my breath away, a tempest of muscle and resolve. Each blow he lands against the scouts reverberates with an intensity that sends ripples through the air. There's a raw power in his movements, a dance of survival that draws my eyes like a moth to a flame. I'm torn between fear and an unexpected admiration for his skill, the way he defends me as if my life holds more weight than his own. I can see the blood spattering across his skin, the grit of the fight hardening his features, and yet he doesn't falter.

"Move!" he roars again, his voice strained, and finally, I snap out of my stupor. I dive into the nearest alley, my pulse racing, the adrenaline igniting every nerve in my body. I can hear the scuffle behind me, the clash of bodies and the desperate sounds of survival. I want to turn back, to help him, but I know I'll only be a liability—a weight dragging him down when he needs to soar.

The alley is narrow and dim, filled with the scent of damp earth and decay. I press against the cold, rough wall, breathless, listening for any sign of Vincent. The silence is deafening, punctuated only by the distant sounds of the fight, which seem to echo like a war drum in my ears. I can't shake the image of him, blood-stained and fierce, battling our enemies while I cower in the shadows. An overwhelming tide of guilt washes over me, pulling me under like a heavy blanket. I can't let him fight alone.

Just as I muster the courage to return, a figure emerges from the end of the alley. My heart stutters, caught between fear and hope, as I strain to see if it's him. The silhouette is familiar, moving with a desperate grace that ignites something deep within me. And then he appears, battered but unbroken, the flicker of determination in his gaze cutting through the fog of uncertainty. He's alive, and I've never been more grateful for the chaos that brought us together in this fractured world.

Vincent emerges from the chaos, his presence a palpable force that fills the narrow alley with an energy both fierce and protective. There's a wild look in his eyes that sends a jolt of electricity through me. I realize that beneath the layers of grit and battle-worn exterior lies a man who is fighting not just for survival but for something larger than either of us can comprehend. The air is thick with the smell of iron and sweat, mingling with the earthy scent of the alley, and I can't help but feel the weight of everything hanging in the balance.

"Are you hurt?" The words tumble out of my mouth before I can stop them, revealing the concern I can no longer contain. My fingers twitch, wanting to reach out and touch the places where his skin is marred with blood and bruises, to offer some kind of comfort or solace amidst the wreckage of our lives.

He shakes his head, though the movement is labored, and a hint of a smile flickers across his face—a flash of defiance amid the chaos. "Only my pride. I'm not much of a morning person," he quips, and the wryness of his tone pulls a reluctant chuckle from my lips, a momentary reprieve from the darkness surrounding us.

We stand together for a heartbeat, two lost souls tethered by circumstance. The fear and adrenaline coiling in my gut intertwine with something unexpected—a burgeoning connection that both thrills and terrifies me. It's maddening to realize how easily he slips past my defenses, unearthing emotions I never intended to explore. Yet, as I take in the breadth of his injury, the stark contrast of his strength and vulnerability, I'm reminded that the shadows he carries are not mine to bear.

"Where do we go from here?" I ask, my voice steady despite the whirlwind inside me. I'm surprised by my own resolve. Perhaps it's the adrenaline still thrumming through my veins, or maybe it's something deeper—a recognition that we're in this together, whether I like it or not.

He glances around the alley, eyes scanning for threats, ever the strategist. "We need to get off the streets. There's an old church a few blocks from here—abandoned, but it should give us some cover for a while." The way he speaks, with that mix of confidence and urgency, makes my heart race for reasons beyond fear. I nod, though uncertainty curls at the edges of my thoughts like smoke.

As we step out from the shelter of the alley, the world feels sharper, colors brighter against the grayness of dawn. The city's pulse thrums beneath our feet, a reminder of the life that continues unabated around us. Every rustle, every distant shout, sends a jolt through my senses, the reality of our situation crashing over me anew. We move in tandem, an unspoken rhythm guiding us as we navigate the twisted streets.

"What's it like to live in a world like this?" I ask, hoping to pry a little more into the shadows of his past, a curiosity that gnaws at me despite my better judgment. The question hangs in the air, delicate yet heavy, as if I'm opening a door to a realm I have yet to fully understand.

Vincent's jaw tightens, the momentary light in his eyes dimming as he considers my words. "It's a gamble," he replies at last, his voice low, thoughtful. "Every day is a question of survival—who to trust, who to betray. It's a game of chess with real lives at stake." There's a weight to his words, a somber truth that settles between us like an unwelcome guest. "You learn to keep your enemies close and your friends closer, but in the end, you're still just a pawn on someone else's board."

A chill creeps through me at the implication of his thoughts, the realization that in this fractured reality, trust is a fragile commodity. "And what about you?" I probe, emboldened by the moment. "Where do you fit in all of this? Are you the pawn, or the player?"

Vincent glances at me, a flicker of something unreadable passing across his features before he laughs softly, though it's tinged with bitterness. "Maybe I'm both. Sometimes it's hard to tell. You start out with one idea of who you are, and then life shows you how wrong you can be."

Before I can respond, we round a corner and the church looms before us, its weathered stones standing sentinel against the encroaching chaos of the world outside. The façade is crumbling, vines snaking through the cracks, a testament to time's relentless march. There's an eerie beauty to it, a stillness that contrasts sharply with the chaos of the city.

"Here," Vincent whispers, motioning for me to follow him through the heavy wooden doors. They creak ominously as we push them open, the sound echoing in the hollow space within. Dust motes dance in the shafts of light that filter through broken stained glass, casting colorful patterns on the floor.

Inside, the air is thick with the scent of must and memories long forgotten. Shadows cling to the corners, wrapping around us like a shroud. We step further into the nave, the silence enveloping us, and I can't help but feel the weight of history pressing down, the echoes of prayers and hopes that linger in the walls.

"We'll be safe here for a bit," Vincent assures me, his voice low as he surveys our surroundings. I nod, but the unease clings to me like a second skin. The stillness is too profound, too perfect, as if it's anticipating something.

"What if they find us?" I whisper, instinctively moving closer to him.

Vincent's gaze sharpens, the protective instinct flaring in his expression. "Then we'll deal with it. Together." His words are steady, a lifeline in the growing uncertainty, and in that moment, I realize that whatever shadows lurk in the corners of this sanctuary, we're no longer facing them alone.

But even as I grasp that truth, a chill snakes down my spine—a nagging sense that this place is not as safe as it appears, that the echoes of the past might yet become the specters of our present. And just as that thought settles in, a low rumble reverberates through the building, shaking dust from the rafters above, as if the very structure itself is warning us of an approaching storm.

The low rumble reverberates through the church's crumbling walls, shaking the dust from above like an ominous warning. My heart races as I glance at Vincent, whose expression shifts from fierce determination to cautious alertness. The tension in the air thickens, wrapping around us like a noose, and I can't help but wonder what other secrets this ancient place might harbor. The stained glass windows, fractured and dim, cast fragmented rainbows on the stone floor, a stark contrast to the growing dread pooling in my stomach.

"Did you feel that?" I ask, my voice a whisper, barely piercing the stillness that clings to the air.

Vincent nods, his eyes narrowing as he surveys the shadows. "Something's not right." His words hang between us, heavy with unspoken fears. The bravado he had shown earlier now feels like a fragile veneer, and I can't shake the sense that the past is closing in, its tendrils creeping out of the very stones that surround us.

"Great, just what I needed today—a little drama from the universe," I murmur, attempting to inject some levity into the moment, though it falls flat in the face of uncertainty. Vincent glances at me, the corners of his mouth twitching upwards, and I take a small comfort in the flicker of humor in his eyes, even as we stand on the brink of something dangerous.

Before we can catch our breath, a loud crash echoes through the church, followed by a scuttling noise. I turn, eyes wide, and the hair on the back of my neck stands up. "What was that?"

Vincent moves swiftly, stepping in front of me, his body tense like a coiled spring. "Stay behind me." The command is firm, but there's an undercurrent of protectiveness that sends warmth flooding through me, even as my pulse races.

We stand in a defensive posture, scanning the dim recesses of the church, shadows dancing like specters in the flickering light. The sound grows closer, a series of sharp movements, like something—or someone—navigating the dark corners of our sanctuary. A glimmer catches my eye, and my breath hitches as I spot movement in the alcove near the altar.

"Vincent, over there!" I gasp, pointing as I edge closer to him, my heart thudding in my chest.

He turns sharply, instinctively reaching for the knife at his belt. "Stay back!" he warns, but it's too late. The figure emerges from the shadows, and I let out a gasp, my hand flying to my mouth as recognition washes over me.

It's a girl, no older than sixteen, with wild hair and a smudge of dirt across her cheek. Her clothes are tattered, and she moves with a feral grace that speaks of a life lived on the margins. "You shouldn't be here," she hisses, darting towards us, eyes wide and darting like a cornered animal.

"Who are you?" Vincent's voice is low and cautious, his stance still protective as he observes her every movement.

"I don't have time to explain! They're coming!" she shrieks, glancing over her shoulder, fear etched into every line of her young face. "You need to hide!"

I look at Vincent, confusion swirling in my mind. "Hide? From what?"

"From them! The Breed—they'll find you! You need to get out!" Her words come in a frantic rush, and I can see the desperation in her eyes. There's something unsettling about her urgency, something that makes me want to believe her, even as reason tells me to be wary.

Vincent exchanges a glance with me, and I can almost see the gears turning in his mind, weighing our options. "What do you mean they're coming? How do you know?" he demands, stepping forward, his protective instincts flaring again.

"They've been tracking you," she says, her voice trembling. "I saw you in the market. I heard them talking—whispers about a traitor." Her gaze flickers nervously towards the entrance, the shadows almost seeming to pulse around her. "They know you're here. You have to leave now!"

A wave of dread crashes over me, mingling with the flicker of hope that maybe we're not as alone as I feared. "We can't just run," I argue, glancing at Vincent, searching for the reassurance I desperately need. "We need to find a way to defend ourselves, to fight back."

His eyes soften for a brief moment, a flash of understanding as he regards the girl, who seems so small and lost against the towering walls of the church. "Do you have somewhere safe?" he asks, his voice gentler, the fierce protector giving way to a reluctant ally.

"Not for long," she replies, the urgency creeping back into her voice. "But you can't stay here. You don't understand what they'll do to you if they find you."

Before we can respond, another crash echoes from the entrance, louder this time, reverberating off the stone walls. The sound of boots hitting the floor fills the air, heavy and purposeful. My heart races, a wild drumbeat that thrums through my entire being.

"Go!" Vincent commands, pushing the girl toward a side door. "Get out while you can!"

"No!" I cry, torn between the instinct to run and the growing bond I feel with this strange girl, this child who has suddenly thrust herself into our lives. "We can't leave you here!"

"I can take care of myself!" she snaps, her eyes flashing with defiance. "But you won't last a minute if you don't go now!"

The urgency in her voice pierces through the haze of uncertainty, and I can see the resolve settle into Vincent's expression, a grim acceptance of the fight we're about to face. "Alright," he says, taking my arm, guiding me towards the door. "We'll find another way."

Just as we reach the threshold, the door bursts open, and a group of scouts floods into the church, their dark uniforms stark against the chaos of stained glass and ancient stone. My breath catches in my throat as they sweep into the nave, eyes scanning, weapons drawn.

"Run!" Vincent shouts, pushing me forward even as he draws his knife, ready to face the storm.

I sprint into the unknown, heart pounding in my chest, the shadows of betrayal closing in behind us. The girl darts to the left, disappearing into the darkness, and I can't shake the feeling that the chase is only just beginning. As I look back over my shoulder, I see Vincent standing his ground, a solitary figure against a tide of darkness, and in that moment, I realize how deep this web of danger has woven around us.

With a final glance at the man who has somehow become my anchor in this storm, I plunge into the depths of the church's shadows, a flicker of fear igniting in my gut. The realization hits me like a thunderclap: in this world of betrayal, trust is as fragile as glass, and we are all just one misstep away from falling apart.

Chapter 11: Whispers in the Dark

The air in the tunnels was thick with a damp chill, wrapping around me like a foggy embrace. Each footstep echoed ominously against the stone walls, a reminder of how deep we had ventured beneath the world above. The flickering light from Vincent's torch danced across the rough-hewn surfaces, casting elongated shadows that seemed to stretch and twist, almost as if they were alive, hungry for secrets. I kept close to him, not just for the warmth that radiated from his body but for the strength I found in his presence—a silent fortress against the perils we had narrowly escaped.

Vincent moved with a deliberate calm, though I sensed the tension coiling beneath his skin like a tightly wound spring. I caught glimpses of his profile: the sharp line of his jaw, the way his brow furrowed in concentration, and the faint glimmer of regret that lingered in his dark eyes. I had known him as a man of few words, but now, as we navigated the damp labyrinth, I felt an urge to unravel the layers of his history. It was as if the very walls around us whispered tales of sorrow and sacrifice, begging to be heard.

"Tell me," I urged softly, breaking the heavy silence. My voice barely penetrated the stillness, but it felt vital, like a lifeline thrown into the abyss. "What happened? What promise did you break?"

He paused, the light flickering as if it too held its breath. I could see him wrestle with the words, his gaze drifting down the dark passageway, perhaps searching for a way to distance himself from the shadows of his past. Finally, he turned to me, his expression raw and unguarded, a side of him I had never seen before. "It was many years ago," he began, his voice low, laced with the weight of memories. "Before the world fell apart, before I became what I am now."

He shifted slightly, the muscles in his arm tensing beneath my touch, yet I didn't pull away. I needed him to feel my presence, my support, even as the shadows of his past clawed at his heart. "I made a vow to protect someone—someone I cared for deeply. But circumstances... they conspired against me. I failed her when she needed me the most."

I felt a shiver ripple through me, not just from the chill in the air but from the anguish that dripped from his words like the water seeping from the walls. "What happened to her?" I pressed, heart racing. There was a gravity in his confession that anchored me to the moment, drawing me deeper into his world.

"She was taken," he said, a bitter edge creeping into his voice. "By those who wanted to exploit her gifts. I should have fought harder, should have found a way to save her. But I was... I was weak." His admission hung in the air, heavy and suffocating. "Every day since, I've paid the price for that weakness. I've hunted them, driven by the need to make amends."

The dim light flickered, and I felt the urge to reach for him again, to remind him that he was not alone in this darkness. "You weren't weak," I said firmly, the words spilling out before I could second-guess myself. "You're doing everything you can now, fighting for those who can't fight for themselves. That takes strength."

Vincent turned his gaze back to me, his dark eyes searching mine, as if trying to gauge the truth in my assertion. "You don't know what it's like to carry such a burden," he replied, his voice tinged with a sorrow that made my heart ache. "To live with the knowledge that someone else is suffering because of your failure."

"Then teach me," I urged, my spirit rising against the shadows that threatened to engulf us. "You're not just a solitary warrior; you have allies now. You have me. Let me help you carry this."

He fell silent, the weight of his thoughts palpable. The dripping of water was the only sound, a steady metronome keeping time with the tumult of our emotions. Just then, a distant rumble echoed through the tunnels, sending a chill skittering down my spine. I felt the shift in the air—the tension coiling tighter around us, urging us to move forward.

Vincent seemed to snap back to the present, shaking off the ghosts of the past like a dog shaking off water. "We need to keep moving. The longer we linger, the more likely we'll be found." His tone shifted back to its familiar steadiness, but I could sense the lingering shadows clinging to him, a dark cloak he couldn't quite shed.

As we continued down the corridor, the atmosphere thickened with anticipation. I could feel the walls closing in, each step echoing like a countdown, drawing us closer to an uncertain fate. The flickering torchlight illuminated patches of mold and dampness, a reminder of how long this place had been forgotten—much like the promises Vincent had made long ago. I wondered how many other lost souls lingered in the dark, each with their own burdens, their own whispers of despair.

"Do you ever think about what lies ahead?" I asked, trying to keep the conversation alive, to stave off the encroaching dread. "When this is all over?"

Vincent's gaze softened for a moment, a glimpse of the man beneath the weight of his scars. "I try not to," he replied, a hint of vulnerability creeping into his voice. "Hope can be a dangerous thing in a world like this. But... if I do allow myself a vision, it's one of peace. A place where I can lay down my sword and no longer be haunted by the past."

I wanted to reach for his hand, to promise him that we would find that peace together. But instead, I simply nodded, taking in the warmth of his words as they brushed against the chill that surrounded us. And as we pressed onward, deeper into the heart of darkness, I made a silent vow of my own. I would stand by him, through the shadows and the light, fighting for our future against the lingering whispers of the past.

The chill in the air settled around us, thick as a blanket, as we navigated deeper into the tunnels. I could feel Vincent's tension shifting with each step, a palpable force that threatened to consume us both. The dampness of the stone walls seeped into my bones, mingling with the heaviness of his memories. I had stepped into a world of shadows, and I wasn't sure if I could guide us back to the light.

"Tell me about her," I urged, drawing on every ounce of courage I possessed. "The one you tried to save. What was she like?" I wanted to understand what had driven him, what had forged the man standing next to me, burdened yet resilient.

His breath hitched slightly, a momentary crack in his stoic façade. "Her name was Lila. She had this light about her—an infectious laugh that could brighten even the darkest corners. She was brilliant, you know? A natural at everything she touched." He paused, his voice softening, the weight of affection evident in his tone. "She could heal with just a touch. The kind of person who could mend a broken heart with her smile."

A flicker of warmth danced in the cold, sterile air, and I felt an unexpected pang of jealousy mixed with admiration. "What happened to her?" I pressed gently, not wanting to pry too deeply but needing to understand the magnitude of his loss.

"I was too late," he replied, his voice strained as if he were recounting a painful confession. "By the time I realized what was happening, she had already been taken by the Breed. They wanted to exploit her abilities, to use her as a weapon. I didn't even have the chance to say goodbye."

I inhaled sharply, the reality of our adversaries hitting me like a wave. The Breed were not just faceless monsters; they were predators, hunting down the innocent for their gain. "You said you've been hunting them," I reminded him, urgency creeping into my words. "What if they're still after her? What if she's still alive?"

Vincent's eyes darkened, the flicker of hope extinguished beneath the weight of despair. "If she is alive, she's in a place far worse than this," he said, gesturing to the damp walls that felt like a prison. "These tunnels were once safe havens. Now they're just remnants of a forgotten world, echoing with the ghosts of those who couldn't escape."

An unsettling quiet enveloped us, the silence stretching as long as the dark corridors that twisted around us. I could see the struggle etched into his features, the clash between the man he was and the man he had been forced to become. "You can't give up hope, Vincent," I insisted, my voice steady against the growing darkness. "Hope is the one thing they can't take from us."

He turned to me, surprise flickering across his face. "What do you know about hope?" His voice was sharp, a protective shield against the vulnerability that threatened to break through. "Hope is a double-edged sword. It can drive you to fight, but it can also cut deeper than any blade when you realize it was in vain."

"You sound like a poet," I shot back, unable to resist a playful grin, even in this grim situation. "I thought warriors preferred swords to sonnets."

Vincent chuckled softly, the sound like a warm ember in the coldness of the tunnels. "Perhaps a little poetry wouldn't hurt. You might have something there."

As we moved forward, the tight corridor opened up into a wider chamber, the walls glistening with moisture as if they were alive. In the dim light, I could see markings etched into the stone—runes, symbols of protection and warding. "This place is ancient," I breathed, running my fingers over the cool surface. "What is this? A sanctuary?"

"It was," Vincent said, his tone shifting again, laden with nostalgia. "Before the Breed turned it into a hunting ground. We used to gather here, share stories, fortify our resolve. Each mark tells the tale of those who came before us, a testament to their struggles and sacrifices."

"Then we're not just fighting for ourselves," I said, the realization dawning on me like the first rays of dawn. "We're fighting for all of them, too. For their memories."

Vincent nodded, the flicker of hope igniting once more in his eyes. "Exactly. We need to remind ourselves of what we're up against, the cost of inaction. The world above may have forgotten, but down here, we remember."

"Then let's make sure they remember us," I replied, the fire of determination sparking in my chest. "Let's take back what they've stolen."

He smiled then, a rare, genuine smile that chased away some of the shadows clinging to him. "You've got a fierce spirit, you know that? It might just be what we need to turn the tide."

Before I could respond, a faint sound echoed through the chamber, a rustle that sent a jolt of adrenaline coursing through me. I turned toward the source, every instinct on high alert. "What was that?"

Vincent's expression hardened, the warrior surfacing once again. "Stay close," he instructed, his voice a low whisper as he scanned the darkness. "We're not alone."

The tension in the air thickened, the silence now heavy with anticipation. I could hear my heart racing, each thump echoing in my ears. We had ventured into the depths of the unknown, and I could feel the shadows pressing in on us, eager to ensnare us in their clutches.

"Vincent," I whispered, my voice barely audible over the pounding of my heart. "What if it's the Breed? What if they've found us?"

"We'll face them together," he assured me, his eyes fierce and unwavering. "We have to be ready for anything. We can't let fear dictate our actions."

As the rustling grew louder, I caught a glimpse of movement in the darkness, a shadow flickering just beyond the edge of the torchlight. I braced myself, adrenaline flooding my veins as I prepared to confront whatever lay ahead.

"Whatever it is, we stand firm," I stated, my voice steadier than I felt. "We'll fight, and we'll survive."

Vincent's gaze locked onto mine, a silent agreement passing between us. Together, we would face the unknown, and together, we would carve our place in this darkened world. The shadows might whisper of despair, but we were the storm that could drown out their voices, rising with a renewed purpose as we plunged deeper into the night.

The rustle in the shadows intensified, an eerie symphony of movement that sent a shiver down my spine. Vincent's body shifted instinctively closer to mine, an unspoken protection forming between us. The flickering torchlight illuminated the chamber just enough to create a surreal atmosphere, as though we had stepped into a scene from a forgotten legend, poised between the living and the spectral.

"Are we sure we want to find out what's lurking in the dark?" I quipped, forcing a lightness into my voice to mask my own apprehension. The corner of Vincent's mouth quirked upward, a fleeting smile that brightened the oppressive gloom, and for a moment, I felt a surge of courage.

"Curiosity killed the cat," he replied, a hint of mischief in his tone, but the shadows in his eyes betrayed the seriousness of our situation. "But satisfaction brought it back. So, let's hope we have nine lives to spare."

A scuffling noise emerged from deeper within the tunnel, more pronounced now, and I felt my heart leap into my throat. "That doesn't sound like a friendly greeting," I murmured, inching closer to Vincent, who had assumed a protective stance, his muscles coiled like a spring ready to explode.

"Stay behind me," he instructed, his voice dropping to a whisper, firm yet laced with urgency. I nodded, my resolve solidifying as I prepared to face whatever horrors awaited us in the depths of this underground labyrinth.

With a slow, deliberate movement, Vincent turned to face the darkness, his posture radiating an air of quiet determination. The tension was palpable, thickening the air until it felt as if I could reach out and touch it. My senses heightened, the world around us faded into a muted blur, and all I could focus on was the sound—scratching and shuffling, growing closer with each heartbeat.

Suddenly, a figure emerged from the shadows, stumbling into the torchlight. My breath caught in my throat as I registered the familiar silhouette. "Lila?" I gasped, the name escaping my lips like a prayer.

But as the figure drew nearer, my hope twisted into confusion. The woman before us was a ghost of the vibrant girl Vincent had described. Her hair hung in disarray around her face, eyes wide and wild, a haunted look reflecting the depths of her torment. "You shouldn't have come here!" she cried, her voice echoing off the stone walls, a desperate plea that resonated in my chest.

Vincent stepped forward, disbelief etching lines across his features. "Lila, is it really you?" His voice trembled with emotion, and the protective walls he had built around his heart began to crack, revealing the vulnerability beneath.

"Yes!" she shouted, frantically glancing over her shoulder as if the darkness itself might come alive. "But you have to leave! They'll come for you, too. You don't understand—this place is a trap!"

I exchanged a glance with Vincent, the air thickening with unspoken questions. "Who? Who is coming?" I asked, stepping cautiously toward Lila, drawn by the urgency in her voice.

"The Breed," she said, her eyes darting to the shadows, panic flooding her features. "They're always watching. They know this place. They're just waiting for the right moment."

Vincent clenched his jaw, the weight of the world pressing down on him. "We can't leave you here," he said firmly, his voice filled with resolve. "You shouldn't have to face them alone. We can help you."

Lila shook her head violently, her expression morphing from fear to fury. "You don't get it! They're not just looking for me—they want you, Vincent! You're the one they want!" Her words struck like a blow, the truth hanging heavily in the air between us.

"Then let them come," Vincent replied, a steely glint in his eyes. "I've fought them before; I'll fight them again."

"Fighting won't save you!" Lila cried, her voice breaking. "They'll use you against each other! They thrive on our weaknesses, and they know your history."

"I don't care about my past," he shot back, frustration lacing his words. "What matters is the present, and I'm not leaving you here to face this alone."

Before Lila could respond, the shadows shifted again, a darker presence emerging from the gloom. My heart raced as figures began to materialize, the sinister forms of the Breed stepping into the dim light, their faces cloaked in malevolence. Their eyes glimmered like shards of glass, and the air around us crackled with the promise of violence.

"Ah, how touching," one of them sneered, stepping forward. His voice dripped with mockery, a chilling sound that sent dread coursing through me. "Reunions in the dark, how poetic. But you've all forgotten one simple fact—you cannot escape what you are."

"Stay back!" Vincent growled, stepping protectively in front of me and Lila, his muscles tensed for a fight.

Lila's face paled as the Breed advanced, fear twisting her features. "They've come for you, Vincent! They won't stop until you're destroyed!"

I felt the weight of her words settle heavily on my chest, a reminder of the stakes we faced. "We can't let them take you again," I murmured, my resolve hardening as I stepped to Vincent's side. "We're not letting fear dictate our actions."

The lead figure raised his hand, a flicker of power crackling in the air. "You don't have a choice. The past will always catch up to you, Vincent. It's time to pay your debt."

With a sudden surge, the shadows coalesced into a swirling mass, and I felt the very air around us pulse with danger. I reached for Vincent's hand, squeezing it tightly. "We'll find a way through this," I whispered fiercely, unwilling to let despair claim us.

The first attack came like a gust of wind, shrouded in darkness and malice. I barely had time to brace myself as the air exploded with a violent force. Vincent and I stood shoulder to shoulder, our connection unyielding as we faced the encroaching darkness.

"Whatever happens, don't let go!" he shouted, and just as the shadow lunged forward, I felt the world tilt on its axis.

The darkness engulfed us, a cacophony of whispers rising to a fever pitch. Time itself seemed to fracture as we prepared to confront our enemies, the air crackling with energy and uncertainty. I could feel Vincent's presence beside me, fierce and unwavering, and in that moment, we were not just fighting for our lives; we were battling the very fabric of our destinies.

And just as the shadows seemed poised to swallow us whole, a blinding light burst forth from the depths of the tunnel, illuminating everything in a brilliant glow. The air thrummed with energy, and I caught a glimpse of something—someone—charging toward us from the depths of the light, a figure poised to change the course of our fate forever.

"Lila, Vincent, hold on!" the figure shouted, their voice cutting through the darkness like a knife.

But before I could make sense of what was happening, the shadows recoiled, and everything faded into chaos.

Chapter 12: The Edge of Desire

The kiss ignites something inside me, a wildfire that consumes the careful barriers I've built around my heart. I can hardly breathe as his lips move against mine, soft yet insistent, as if he were carving a space for himself in my very soul. It's dizzying, the way he pulls me into his orbit, the world outside the warehouse fading into an indistinct blur. The air is thick with the scent of dust and the faint metallic tang of rust, but all I can focus on is the warmth radiating from his body, the way it envelopes me in a cocoon of raw, untamed emotion.

As our kiss deepens, I sense the hesitation in him, a flicker of uncertainty that almost breaks the spell. His hand, still resting against my cheek, trembles slightly, and it pulls me back from the edge of oblivion. I pull away, breathless, and search his face, that handsome, rugged face that holds shadows I long to chase away. "Vincent..." I start, but the words catch in my throat. What do I even say? That I'm terrified of this connection we've stumbled into? That I've spent years building walls to keep people like him out?

He searches my eyes, the intensity of his gaze making me feel exposed. "What are we doing, Lynn?" he asks again, and there's a vulnerability in his voice that stirs something deep within me. His question hangs between us, charged with unspoken fears and uncharted territory. I know he feels it too—the pull that draws us together, yet threatens to tear us apart with its ferocity.

"I don't know," I admit, my voice barely above a whisper. "I've never felt this way before." It's true; I've danced on the fringes of desire, always keeping my heart under lock and key. But here, in this crumbling edifice that used to be a place of industry, everything feels different. It's as if the universe conspired to shove us together, forcing us to confront the undeniable chemistry sparking in the air around us.

His expression softens, and for a moment, the fierce resolve I've come to admire gives way to something tender, almost vulnerable. "Neither have I," he confesses, his thumb brushing over my cheekbone in a gesture so gentle it nearly steals my breath. "I'm scared, Lynn. Scared of what this means."

"Scared?" I echo, the word slipping out before I can stop it. "You're the fearless one. The one who charges into the fray without a second thought."

He chuckles softly, but there's a tightness in it. "Fear doesn't mean you don't act; it just means you're aware of the stakes." He pulls back slightly, and I can see the flicker of doubt in his eyes. "And right now, the stakes feel high."

His words hang heavy between us, but as I study him, I realize that fear is something we both understand. I've built my life around it, carefully curating a world where the familiar is safe and predictable. But the ache in my chest when he's near tells me that perhaps it's time to tear down the walls, to leap into the unknown. "What if we just... embraced the fear?" I suggest, my heart racing at the thought. "What if we just let it happen?"

His brow furrows, as if contemplating the weight of my proposition. The silence stretches, thick and palpable, each heartbeat echoing the uncertainty that thrums in the air. I'm terrified of where this could lead—what if we crash and burn? But the thought of stepping back, of retreating into my solitary existence, fills me with an even deeper dread.

Vincent's hand drops to his side, but he takes a step closer, closing the space between us. "You're talking about a leap, Lynn. A leap I've never taken before. But..." He pauses, his gaze piercing into mine as if trying to read my very thoughts. "But I can't deny what I feel."

That simple admission sends a rush of warmth through me, wrapping around my heart like a warm blanket. It's exhilarating and terrifying all at once. "Then why not take that leap together?" I propose, my voice steadier than I feel. "Let's face whatever comes next as a team."

He hesitates, his expression conflicted, but then something shifts in his eyes—an understanding, perhaps, or the dawning realization that we might be standing at the precipice of something monumental. "You make it sound easy," he replies, a hint of a smile breaking through the tension. "But it's not, is it?"

"No," I admit, laughter bubbling up in me, buoyed by the shared weight of our fear. "But then again, nothing worthwhile ever is."

As the moonlight spills through the broken windows, illuminating the dust motes dancing in the air, I take a breath, grounding myself in the moment. The warehouse, once a relic of abandonment, now feels like a sanctuary—a place where we can shed our fears, even if just for a little while. The reality of what's to come is uncertain, but standing here with him, I can almost convince myself that we might just make it through the darkness together.

"Okay," he says, and there's a new lightness in his voice. "Together, then."

And just like that, the weight of the world shifts, the air crackling with the promise of new beginnings. I smile, feeling the last remnants of doubt fade away as I reach for his hand, intertwining our fingers, sealing our unspoken pact. The future may be unpredictable, but in this moment, surrounded by the shadows of the past, I know we're ready to face whatever comes next.

The kiss feels like a spark igniting a long-dormant fire, and for a moment, I lose myself in the sensation, the world around us dissolving into a haze of warmth and possibility. But as I pull away, breathless and dazed, the enormity of our decision rushes back like a cold wave, grounding me in reality. "What now?" I whisper, my heart racing as I wrestle with the uncertainty that lies ahead.

Vincent studies me, his brow furrowed in thought. "Now?" he echoes, a hint of amusement dancing in his eyes, which softens the tension in my chest. "Well, we could start with not getting caught by whoever owns this place."

I chuckle, a nervous sound that fills the stillness of the warehouse. "I suppose that would be a solid plan." The remnants of dust swirl around us, caught in the beams of moonlight that filter through the cracks in the dilapidated walls. It's an odd sanctuary, one filled with echoes of the past, and yet, in this moment, it feels like our own secret world.

"I've always liked the idea of secret rendezvous," he says, his voice low and teasing. "But maybe we should find somewhere a little less likely to collapse on us."

"Are you saying I'm a liability?" I feign shock, clutching my chest dramatically. "I thought I was a delightful partner in crime."

"More like an unpredictable variable," he retorts, an impish grin spreading across his face. "But that's what makes you interesting, isn't it?"

"Interesting? I prefer 'fascinating.' Much more dramatic." I can't help but smile back at him, feeling the tension lift slightly as laughter dances between us. The warmth of our exchange chases away the chill of fear, reminding me why I took this leap in the first place.

We linger for a moment, caught in a shared breath of possibility, before Vincent breaks the silence. "But really, I want to know what this means for us. If we're doing this—whatever 'this' is—then we need to be honest with each other."

His sincerity pulls me back to the gravity of our situation. "Honesty, huh?" I raise an eyebrow. "Aren't you getting a bit ahead of yourself? We've only just started making out in abandoned buildings. Don't you think we should work up to the deep, emotional stuff?"

He chuckles, but the seriousness returns to his expression. "I'm serious, Lynn. I can't pretend that everything is just casual. Not when you're involved."

The warmth in my chest flickers, battling with the weight of his words. "I get it. I do. But I've spent so long building my walls, I'm not sure how to let them down. What if I ruin this? What if I'm just a passing phase for you?"

"I could say the same about myself," he counters, stepping closer, his eyes narrowing with intent. "What if I'm just a momentary distraction in your grand plan? You're about to launch into a new chapter of your life. You have dreams, goals, and here I am—just a guy in a warehouse."

"A guy who's definitely more than just a guy," I interject, a smile creeping onto my face despite the seriousness of the conversation. "You're practically a romantic lead in a novel."

"Is that so?" He feigns deep thought, stroking his chin with exaggerated deliberation. "I suppose I do have the brooding good looks."

"Oh, definitely. And the mystery," I add, gesturing around us. "Who wouldn't swoon for a man who hangs out in a decrepit warehouse at night?"

Vincent's laughter fills the air, and it feels like a balm. But as the laughter fades, the reality looms over us once more. "In all seriousness," he says, his tone shifting, "I'm not going anywhere. If you decide to take this leap with me, I promise to be here, to figure it out together."

"Even if I drag you into the chaos of my life?"

"Especially then," he replies, a fire igniting in his gaze that makes my heart flutter. "I want to see the chaos. I want to know the real you."

The sincerity in his voice sends a rush of warmth through me, a strange sense of safety wrapped in vulnerability. "Then let's do it.

Let's embrace the chaos," I say, my heart pounding in my chest, the thrill of this decision coursing through my veins.

"Chaos, it is," he agrees, and there's an unmistakable spark in his eyes as he leans in closer again. This time, the kiss feels different—deeper, richer with the promise of uncharted territory. I melt into him, surrendering to the moment, to the wild heartbeats echoing in the hollow spaces of the warehouse.

Just as our lips meet, a loud crash interrupts us, reverberating through the building like thunder. We pull apart, wide-eyed, adrenaline flooding my system. "What was that?" I hiss, my heart racing with a mixture of excitement and fear.

Vincent's expression shifts from playful to serious in an instant. "I don't know, but we should probably check it out. Or run. Running is a valid option."

"Let's go with option one for now. I don't want to get caught doing something we probably shouldn't be doing," I whisper, a mix of apprehension and thrill surging through me as we inch toward the source of the noise.

We creep through the shadowy expanse of the warehouse, the silence amplifying the sound of our footsteps against the concrete floor. My heart races, a pounding drum echoing my trepidation. The shadows seem to shift around us, each creak of the building making me jump as we approach the source of the disturbance.

As we round a corner, a figure emerges from the darkness—a shadowy silhouette moving cautiously, its back to us. "Who's there?" I call, my voice steady despite the tremor of fear.

The figure turns slowly, and recognition floods through me. "What the hell are you doing here?" I gasp, shock coursing through my veins as I step back, my heart racing for an entirely different reason now.

The figure in front of us steps into the moonlight, revealing a face I never expected to see here—Carter, the very embodiment of chaos in my life, and a walking reminder of my past mistakes. "Lynn? Vincent?" he says, a mix of surprise and annoyance contorting his features. "What the hell are you two doing in my warehouse?"

"Your warehouse?" I echo incredulously, my mind racing to catch up. "Since when did this become your territory?"

"I've been working on a project," he shrugs, as if his presence here isn't a complete violation of my newfound moment of connection with Vincent. "What are you doing here? I didn't expect to find you two playing house."

Vincent's jaw tightens beside me, his muscles tensing as he assesses the situation. "We were just leaving," he says, his voice low and steady, a subtle warning threading through his words.

"Leaving?" Carter scoffs, crossing his arms over his chest, and the tension in the air thickens like the shadows around us. "You think I'm going to let you just walk out? You don't get to sneak around here without a conversation."

I take a step forward, heart pounding, bracing myself for what might come next. "Carter, we're not here to cause trouble. This is just a misunderstanding."

"Is it?" His gaze darts between us, a mix of accusation and curiosity. "Because it looks to me like you're having a moment. In my warehouse."

"It's not what you think," Vincent interjects, stepping slightly in front of me, a protective barrier against the tension radiating from Carter. "This is none of your business."

Carter's lips curl into a smirk, the kind that makes my skin crawl. "Oh, it's definitely my business when my ex shows up with her new boyfriend—"

"Ex?" Vincent's voice is sharp, cutting through the air like a blade.

"It's not—" I start, but Carter talks over me, a gleam of mischief in his eyes. "Oh, it is. Lynn and I had quite the adventure once upon a time. You could say we have history."

"History doesn't define us," I snap, anger flaring in my chest. "And what I do now is not your concern."

Carter shrugs, the casual demeanor only infuriating me further. "Whatever helps you sleep at night. But you can't just walk into my space and expect me to ignore the elephant in the room."

Vincent shifts slightly, his presence a comforting weight beside me, but I can feel the tension radiating from him. "We weren't looking for trouble," he repeats, his voice calm but firm. "But if you're going to make it an issue, then perhaps we need to rethink how we handle this."

"Is that a threat?" Carter challenges, his bravado masking the tension simmering beneath.

"Not at all," Vincent replies, and I can hear the deliberate patience in his tone. "But I won't stand here and let you bully us into a corner. This doesn't have to escalate."

Carter's expression darkens, and for a moment, I wonder if he'll push this confrontation further. "You think I'm bullying you?" he says, incredulity lacing his words. "You're the one trespassing, not me."

"Let's not make this worse than it needs to be," I implore, stepping between the two men, hoping to defuse the tension. "Carter, we can talk about this like adults. We don't have to turn this into a fight."

"Talk?" He scoffs, but I see a flicker of doubt in his eyes. "What is there to talk about? You two look cozy enough."

"Cozy is one way to put it," I reply, trying to inject some levity into the situation. "More like two people exploring options in a—"

"In a dilapidated warehouse?" he finishes, rolling his eyes. "You must have a thing for the dramatic."

"Drama is my middle name," I quip, hoping to steer the conversation back to calmer waters. But the moment hangs heavy with unspoken words, and I know that deep down, it won't be that easy.

Carter shifts on his feet, and I can sense the inner conflict. "Look," he says slowly, "I didn't come here to start a fight, but you need to understand something."

Vincent narrows his eyes, clearly wary. "And that is?"

"I know you, Vincent. You don't stick around. You disappear when things get tough." His words cut through the air, each syllable sharp with accusation.

I feel Vincent tense beside me, and I step closer to him, willing to be a buffer against the barbs. "That's not fair, Carter. Everyone has their reasons. Vincent is here now, with me."

"Here's the thing," Carter continues, his voice lowering as if he's about to impart some wisdom. "I've been in Lynn's life long enough to know she has a penchant for falling for the wrong guys."

"Which would make you the poster child for wrong choices," Vincent shoots back, his eyes narrowing. "Do you want to revisit your own history?"

A flicker of anger passes over Carter's face. "I'm not the one in danger here. You are, Vincent. You're playing with fire, and I'm not just talking about Lynn's heart."

"What's that supposed to mean?" I ask, my voice rising as confusion mixes with a fresh wave of anxiety.

"It means—" Carter begins, but the sound of footsteps echoing in the distance interrupts him, sharp and jarring.

We all turn, straining to see through the shadows, and a chill races down my spine. "Who's there?" I call, my voice wavering slightly as the footsteps draw closer.

Vincent moves instinctively, placing himself between me and the direction of the noise. "Stay behind me," he whispers, and the protective instinct in his voice sends a shiver of warmth through me, even amidst the growing fear.

"Great, now we've got uninvited guests," Carter mutters, scanning the darkness as the footsteps grow louder, a deliberate cadence that feels menacing in the dim light.

As the figure steps into view, I freeze, recognizing the familiar silhouette. My breath catches in my throat, dread pooling in my stomach as the reality of our situation solidifies. The tension in the air thickens, and I realize that what I thought was a moment of connection has transformed into something far more perilous, where past choices and unexpected alliances converge in an uncertain climax.

"Lynn," the figure says, voice cold and steely, "we need to talk."

Chapter 13: Fragile Trust

The kiss still tingles on my lips, a sweet ache that teeters on the precipice of something profound yet terrifying. It hangs in the air between us, a delicate thread spun from unshed emotions and untold fears, binding us together even as shadows loom ever closer. In the dim light of our sanctuary, I can hear the whispers of the outside world, a place where danger lurks just beyond our fragile walls. Vincent's footsteps echo against the cold stone floor, each stride filled with an urgency that gnaws at my insides. He moves with a restlessness that mirrors my own turmoil, the tension coiling tighter with every passing second.

I can't help but admire him; even in his anxiety, there's a grace to his movements, a fierce determination etched into the set of his jaw and the intensity of his gaze. The air is thick with unspoken words, the kind that cling to the back of your throat like smoke. I can see the weight of our circumstances etched on his brow, a stark reminder that we're not simply two people tangled in the threads of a burgeoning romance. We're fugitives, hunted by the Breed, their insatiable hunger for power spilling over into our lives like a creeping poison.

"Lynn," he finally says, his voice low and steady, cutting through the tension like a knife through butter. "We need to go back. To where it all began."

The words hang heavy in the air, reverberating in my chest with a mix of dread and longing. The thought of returning to the Breed's stronghold feels like a plunge into icy water, a reckless abandonment of everything I've fought to escape. But as I meet his gaze, those stormy eyes brimming with conviction, I feel the trepidation shift into something else—something warmer, a flicker of hope that perhaps we could rewrite our story.

But that hope is a fragile thing, easily shattered by the cruel reality of our situation. "Are you out of your mind?" I snap, a surge of adrenaline pushing me to confront him. "That place is a death trap. We'll be walking right into their hands."

His expression doesn't falter, and for a moment, I wonder if he's even hearing me. "We're running out of time. They know we're here, and if we don't act now, we'll be hunted down like animals. We have to take the fight to them."

There's a fire in his words, a passion that ignites something deep within me. I want to believe in him, to trust that we can find a way to turn the tides in our favor, but fear gnaws at my resolve. "And what if we fail? What if they catch us?"

He steps closer, the warmth of his presence enveloping me, and for a fleeting moment, the world outside disappears. "We won't fail. Not with you by my side."

His words dance in the air between us, wrapping around my heart like a vine, squeezing tightly until I can't breathe. There's an intoxicating pull to him, a magnetic force that makes me feel alive yet utterly terrified. I want to cling to the safety of our sanctuary, to bask in the glow of what we could become, but the reality is a monstrous beast lurking just outside our fragile haven.

"What's the plan then?" I ask, my voice softer now, laced with curiosity rather than fear.

Vincent exhales, a mixture of relief and apprehension. "We gather intelligence, figure out their movements. If we can anticipate their next move, we can strike first."

"Intelligence?" I arch an eyebrow, half-smirking, half-serious. "You make it sound so... James Bond. Are we supposed to infiltrate a gala, drink martinis, and shake hands with villains?"

He chuckles, a low, rumbling sound that warms the space between us. "Not quite, but we do need to blend in. I know a few contacts who can help us get inside."

I watch as he leans against the rough stone wall, the shadows playing across his features, highlighting the determination etched into his every line. The thought of slipping back into the heart of the enemy's lair, mingling with the very people who wish to see us dead, sends a shiver down my spine. Yet, despite the fear clawing at my insides, something stirs within me—a rebellious urge to fight back, to take control of my fate instead of letting it be dictated by those who would see us fall.

"What's the worst that could happen?" I say, attempting to sound braver than I feel. "A little espionage? A dash of charm? I'm not saying it's a great idea, but if it means sticking it to the Breed, I'm in."

His eyes flash with something akin to pride, and I can't help but smile back, feeling a surge of warmth bloom in my chest. "That's the spirit."

Just then, a distant sound interrupts our moment—an ominous crash that reverberates through the walls of our sanctuary, sending a jolt of adrenaline coursing through my veins. My heart races as I meet Vincent's gaze, the playful banter shattered like glass, replaced by a stark realization that our time is running out. The Breed is here, and we have to move—now.

"Get ready," he murmurs, urgency infusing his voice as he pulls away, determination setting his jaw. "We don't have much time."

I nod, the weight of the world settling on my shoulders as I prepare to step back into the fray, knowing that with every choice we make, we tread a fine line between hope and despair. I take a deep breath, steeling myself for the challenges ahead, the kiss still lingering like a promise of what we could fight for—a love forged in the flames of battle, fierce and unyielding.

Adrenaline thrummed through my veins as I adjusted to the sudden shift in atmosphere, the air around us thickening with the promise of imminent danger. The distant crash faded into an unsettling quiet, a precursor to the chaos I could feel lurking just beyond the shadows. I stole a glance at Vincent, his silhouette sharp against the dim light. The way he held himself—shoulders squared, fists clenched—spoke volumes about his resolve, and it ignited a fire within me that battled fiercely against my fear.

"Okay, so we're going back," I said, the words rolling off my tongue like a dare. "But if we're going to make it out of this alive, we need a plan. No more Mr. Hero running in blindly. Got it?"

Vincent shot me a sideways glance, an amused smirk tugging at the corners of his mouth. "Mr. Hero, huh? I'll take that as a compliment. But really, you're right. We need to think this through."

I felt the tension ease slightly as we shared a moment of levity, but it was quickly swept away by the grim reality of our situation. "You have any ideas on how we're supposed to get back in there without being caught? Maybe we can disguise ourselves as villains. That could work."

He chuckled, a deep sound that resonated in the quiet. "I'd pay good money to see you dressed as one of them. You'd need a cape for the full effect."

I grinned, shaking my head. "Capes are so last season. I was thinking more along the lines of something sleek and shadowy. Maybe a leather jacket? Or, better yet, something in a darker palette—just to fit in with their whole 'brooding villain' aesthetic."

Vincent's laughter faded, replaced by a more serious tone as he reached for my hand, our fingers intertwining. "Jokes aside, we need to be smart. They'll be on high alert, which means we'll need to be stealthy. I have a contact in the city who can help us get access to their intel. If we can learn their schedules, we'll know when it's safest to move."

"Contact, huh?" I raised an eyebrow. "Is this person likely to get us killed or just mildly inconvenienced?"

"Let's go with mildly inconvenienced. Lydia's a bit... eccentric, but she's reliable."

"Eccentric? That's comforting. I can't wait to meet our new best friend." I squeezed his hand, more to reassure myself than him. "Just promise me one thing—if she offers us tea, we decline. It's always the tea."

He nodded, a twinkle in his eye. "Noted. No tea."

The moment of humor broke, as if a weight had descended upon us again. We were racing against time, and I felt it in my bones. As we moved through the makeshift sanctuary, I caught a glimpse of the city beyond the small, barred windows, the evening sky painted in hues of purple and gray. Somewhere out there lay the Breed's stronghold, a place that felt more like a fortress than a home. My stomach twisted at the thought of what awaited us.

"Are you ready?" Vincent asked, his voice a low rumble, a steadying force amidst the chaos brewing inside me.

"Ready as I'll ever be," I replied, forcing a smile even though my heart hammered against my ribcage. "Let's go give Lydia a visit."

With a final glance around our refuge, we slipped out into the night. The streets of the city were alive with sounds—a cacophony of laughter, distant music, and the hum of cars cutting through the cool air. Under the dim glow of streetlights, we moved quickly, hearts pounding in sync, bodies attuned to the electric tension of being so close to the enemy.

Vincent led the way through winding alleys, past crumbling buildings cloaked in shadow, until we arrived at a door that seemed almost too unassuming to lead to anything of consequence. He knocked twice, a rhythm that seemed both familiar and strange, and I held my breath, the anticipation thickening the air.

The door creaked open, revealing a woman with wild hair and an even wilder grin. Lydia was an explosion of color amidst the muted surroundings, her bright red coat standing out against the drab backdrop of the city. "Finally! I was beginning to think you'd gotten lost!"

"Or caught," Vincent replied, stepping inside. I followed, feeling the warmth of her space wash over me. The walls were plastered with maps and photographs, a chaotic array that somehow felt inviting.

"Lydia, this is Lynn," Vincent introduced, gesturing toward me. "We need your help."

"Help? I'm all about help! What do you need?" She clasped her hands together, eyes sparkling with excitement.

"A map of the Breed's stronghold," Vincent said, cutting straight to the chase. "We need to know their movements—anything you can share."

"Oh, sweetie, you're in luck! I just received a shipment of intel that's positively juicy." She rummaged through a pile of papers, her fingers dancing over the sheets until she produced a map, its edges frayed and marked with annotations.

I leaned closer, tracing the lines with my eyes, absorbing the information like a parched traveler at an oasis. "You've got everything mapped out, haven't you?" I murmured, impressed.

"Of course! I live for this! Now, you'll want to avoid the eastern wing—it's crawling with guards, but if you sneak through the old maintenance tunnels here..." She pointed to a narrow, winding line that disappeared into a shadowed corner.

Vincent nodded, absorbing every detail, but I couldn't help but interject. "Wait, hold on. Maintenance tunnels? Are we going to be crawling through grime and who knows what else? What is this, a horror movie?"

"More like a heist flick," Lydia said, winking at me. "And don't worry; I'm sure it'll be thrilling. You'll be in and out before you know it."

Thrilling. The word echoed in my mind, but all I could think about was the uncertainty of what lay ahead. "And if things go sideways?"

Lydia waved a hand dismissively, as if that possibility was merely an afterthought. "That's why you have Vincent! Just stick to the plan and you'll be fine."

I shot Vincent a glance, and the glint in his eye reminded me of the promise he'd made earlier—to keep us safe. I had to trust him. "Right. Just stick to the plan," I echoed, my voice steady despite the flicker of doubt inside.

As we huddled closer to the map, the weight of our task loomed over us. The tension was palpable, each of us aware that this moment could change everything. I took a deep breath, ready to embrace the chaos of the path ahead.

The map lay spread out before us, an intricate web of corridors and hidden routes that seemed to pulse with possibilities. Lydia's fingers traced the lines as if conjuring a spell, her excitement palpable. "This is your lifeline," she said, her voice rising with enthusiasm. "If you go through the maintenance tunnels, you can access the mainframe without being spotted. Just be cautious—those tunnels haven't seen light in years."

Vincent nodded, his focus unwavering as he studied the details. "So we enter here, through the service door in the alley, and navigate through the lower levels." He pointed at the dimly lit area marked on the map. "We'll need to be quick. The guards rotate every twenty minutes."

"Twenty minutes?" I echoed, incredulous. "That's practically an eternity for us! Do they take coffee breaks in there?"

"They might," Lydia interjected, a playful glimmer in her eyes. "If you happen to bump into them, just distract them with small talk about the weather. Works like a charm."

"Right, because nothing disarms a guard like a riveting discussion on precipitation," I quipped, earning a laugh from both Vincent and Lydia. But beneath the banter, a current of anxiety twisted in my stomach.

Lydia continued, her voice now serious. "In all seriousness, once you're in, you'll need to access the mainframe quickly. There's a trove of information there that could turn the tide in your favor."

"Information, right. The holy grail of our operation," I replied, mentally steeling myself for what was to come. "Let's just hope it doesn't come with a side of death."

Vincent squeezed my hand, his touch grounding me. "We can do this, Lynn. We have to do this."

With the plan taking shape, we set our departure for the late evening, when the shadows would cloak our movements. As night fell, the city transformed into a vibrant tapestry of lights and sound, bustling with life yet filled with an undercurrent of danger that tinged the air. I glanced at Vincent, whose expression was a mix of determination and a touch of concern.

"Stay close," he murmured as we stepped into the cool night, the familiar weight of our mission settling heavily on my shoulders.

Navigating through the alleys, we kept our voices low, our steps careful as we approached the service door. The distant sounds of laughter and clinking glasses from a nearby bar filled the air, a stark reminder of the normalcy we'd once known, now a mere echo of a life that felt light-years away.

"This is it," Vincent whispered, gesturing to the door, its surface worn and unassuming. I took a deep breath, my heart thundering in my chest.

"Ready?" I asked, though the tremor in my voice betrayed my nerves.

"Ready," he confirmed, and we pushed through the door into the darkness beyond.

The corridor was narrow, the air stale and thick with the scent of dust and decay. We moved quickly, guided only by the dim light filtering in from above. My heart raced, each thump echoing in my ears as I stole glances at Vincent, who was scanning every corner with hawk-like intensity.

"I can't believe we're doing this," I muttered, the absurdity of our situation hitting me like a wave. "I mean, who thought crawling through dark tunnels would be a fun Saturday night?"

"Right? I had different plans, but this works too," he replied, a smirk playing at the edges of his lips, his attempt at humor cutting through the tension.

As we ventured deeper, the air grew colder, and the oppressive silence of the tunnel wrapped around us like a heavy cloak. The walls seemed to close in, the shadows stretching menacingly as if watching our every move. Just when I thought the darkness might swallow us whole, we stumbled upon a small maintenance room filled with equipment and ancient machinery that had long since gone to seed.

"This must be it," Vincent said, stepping inside cautiously, his breath hitching as he took in the surroundings. "We can access the mainframe from here."

I moved beside him, squinting at the mess of wires and outdated tech. "You know, I always thought being a spy would be a little more glamorous than this. Where's the high-tech gadgetry?"

"Right? I was hoping for exploding pens or something." He chuckled, but his expression quickly shifted to focus. "Help me with this."

I nodded, rolling up my sleeves as we began sifting through the clutter. The tension crackled in the air, a palpable energy that underscored the weight of our mission. With each passing moment, the sense of urgency grew, a ticking clock counting down to who knew what.

"Here, I found a terminal," Vincent said, excitement mingling with apprehension as he brushed dust off a monitor. "If we can get this online, we might be able to access their network."

As he worked, I kept watch, my senses heightened, every creak and distant sound amplified in the eerie silence. "Hurry, please," I whispered, stealing a glance at the door, my instincts screaming at me to be vigilant.

Vincent's fingers danced over the keyboard, frustration flickering across his features. "It's taking longer than I thought. Come on... come on."

"Any day now would be great," I muttered under my breath, willing the technology to cooperate.

Finally, the screen flickered to life, illuminating his face in a ghostly glow. "Got it!" he exclaimed, a spark of triumph igniting in his eyes. The screen displayed a maze of files, all labeled with ominous titles.

"Okay, this is it. We're looking for anything on their operations, their personnel—anything that can help us."

I leaned closer, scanning the files, my heart pounding in rhythm with the urgency of the moment. "There has to be something here."

Just as I began to scroll through the documents, a sudden noise echoed from the corridor behind us—a distant thud that sent a jolt of adrenaline coursing through my veins.

"Did you hear that?" I asked, my voice a sharp whisper.

Vincent's head snapped up, his face pale. "Yeah. We need to move, now."

Before I could respond, the door burst open, and a figure stood silhouetted against the light—a guard, his eyes narrowing as he spotted us. Panic surged through me as Vincent sprang into action, his instincts kicking in.

"Run!" he shouted, grabbing my arm and pulling me toward the back of the room.

My heart raced as I stumbled after him, the reality of our situation crashing down. Just as we reached the rear exit, more footsteps thundered in the hall, and I felt the weight of inevitability settle in.

"Vincent, they're coming!" I cried, fear lacing my voice as we scrambled through a narrow doorway, hearts pounding with the knowledge that there was no turning back now.

We burst into another corridor, the sound of pursuing footsteps echoing behind us like a countdown to chaos. In that moment, as we raced forward, I couldn't shake the feeling that we were running toward a precipice—one that might lead to salvation or plunge us into darkness.

And as I glanced back at Vincent, determination etched on his face, I realized that we were on the brink of something monumental, a decision that would alter our fates forever. The echo of the footsteps grew louder, merging with my frantic heartbeat, until I could almost hear the Breed's breath on my neck, hot and threatening.

"Lynn!" Vincent called, and as I turned to him, I saw the glint of something metallic in his hand. "This way!"

But before we could take another step, a shout rang out behind us, followed by the blare of alarms echoing through the halls, shaking the very foundations of our escape. My breath caught in my throat as the realization hit—a stark, cold certainty that this was only the beginning of a fight that would determine everything.

Chapter 14: The Heart of the Abyss

The air was thick with tension as we navigated the dimly lit streets, the world around us teetering between the familiar and the foreboding. Each footfall echoed like a heartbeat, and I wondered if the shadows were conspiring against us, whispering secrets that would betray our every move. Vincent and I slipped past flickering streetlights, the yellowed glow casting elongated shadows that danced and morphed like specters on the pavement. The city, once a vibrant tapestry of life, now felt like a labyrinth, each corner a new possibility of peril.

Vincent's hand was a reassuring anchor in the swirling uncertainty. His fingers intertwined with mine, their warmth radiating an unspoken promise. I could feel the strength in his grip, a silent message that we would face whatever awaited us together. It was a sentiment that bolstered my courage, even as unease twisted in my stomach like a coiled serpent. The Breed's headquarters loomed ahead, an ominous structure hidden beneath layers of concrete and secrecy, its very existence a reminder of the tangled web we had entered.

As we rounded the last corner, the entrance to the stronghold came into view—a weathered door embedded in an unremarkable wall, marked only by the faintest scratches of what once might have been a sign. My heart raced. It felt like stepping into the belly of a beast, knowing it could swallow us whole without a moment's hesitation. I hesitated, my feet rooted to the ground, but Vincent's unwavering gaze urged me on. "We have to keep moving," he whispered, his voice low and firm.

"Right," I managed to reply, swallowing hard. The moment felt monumental, a crossing of thresholds that would change everything. I could sense the weight of what lay ahead—secrets tangled in lies, the past clawing its way into the present. Yet beneath the fear, a spark of determination ignited within me. We were survivors, and if the Breed had anything to say about it, we would fight for our future.

The door creaked open, revealing a narrow staircase spiraling downward into a well of darkness. I glanced back, catching a fleeting glimpse of the city above—a chaotic mosaic of life I knew I was about to leave behind. Taking a deep breath, I stepped inside, drawn by an inexplicable force, the darkness welcoming me like an old friend. Each step we descended seemed to strip away the last remnants of my former self, the light of the world above fading into nothingness.

Vincent followed closely, his presence a constant reassurance against the encroaching shadows. The air grew cooler as we descended, tinged with the scent of damp stone and something metallic—a hint of danger that made my skin prickle. Just as I began to question the wisdom of our descent, the staircase opened up into a vast underground chamber, illuminated by flickering overhead lights that cast long shadows across the rough-hewn walls.

The space was filled with activity. Figures moved about, their faces obscured by hoods or turned away, yet I could sense the tension in the air. Whispers flitted like moths around a flame, secrets shared in hushed tones, the atmosphere thick with anticipation. I felt a knot of apprehension tighten in my chest; we were not alone in our quest. Here, in the heart of the Abyss, alliances were forged and broken in the blink of an eye.

"Stay close," Vincent murmured, and I nodded, fighting the urge to shrink back. He led me through the crowd, weaving between bodies until we reached a makeshift table at the far end of the chamber. It was cluttered with maps and strange devices, remnants of plans drawn in haste. A woman stood behind it, her sharp features illuminated by the soft glow of a nearby lamp. She was fierce, with eyes like shards of ice, and I could sense the authority that radiated from her.

"Vincent," she greeted, her voice a low growl. "You're back sooner than expected."

"We encountered some complications," he replied, his tone clipped. "I needed to bring her here."

Her gaze shifted to me, assessing, as if trying to peel back the layers of my facade. "You're the one he spoke of—the wildcard in this dangerous game."

I felt a flush rise to my cheeks, both pride and embarrassment swelling within me. "I'm no wildcard," I asserted, lifting my chin. "I'm here because I want to help."

"Help?" The woman's lips curled into a sardonic smile. "Do you even know what you're stepping into? This isn't a game of chance; it's survival. You'll need more than courage if you want to make it through this."

Before I could respond, a commotion erupted nearby. Voices raised in alarm, and my pulse quickened as a figure broke through the crowd, urgency etched across their face. "We've got a breach! They're coming!" The words hung in the air like a gunshot, drawing every gaze toward the entrance.

My heart raced as I turned to Vincent, his expression hardening, eyes alight with a fierce determination. "We need to prepare," he said, and I felt a wave of adrenaline crash over me. This was it—the moment we had feared was finally upon us. The Abyss was about to test us in ways we could never have imagined.

"Prepare for what?" I asked, my voice steadier than I felt.

"Battle," he replied, his grip tightening around my hand. "It's time to show them what we're made of."

In that instant, the weight of our choices settled over me like a shroud. Whatever lay ahead, we would face it together, bound by the fierce resolve that had brought us this far. The flickering lights dimmed further, casting us into uncertainty, but I felt something shift within me—a steely determination to emerge victorious, no matter the cost. We were on the brink of a fight that would define us, and I refused to back down.

The chaos erupted like a lightning strike in the heart of the Abyss, the suddenness of it igniting a spark of primal fear in the air. Voices raised in urgency sliced through the tense atmosphere, drawing every set of eyes to the entrance where a figure stood, panting and disheveled. My stomach dropped as I watched men and women alike spring into action, their previous conversations forgotten, replaced by a fevered energy that thrummed with anticipation.

Vincent's hold on my hand tightened as he turned to face the commotion. "We need to organize," he said, his tone shifting from apprehensive to commanding, an authority rising within him that I had not fully appreciated until now. He exuded a sense of purpose that ignited something within me, a yearning to be a part of this fight, however daunting it seemed.

I squeezed his hand, a silent pact that echoed louder than words. We were in this together, no matter how treacherous the waters ahead. Vincent turned to the woman at the table, her icy demeanor now softened by the urgency of the situation. "What's the status?" he asked, his voice steady despite the turmoil around us.

She met his gaze, her expression hardened into a mask of resolve. "A faction of the Breed has discovered our location. They're armed and coming fast. We have less than ten minutes to prepare." The gravity of her words sank in, and I felt a cold sweat break out across my brow. The fear that had lingered in the back of my mind transformed into a fierce determination.

"Ten minutes?" I echoed incredulously. "What do we do with ten minutes?"

The woman shot me a glance, her eyebrows arching in skepticism. "We gather weapons, fortify the entrances, and pray to whatever gods you believe in that they're not as prepared as we are."

Vincent turned to me, his eyes gleaming with a mix of excitement and adrenaline. "Let's go," he urged, and with a nod, we raced toward the nearest supply table. I had never thought of myself as the type to charge into battle, but the weight of the situation infused me with a surge of adrenaline I had never felt before.

We reached the table, a haphazard assortment of weapons strewn about—knives glinting in the low light, makeshift shields crafted from scrap metal, and a few pistols that looked as though they had seen far too many skirmishes. I grabbed a knife, its handle cool and solid in my palm, the weight reassuring. "Do you think this will be enough?" I asked, looking at Vincent, who was busy collecting ammunition.

He flashed a wry smile, one that cut through the tension like a warm knife through butter. "We'll make it enough. It's not the size of the arsenal; it's how we use it, right?"

I couldn't help but laugh, despite the dire circumstances. "So, you're saying we need to be creative?"

"Exactly." He grinned, and in that moment, I felt a flicker of hope, a reminder that in the depths of darkness, humor could still pierce through like sunlight.

We joined the throng of people bustling about the chamber, voices rising and falling as they prepared for the impending confrontation. I could see fear etched in the lines of their faces, but it was counterbalanced by an undeniable camaraderie. These were not just warriors; they were a family, bound by loyalty and a shared mission.

As we gathered weapons and supplies, I couldn't shake the feeling of impending doom that hovered over us like a storm cloud. The air felt charged, electric with anticipation, and every footfall echoed the ticking clock of our fate. "What if they're too strong?" I whispered to Vincent, the doubt creeping in despite my efforts to remain resolute.

"We'll find a way," he replied, his voice steady as steel. "We have to."

With the clock still ticking, we finished our preparations. I found myself drawn to a makeshift barricade being assembled against one of the walls, filled with boxes and scrap metal. "What's the plan?" I asked a burly man who was anchoring a large piece of debris into place.

"Hold the line," he grunted, sweat glistening on his brow. "When they come, we push back. No one gets through without a fight." His fierce determination sent a shiver of conviction through me.

Vincent joined me, resting a hand on my shoulder. "Stick close. We'll cover each other. Just remember what we practiced."

I nodded, adrenaline surging through my veins. "Right. Creative solutions, remember?"

He chuckled softly, the sound a buoy in the rising tide of anxiety. "Exactly. Just keep your wits about you, and we'll be fine."

Suddenly, the heavy thud of boots echoed from the entrance, a sound that reverberated like a drumroll announcing the arrival of our fate. My heart raced, and I could see others around me tense, every muscle coiled tight with anticipation.

The doors burst open, and a wave of figures surged into the chamber, the dim light catching on their weapons. They were a blend of fierce determination and chaotic energy, eyes wild with the thrill of battle. I could feel Vincent's presence at my side, a calm amidst the storm, as we faced this unyielding tide together.

"Get ready!" Vincent shouted, his voice cutting through the noise. "We're not backing down!"

The air crackled with tension as our opponents rushed forward, and I could feel the world narrowing to that single moment—their presence, our resolve, the electrifying push and pull of chaos about to erupt. The atmosphere thickened with the impending clash, a heady mix of fear and exhilaration that promised to change everything.

"Let's show them what we're made of!" I yelled, surprising even myself with the fervor in my voice. I gripped the knife tighter, the cold steel grounding me in a moment that could define our very existence. We were more than just bodies in the fray; we were a force—a united front determined to carve out our fate amid the shadows.

And as the first clash rang out, reverberating through the chamber, I knew one thing for certain: I was ready to fight.

The moment the first clash erupted, the world around me transformed into a chaotic symphony of shouts and clattering metal. Adrenaline surged through my veins, igniting every sense as the air thickened with the smell of sweat and impending conflict. I barely had time to process the chaotic scene unfolding before me; figures rushed past, shadows of determination and desperation flickering in the dim light.

I stood shoulder to shoulder with Vincent, our weapons at the ready, hearts synchronized in the chaos. The initial wave of attackers crashed against our makeshift defenses like a storm battering a fragile coastline. Bodies collided, and the sharp sound of metal meeting metal reverberated in my ears, creating a pulse that matched the frantic beat of my heart.

"Stay sharp!" Vincent shouted, lunging forward as an opponent swung a heavy baton in our direction. I could feel the force of his resolve at my back, and with a quick pivot, I ducked under the arc of the swing, my knife finding its mark with a surprising accuracy I didn't know I possessed.

"Nice move!" Vincent called, a hint of pride in his voice. "You're a natural."

"Let's hope I'm a natural at survival," I replied, my voice steady despite the whirlwind of action surrounding us. The energy in the room was electric, the chaos a dance we hadn't chosen but were determined to master.

The clash continued, our side pushing back against the intruders with fierce resolve. The woman at the makeshift table had rallied the troops, her voice cutting through the din with a fierce clarity. "Form a line! Hold your ground!" she commanded, her presence a beacon of strength amid the tumult. I caught her eye, and in that moment, I saw the weight of her leadership reflected in the depths of her gaze—she was as much a warrior as anyone in this room.

As we fought, I felt a primal instinct take over, a survival mode kicking in that transcended fear. I moved with fluidity, weaving through the crowd, thrusting my knife with precision, my body responding to the rhythm of battle as if it were a long-forgotten dance. But just as I began to feel a sense of control, a sharp shout drew my attention.

"Cover the rear!" someone yelled, and I turned just in time to see another group of attackers burst through an unguarded entrance, a menacing wave of bodies pouring in. Panic surged in my chest, but Vincent's steady hand grasped my arm. "We can't let them flank us!"

"Right!" I yelled, adrenaline surging anew as I followed his lead. We pivoted, joining a line of defenders who stood ready to absorb the impact. "On my count," Vincent said, his voice steady and commanding. "One, two—"

The moment he shouted, we charged forward, meeting the new threat head-on. The clash was intense, a cacophony of growls and shouts filling the air as we fought for our lives and our home. It was in the heart of this chaos that I felt the connection between us deepen—a bond forged in the fires of conflict, where each of us fought not just for ourselves, but for the others standing beside us.

A sudden movement caught my eye—a flash of silver slicing through the throng. My heart plummeted as I recognized the familiar figure of a foe I had encountered before, a ghost from the past. A sharp knife glinted menacingly in their grip, and before I could shout a warning, they lunged for Vincent.

"Vincent!" I cried, panic slicing through me like a blade. I lunged forward, propelled by instinct and sheer desperation, but time seemed to slow as I raced to intercept. My feet pounded against the ground, my breath a frantic rhythm as I hurled myself between them.

The impact knocked me off my feet, the force of it sending shockwaves through my body. I twisted as I fell, managing to deflect the blade just inches from Vincent's side, but it came at a price. The knife grazed my arm, pain blooming like a flower unfurling its petals.

"Are you okay?" Vincent's voice was a mix of concern and urgency, and he was at my side in an instant, worry etched into his features. I clenched my teeth against the pain, adrenaline dulling the edges as I pushed myself up.

"Just a scratch," I replied, forcing a smile even as blood trickled down my forearm. "Nothing I can't handle."

"Nothing you can't handle?" He shot me a disbelieving look. "You just saved my life!"

"Yeah, well, saving you is sort of my job now," I said, trying to lighten the mood despite the rising stakes.

Just then, the tide of the battle shifted. The initial wave of attackers began to retreat, their confidence faltering in the face of our determination. Cheers erupted from our side, a collective surge of hope coursing through us. But before I could allow myself to relax, I felt a sudden chill, an instinctive awareness that something wasn't right.

"Don't let your guard down!" the woman commanded, her voice cutting through the celebratory shouts. "They're regrouping!"

In that moment, the atmosphere shifted, an unsettling tension hanging in the air like a storm cloud on the horizon. I exchanged a glance with Vincent, the unease mirrored in his eyes.

"Something's coming," I murmured, and before he could respond, the ground beneath us trembled with an ominous rumble, a deep growl resonating from the very bowels of the Abyss.

"What the hell is that?" Vincent's eyes widened, his grip on my hand tightening as we turned to face the entrance.

The walls vibrated, dust cascading from the ceiling as the noise intensified, a roar that seemed to shake the very foundations of our refuge. Suddenly, the front wall cracked, a jagged fissure splitting the stone like a wound, and from the darkness beyond, a massive silhouette loomed, backlit by the flickering lights of the chamber.

"What is that?" I breathed, fear clawing at my throat as the creature emerged from the shadows, a monstrous figure far larger than any we had faced.

The air grew thick with dread as the room fell silent, all eyes drawn to the looming presence before us. It wasn't just a fighter; it was something otherworldly, something that promised destruction.

"Everyone, brace yourselves!" the woman shouted, her voice breaking through the frozen moment.

I felt the ground tremble beneath my feet as the creature stepped forward, and the world around me fell away, leaving only the weight of uncertainty. We were at the edge of an abyss, not just of stone and earth, but of fate itself, and as the shadows loomed larger, I realized we were teetering on the brink of something catastrophic.

"Vincent," I whispered, the fear in my voice palpable. "What do we do now?"

But before he could respond, the creature unleashed a deafening roar, and all hope fractured like glass shattering under pressure. In that moment, the Abyss seemed ready to consume us whole, and as the darkness surged forward, I knew this was a fight we might not win.

Chapter 15: Secrets Unveiled

The hidden chamber is a world apart from the sterile, imposing corridors that led us here. The air hangs heavy with secrets, a musty scent that whispers of time forgotten and stories buried. Flickering shadows dance along the walls, the only light emanating from a single, flickering bulb overhead, casting an eerie glow on Vincent's anxious face. I can see the conflict etched in the lines of his forehead, the tension in the set of his jaw, and it dawns on me that whatever he's about to reveal has the potential to change everything.

"Vincent," I say, my voice a blend of concern and curiosity. "What is this place?"

He hesitates, swallowing hard as if the words he's grappling with might choke him. "It's a repository of... information. About us. About those who went missing." His eyes dart around the room, as if the very walls might betray him, or worse, reveal the enormity of what he has to share.

I step closer, the chilling reality of his words settling in like a dense fog. Each file, meticulously stacked, carries a name I once whispered in laughter, shared dreams with, or held in the safety of my heart. "What do you mean, about us?" The pit in my stomach deepens, a sensation akin to standing on the edge of a precipice, the ground crumbling beneath me.

Vincent pulls out a file, its corners frayed, the name on the cover causing my breath to hitch in my throat. "Samantha Albright," he reads softly, as if the name were a sacred incantation. "She disappeared three years ago. No one knew what happened to her." His fingers trace the outline of the folder, his expression haunted by a past he seems unable to escape.

I feel the air leave my lungs, replaced by a creeping dread that wraps around my heart like a vice. "Samantha... I used to play in the park with her as a child. We promised we'd always look out for each other." The memories flood back—sunlit afternoons filled with laughter, the taste of cotton candy on our tongues, the innocence of childhood dreams. The stark reality of her absence casts a long shadow over those moments.

Vincent's gaze sharpens, a flicker of determination igniting behind his eyes. "She wasn't the only one. They've been collecting us—each name a piece of a larger puzzle." He gestures to the other files, the weight of his words pressing heavily against the fragile walls of my mind. "They're hunting people with our... abilities. And it goes deeper than you know."

"Abilities?" My heart races, a wild drum echoing in my ears. "What abilities are you talking about?"

His silence answers me more than words ever could. The truth lies heavy between us, a tangible entity that vibrates with unspoken fears and half-formed revelations. "You have to understand, I didn't know. I didn't think it was real until I started seeing the patterns, the disappearances. I thought it was just coincidence, but..." His voice trails off, laden with guilt.

"Vincent, please. You need to tell me everything." The urgency in my voice rings through the chamber, and I can see his resolve falter.

Taking a deep breath, he opens another file, revealing a photo of a woman I don't recognize, her eyes wide with a mixture of fear and defiance. "This is Lena. She had a gift for healing—unusual, right? They took her last year."

I shiver at the thought of someone with such a remarkable ability being hunted, snatched away from the world like a fleeting dream. "How do you know this?"

"I have connections—people who keep their ears to the ground. But I didn't connect the dots until I met you." His voice drops to a near whisper, the gravity of his confession anchoring us both. "You're part of this, part of something bigger. I didn't want to believe it."

I step back, the implications of his words sinking in like stones dropped in water, creating ripples of unease. "So what does that mean for me? For us?"

Vincent looks at me, a storm of emotions swirling behind his gaze—fear, protectiveness, and something I can't quite place. "It means we need to get out of here. Now."

Before I can respond, the sound of footsteps echoes in the distance, growing closer, a discordant rhythm that sends a jolt of adrenaline through my veins. Vincent's eyes widen, and he shoves the files back into the hidden compartment, urgency transforming his earlier hesitation into a fierce determination.

"Stay close to me," he instructs, his voice firm as he takes my arm. I can feel the tension radiating from him, and I nod, every instinct screaming at me to trust him, to follow him into the unknown.

We slip back into the corridor, the shadows our only companions. The atmosphere is electric, every sound amplified, every heartbeat a reminder of the peril we're in. As we move through the maze of halls, the weight of our unspoken truths hangs between us, an invisible tether that binds us together even as we navigate the dangers ahead.

Vincent glances over his shoulder, his expression a mixture of concern and resolve. "I'm not going to let them take you. Not now, not ever."

His words are a lifeline, a promise that ignites a flicker of hope in the darkness. I want to believe him, to cling to the idea that together we can unravel the secrets that threaten to consume us. But as we reach a junction, I can't shake the feeling that the worst is yet to come, that the path ahead is fraught with even greater challenges.

Yet there's something electric in the air, a sense of possibility intertwined with danger, and I can't help but feel that perhaps, just perhaps, we're destined to uncover the truth that lies beneath the surface, hidden away from the world—like us.

The corridor seems to stretch endlessly, a snaking path that twists and turns into shadowy corners, each step echoing with a sense of impending doom. I can feel the pulse of the building around us, its very walls saturated with the whispers of those who came before, lost to the machinations of the Breed. Vincent pulls me along, his grip firm yet reassuring, a silent promise that he won't let go until we're safe. The flickering lights overhead create a staccato rhythm of illumination and darkness, mimicking the racing thoughts in my mind.

"Do you think they know we're here?" I whisper, glancing back at the corridor behind us, the ominous silence almost too heavy to bear.

"I hope not. We can't afford to be discovered." His voice is tight, and I can see the tension radiating off him like heat from a flame. "We need to reach the exit before anyone notices."

Every instinct tells me to trust him, yet a nagging doubt lingers in the back of my mind, like a persistent itch I can't scratch. "You said they were hunting us. How do we know they won't catch up to us?"

Vincent stops suddenly, his eyes narrowing as he scans our surroundings. "That's why we have to stay quiet and quick. If we're caught, there's no telling what they'll do."

The very idea sends a shiver down my spine. "What do you mean by that?" I ask, feeling the weight of every unspoken threat looming in the air.

"I mean, this isn't just about us. It's bigger than I ever thought," he replies, his voice barely above a murmur. "We're part of something they consider... expendable."

Those words linger in the air, and I swallow hard against the bitterness rising in my throat. "Expendable? Is that what you think of me?"

He whirls around to face me, his expression fierce. "No! That's not what I meant, and you know it." The intensity in his gaze softens slightly, a flicker of vulnerability breaking through the tension. "You're anything but expendable to me."

The sincerity in his voice washes over me like a wave, and I feel a flicker of hope in the midst of chaos. "Okay, then. What's the plan?"

He takes a deep breath, clearly collecting his thoughts. "There's a service entrance at the end of this corridor. If we can reach it undetected, we'll have a chance to escape."

"Lead the way," I say, trying to inject a note of confidence into my tone.

As we move forward, the shadows deepen around us, the air thick with the scent of concrete and something metallic, a reminder of the secrets locked within these walls. Each footfall feels weighted, as if the very ground is trying to hold us back, to tether us to the past that is closing in on us.

Vincent slows as we approach a door, his body tense, every muscle coiled like a spring. "Stay behind me," he murmurs, pushing the door open just a crack. The light spills into the corridor, illuminating his features, the determined set of his jaw highlighting the lines of worry etched into his skin.

I peek around him, and my heart races at the sight of a bustling room filled with agents, their chatter low but urgent, punctuated by the occasional ringing of phones and the clatter of keyboards. "Looks like a war room," I whisper, my breath hitching in my throat.

Vincent nods, eyes scanning the room for any signs of danger. "We'll need to wait for a moment when they're distracted."

Just then, a loud voice cuts through the murmur—a woman with an authoritative tone. "We need to ramp up the search for any remaining individuals. They can't have gone far."

My stomach drops at her words, and Vincent's grip on my arm tightens. "This isn't just about Samantha or Lena anymore. They're hunting all of us."

Before I can respond, the agents around us erupt into chaos, a sudden surge of urgency as they begin to scramble for their weapons, a stark contrast to the earlier calm. "What's happening?" I hiss, panic rising like bile in my throat.

"They must have received a tip-off," Vincent says, his voice low and urgent. "We need to go, now."

He pushes the door open wider, and we slip through just as the agents begin to disperse, confusion palpable in the air. My heart races as we find ourselves in a narrow corridor leading to an unmarked exit. Each step feels precarious, the tension crackling around us like static electricity.

"Vincent," I whisper, pulling him to a halt, "if they're really hunting us, how do we know this exit isn't just another trap?"

He turns to me, his expression resolute. "It's a risk we have to take. I'd rather face whatever's waiting out there than stay here."

"Then let's do it," I reply, steeling myself against the uncertainty.

As we approach the exit, the tension morphs into something electric, an undercurrent of danger and possibility intertwined. I can feel the weight of the world pressing down on us, the anticipation a heady mix of fear and hope. "Ready?" he asks, and I nod, my pulse racing in sync with his.

The door swings open, revealing the dim light of a deserted alley, the night air cool against my skin. We step into the unknown, the world outside alive with sounds—the distant hum of traffic, the rustle of leaves, the very breath of freedom tantalizingly close yet heartbreakingly far.

But before we can fully step into the light, a figure emerges from the shadows, blocking our path. My heart skips a beat as I take in the unfamiliar face, a stranger who seems to hold the key to the next phase of our journey. "You two look like you're in quite a predicament," the figure says, a sly smile curling on their lips, their voice dripping with something that feels like menace mixed with mischief.

"Who are you?" I demand, my voice shaking slightly despite my efforts to sound assertive.

The stranger chuckles, a sound both charming and unsettling. "Just a friend. Or perhaps a foe. It all depends on how you play your cards."

Vincent steps protectively in front of me, his demeanor shifting from cautious to combative. "We don't have time for games. We need to leave, now."

"Ah, but you might want to hear what I have to say first," the stranger replies, a glint of mischief in their eyes. "What if I told you that the Breed isn't the only player in this game?"

I exchange a glance with Vincent, the uncertainty between us palpable. "What do you know?" I ask, curiosity outweighing the instinct to run.

The stranger's smile widens, a cat playing with a particularly intriguing mouse. "More than you can imagine. And if you want to survive, you might want to listen closely."

With that, the tension spikes again, the air thick with anticipation as we stand on the precipice of an unexpected revelation, the choices we make here potentially rewriting the very fabric of our existence.

The stranger's presence, a perplexing mix of charm and danger, hangs in the air between us like a taut wire ready to snap. Their smirk reveals nothing, but the glint in their eyes speaks volumes, a silent invitation to tread deeper into the unknown. I glance at Vincent, who stands rigidly beside me, a shield of uncertainty.

"What do you want?" I ask, my voice steadier than I feel.

"Straight to business, I see. I like that." The stranger leans against the wall, arms crossed casually, as if we're simply discussing the weather rather than our lives hanging in the balance. "I want to help you, but first, I need something from you."

Vincent's brow furrows, suspicion swirling in the air like smoke. "What could you possibly want from us?"

The stranger shrugs, feigning indifference, but I catch a glimpse of something deeper beneath the surface—an urgency that belies their calm demeanor. "Information. You have something I need, something that could shift the power dynamics in this game."

"What are you talking about?" I demand, my patience waning.

"Let's just say you've drawn the attention of the wrong people, and if you're not careful, it won't be long before they come knocking."

"What does that mean?" Vincent interjects, stepping forward, his protective instincts flaring. "Who are you working for?"

The stranger rolls their eyes in a dramatically exaggerated manner, as if our questioning is a tedious game. "Honestly, it's quite exhausting keeping track of who's who in this murky underworld. Let's just say I'm a free agent, a mercenary of sorts. And right now, my interests align with yours."

"Your interests?" I scoff. "And what might those be? A little backroom deal to save your own skin?"

"Touché," they reply, a glimmer of respect flashing across their face. "But make no mistake, I'm not without my own motives. The Breed has a larger agenda than even you know. And if you're still in the dark, you'll find yourself part of their collateral damage in no time."

The weight of their words sinks into my bones, the realization dawning on me that we're tangled in a web far more intricate than I ever imagined. "So, what do you propose?"

"Simple. You give me access to the files you found—names, connections, anything that will lead me to the core of this operation.

In return, I can help you both disappear before they catch wind of your little adventure."

Vincent's jaw clenches, his instincts screaming that this could be a trap. "And why would we trust you? You could be working with them for all we know."

"Trust is a fragile thing, isn't it? But consider this: if I wanted you dead, you would be by now." The stranger pushes away from the wall, stepping closer, their expression earnest for the first time. "I'm offering you a lifeline, a way to break free from this nightmare."

I glance at Vincent, who is still processing this new development. "What do you think?" I whisper, the tension crackling in the air like static before a storm.

"I don't like it," he replies, his voice low and cautious. "But if we don't act soon, we may not have another chance."

"Exactly," the stranger interjects, their tone brightening. "So what'll it be?"

Vincent's expression hardens, his resolve palpable. "If we do this, we need your word that you'll help us find the others who have gone missing. I won't just walk away without knowing we've done something to stop this."

The stranger raises an eyebrow, a playful glimmer returning to their gaze. "Ah, the noble knight in shining armor. How quaint. But fine, I can't deny that my interests might align with that as well."

"Then it's settled," I say, adrenaline coursing through me, the thrill of risk igniting a fire in my chest. "But if you try anything—"

"I know, I know. You'll cut me down where I stand. Very dramatic," they say, waving a dismissive hand. "Now, let's get to work. Time is of the essence."

We step back into the alley, the chill of the night wrapping around us like a cloak, and I can't help but feel the weight of what we're about to undertake. The stranger leads the way, their confident stride punctuating the gravity of the situation.

"What's your name?" I ask, needing something more to anchor this bizarre alliance.

"Call me Kai," they reply, throwing a glance over their shoulder with a smile that doesn't quite reach their eyes.

"Nice to meet you, Kai. Let's just hope we don't end up regretting this," I say, trying to inject some levity into the air.

"Regret is part of the fun," Kai quips back, their tone light even as we navigate the shadows.

As we move deeper into the labyrinth of the city, I can feel the tension shifting. The weight of our decision hangs heavily, every step echoing with the uncertainty of our fate. The streets are alive with the distant sounds of laughter and the flicker of neon signs, but all of it feels distant, a world removed from the one we've just escaped.

Kai leads us to a nondescript building, its façade blending seamlessly into the surroundings, a facade of normalcy hiding the chaos within. "This is where the files are kept," they say, glancing around before pushing open the door.

The interior is dimly lit, the hum of machinery filling the air, and I feel an uneasy mix of excitement and dread. "How did you find this place?" I ask, my voice barely a whisper.

"A little bird told me," Kai replies cryptically, a hint of mischief dancing in their eyes.

Vincent shifts beside me, tension radiating off him as he scans the room. "Let's just get what we need and go. I don't like being exposed."

As we step inside, the atmosphere thickens, a sense of foreboding creeping in with every passing second. Rows of cabinets line the walls, each one promising secrets and revelations that could change everything.

"Start looking," Kai instructs, the urgency in their voice cutting through the haze of uncertainty. "We don't have much time."

Vincent and I fan out, the flicker of a fluorescent light overhead casting long shadows that feel alive, watching us as we search. My hands tremble slightly as I pull open drawers, the musty scent of paper and ink filling my nostrils. I sift through the contents, my heart racing as names and faces swim before my eyes, each one a story untold, each one a life shattered.

"Here!" I call out, pulling a folder marked with familiar handwriting, the name emblazoned across the front striking me like a blow to the chest. "It's one of them!"

Vincent rushes over, his expression fierce as he scans the contents. "This is what we need. Let's grab as much as we can."

But before we can act, the room erupts into chaos. The door bursts open, and agents flood in, their expressions a mix of surprise and fury. "Stop right there!" one of them shouts, a gun drawn and aimed directly at us.

My heart drops into my stomach, adrenaline surging through my veins as I glance at Vincent. "What do we do?" I gasp, panic threatening to overtake me.

"Run!" he yells, grabbing my arm, but as we turn to flee, a second agent blocks our path, his expression cold and unyielding.

In that moment of paralyzed disbelief, a voice cuts through the air, smooth and authoritative. "Now, now, let's not be hasty."

I turn to see another figure step into the fray, the silhouette familiar yet ominous. The chill that runs down my spine is unmistakable. This time, the Breed isn't just watching from the shadows; they've stepped into the light, and everything is about to change.

"Welcome to the final game," the newcomer says, a smile twisting their lips, and I realize with dawning horror that the stakes have never been higher.

Chapter 16: Bound by Blood

Confronting Vincent about the files feels like stepping onto a battlefield where the air is thick with the acrid scent of betrayal. I stand across from him, my heart pounding so loudly I can scarcely hear the echo of my own voice. "You lied to me!" The accusation lingers between us, sharp as broken glass, shimmering with anger and disbelief. His face, usually a mask of cool confidence, twists momentarily as confusion washes over him.

"Lied?" His voice wavers, the syllables struggling to hold their usual steadiness. "You don't understand—"

"No, you don't understand!" I cut him off, the desperation in my tone cracking like a whip. "You kept this from me. You let me believe you were fighting for something noble, but all along, you were dancing with the enemy."

His eyes flash, a storm brewing just beneath the surface. "You think I had a choice?" His voice drops to a low murmur, raw and vulnerable. "The Breed didn't give me one. They threatened her—my sister."

The way he says it, "my sister," sends a ripple of empathy through me, softening the edges of my anger. I remember the moments we shared—the laughter, the warmth that flickered between us like a flame threatening to ignite. In this tense standoff, I see not just the man who deceived me, but a tortured soul twisted by the weight of his own choices.

"I can't even imagine what that must have felt like," I say, my voice lowering as the truth washes over me like a sudden wave, pulling me under. "To be forced into such a world." The pain etched in his features speaks volumes, each line a testament to his struggle. "But we can't keep doing this, Vincent. This dance of shadows... it's suffocating."

He rubs the back of his neck, an unconscious gesture of vulnerability that further unravels the armor he wears so well. "Every decision I made was to protect her. I thought..." He trails off, the admission a heavy weight that hangs in the air, settling like dust. "I thought if I played their game long enough, I could find a way out. A way to save her."

"Instead, you became one of them." The bitterness of that truth is bitter in my mouth. I want to reach out, to touch him, to bridge the chasm of secrets that has widened between us. "You didn't just lose your sister, Vincent. You lost yourself."

For a moment, silence envelops us, thick and suffocating. The weight of his decisions, like a leaden cloak, wraps around him. I watch him, eyes searching for the flicker of the man I once admired. "What do we do now?"

His gaze flickers to mine, the intensity there almost palpable. "I have to make this right. I won't let them take anyone else from me."

"Do you even know how?" I ask, the skepticism in my voice betraying my uncertainty.

"I don't know," he admits, and the honesty in his tone cuts through the tension like a knife. "But I'm willing to fight. For her. For us."

The last word hangs in the air, an unspoken promise that sends a shiver down my spine. For us. The idea feels both terrifying and exhilarating, as if the ground beneath my feet has shifted into something solid yet unpredictable.

"Then we fight together," I say, my resolve sharpening into something fierce. "We uncover the truth, find a way to outsmart the Breed. If we're going to do this, we do it side by side."

He steps closer, the air crackling with tension as his eyes search mine for sincerity. "You really mean that? After everything?"

"Blood binds us, Vincent. But trust is forged in fire." The truth of my words hangs heavy between us, an unbreakable thread pulling tighter. "We can't let fear dictate our actions any longer."

"I want to believe that," he says, a flicker of hope igniting in his gaze. "But the Breed—they're ruthless. They won't stop until they have what they want."

"Then we need a plan," I reply, determination coursing through my veins like wildfire. "We can't keep playing their game by their rules."

As we strategize, the air shifts, the tension morphing into something charged with possibility. Each word exchanged feels like a step toward reclaiming our power, a shared mission that transcends the betrayals and scars we bear.

The night stretches before us, dark and heavy, but within that darkness lies the potential for rebirth. I can feel the fire of our newfound alliance burning bright, illuminating the path ahead. Each whispered strategy becomes a promise that we won't back down, that we won't let the shadows consume us.

His fingers brush against mine, an innocent gesture that sends a jolt through me. I catch my breath, the weight of what lies ahead pressing down on us like an impending storm. The resolve in his eyes reflects back at me, and I realize that I am no longer standing alone. We are bound by more than blood; we are bound by choice, by shared scars, and the burning desire to rewrite our destinies.

The Breed may have cast their shadows long and dark, but together, we will carve out our own light. As the night deepens, so too does our resolve, the world around us shimmering with the promise of rebellion and the intoxicating thrill of the unknown.

The quiet tension that had settled between us crackled like static electricity, charged with unspoken words and shared histories. As Vincent stood there, the shadows of his past flickering behind him like ghosts, I felt the weight of our newfound alliance pressing down upon us. “We need to get moving,” I said, breaking the silence that threatened to suffocate us both. “The longer we stay here, the more exposed we become.”

“Right.” He nodded, his expression shifting from vulnerability to determination. “We’ll need to gather supplies. There’s a place I know.”

“Great, just as long as it isn’t a trap.” I couldn’t help but tease, trying to lighten the mood. “If you lead me into a den of vicious cats, I might reconsider this trust thing.”

A flicker of amusement broke through his brooding demeanor. “Noted. I promise you there are no vicious cats. Just a few very angry people.”

“Wonderful,” I replied, rolling my eyes dramatically. “Sounds like a party.”

With a determined nod, Vincent turned, leading the way through the darkened halls of the abandoned building. Each step echoed like a heartbeat, the dim light casting long shadows that danced along the walls. The flickering fluorescent bulbs above struggled against the encroaching darkness, and I felt as if we were moving through a living entity, each step stirring the dust of forgotten dreams.

Vincent glanced back, catching my eye. “You know, we’re in this together now. There’s no turning back.”

“I wouldn’t dream of it,” I replied, my voice steady despite the flutter of nerves in my stomach. “I didn’t come this far to back down. I’m in.”

He studied me for a moment, something akin to admiration flickering in his gaze. “That’s good to hear. I was worried you’d want to run away screaming.”

“Oh, I might do that too, but only after I’ve caused some serious chaos.” The corner of his mouth quirked up in a smile, and for a moment, the weight of our situation lightened.

As we navigated through the debris-laden corridors, I couldn't shake the feeling that the walls themselves were watching us. They held secrets, whispered stories of those who had come before—people who had made choices and faced consequences that had rippled through time. The thought sent a shiver down my spine, but I pushed it aside, focusing on the path ahead.

We finally reached a rusted door at the end of the hallway, the kind that looked like it hadn't been opened in years. Vincent paused, placing a hand against the cool metal, his expression serious. "This leads to a basement level. It's where they store... things."

"Things?" I raised an eyebrow, skepticism creeping in. "What kind of things? I'm not sure I want to know."

"Let's just say the Breed has a penchant for keeping items that can be used against their enemies." He pushed the door open, and a musty odor wafted up, mingling with the damp air.

I wrinkled my nose, stepping inside. "And you trust this place? Because it feels a little like stepping into a horror movie."

"Trust is a strong word," he admitted, stepping cautiously into the gloom. "But I've been here before. I know what's down here."

I followed closely behind him, scanning the shadows for any signs of danger. The basement was a cavernous space, lined with shelves piled high with old crates and boxes, their contents hidden beneath layers of dust. A single bare bulb swung overhead, casting erratic shadows that seemed to dance in the corners of my vision.

"Let's hope these 'things' are useful," I murmured, brushing my fingers over the surface of a crate. "What are we looking for?"

"Supplies, weapons, anything we can use to level the playing field." He moved with purpose, rifling through boxes and casting aside the debris of forgotten lives. "The Breed won't hesitate to eliminate us. We need to be prepared."

"Don't worry," I said, my determination flaring as I joined him in the search. "I'm not about to go down without a fight. You might be the one with the tragic backstory, but I have a few surprises up my sleeve too."

Vincent chuckled softly, the tension in his shoulders easing just a fraction. "I like surprises. Especially the good kind."

As we dug deeper into the clutter, I unearthed a collection of weapons: an old crossbow, a few knives, and something that looked suspiciously like a smoke bomb. "This looks promising." I held up the smoke bomb, inspecting it closely. "What do you think? Should we toss one of these at the next group of angry cats?"

"Not cats, remember?" he reminded me, smirking as he surveyed our growing pile of gear. "But yes, that could work. If we're going to confront the Breed, we need every advantage we can get."

With our arms laden with the remnants of past battles, we turned to leave the basement. Just as we reached the door, a loud crash echoed through the space, reverberating like thunder. I froze, the sound slicing through the air with an icy dread.

"Did you hear that?" My heart raced, instincts kicking in.

Vincent nodded, his expression darkening. "They've found us. We need to move, now."

Adrenaline surged as we sprinted toward the exit, the fear and urgency propelling us forward. The walls seemed to close in, each footfall echoing in the confined space, urging us to escape before the shadows caught up.

Bursting through the door, we emerged back into the dimly lit hallway, panting and wide-eyed. The tension in the air felt palpable, thick as fog, and I could feel the presence of danger lurking just out of sight.

"Quick, this way!" Vincent urged, grabbing my hand and pulling me into a side corridor. I barely had time to register the warmth of his grip before we were running again, the thud of our footsteps a desperate rhythm in the night.

With every twist and turn, the anticipation crackled around us, the adrenaline firing my senses. There was no turning back now. We were racing into the unknown, united against an enemy that would stop at nothing to tear us apart. Together, we would face whatever lay ahead, the storm closing in around us.

We plunged through the corridor, Vincent's grip a lifeline as we navigated the twisting hallways. The echo of our hurried footsteps reverberated against the grimy walls, a heartbeat echoing in a world that had grown far too quiet. My mind raced, weighing our options with the cold clarity of fear and adrenaline. With every corner we rounded, I expected to see the shadows of our pursuers materialize, looming like harbingers of doom.

"Do you know where we're going?" I gasped, trying to keep up with his long strides.

"Not exactly," he admitted, glancing back at me with a mixture of determination and worry. "But anywhere is better than here."

"Perfect. We're going with the 'anywhere but here' strategy. Very reassuring," I shot back, forcing a breathless laugh despite the rising tension.

"Trust me," he urged, and the sincerity in his eyes sent a jolt through me. "We'll find an exit. Just keep moving."

The hallways twisted and turned, each corner revealing new passages that seemed to stretch endlessly before us. The faint hum of machinery vibrated in the air, a reminder of the dark undertones lurking in the corners of our world. We ducked into a side room, quickly shutting the door behind us, the wood shuddering under the force of our breaths.

"Let's listen," he whispered, pressing his ear against the door. I joined him, my heart pounding in sync with the ominous silence outside.

Time stretched in those agonizing moments, the stillness amplifying every creak and groan of the building. I could almost hear the pulse of the night, an electric energy coursing through the walls, as if the very structure of the building knew we were trapped within it.

"What if they catch us?" I asked, my voice barely above a whisper. "What if they know we're here?"

"They won't," he replied with confidence that felt like a fragile mask. "At least, not yet. We just need to stay one step ahead."

I nodded, though uncertainty clawed at my insides. I was still piecing together what this meant for us, the implications of our choices looming like a storm cloud on the horizon. Just as I was about to voice my thoughts, a sharp noise sliced through the quiet—a sound unmistakably human.

Vincent's eyes widened, his body tense as he backed away from the door. "We need to move," he hissed.

But before we could turn, the door burst open, and a figure stepped inside, silhouetted by the dim light from the hallway behind. My breath caught in my throat as I recognized the intruder: a tall woman with raven-black hair and eyes that glinted like steel. Her presence filled the room, radiating authority and danger.

"Nice to see you both again," she said, her voice smooth like velvet but laced with malice. "You didn't think you could run forever, did you?"

"Aria," Vincent said, barely concealing his contempt. "What are you doing here?"

"Oh, just checking in on my favorite little rebels." She stepped further into the room, the door swinging shut behind her with an ominous thud. "You know, the Breed doesn't take kindly to defection."

"What do you want?" I snapped, summoning every ounce of bravado I could muster. "You think we're going to surrender?"

"Ah, so feisty. I've always admired that about you," she replied, a smirk curling her lips. "But this isn't about surrender. It's about choices."

Vincent moved slightly in front of me, a protective gesture that ignited something fierce within me. "You don't have to do this, Aria. We can find another way."

Her laughter echoed off the walls, cold and dissonant. "You don't get it, do you? There is no other way. The Breed's demands are non-negotiable." She leaned in closer, her eyes narrowing. "And you both are in far too deep."

A sudden anger surged within me, fueled by the realization that Aria wasn't just a voice of the Breed—she was a part of it. "You're nothing but a puppet, Aria. You've given up your humanity for power."

"Humanity is overrated," she shot back, the malice in her gaze a testament to her choices. "Power is what keeps you alive in this world. You should know that by now."

"What's your plan, then?" I pressed, stepping out from behind Vincent, emboldened by a defiance that coursed through my veins. "Do you really think you can intimidate us into submission?"

"Oh, sweet naïve girl." She smiled, but it didn't reach her eyes. "Intimidation isn't my game. I'm offering you a choice."

"What kind of choice?" Vincent asked, his voice steady yet strained.

"Join us. Help us eliminate those who threaten the Breed. Think of the power you could wield." Her tone shifted, weaving an enticing web of possibilities. "You could be someone important, someone who matters."

"And if we refuse?" I challenged, heart pounding in anticipation of her answer.

"Then we'll have to make an example of you both." Her expression darkened, the playful veneer shattering into something much more sinister.

Vincent's grip on my arm tightened, and I felt the weight of his concern washing over me. "We're not afraid of you, Aria. You're not the only one who can make threats."

"Oh, but you should be afraid. You have no idea what the Breed is capable of."

Suddenly, a loud crash echoed from down the hallway, reverberating through the room like a harbinger of chaos. I exchanged a glance with Vincent, a mutual understanding passing between us.

"Let's go," I said, breaking away from his grip. "We can't let her keep us here."

Vincent hesitated, his eyes darting between me and Aria, but I could see the resolve building in him. "You're right."

Before we could retreat, Aria stepped forward, a menacing smile creeping across her face. "You think you can escape so easily?"

"Try us," I shot back, adrenaline surging as we rushed toward the door. But just as we reached it, the lights flickered and plunged us into darkness.

Panic surged, and I felt Vincent's hand find mine, anchoring me in the chaos. "Stay close," he whispered, his breath warm against my ear.

"Where do we go?" I shouted, the sound of my voice swallowed by the darkness.

Suddenly, the sharp crack of gunfire rang out, splintering the silence like glass shattering. My heart raced as I realized we were no longer just running from Aria. The hunt was on, and the stakes had just been raised.

In the pitch black, we darted toward the sound of chaos, hoping against hope that we could find a way to escape this nightmare. With every ounce of strength, I pulled Vincent along, our shared breaths mingling with the encroaching darkness.

Just when it felt like we might find our way, the world erupted around us. The blaring of alarms filled the air, red lights flashing like angry fireflies, and in that moment, I realized: we were not just fighting for our lives. We were fighting for something much larger than ourselves, something that could ignite a rebellion against the shadows that threatened to consume us.

And then, from the darkness, a voice called out—a familiar voice, one that sent chills racing down my spine. "You didn't think you could escape without me, did you?"

I turned, the blood draining from my face as I faced the very last person I expected to see. The walls around us seemed to close in, and with a jolt of realization, I understood: our world was about to get even more complicated.

Chapter 17: The Ties that Bind

The air was thick with the scent of damp earth and the faint echo of our whispered conspiracies. A sliver of moonlight slipped through the gaps in the ancient oak branches, illuminating the clearing where Vincent and I had set up our makeshift headquarters. This place had once been a sanctuary, a spot where childhood dreams of adventure had danced through my mind. Now, it felt more like a battlefield, littered with the remnants of our past and the weight of our uncertain future. We huddled together, hearts pounding as we mapped out the labyrinthine schemes of the Breed, the very organization that had forged chains around our souls.

"Are you sure this is the right way?" Vincent asked, his voice low and laced with skepticism. The shadows of his brow furrowed deeply, but the light from the lantern flickered softly against his chiseled jaw, reminding me of how the darkness could be beautiful if you looked closely enough.

I leaned in closer, my fingers brushing against the paper as I traced the routes we had charted. "It's the only way we've got," I replied, the confidence in my tone belying the uncertainty curling in my stomach. "If we're going to take them down, we have to infiltrate their ranks. Start from the inside and work our way out."

Vincent's gaze flickered over my face, searching for something—reassurance, perhaps, or maybe just an understanding of how I could be so resolute in the face of such peril. "And what makes you think they'll let us in? They don't take kindly to traitors."

A small laugh escaped me, both incredulous and defiant. "Well, we're not exactly calling ourselves traitors. Think of it as... strategic positioning." I winked, trying to lighten the weight of our conversation, but the truth hung heavy between us. The Breed had left scars not just on our bodies but on our spirits, leaving us both with a hunger for vengeance that gnawed at us relentlessly.

He smirked, but it didn't reach his eyes. "Strategic positioning. Sounds like you've been reading too many spy novels."

"Maybe I have," I shot back, a playful glint in my eyes. "I like to think I've got a flair for the dramatic." The banter felt like a balm, soothing the churning turmoil within me. It was easier to jest than to confront the reality that every step we took could lead us into a trap, the noose tightening with each calculated move.

As we leaned over the hastily drawn map, a subtle tension crackled in the air—one that felt as palpable as the static before a storm. Our shoulders brushed against each other, a touch that sent unexpected warmth spiraling through me. It was disarming, this intimacy. Here, amid the chaos of our lives, was a small sliver of normalcy—a shared mission, a common purpose.

"What if we're caught?" Vincent's voice was a mere whisper now, a thread of vulnerability woven into the fabric of his bravado. "What if we're not just killed but taken back?"

The thought sent a shiver coursing through me. I had seen too many friends vanish, too many who had been swallowed whole by the very darkness we sought to combat. "We won't be," I said firmly, more to convince myself than him. "I refuse to let them have that power over us again. We're stronger than they think."

His eyes locked onto mine, fierce and penetrating. "You're right. We are stronger." There was a determination that flared in him, a fire that was too bright to ignore. It ignited something within me, pushing me to stand taller and face the uncertainties with a boldness that was just beginning to take root.

"What's the first step then, fearless leader?" he teased, but the twinkle in his eye showed he was ready to follow wherever this path would lead us.

"We gather intel," I replied, excitement bubbling beneath the surface. "I have contacts—people who can get us closer to their operations. We blend in, earn their trust. And when the moment is right..." I let the sentence dangle, letting the weight of what that meant settle in.

He nodded slowly, his expression shifting to one of deep contemplation. "And what about when we find out things we don't want to know? What if we're not prepared for the truth?"

"Truth?" I echoed, my heart clenching. "Truth is a double-edged sword, Vincent. Sometimes it cuts deep, but sometimes it can set you free." I meant it, though the realization of how intertwined truth and pain were filled me with a hesitant dread.

"Let's hope we're prepared then," he said, the tension easing slightly. "We have to be."

A rustle in the underbrush snapped us both to attention, adrenaline surging as we exchanged tense glances. The world around us fell silent, and in that moment, it felt as if the universe itself was holding its breath, waiting for our next move.

"Do you hear that?" I whispered, my voice barely more than a breath.

Vincent's expression hardened, and he nodded, his hand instinctively reaching for the dagger at his side. "Stay close," he murmured, the warrior in him awakening.

As the sound drew closer, my heart raced, a cacophony of hope and dread pulsing through me. Whatever it was, it could either spell doom or offer a twist in our story—perhaps the very opportunity we needed. In this fragile alliance, we had to embrace every uncertainty, every risk, for the stakes were nothing less than our lives and the freedom we craved.

As the shadows deepened around us, I felt a rush of resolve. No matter what lay ahead, we would face it together, bound by a shared purpose and a burgeoning trust that could either save us or shatter us entirely.

The rustle in the underbrush turned into a shuffling that drew nearer, almost uncomfortably so, each sound amplified in the stillness of the night. Vincent's body shifted, instinctively putting himself between me and the encroaching noise, his posture tense with anticipation. The air was electric, crackling with possibilities, both thrilling and terrifying.

I held my breath, straining to catch any further sound—footfalls, a voice, anything that could give us a clue. Just as a figure emerged from the shadows, cloaked in the dim light, I felt the urge to dart back into the trees, to blend with the night like a ghost. But the choice was taken from me; it was already too late for retreat.

"Vincent? Is that you?" The voice cut through the silence like a knife, sharp and familiar. I relaxed slightly as the figure stepped into the weak moonlight. It was Lena, a woman I had known from the resistance, someone whose resilience was matched only by her quick wit. Her face was smudged with dirt, hair tangled as though she'd just escaped a brawl with a particularly nasty thicket.

"Lena!" I exclaimed, stepping forward, relief washing over me. "What are you doing here? You shouldn't be out alone."

Vincent lowered his guard slightly but kept his body angled toward her, a protective instinct lingering even as he recognized her.

Lena laughed, a sound that was both light and edged with fatigue. "Trust me, if I could have avoided this particular escapade, I would have. But desperate times and all that." She looked between us, her expression shifting from relief to curiosity. "What are you two plotting in the middle of the woods at this hour?"

"Nothing much, just a little treason," I replied with a smirk, trying to lighten the tension in the air. "You know, the usual."

"Ha! Well, if it involves the Breed, count me in." She straightened, her energy rekindled by our shared purpose. "I've got some information that might help you both."

Vincent and I exchanged a quick glance, the weight of our mission settling back into focus. "What did you find out?" Vincent asked, his tone serious now, every ounce of his focus on her.

"There's talk of a meeting," Lena began, her eyes sparkling with a blend of mischief and determination. "An internal summit of sorts. They're shifting personnel, and there's a rumor about a transfer of power at the top. If we can get eyes on that, we might be able to figure out who's really calling the shots."

"Where?" I pressed, feeling the pulse of adrenaline quicken in my veins. This was the kind of lead we needed, the thread we could pull to unravel the fabric of their operation.

"Near the old factory by the river," she replied, biting her lip as she recalled the details. "They've been using it as a front for their operations. I overheard two of their lackeys talking while I was hiding in the supply shed. It's heavily guarded, but if we play our cards right..." She let the thought dangle, a glimmer of hope shimmering in her voice.

"Are you sure about this?" Vincent asked, skepticism creeping into his tone. "The Breed is notorious for its traps. It could be a setup."

Lena's eyes narrowed, her resolve unwavering. "I wouldn't put my life on the line for something that didn't have a chance of being true. We have to take risks. That's how we'll win."

"Then let's do it," I said, the words bursting from me with an urgency that surprised even myself. The thrill of danger surged within me, entwining with the hope that perhaps, just perhaps, this could be our moment to turn the tide. "We gather intel, find out who's involved, and then—"

"And then we make them regret ever crossing us," Vincent finished for me, a smirk ghosting his lips. The fire that had been kindling between us flared again, igniting the spark of a plan, a mission that felt increasingly possible.

Lena grinned, her enthusiasm infectious. "Okay, then it's settled. We move at first light. But we need to be cautious—no heroics, no flashy entrances."

"I don't do flashy," I replied, raising an eyebrow at her. "I prefer a more... subtle approach."

"Right," she laughed, rolling her eyes. "Because wandering through the woods in the dead of night with your life on the line is the epitome of subtlety."

"Touché," I conceded, unable to suppress a smile.

As we strategized further, weaving through the intricacies of our plans, I felt a sense of belonging blossom within me—a connection that grew not only with Vincent but also with Lena. This trio, formed by shared experiences and aspirations, was something I hadn't realized I craved so deeply.

Before long, our plans morphed into something tangible, a roadmap filled with action points and contingencies, the kind of outline that would normally have felt insurmountable but now seemed attainable. I found myself imagining the moment we would break through the Breed's defenses, the thrill of liberation, the taste of victory.

Then, in the midst of our plotting, the shadows shifted again. A low growl erupted from the underbrush, cutting through our camaraderie like a blade. The sound sent a chill racing down my spine, instincts kicking in as we braced for whatever danger lurked just out of sight.

"Stay close," Vincent murmured, his hand moving to his dagger once more, the playfulness of our earlier banter evaporating in an instant.

As the growling escalated, a figure broke through the treeline, low to the ground, fur bristling, eyes glinting with an unsettling intelligence. A wolf. My heart raced, caught between fear and awe as it stood before us, an embodiment of raw power and untamed beauty. It was magnificent yet terrifying, a reminder of nature's unpredictability and our own frail humanity.

"Is it just me, or is it getting a bit too wild out here?" Lena whispered, her voice barely above a hush, eyes wide with a mix of fear and excitement.

"Definitely not just you," I breathed, my pulse quickening, both exhilaration and trepidation crashing through me. This was not the kind of encounter I'd anticipated during our midnight planning session.

As the wolf studied us, its gaze sharp and assessing, I felt an inexplicable connection, an understanding that transcended the boundaries of our worlds. In that moment, we were not just a ragtag team of insurgents plotting against a formidable enemy; we were all creatures of the night, navigating our own treacherous paths in search of freedom, however fleeting it might be.

"Maybe we should offer it a deal," I quipped, attempting to dispel the tension. "Join our side, and we'll promise to leave the rest of your pack alone."

Lena snorted, half-laughing, half-sobbing, while Vincent kept his eyes locked on the wolf, both of us caught in a surreal standoff. Whatever was about to unfold, one thing was clear: the night was far from over, and our resolve would be tested in ways we could never have imagined.

The wolf stood before us, its golden eyes glinting with a fierce intelligence that made my heart pound. Time stretched, each second dragging as I considered whether we were about to become its next meal or find an unlikely ally in the darkness. I could almost hear the racing of our hearts, three beats in sync as we collectively held our breath.

"Anyone have a snack?" I whispered, attempting to inject some humor into the situation, though my voice trembled slightly. The wolf shifted, muscles coiling beneath its fur, but instead of lunging, it simply observed us with an unnerving calm.

"Seriously?" Vincent shot back, his eyes narrowing as he remained poised, ready for anything. "You think it's interested in your rations?"

"Well, it wouldn't hurt to ask!" I replied, crossing my arms defiantly. "I mean, what if it has a taste for adventure? We could form a new pack."

"Not sure that's how it works," Lena added, a nervous chuckle escaping her lips. "But hey, if it helps, I have some jerky in my pocket."

The wolf's ears perked up, as if it had understood us perfectly, and it stepped closer, inching forward with a grace that was both mesmerizing and alarming. Its gaze flickered between us, as if weighing our intentions, assessing our worth.

"Stay still," Vincent cautioned, his voice a low growl. "If it thinks we're a threat—"

"I get it, I get it," I said, trying to rein in my instincts to step forward and pet the magnificent creature. "No sudden movements."

The wolf tilted its head, and in that moment, I could almost believe that it was curious, not hostile. It took another cautious step, then paused again, studying us intently. There was an unspoken connection in the air, a tension that felt like an invitation.

"Maybe it knows something," I suggested, my heart racing with a mixture of excitement and dread. "It could be a sign. Maybe it's here to guide us."

"Or it's hungry," Vincent replied dryly, keeping his eyes fixed on the wolf. "I don't think 'guidance' is on the menu."

Just then, the wolf let out a low growl, vibrating through the clearing. It turned its head sharply, ears pricked, as if responding to a sound only it could hear. The shift in its demeanor sent a jolt through me, and my instincts flared, urging me to retreat.

"What is it?" I whispered, tension coiling tight in my chest.

Before Vincent could answer, the underbrush erupted with movement, and from the shadows emerged a group of men, clad in dark uniforms, their faces obscured by masks. The sight of them sent a chill through my bones. They were part of the Breed, the very organization we had sworn to dismantle.

"Now would be a great time for that snack," Vincent muttered under his breath, positioning himself protectively in front of me and Lena.

The wolf reacted instantly, its growl escalating, a fierce sound that resonated with the very air around us. The men paused, surprised by the unexpected presence of the creature, and in that moment, time seemed to suspend itself.

"Back off, wolf!" one of the men shouted, brandishing a weapon, but the wolf didn't flinch. Instead, it snarled, teeth bared, a creature of instinct and fury ready to defend its territory.

"Vincent, we need to get out of here!" I urged, my heart pounding in my chest. This was not how I had envisioned our night unfolding.

"Stay close," he said, his voice steady as he gestured for Lena to follow. "On my count—"

Before he could finish, the wolf lunged, darting towards the nearest man with a speed that took us all by surprise. It was a flash of fur and muscle, a savage dance that left the intruder stumbling back, eyes wide with shock.

"Go! Now!" Vincent shouted, grabbing my arm and pulling me away from the chaos. The sudden urgency propelled me forward, adrenaline coursing through my veins as we bolted into the thicket.

Branches whipped at my face, and the underbrush crunched beneath our feet, but I couldn't shake the image of the wolf engaging with our enemies from my mind. I glanced back just in time to see it launch itself onto another man, fierce and powerful, a primal force of nature battling against the odds.

"I never thought I'd see a wolf take on the Breed," Lena gasped, breathless as we weaved between the trees, our hearts racing.

"Neither did I," I admitted, stealing a glance back. The wolf had the upper hand for now, but I knew better than to think we were safe. More men would come; they always did.

"Where do we go?" Lena called, her voice strained with exertion.

"Towards the river!" Vincent directed, his breath steady despite the chaos. "If we can reach the water, we can find a place to regroup."

The shadows danced around us, and the night felt alive with the thrill of our escape. Every rustle in the foliage seemed to promise danger, but the wolf's growls echoed behind us, an unexpected ally battling fiercely against our pursuers.

As we approached the riverbank, the moonlight glinted off the water, a silver ribbon winding through the trees. It was a beautiful sight, but beauty felt misplaced amid the urgency of our flight.

"We'll hide here for a moment," Vincent said, motioning for us to duck behind a cluster of rocks. The river flowed beside us, its sound soothing and relentless, like a heartbeat that thrummed with life.

Once we were concealed, I leaned against the cool stone, my lungs heaving as I tried to catch my breath. "Do you think they saw us?" I whispered, peering out into the darkness.

"Let's hope not," Vincent replied, his voice low. "We need to give them a moment to pass before we make any moves."

Lena rubbed her arms as though trying to erase the lingering fear. "That wolf... it was incredible. I've never seen anything like it."

"Nor will we again if we don't keep moving," Vincent said, urgency creeping back into his tone. "We need to find shelter and a way to regroup. If we're caught here..."

"Yeah, let's not think about that," I interjected, forcing a grin to mask my anxiety. "We've faced worse odds, right?"

"Right," he agreed, but I could see the tension in his jaw.

A sudden howl pierced the air, echoing off the water, and we all froze. It was the wolf, a haunting sound that resonated in the night, stirring something deep within me. It was a call to arms, a promise of resilience, but it also signaled the danger that was drawing near.

"That's not just a howl," Vincent said, his expression darkening as he listened intently. "It's a warning."

Before I could respond, the brush crackled again, the sound of hurried footsteps rushing toward us. Panic surged through me, the reality of our situation pressing down like a weight. We couldn't stay here; we had to move.

"Run!" Vincent ordered, his voice laced with urgency.

We took off once more, my heart pounding in sync with the thunderous roar of the river. Branches snagged at my clothes, but I didn't stop to check for tears or scratches. There was no time for hesitation.

As we sprinted along the water's edge, the sound of pursuit grew louder, the men from the Breed hot on our trail. I could feel them closing in, shadows on our heels, and I dared to glance back, only to see the dark figures emerging from the tree line, eyes glinting with malice.

"Head for the cliffs!" Vincent shouted, pointing to a rocky outcrop ahead, and without question, we veered toward it, the promise of elevation feeling like our only hope.

As we reached the base of the cliffs, I turned again, just in time to see the wolf charging toward us, moving with an agility that was nothing short of breathtaking. But behind it, the men followed relentlessly, their intentions clear.

"Get up!" I urged, scrambling to find a foothold on the jagged rocks. "We need to climb!"

Lena and Vincent started to ascend, but the wolf was caught in a frantic skirmish with two men, a flurry of fur and teeth.

"Go! We'll help it!" Vincent shouted back, his voice full of conviction.

"Are you insane?" I yelled, panic lacing my words.

"Just do it!" He didn't wait for a response, plunging back into the fray, determination etched into his every move.

"Vincent, no!" I cried, but the moment hung heavy as I grappled with the impossible choice. The wolf needed help, but so did we.

I felt torn, my heart screaming at me to join him, but instinct pushed me to climb higher. The growls and shouts rang in my ears, a cacophony of chaos that threatened to consume us all.

I turned back one last time, witnessing the struggle between our unexpected ally and the men who sought to capture or kill it. Vincent was fighting fiercely, but the odds were against him.

With a final glance, I forced myself to look away, scrambling up the rocks, desperation fueling my ascent. I was leaving behind a battle, but my mind raced with what it all meant—a crossroads of loyalty and survival, of love and duty.

As I reached the ledge, the air became thick with tension

Chapter 18: The Beast Within

I stood at the edge of the old rooftop garden, a place where concrete met greenery in a defiant embrace, trying to breathe through the thick tension that coiled around me like smoke. It was a sanctuary amid the chaos of the city below, where the clamor of horns and shouting voices faded into a dull murmur. The sky above was painted in hues of lavender and rose, the sun sinking low, casting long shadows that danced across the uneven stone path. This garden was our refuge, a secret space we had carved out in a city that felt like it was always on the brink of something catastrophic.

But today, the air felt different. There was an electric charge, a portent of trouble that sent prickles down my spine. Vincent stood a few paces away, his back rigid, hands shoved deep into the pockets of his worn leather jacket. I could see the lines of worry etched into his brow, the way his jaw clenched tight enough to break. It was as if the weight of the world rested on those broad shoulders, and I wished more than anything to lift it, to banish whatever demons haunted him.

"Are you okay?" I ventured, my voice barely above a whisper, as if louder words might shatter the fragile peace around us. I stepped closer, the soft crunch of gravel underfoot barely registering against the frantic drumming of my heart.

He turned, his blue eyes flickering with an intensity that made me hold my breath. "I'm fine," he replied too quickly, a hint of an edge in his tone that sent alarm bells ringing in my head. I could read him like an open book, and the words he chose felt like the ink was barely dry, a flimsy cover over the storm brewing within.

"Vincent," I pressed, daring to reach out and touch his arm. "You don't look fine."

With a sharp inhale, he stepped back, the distance between us suddenly vast. "It's just..." He paused, searching for words that were clearly stuck in his throat. "I didn't expect to see him again."

There it was—the unspoken name of the shadow looming over us. The Beast. Just saying it felt like a curse, heavy and foreboding. I knew enough about Vincent's past to understand that this wasn't just another name; it was a specter that had haunted him, a tangible reminder of the darkness he'd once fought to escape. "What does he want?" I asked, the very idea making my skin prickle.

"Destruction," Vincent murmured, his voice low, almost reverent. "He's a harbinger of chaos, a destroyer of worlds."

I felt the air thicken as the implications settled in. This was more than just a personal vendetta; the arrival of The Beast threatened everything we had built, our plans for the future, the fragile hope that we could escape the shadows. "We can't let him come between us," I urged, the steel in my voice surprising even me. "We've fought too hard to get this far."

Vincent looked at me, and for a moment, the storm within him quieted, replaced by something softer. "I know," he said, the vulnerability in his eyes making my heart ache. "But he knows how to exploit weakness. He knows how to make people break."

We fell into a heavy silence, the kind that drapes over you like a shroud. The wind whispered through the garden, rustling the leaves of the small trees, and for a moment, I allowed myself to imagine a world where we didn't have to face The Beast, a world where Vincent was free from his past. But the thought slipped through my fingers like sand, and I could see the shadows creeping back into Vincent's expression.

"Tell me about him," I urged, even as I braced myself for the onslaught of memories that would surely follow.

Vincent's eyes clouded with recollection, and I could feel the shiver of dread that rolled off him in waves. "He was... merciless. The kind of guy who makes you wish you'd never been born. He enjoys the hunt, the power. And he has a way of getting under your skin, twisting your fears against you."

My heart ached for him, the burden of those memories weighing heavy on his soul. "What did he do to you?" I asked, my voice gentle, but firm.

Vincent clenched his jaw, the muscle ticking with tension. "It's not just me he goes after," he said, his gaze distant. "He takes what you love, uses it against you. He'll come for us, and he won't stop until he's made us suffer."

A shiver ran down my spine, but I refused to let fear paralyze me. "Then we face him together," I said, the determination in my voice sharpening with each word. "We won't let him tear us apart. I won't let him take you from me."

For the first time, a flicker of something akin to hope ignited in Vincent's eyes. "You don't know what you're asking," he said, but the protest was weak, nearly drowned out by the fierce light in my own heart.

"Maybe I don't," I admitted, stepping closer until I could see the tumult swirling in his eyes. "But I do know that you're not alone anymore. You have me."

The moment hung between us, fragile and precious, like the first glimmer of dawn after a long, dark night. Vincent's expression softened, the hard lines of worry giving way to something gentler, more vulnerable. He reached out, brushing a strand of hair behind my ear, his touch lingering. "You're too good for this world, you know that?"

"Goodness has nothing to do with it," I said, a teasing smile breaking through my resolve. "I just refuse to be the damsel in distress."

He chuckled softly, the sound easing some of the tension that had gripped us both. "Damsel? No. You're more like a warrior princess, ready to storm the gates."

"Warrior princess?" I laughed, the lightness of the moment a welcome reprieve. "I'll take that. But we need a plan."

And with that, as the sun dipped below the horizon, casting a warm glow over our clandestine sanctuary, we began to devise our strategy. The Beast was coming, but together, we would face whatever darkness lay ahead.

The darkness seemed to seep into every crevice of our sanctuary, making the once-vibrant rooftop garden feel like a forgotten relic. As Vincent and I began to outline our plan, the lingering sense of dread hung over us like storm clouds ready to burst. I paced back and forth, the gravel crunching underfoot, while Vincent leaned against the rough-hewn wooden railing, his gaze fixed on the horizon.

"Alright, we need to think about how The Beast will come at us," I said, trying to keep my voice steady, but the tremor in it betrayed the tension brewing beneath the surface. "He's not just going to walk in and announce himself. He'll be calculating, looking for weaknesses."

Vincent nodded, but his expression was distant, lost in the tumult of his past. "He always was good at that. He knows how to play mind games, how to use people's fears against them."

I stopped pacing and turned to him, searching his face for any sign of the brave warrior I knew lay beneath the burden of those memories. "What are you afraid of?" I asked, stepping closer, my voice soft yet insistent. "Is it just him, or is it something deeper?"

Vincent's eyes darkened, shadows flickering behind them as if the ghosts of his past were battling for control. "Both," he admitted, his voice barely above a whisper. "The Beast is a reminder of everything I fought to escape, but he's also a reminder of how easily everything can be taken away. I can't let him hurt you."

"Then let me help you fight back," I replied, firming my resolve. "You're not the only one who has something to lose here. I refuse to stand on the sidelines while you do this alone."

He regarded me with a mixture of admiration and concern, his fierce loyalty battling against the instinct to protect me from the darkness he carried. "You have no idea what he's capable of. I don't want you to face him."

"Believe me, I have a pretty vivid imagination," I shot back, a smile creeping onto my lips to break the weight of the moment. "And I'd rather take on The Beast than face another night of you brooding in silence."

Vincent chuckled, a rich sound that filled the air like a warm blanket. "You have a knack for making the impossible seem trivial."

"Maybe it's the other way around. You're just making this far too dramatic." I feigned a swoon, throwing my arm over my forehead in mock despair. "What's next? A sonnet about the tragic hero haunted by his past?"

He laughed, and I could see the tension in his shoulders ease, if only for a moment. "You'd be surprised. I've got a couple of verses hidden away."

"Please, spare me," I said, rolling my eyes playfully. "But seriously, we need to come up with a plan. What if we lure him out? Get him away from the places he knows best."

Vincent's brows knitted together, a hint of intrigue breaking through the cloud of dread. "Luring him out could work, but we'd need to make it look enticing enough for him to take the bait. He thrives on chaos."

"Then let's give him what he wants," I replied, my mind racing with possibilities. "We could create a diversion, something that screams danger or draws attention. That's what he feeds on, isn't it?"

He studied me, a mixture of admiration and caution in his eyes. "You're suggesting we make ourselves a target?"

"Not just a target—an irresistible challenge." I grinned, feeling the thrill of the plan taking shape. "We need to show him that we're not afraid, that we're ready to fight back. You have to remember, Vincent, fear is just another weapon, and we can turn it against him."

Vincent smiled, the ghost of a true grin lighting up his face, and it felt like sunshine breaking through the clouds. "You really are something, you know that? I've been around a lot of darkness, but you somehow manage to find the light."

"And you're not so bad yourself," I shot back, the banter weaving a fragile thread of connection between us. "Now, if we're going to execute this brilliantly bold plan, we need to figure out where to stage our little show."

"We'll have to pick somewhere he'd least expect," Vincent said, a thoughtful look crossing his face. "Somewhere he wouldn't consider us to be."

I glanced around the garden, taking in the wildflowers that bloomed defiantly among the cracks in the pavement. "What about the old docks? It's secluded, but there's enough history there to draw him in. The chaos of the shipping yard could mask our movements."

Vincent nodded, his eyes sparking with determination. "That could work. We could create an illusion of vulnerability, draw him in like a moth to a flame."

"Then it's settled," I declared, a surge of adrenaline coursing through me. "We'll meet there tomorrow at dusk. But first..."

"First?" He raised an eyebrow, intrigued.

I took a step closer, feeling the magnetic pull between us. "First, we need to get you some new gear. You're not going into battle dressed like a brooding artist from the '90s."

Vincent laughed, and the sound washed away some of the tension, leaving behind the warmth of connection. "I suppose my fashion choices could use some updating."

"Definitely," I said, nudging him playfully. "And we should probably scout the area as well, just to familiarize ourselves with the layout."

"I'm beginning to think I've underestimated you," he admitted, a teasing glint in his eyes. "You're quite the strategist."

"And you're quite the reluctant hero," I countered, a challenge lacing my tone. "Now, let's get to work. The Beast won't know what hit him."

As the sun dipped below the skyline, casting a golden hue across the rooftop, we began to forge our plans, weaving together threads of hope and determination. The looming threat of The Beast felt less insurmountable in that moment, our shared laughter echoing through the garden like a promise. Together, we were ready to face whatever darkness lay ahead.

The following day dawned with an unsettling blend of excitement and anxiety as I made my way to the old docks. The air was thick with the scent of salt and rust, the distant cries of seagulls weaving through the lingering fog that clung to the shore like a reluctant secret. It was a place steeped in stories, the kind that whispered of both hope and despair, a fitting backdrop for the clash we were about to instigate. My heart raced in tandem with the waves crashing against the battered wooden pilings, each swell a reminder of the challenge that lay ahead.

Vincent had been uncharacteristically quiet on our way here, his mind clearly occupied with thoughts of The Beast and the shadows of his past. I had insisted on taking the lead in our plan, trying to deflect some of the weight pressing on his shoulders. It was my way of being useful, of proving that I could stand alongside him as an equal rather than simply a bystander in this dangerous game. As I approached the meeting spot, I turned to him, determination setting my jaw. "You ready for this?"

He looked at me, those stormy blue eyes searching mine for a moment before he nodded, though the tension around his mouth told me he wasn't entirely convinced. "Just promise me you won't do anything reckless."

"Me? Reckless?" I feigned innocence, placing a hand dramatically on my chest. "I'm a model of restraint and caution."

His lips twitched into a reluctant smile, but the shadows still loomed behind his eyes. "Right. Just remember, this isn't a game."

"I'm aware," I replied, my tone turning serious. "But we need to show him we're not afraid. That's our only advantage."

We walked further into the docks, the wooden planks creaking beneath our feet as we maneuvered through crates stacked high, remnants of a bustling trade long past. The docks were quiet, an eerie stillness settling over the scene that made my skin prickle. The sun hung low in the sky, casting long shadows that danced unsettlingly in the corners of my vision.

"Let's set up near the old warehouse," I suggested, pointing toward a structure that loomed like a forgotten giant. Its paint was peeling, and broken windows gaped like empty eyes, but it offered plenty of cover and a clear line of sight.

Vincent nodded, and we crept toward the warehouse, the adrenaline in my veins propelling me forward even as my heart pounded like a drum in my chest. I took a moment to scan the area, every instinct screaming for me to be alert. "We'll wait here," I whispered, crouching behind a stack of crates. "And then we'll create our diversion."

"Right," he agreed, settling beside me. "We'll use those old barrels over there." He gestured to a row of weather-beaten barrels stacked against the wall. "A fire will draw him in. He won't be able to resist."

"Just as long as it doesn't set the entire dock ablaze." I shot him a teasing glance. "But if it does, I'll promise to leave the fire extinguishing to you."

He chuckled softly, the sound grounding me in the moment. "As long as you promise to stay out of the flames."

With our plan laid out, the air crackled with anticipation as we settled in to wait. Time stretched like a taut wire, each minute feeling like an eternity. I could feel the tension building, my thoughts racing back to the previous night's conversation, the weight of Vincent's fears a palpable presence in my mind. I could almost hear the echoes of his past, haunting him like a ghost demanding to be acknowledged.

Minutes turned into hours, and just as I thought the weight of stillness would crush us, a shadow broke the horizon. I spotted movement, the unmistakable figure of a man advancing through the fog. My breath caught in my throat as recognition washed over me like ice water. The Beast. He was tall and imposing, his silhouette framed against the dim light, a harbinger of chaos that felt like a nightmare made flesh.

"Get ready," I whispered urgently, my heart racing. "He's here."

Vincent tensed beside me, his eyes narrowing as he focused on the approaching figure. "We stick to the plan. Draw him in and then..."

Before he could finish, The Beast stopped, scanning the area with an unsettling calm that sent chills racing down my spine. It was as if he could sense us, an animal smelling fear on the wind.

"Show yourself!" he called out, his voice a deep rumble that reverberated through the air.

A chill crawled up my spine as the confidence that had buoyed me began to falter. "Maybe we should have picked a different location," I muttered under my breath.

"I think he already knows we're here," Vincent replied, tension lacing his words.

In an instant, The Beast turned sharply toward us, his gaze piercing through the shadows. "There you are," he said, a predatory smile spreading across his face. "I was wondering when you'd come out to play."

My stomach dropped as I locked eyes with him, the malevolence in his gaze sending shivers racing down my spine. It was a look that promised pain, a reminder that he thrived on fear and chaos.

"Now!" Vincent hissed, igniting the makeshift fire we had prepared. Flames flickered to life, licking at the air, and for a brief moment, the brightness illuminated the docks, chasing away the shadows.

The Beast's expression shifted from amusement to surprise, the fire drawing him closer as we had hoped. "You think a little fire can stop me?" he shouted, advancing toward us, an ominous figure engulfed in the glow of our flames.

"Just stay behind me!" Vincent commanded, positioning himself in front of me as if he could shield me from the impending danger.

But before I could respond, the ground beneath us trembled as the warehouse door burst open, revealing a group of figures emerging from the shadows, clad in dark clothing, their intentions clear. My heart raced as I realized we were not just facing The Beast; we were now surrounded.

"Vincent!" I yelled, panic seeping into my voice as I grabbed his arm, the sense of betrayal flooding my mind. "What are we going to do?"

The Beast laughed, a low, mocking sound that echoed around us. "You're in over your heads, little mice."

And just like that, the world spun into chaos, darkness closing in as the flames flickered uncertainly, casting eerie shadows on the walls around us.

Chapter 19: Flames of Vengeance

The air crackled with tension, a palpable energy that charged the atmosphere as Vincent and I faced the Beast. It loomed before us, a monstrous silhouette against the backdrop of the smoldering ruins, its eyes glowing like embers in the dark. I could feel my heart thrumming in my chest, each beat a reminder of the stakes at hand. This wasn't just a fight for survival; it was a reckoning, the culmination of years spent in the shadows of fear and despair.

Vincent stood beside me, his presence a steady flame amidst the chaos. I watched him, taking in the way his jaw tightened, the way his fists clenched, knuckles white and trembling with the weight of pent-up fury. The memory of our journey surged through me: the whispered confessions shared in the quiet of the night, the tenderness of his touch, the unwavering loyalty that had blossomed between us like wildflowers in a cracked pavement. It was as if the universe had conspired to bring us together, two souls ignited by shared struggles, and now, we stood on the precipice of an all-consuming fire.

The Beast roared, a guttural sound that reverberated through my bones, threatening to swallow me whole. I could see the jagged scars on its body, a map of battles lost and won, each one a testament to its relentless cruelty. But I also recognized the pain etched into Vincent's face, a mirror of the torment he had endured. This creature had haunted his dreams, a specter of his past that had clawed its way into our present. Today, it would be vanquished, but not without a fight.

As if sensing our determination, the Beast charged, a whirlwind of fury and flame. I barely had time to react before Vincent was moving, a blur of muscle and grace. He met the beast head-on, their collision a violent explosion that sent shockwaves through the ground. I felt the heat of the fire as it surged around us, the acrid scent of smoke filling my lungs. My instincts screamed at me to retreat, to seek safety in the shadows, but I couldn't—wouldn't—leave him to face this horror alone.

"Vincent, watch out!" I shouted, my voice barely breaking through the chaos. He glanced back at me, a fierce spark in his eyes that ignited something deep within me. I knew then that we were in this together, that our fates were intertwined in a dance as old as time itself.

With every swing of his weapon, Vincent channeled his fury into precise strikes, each blow a manifestation of years spent trapped in the Beast's grip. I found my own strength rising within me, urging me forward. I had trained for this moment, learned how to harness my fear, how to transform it into something potent. As the Beast reared back, preparing to unleash its fire, I seized my chance. I rushed toward Vincent, my heart racing, and we moved as one, two parts of a whole united against a common enemy.

The flames roared around us, licking at the edges of our resolve, but we were undeterred. The battle raged on, a tempest of clashing wills and ferocious power. Each time the Beast lunged, I felt the ground tremble beneath my feet, but Vincent remained a rock, unwavering in the face of this nightmare. With each clash of our weapons against the creature's hardened hide, a symphony of determination and despair played in the air, the rhythm of our fight echoing the heartbeat of the world around us.

"Remember who you fight for!" I called out, my voice a beacon of hope cutting through the darkness. The weight of my words hung in the air, a reminder of the love and sacrifice that had brought us here. With renewed fervor, Vincent launched into a furious assault, each swing of his weapon a declaration of defiance against the shadows that sought to consume us.

The tide began to turn as the Beast staggered back, its ferocious roars morphing into something less confident, more desperate. I could see the flicker of doubt in its eyes, a realization that its reign of terror was drawing to a close. In that moment, I knew we had the upper hand, but victory was still a heartbeat away.

I moved closer to Vincent, our bodies a synchronized force as we flanked the Beast. The heat of the flames danced around us, but my focus was razor-sharp, my heart pounding with the exhilaration of battle. "Now!" I shouted, and we struck in unison. The impact was breathtaking, a crescendo of sound and fury that reverberated through the very core of the earth.

As the dust settled and silence enveloped the battlefield, I stood, panting and bloodied, alongside Vincent. The Beast lay defeated, a once-mighty figure now reduced to a whisper of its former self. I turned to Vincent, searching his face for any hint of despair, but instead, I found something unexpected—relief, and a flicker of hope. We had done it. We had faced the darkness and emerged into the light.

He reached for my hand, and I grasped it tightly, feeling the warmth of his skin against mine. In that moment, all the pain, the suffering, and the fire that had forged us into who we were today seemed to coalesce into something beautiful. Together, we had rewritten our fate, crafting a narrative steeped in resilience and love.

As we surveyed the wreckage of the battlefield, I realized that the fight was not just against the Beast, but against the shadows of our pasts. We had reclaimed our lives from the clutches of fear, igniting a flame of vengeance that now burned brightly between us. And in that flame, I saw our future—a tapestry woven with threads of strength, tenderness, and an unbreakable bond forged in the crucible of battle.

The aftermath hung in the air like a lingering scent of smoke, heavy and suffocating. As the last flickers of flame faded into the evening, I turned to Vincent, the realization of our victory settling over me like a warm cloak. His face was a tapestry of exhaustion and exhilaration, a testament to the battle we had just endured. We had triumphed over a nightmare, yet the shadows it cast still flickered at the edges of our minds, threatening to ensnare us in their grip.

"Do you think it's really over?" I asked, my voice barely a whisper against the eerie stillness that enveloped us. The remnants of the Beast lay scattered, charred and lifeless, yet an unsettling question nagged at the corners of my mind.

Vincent let out a breath, a low rumble that echoed the weary weight in his chest. "For now," he replied, his gaze scanning the debris, eyes sharp and calculating. "But these things have a way of lingering, don't they? Like a bad smell after a storm."

I nodded, the image of our monstrous foe seared into my memory. The pain it had caused—both physical and emotional—was not something that could be easily forgotten. "And what about the others? The ones it hurt before?" The thought of those still suffering, their lives irrevocably altered, weighed heavily on my heart.

"They'll have to fight their own battles," he said, a hint of bitterness lacing his tone. "I can't save them all." His eyes met mine, a fleeting vulnerability flickering across his features. It was a rare glimpse into the depths of his soul, where pain and hope intertwined, shaping the man I had come to love.

In that moment, I felt an urge to bridge the distance that lingered between us, to remind him that he was not alone in this fight. "But we can help," I insisted, my conviction steady. "We can gather the others, share what we've learned. We can be a force together."

Vincent's brow furrowed, uncertainty clouding his eyes. "A force for what? More battles? More loss?"

"More healing," I replied, stepping closer, my voice a soothing balm against his turmoil. "There's strength in numbers, Vincent. We can be the spark that ignites change."

A flicker of something ignited in his gaze, a tentative spark of hope. "You really believe that?"

"I do," I replied, my heart racing at the intensity of his scrutiny. "If we don't try, we risk letting the darkness win. And I refuse to let that happen."

He took a deep breath, the air between us thick with unspoken emotions. "You're too damn optimistic, you know that?" he said with a half-smile, the corners of his mouth lifting just enough to banish some of the shadows.

"Guilty as charged," I shot back, a grin breaking across my face. "But it's not optimism. It's a choice. I choose to believe we can do something worthwhile."

Vincent studied me, his expression softening as the last remnants of anger faded from his features. "You're one hell of a woman," he murmured, a hint of admiration lacing his words. "I'm lucky to have you."

The warmth of his praise sent a flutter through my chest, but before I could respond, a noise broke the serenity—an urgent rustle from the brush nearby. My heart leapt, adrenaline spiking once again. "What was that?"

Vincent tensed, his instinctual warrior persona returning as he scanned the perimeter, muscles coiling like springs. "Stay behind me," he ordered, his voice low and steady.

As the underbrush parted, a figure emerged, stumbling into view. It was a woman, wild-eyed and breathless, her clothes torn and dirt-streaked. My pulse quickened, and I stepped closer to Vincent, the instinct to protect surging within me.

"Please!" she gasped, her voice a desperate whisper. "You have to help me! They're coming!"

"Who's coming?" Vincent demanded, his tone sharp, authoritative.

"The Beast's followers! They know what you did! They'll stop at nothing to finish the job!" She clutched her side, pain flashing across her features. "You have to—"

Before she could finish, the sound of shouts and heavy footsteps echoed through the trees, growing closer, a sinister promise of retribution. Vincent's grip on my hand tightened, and I felt the rush of adrenaline mix with a newfound fear.

"Run!" he shouted, shoving the woman toward the thicket behind us. "Get to the village! We'll hold them off!"

"No!" I protested, dread pooling in my stomach. "We can't leave you!"

"Don't argue with me!" he snapped, urgency igniting his words. "We can't let them catch you. You need to warn the others. Now go!"

With a sense of foreboding anchoring me in place, I hesitated, torn between the instinct to flee and the desire to stay at his side. "Vincent—"

"Go!" His voice was a blade, sharp and decisive, cutting through my hesitation.

The woman grabbed my arm, pulling me back, urging me forward into the underbrush. "We need to move, or we'll all be trapped!"

Reluctantly, I tore my gaze from Vincent, his silhouette slowly blending into the shadows as I sprinted into the darkness, the sound of pursuit growing louder behind us. My heart raced not only from the exertion but from the knowledge that we were not safe yet.

We dashed through the trees, branches clawing at our skin, the distant roar of chaos echoing in our ears. The fear was palpable, a tangible force that threatened to consume us. But somewhere within that chaos, I felt a flicker of resolve. We had faced the Beast, and while the battle was far from over, I knew that together we could rally our strength.

I had chosen hope. And even in the depths of despair, I would fight to keep that flame alive.

The thrum of fear pulsated through my veins as I sprinted through the underbrush, the woman's panicked breaths mingling with the sounds of pursuit. Each step felt like an eternity, the ground beneath me a blur of fallen leaves and tangled roots that threatened to trip me at any moment. I could hear the shouts of the Beast's followers growing louder, their intentions as clear as the crescent moon illuminating the chaos that engulfed the night.

"Which way?" I gasped, glancing back at the woman, her face pale and streaked with dirt. She was stumbling, but her eyes shone with a fierce determination that mirrored my own.

"Just keep running! We have to reach the village!" she urged, her voice a thin thread of hope in the growing darkness.

I pushed forward, adrenaline propelling me into the unknown, a blend of dread and resolve clashing within me. My mind raced with the realization that while Vincent was engaged in a battle of his own, I was now responsible for ensuring our survival and the survival of those we had left behind. Each breath felt like a rallying cry—fear was a tether I refused to allow to bind me.

As we darted deeper into the forest, the trees closed in around us, their twisted branches clawing at the night sky like desperate fingers. The path became a maze of shadows and whispers, and every rustle in the underbrush sent a shiver down my spine. I could sense their approach, could feel the darkness creeping closer, hot on our heels.

"Keep moving!" I urged, glancing over my shoulder. The shouts had grown into a cacophony of rage, echoing through the trees. It was a terrifying reminder of the power the Beast still wielded, even in death.

Suddenly, the ground beneath me shifted, and I stumbled, twisting my ankle against the unforgiving roots. Pain shot through my foot, but I bit my lip to stifle a cry. "I can't—"

"You have to!" the woman shouted back, her voice firm. "You can't stop now!"

With a deep breath, I pushed through the pain, forcing myself to ignore the burning ache as I fought to regain my footing. The woman was right. Stopping meant giving in, and I refused to let fear dictate my actions.

As we continued, the terrain became more treacherous, the underbrush thickening and slowing our progress. "Do you know a safe place?" I panted, my lungs screaming for air.

"There's an old cabin, a hunter's retreat," she said, her gaze scanning the forest for signs of the pursuers. "It's not far from here, but we need to hurry."

The thought of a temporary refuge sparked a flicker of hope in my chest. "Lead the way!" I urged, my voice stronger now, infused with the adrenaline coursing through my veins.

We pressed on, darting between trees, the shadows around us growing darker, more ominous. But the memory of Vincent's fierce determination spurred me onward, his unwavering strength a balm against my fears. I could almost hear him urging me forward, his voice a steady reminder that we were not alone in this fight.

Just as I thought we might reach the safety of the cabin, the forest erupted into chaos. From the shadows, figures emerged, eyes glinting like polished stones in the moonlight. They were relentless, their faces twisted with rage, remnants of the Beast's loyal followers, still eager for vengeance.

"Run!" I screamed, adrenaline surging as I pushed the woman ahead of me. She stumbled but caught herself, racing toward the distant promise of safety. I turned to confront our pursuers, ready to fight, ready to protect the only hope we had left.

"Come on then! You want a piece of me?" I shouted, trying to project confidence I didn't feel. The hunters advanced, their intentions clear, and a shiver of fear lanced through me as I faced the mob. They were here for revenge, but I would not go down without a fight.

I fought like a whirlwind, dodging blows and retaliating with every ounce of strength I could muster. The first attacker lunged, and I ducked low, striking out with my fist and catching him off-guard. A satisfying crack echoed as my blow landed, sending him stumbling backward.

But there were too many. Even as I fought, more surged forward, their eyes wild with the promise of revenge. I caught a glimpse of the woman sprinting toward the safety of the trees, and a pang of desperation shot through me. "Get to the cabin!" I yelled, my voice hoarse. "Don't look back!"

"Help me!" she cried, her fear palpable even from a distance.

"No!" I shouted, the weight of helplessness crashing down on me. "You need to warn them!"

I turned back to face my attackers, fury igniting my resolve. The world narrowed down to the fight in front of me, the moonlight glinting off weapons raised in malice. I could hear their shouts, feel their desperation, and knew they would not stop until they had their pound of flesh.

Just as I prepared to launch myself at the next figure approaching, a sharp pain flared in my side. I gasped, looking down to see blood seeping through my shirt, warmth spreading against my skin like a cruel reminder of my mortality.

"Vincent!" I gasped, the name a prayer on my lips. The thought of him fighting against this evil, of him needing me, propelled me forward once more. But the darkness was closing in, and I could feel the weight of despair pressing down, threatening to crush my spirit.

I fought, I clawed, I screamed, refusing to be taken down, but the odds were against me. My vision blurred as I swung wildly, trying to fend off the relentless tide. "This isn't the end!" I shouted defiantly, even as my body weakened.

And then, just as I felt myself falter, a loud crash echoed through the trees. The ground shook beneath me, and the familiar roar of flames erupted nearby.

"What now?" I thought, dread pooling in my stomach. The woods lit up with a sudden, blinding light, illuminating the figures around me. I could see their faces contort with confusion, fear, and then—recognition.

In that moment of distraction, the figures hesitated, and I seized the opportunity to push through the crowd, desperate to reach the sanctuary of the cabin. But before I could fully escape, a hand clamped around my arm, yanking me back into the fray.

"Where do you think you're going?" a voice snarled, low and menacing.

I struggled against the grip, heart pounding, panic setting in. I twisted, trying to break free, but as I did, another explosion rocked the clearing. The night exploded in blinding light and searing heat, sending all of us sprawling to the ground.

Through the haze of chaos, I caught a glimpse of flames licking at the trees, the fury of a firestorm consuming everything in its path. "No!" I gasped, horror flooding my senses as I realized the cabin was engulfed, flames dancing high into the night sky.

The hand on my arm tightened, dragging me back from the inferno, and I fought against it, desperate to reach the fire, to find Vincent. "Let go of me!" I screamed, fear lacing my words. "I have to get to him!"

But as I struggled, the shadows closed in around us, the chaos swirling like a tempest. I could feel the heat of the flames, the rush of the inferno battling against the chill of the night, and in that terrifying moment, I knew I was caught between two worlds—one teetering on the brink of destruction, and the other fighting for survival.

Just then, a familiar voice broke through the din, a beacon of strength in the darkness. "I've got you!"

I turned, and there was Vincent, emerging from the smoke and chaos, his presence a fierce contrast to the encroaching shadows. He was a warrior, unyielding, a force of nature—and he was coming for me.

But just as I thought salvation was within reach, the ground beneath us rumbled ominously, and a massive crack split the earth. "Vincent!" I shouted, terror lacing my voice.

As I watched, everything fell into chaos. The ground shifted, the flames erupted higher, and in that fleeting moment, the world spun out of control. Just as I reached for him, the earth gave way, and I felt myself slipping into the abyss, the darkness closing in around me like a shroud.

"Don't let go!" I cried, my heart racing as I plummeted into the unknown, the sound of Vincent's voice echoing in my ears, a final plea to hold on amidst the chaos.

Chapter 20: Echoes of Ashes

The sun dipped low, casting long shadows across the ruined courtyard, remnants of the battle still etched in the stone walls like scars that refused to fade. I stood beside Vincent, who leaned against the cold granite, his jaw tight, a flicker of rage and remorse playing across his features. The air was thick with the scent of charred earth and lingering magic, the remnants of our struggle swirling like ghosts around us. Despite the fragile peace that had settled after the Beast's defeat, an undercurrent of unease pulsed in the air, crackling like distant thunder.

"Do you ever think it would have been easier to give in?" His voice was low, rough, as though the words themselves were a burden he could barely lift. I turned to face him fully, catching the light just right to see the depths of his anguish reflected in his dark eyes.

"Easier?" I echoed, incredulous. "You mean like surrendering to a monster? You fought for our lives, Vincent. You fought for me." My heart tightened as I said it, remembering the moments when he had pushed himself beyond the brink, wielding his pain like a weapon.

"It wasn't just for you." He shifted slightly, breaking our gaze as he stared into the horizon. "It was for all the people I've failed. All the lives I've taken." His voice cracked on the last word, each syllable a reminder of the weight of his past. I stepped closer, the warmth of my body reaching out to him like a lifeline in the chilling dusk.

"You didn't fail them," I murmured, my hand finding his. "You fought for them, for us. That's what matters." I felt the tension in his fingers as he gripped mine, a silent acknowledgment of our connection. But even as I spoke, I sensed the storm brewing within him, a tempest of guilt and anger that was far from quelled.

"You don't understand," he said, his voice tightening as though he were wrestling with the ghosts that haunted him. "I've taken lives that were innocent, lives that had nothing to do with this war. Each death echoes in my mind, and it's like I can feel their screams."

The sky darkened as if the heavens themselves were mourning alongside him. I could see the turmoil in his face, the way his muscles coiled with tension, and I knew that the defeat of the Beast had merely opened the door to his internal struggle. I wanted to reach into the depths of his pain and pull him out, to show him the man I saw—the hero who had risen against the odds, the one who had shielded the vulnerable and fought for the ones he loved.

"Then let me help you carry it," I said, fierce determination coursing through me. "You don't have to do this alone." He looked at me, and for a moment, the shadows in his eyes softened.

"But what if it's too heavy?" he whispered, a vulnerability that caught me off guard. "What if I crumble beneath it?"

I shook my head, willing him to understand. "Then I'll be here to catch you. We'll face it together." In that instant, I saw a flicker of hope—a glimmer that perhaps he could believe in himself as much as I believed in him. But the moment was fleeting, swallowed by the oncoming darkness that seemed to echo the turmoil of our surroundings.

As the sun sank further below the horizon, the winds shifted, carrying with them the scent of rain and something more sinister—an unseen presence lurking just beyond the edges of our fragile peace. I glanced around, senses heightened, feeling the world around us pulse with an energy that seemed almost sentient.

"Do you feel that?" I asked, instinctively moving closer to Vincent. He nodded, his body tense as he scanned the trees that bordered the courtyard, their branches clawing at the sky like skeletal fingers.

"It's like something's coming," he said, the raw edge of worry creeping into his voice. "Something worse."

Just then, a low growl broke the stillness, reverberating through the air like a distant thunderclap. My heart raced as a figure emerged from the shadows—a creature shrouded in darkness, its eyes gleaming with malice. Instinct kicked in; I stepped in front of Vincent, ready to fight whatever threat had dared to approach us.

"Stay behind me," I ordered, my voice steady, though fear clawed at my insides. The creature's growl morphed into a snarl, revealing jagged teeth that glistened in the fading light.

"Are you ready for this?" Vincent asked, his hand sliding to the hilt of his sword. There was a fire in his gaze that hadn't been there moments before, a spark igniting within him as he readied for battle.

"Always," I replied, adrenaline surging through my veins. The looming threat before us felt like a reflection of Vincent's turmoil, a manifestation of his past that had come to haunt him anew. But together, we were stronger than any darkness that sought to divide us. As the creature lunged forward, I drew upon the magic that coursed through me, feeling the energy pulsate with every beat of my heart.

We were about to discover if our fragile peace could withstand the storm, and if the echoes of our past could be silenced by the strength of our bond. The night had only just begun, and the true battle lay ahead, one that would test not only our skills but the very foundation of what we had built together.

The creature lunged, a blur of shadows and primal fury, and my heart pounded like a war drum, echoing in the cavernous silence that enveloped us. I barely had time to register its form before Vincent was moving, his body a well-oiled machine of reflexes and training. He drew his sword with a fluid motion, the blade glinting ominously as it caught the last rays of sunlight. It felt like the world had narrowed down to this single moment—us against a beast that seemed conjured from nightmares.

"Nice doggy," I quipped, trying to inject a bit of levity into the encroaching darkness, though my voice came out steadier than I felt. Vincent shot me a look, half amused, half incredulous, as if to say this was no time for humor. "What? I've always wanted a pet," I added with a wink, trying to mask my nerves.

Before the creature could respond to my audacity, it lunged forward, its powerful muscles coiling beneath sleek fur. I barely had time to brace myself as Vincent charged alongside me, his presence a steady anchor against the chaos. With a fierce battle cry, he swung his sword in a graceful arc, striking the creature's shoulder and eliciting a howl that reverberated off the stone walls, echoing the torment of souls long lost.

I followed Vincent's lead, channeling the energy swirling within me. My hands ignited with a warm glow as I summoned magic, casting a barrier of shimmering light that enveloped us both. "You know," I yelled over the creature's growls, "this is not exactly how I pictured our post-Beast relaxation! Next time, let's just stick to tea and poetry!"

Vincent laughed despite the dire circumstances, the sound a stark contrast to the chaos. "I'll make a note to schedule that for next week, right after we finish slaying the 'insatiable hellhound.'"

We danced around the beast, moving as if choreographed, my magic flaring to life with every spell I cast. Lightning crackled from my fingertips, striking the creature and momentarily stunning it. "See? It's all about the theatrics!" I shouted, adrenaline coursing through me.

The creature shook off the effects of my magic, its eyes glowing like two malevolent suns. It lunged again, this time targeting me, and I barely dodged as it crashed to the ground where I had just stood. "Okay, so maybe less drama next time!" I grunted, scrambling backward as I regained my footing.

Vincent was beside me in an instant, his sword a blur as he redirected the beast's attention. "Keep your distance!" he commanded, his voice a fierce whisper that cut through the tension. "We need to outmaneuver it."

I nodded, my focus sharpening. The bond we shared, forged in battles both won and lost, thrummed like a heartbeat between us. We understood each other without words, our movements synchronized, an unspoken trust bolstering us against the tide of chaos.

"Let's take it down together," I said, my voice steadier now. I gathered my strength, focusing on the spell I'd been refining during our quieter moments. It would take every ounce of power I had, but if it worked, it could turn the tide.

Vincent met my gaze, understanding flickering in his eyes. "On three," he said, lifting his sword high as he prepared to strike. "One... two..."

"Three!"

Together, we struck, a burst of light and steel against darkness. I unleashed my magic, a brilliant flash that engulfed the beast, while Vincent's sword sliced through the air with deadly precision. The creature howled, caught in the radiant storm, and for a moment, it seemed as if time itself had paused, suspended in the balance between light and dark.

Then, with one final, defiant roar, the beast fell. The echo of its defeat faded, leaving behind an eerie stillness, the kind that wraps around you like a heavy blanket. I stood there, panting, feeling the adrenaline drain from my body as the glow of my magic dissipated into the night.

Vincent sheathed his sword, his chest heaving as he turned to me, a mixture of relief and lingering tension in his expression. "Did we just—"

"Take down a hellhound? Yes, yes, we did!" I interjected, unable to contain the surge of triumph. "See? Who needs poetry when you have magical battle tactics?"

Vincent chuckled, but the laughter quickly faded as the weight of what had just happened settled over us. The silence felt thick with unspoken questions, ghosts still whispering in the shadows. "That was too easy," he murmured, looking around cautiously, as if the very ground might crack open to reveal more lurking horrors. "Something doesn't feel right."

I stepped closer to him, noting the way his eyes flickered with unease. "We should move. Whatever that was, it was only a piece of something larger."

As we retreated from the courtyard, the moon rose high in the sky, casting an ethereal glow on the remnants of our battlefield. My mind raced, thoughts tumbling over each other like leaves in the wind. The echoes of the past were not done with us; I could feel it in my bones.

"Vincent," I began, my voice softening as we walked, the warmth of his presence beside me a comfort against the chill of the night. "Tell me about them. The lives you couldn't save."

He hesitated, his expression clouded with memories, shadows flickering across his features like ghosts. "They weren't just lives. They were... people." His voice faltered, and I could see the anguish etched in the lines of his face. "Each one was a choice I made, and every choice came with consequences."

"Then we'll make new choices," I said firmly, grasping his hand tighter. "Ones that lead us toward the light instead of dragging us into darkness. You're not those choices, Vincent. You're here with me now, and that matters."

He looked at me, something softening in his gaze, and for the first time, I saw a flicker of hope. "You make it sound so simple."

"Life rarely is," I replied, a smile tugging at my lips. "But you and I, we've made it this far. Together, we can face whatever is lurking out there. I promise."

And as we continued onward, the path ahead uncertain, I felt the storm within us begin to settle, weaving threads of resilience into the fabric of our shared journey. We would navigate the darkness together, forging a future that shimmered just beyond the horizon—a future where the echoes of the past could finally find peace.

The forest enveloped us as we retreated from the remnants of the battle, its trees standing like ancient sentinels, guarding secrets that whispered through the night air. Moonlight filtered through the branches, casting a silvery glow on the path ahead, where shadows danced with the flickering of leaves. I could hear the soft rustle of the wind, a gentle reminder that nature continued its rhythm, even as our world threatened to unravel.

Vincent walked beside me, his presence a solid reassurance against the encroaching darkness. The weight of his past hung around us like an uninvited guest, and I could see the way his muscles tensed as we navigated the underbrush, ever alert for new threats. The silence was unnerving, punctuated only by the occasional crack of a twig underfoot. "I can't shake this feeling," he said, his voice low, laced with unease. "It's like we've stirred something we shouldn't have."

"Yeah, like a hornet's nest," I replied, trying to lighten the mood, though I felt it too—a prickling awareness that we were being watched. "Maybe next time, we'll just throw a picnic instead of hunting monsters." I shot him a sideways glance, hoping to coax a smile from him.

"Picnics won't keep us safe, but I appreciate the optimism," he said, a hint of a smirk tugging at the corners of his mouth. "You think we'd attract a hellhound with sandwiches?"

"Only if the sandwiches are really, really good," I quipped back, my heart racing at the sudden thrill of banter. For a moment, the tension between us dissipated, if only slightly.

But then, the air shifted. The whisper of the wind turned into a growl, reverberating through the trees. It felt almost sentient, a creature of darkness gathering itself to spring. I stopped abruptly, raising my hand to signal Vincent. "Did you hear that?"

He nodded, his expression shifting from light-hearted to grave in an instant. "Yeah, we're not alone."

Before we could react, the underbrush exploded into chaos as another creature burst forth—a hulking mass of fur and fangs, larger than the last, its eyes burning with an intelligence that sent chills down my spine. The creature's form was shrouded in shadows, like it had stepped out from the depths of Vincent's nightmares, and I knew we were outmatched.

"Great, just what we needed," I muttered, backing away instinctively. "Another guest for our little soirée."

Vincent tightened his grip on his sword, his muscles coiling like a spring. "We can't let it get the upper hand. It's fast; we need to work together."

"Right, teamwork makes the dream work!" I said, my voice shaking a little, a wry grin masking the panic simmering beneath the surface. "But how do you feel about the dream of fleeing? It's always been a favorite of mine."

"No running," he said firmly, his eyes locked onto the creature. "We stand and fight. This one's different, and we need to know why."

I swallowed hard, feeling the weight of his resolve. There was no escaping this; we were bound to face whatever dark force had been unleashed. "Fine. But if we survive, I'm insisting on that picnic," I replied, channeling my anxiety into determination.

Vincent nodded, and we fell into our rhythm, moving as one. He lunged first, the sword slicing through the air, a glint of silver against the darkness. I summoned my magic, weaving it into a barrier, the energy thrumming through my veins as I prepared for the impact. The creature lunged, its massive form barreling toward us, and I released my spell, a wave of light that collided with its snarling face.

The creature staggered back, howling in anger, but it quickly regained its footing. With a flick of its powerful legs, it charged again, and I felt the ground tremble beneath us. "This is one angry furball!" I yelled, barely dodging its swipe as it barreled past. "What did we do to deserve this? I only wanted a peaceful evening!"

"Save your energy for the fight!" Vincent called, his focus unyielding as he pivoted, striking at the beast with all his might.

I felt a rush of power surge through me, and I began to chant, weaving a spell to bind the creature. "By light and shadow, hold fast this beast!" The air shimmered around me, and tendrils of magic snaked toward the creature, wrapping around its legs.

For a moment, it paused, confusion crossing its features as the bindings took hold. "Yes! It's working!" I exclaimed, but before I could celebrate, the creature let out a deafening roar, its rage intensifying, the magic beginning to falter.

"It's stronger than I thought," I shouted, panic creeping in. "I don't think I can hold it!"

"Then let's distract it!" Vincent shouted, swinging his sword in a wide arc, aiming for its neck. The creature dodged, but the movement gave me just enough time to gather my strength.

"Okay, how about a little flash?" I called, channeling my magic again, this time focusing on creating an explosion of light, blinding the creature momentarily. The air crackled with energy as the explosion erupted, filling the clearing with a blinding brilliance.

The beast howled, disoriented, and I seized the moment. "Now, Vincent!" I cried.

He surged forward, aiming for the creature's heart, but just as he struck, the beast recovered, swatting him aside with a powerful swipe. He hit the ground hard, the sword skittering from his grasp. "Vincent!" I screamed, fear gripping my throat.

I darted toward him, heart pounding, but the creature was already turning its attention back to me, a sinister glint in its eyes as it readied to pounce. "No, no, no!" I chanted, panic flooding my senses.

With a surge of desperation, I reached for the last reserves of my magic. "Get away from him!" I screamed, and in that moment of raw emotion, I unleashed everything I had. The light exploded forth, enveloping the creature, but instead of retreating, it only seemed to grow stronger, its form darkening as it drew closer, eyes locked on me with an intensity that sent shivers through my spine.

I took a step back, adrenaline coursing through me as realization hit. "This isn't just a creature, is it?" I breathed, dread pooling in my stomach. "It's something more."

And then, just as it lunged forward, a voice echoed through the darkness, smooth and taunting, slicing through the tension like a blade. "Oh, how delightful to see you again, my little warriors."

The shadows shifted, and from the depths emerged a figure cloaked in darkness, eyes glinting with amusement. "Did you think defeating the Beast would free you? This is just the beginning."

Panic surged through me as the realization settled like ice in my veins. We weren't just battling creatures of the dark; we had awakened something far more dangerous, and now, it had come to claim us. As the creature lunged, I realized that our fight was far from over, and the true horror was only just beginning.

Chapter 21: The Gathering Storm

The room was steeped in the kind of silence that has a weight of its own, heavy and suffocating, as if the very air was bracing for the storm about to break. I sat on the edge of my worn leather chair, fingers drumming against its armrest, the rhythm of my anxiety echoing in the stillness. Vincent leaned against the doorframe, his silhouette cutting a stark figure against the light that spilled in from the window, a soft halo framing his sharp features. Even in the face of the uncertainty creeping into our lives, he held an aura of calm, his dark hair tousled, the late afternoon sun catching the glint of worry in his eyes.

"You know they're not going to stop until they get what they want," he said, his voice low, almost a whisper, but it struck through the tension like a knife. "We need to figure out what this ritual is and how to stop it."

A shiver ran down my spine as I recalled the cryptic message that had arrived just hours ago, delivered by a shadowy figure who vanished as quickly as he appeared. The parchment had been weathered, its edges singed as though it had barely escaped a fire. Scrawled in a hurried, jagged script were warnings about the Breed—their insatiable hunger for power, their machinations hidden beneath layers of deception. It spoke of a gathering, of a ritual that would unleash chaos, and I felt the blood drain from my face at the implications.

"What if they're too strong?" I ventured, the words escaping my lips before I could catch them. The thought of facing the Breed, their leaders with their ruthless ambition, was enough to make my stomach churn. I had seen the destruction they left in their wake, the ruin that came from their pursuit of power, and the very idea of their intentions unearthing an even darker force sent icy fingers curling around my heart.

Vincent stepped closer, his presence warming the chilled air around us. "We can't afford to think like that," he said, firm yet tender, his eyes boring into mine with an intensity that steadied my spiraling thoughts. "Fear is what they thrive on. We can't let it paralyze us."

A surge of determination ignited within me, and I squared my shoulders. He was right; we had faced danger before, and we had survived. It was a fragile thread we walked, but as long as we were together, it felt like we might just find a way to outmaneuver the looming darkness. "Then let's uncover their plans. We need to gather intel, find allies, anyone who can help."

Vincent nodded, and a flicker of something—hope?—passed between us. We were not just two people caught in the crossfire of a battle; we were a team, and together we could navigate this treacherous landscape. "We need to get to the old archives. If the Breed are planning something, they're bound to have left clues there," he suggested, already moving toward the door.

The archives were a labyrinth of dusty shelves and forgotten tomes, filled with the whispers of history that had long since settled into silence. They were also rumored to be haunted, but I couldn't care less about specters when faced with the living menace of the Breed. As we made our way through the winding streets, the city was an echo of its usual self—people moving about their business, laughter ringing out from cafes, the scent of freshly baked bread wafting through the air. It all felt absurdly normal, as though the world hadn't caught wind of the storm brewing just beneath the surface.

Upon arriving at the archives, I pushed open the heavy oak door, the creak echoing in the dim light. Dust motes danced in the beams of sun that filtered through the windows, and the scent of old paper and leather wrapped around me like an embrace. I took a deep breath, grounding myself in the familiarity of the space, while Vincent moved with purpose, scanning the titles lining the shelves.

"What do you think we're looking for?" he asked, his brow furrowed in concentration. "An ancient prophecy? A dark spell?" His wry smile teased the corners of his mouth, a reminder that beneath the seriousness, there was always room for levity.

"Preferably something that doesn't involve summoning demons or causing apocalypses," I shot back, searching through the tomes with an urgency that thrummed in my veins. "Maybe something about their hierarchy? Their weaknesses?"

Vincent grinned at my wit, and together we began to sift through the clutter of books and scrolls, each one a potential lifeline. As I pulled out a particularly ancient volume, the spine cracked, releasing a cloud of dust that tickled my nose. I sneezed, a sound that echoed in the stillness, and Vincent chuckled softly.

"Bless you. At least we know we're not dealing with ghosts just yet."

"Unless they're allergic to dust," I replied, a smile breaking through my earlier tension. The playful banter felt like a balm against the mounting anxiety, reminding me that amidst the chaos, we still had each other's backs.

But our light-hearted moment was shattered when I turned a page and a folded piece of parchment slipped out, fluttering to the floor. As I bent to pick it up, my heart raced, sensing it was important. Unfolding it, I gasped as the words jumped out at me, describing a dark gathering meant to channel unimaginable power through a ritual designed to bind the very essence of the city itself.

I glanced at Vincent, the gravity of our discovery sinking in. "This isn't just a threat. It's a countdown." The realization hit me with the force of a tidal wave, and I felt the air grow heavy around us once more. The Breed were not merely plotting; they were preparing for something cataclysmic. And with every moment that slipped away, the storm drew nearer, promising destruction if we didn't act swiftly.

Vincent's expression turned fierce, his determination mirroring mine. "Then we need to mobilize. We'll rally our allies, anyone who will listen. They can't succeed if we stand together."

With his words igniting a flame of hope within me, we gathered what we could from the archives, ready to face the chaos ahead.

The weight of the parchment in my hands felt like a tether to reality, the ink scrawled across its surface a chilling reminder of the impending chaos. I folded it carefully, slipping it into my pocket as Vincent and I exchanged a glance that spoke volumes—our bond forged in fire, stronger than the darkness threatening to engulf us.

"Let's get moving," Vincent urged, his voice steady, but I could sense the urgency thrumming just beneath the surface. We stepped out of the archives, the sun still shining in a mockery of our grim discovery, the city alive with sounds that felt dissonant against the storm brewing in our hearts. The bustling streets were vibrant, a tapestry of life that seemed blissfully unaware of the shadows creeping closer, and I couldn't help but feel a pang of envy. How could they go on with their laughter and chatter when we were spiraling into chaos?

We navigated through the crowded marketplace, the air fragrant with spices and fresh produce. A vendor shouted cheerfully about his ripe tomatoes, while children darted past us, shrieking with delight as they chased one another. It was a scene of normalcy, a slice of life that felt like a cruel illusion. I glanced at Vincent, who was watching me, a slight frown pulling at his lips.

"What's on your mind?" he asked, his tone gentle, though the concern etched in his features was unmistakable.

"Just... everything. What if we're too late? What if we can't stop them?" The words slipped out, tinged with a vulnerability I rarely allowed myself to express.

Vincent paused, taking my hands in his, his grip warm and reassuring. "Then we'll make sure we do everything we can. We can't predict the future, but we can prepare for it." His gaze bore into mine, the sincerity in his eyes igniting a flicker of hope within me.

With a determined nod, I pulled away, taking a deep breath. "Right. We need to find others who can help us. If the Breed is gathering their forces, we need to counteract that with our own."

As we wove our way through the streets, I mentally compiled a list of our allies. There was Celeste, a sorceress with a sharp tongue and sharper wit, who had a knack for gathering information. Then there was Gideon, a grizzled warrior with scars that told stories of battles fought and won, whose strength would be invaluable. The thought of rallying our motley crew sent a thrill through me; we were not alone in this fight, not yet.

We arrived at a small café tucked away in a narrow alley, its entrance flanked by flowering vines that seemed almost magical in their vibrancy. The familiar sound of clinking cups and murmured conversations spilled out, a comforting background noise amidst our urgency. As we stepped inside, the air was warm and fragrant, the scent of coffee mingling with something sweet—probably freshly baked pastries.

Celeste was already seated at our usual table, her vibrant red hair a stark contrast against the muted tones of the café. She looked up, her green eyes sparkling with mischief as she noticed us. "Well, if it isn't my favorite do-gooders! What's got you two looking so serious? Planning to overthrow a small kingdom?"

I chuckled, a welcome relief from the tension clinging to my skin. "You could say that. We've got some urgent news about the Breed."

Her smile faded, replaced by a look of understanding. "I figured as much. You wouldn't come here with that expression unless it was serious. Spill it."

Vincent and I exchanged glances before diving into the details, outlining the message we had received and the potential for a catastrophic ritual. Celeste listened intently, her expression shifting from concern to determination as we spoke.

"So, they're attempting something big," she said, her voice firm. "We can't let that happen. What do you need from me?"

"Information," Vincent replied. "Any intel you can gather about the Breed's movements, their leaders—anything that might give us an edge."

Celeste nodded, her fingers drumming against the table as her mind raced. "I can reach out to my contacts. There are whispers about an underground meeting, a gathering of those loyal to the Breed. If we can infiltrate that, we might learn more about their plans."

The thought sent a shiver down my spine. "Infiltrate? Do you think that's wise? What if they catch you?"

She waved her hand dismissively, a smirk on her lips. "I'm not a delicate flower, you know. I've dealt with worse than the Breed. Plus, I've got a few tricks up my sleeve. Just promise me you'll keep your heads down while I do this. No heroics, okay?"

Vincent and I nodded, and I couldn't help but feel a swell of gratitude toward her. "Thank you, Celeste. We'll do our part. Just be careful."

As we finished our discussion, I felt a flicker of hope reigniting within me. If we could unite our strengths, perhaps we stood a chance. With our spirits bolstered, we made our way back to the streets, determined to gather the rest of our allies.

The sun dipped lower in the sky, casting an amber glow that made the city look almost ethereal. The shadows lengthened, and with them came the weight of impending darkness. We sought out Gideon next, a stalwart figure known for his unwavering loyalty and relentless strength.

His training grounds were a sight to behold—a vast, open space filled with the clang of metal against metal and the grunts of exertion. The air was thick with the smell of sweat and determination, a testament to the dedication of those who trained there. Gideon spotted us immediately, a broad grin spreading across his face as he wiped his brow with the back of his hand.

"What brings you two to my humble domain? Come to test your mettle against my latest recruits?"

I returned his smile, though it felt more strained than usual. "Actually, we need your help. The Breed is planning something catastrophic, and we're gathering everyone we can to stand against them."

The joviality in his eyes faded, replaced by a steely resolve. "What do you need me to do?"

"Gather your best fighters, and anyone you trust. We're going to need all the strength we can muster to counter whatever they have planned," Vincent replied, his tone serious.

"Consider it done. I'll rally the troops and meet you back at the café. We'll strategize from there."

As we parted ways, I felt a sense of purpose settling over me, each ally we gathered adding weight to our resolve. But as we headed back to the café, the knot of dread in my stomach tightened again. The Breed was out there, plotting, their shadows inching ever closer to our fragile light. Yet, amidst the uncertainty, the unwavering bond between Vincent and me flickered like a candle against the encroaching dark. Together, we would face the storm.

As the sun dipped below the horizon, the sky blazed in a riot of colors—fiery oranges and deep purples swirling together like a painter's chaotic brushstrokes. But the beauty was lost on me, overshadowed by the weight of our task. Vincent and I made our way back to the café, the sounds of the bustling city fading into a distant hum. The air felt thick, charged with the anticipation of what was to come, and every step echoed the urgency thrumming in my veins.

When we arrived, the café was already filled with our gathering of allies. The atmosphere buzzed with a mixture of tension and resolve, the weight of our shared mission uniting us in a way that felt both empowering and terrifying. Celeste was seated at the head of the table, a stack of papers sprawled before her, her expression fierce and focused. Gideon stood nearby, a broad-shouldered sentinel surveying the room, ready to spring into action at a moment's notice.

"Glad to see you both made it back in one piece," Celeste remarked, her eyes glinting with mischief as she leaned back in her chair. "Did you manage to charm anyone into joining our merry band of misfits?"

"Gideon is gathering his fighters as we speak," Vincent replied, pulling out a chair and motioning for me to sit. I settled in, the familiar creak of the wood a small comfort against the brewing storm outside. "And we might have a lead on the Breed's movements."

I placed the parchment from the archives on the table, smoothing out its edges as I explained what we had uncovered. The atmosphere shifted as the group leaned in, the significance of our discovery sinking in. Each face reflected a spectrum of emotions—concern, determination, and a spark of defiance.

"So, they're planning to gather their strength at the old cathedral," Gideon said, his voice deep and steady, cutting through the murmur of conversations. "That place is a relic. It holds power, but it's also a perfect trap."

"Exactly," Celeste replied, her fingers tracing the edge of the parchment. "If they manage to complete their ritual, we won't just be fighting the Breed—we'll be contending with forces far beyond our understanding. We need to strike first."

The tension in the room thickened, an electric pulse that connected us all. "What's the plan?" I asked, the urgency of our situation igniting my resolve.

"First, we need eyes on the cathedral," Vincent said. "Celeste, can you send someone to scout? We need to know who's there and how many. Gideon, can your fighters prepare to engage if things go south?"

"Consider it done," Gideon replied, his voice laced with confidence. "We'll be ready to move as soon as we know the lay of the land."

"And I'll work on gathering more intel," Celeste added, her demeanor shifting to one of fierce determination. "We'll use every resource we have."

Just as we began to strategize further, the café door swung open with a crash, and a gust of wind swept through the room, snuffing out a few flickering candles. The atmosphere shifted, charged with an unsettling energy. We turned to see a figure standing in the doorway, silhouetted against the dying light.

"Sorry for the interruption," the newcomer said, stepping inside with an air of confidence. "But I think you might want to hear what I have to say."

It was Alaric, the enigmatic leader of a rival faction that had long been at odds with the Breed. His reputation preceded him, a man shrouded in mystery, known for his cunning and the unpredictable nature of his loyalties. I exchanged wary glances with Vincent and Gideon, both of whom looked equally surprised.

"Alaric," Vincent greeted cautiously, his eyes narrowing. "What brings you here? Your kind doesn't usually mingle with ours."

"I heard rumors of the Breed's plans and figured you'd be a good place to start." Alaric's dark eyes swept across the room, assessing the tension simmering just beneath the surface. "We have a common enemy, and I believe we could help each other."

"Help us?" I echoed, skepticism lacing my tone. "Why would you want to do that?"

"Because," he replied, stepping closer, "if they succeed, we're all done for. And I'm not quite ready to face the void just yet." His words dripped with a mix of bravado and sincerity, and I felt a flicker of intrigue despite my caution. "I'm willing to share what I know—if you're willing to work together."

Vincent exchanged glances with Gideon, the tension in the air thickening with uncertainty. "And what's in it for you?" Vincent asked, his voice low and guarded.

"Survival," Alaric said simply. "And perhaps a bit of glory. I'm not a fool; I know this fight will be difficult. But with your resources and my knowledge, we might just stand a chance."

I could see the gears turning in Vincent's mind, the weight of the decision looming over us. Alaric was known for his ability to manipulate situations to his advantage, and yet, the gravity of his offer hung in the air like a storm cloud, promising both danger and potential salvation.

"Fine," Vincent finally said, his voice steady. "We'll hear you out. But any false moves and you'll find yourself on the wrong side of a blade."

"Duly noted," Alaric replied, a sly smile playing at the corners of his mouth. He leaned forward, lowering his voice as if sharing a dangerous secret. "The Breed plans to perform the ritual during the next full moon. They're gathering a force strong enough to harness the city's energy, and if they succeed, they'll unleash chaos like we've never seen."

I felt a chill creep up my spine. "And you know this how?"

"I have my sources," he said cryptically, his eyes glinting with secrets. "But there's something else. The leaders of the Breed are not just ruthless; they're desperate. They believe this ritual will grant them the power to transcend our world."

A ripple of unease passed through the room, the implications settling heavily on our shoulders. "Transcend? What does that even mean?" I asked, dread coiling in my stomach.

Alaric leaned back, crossing his arms. "It means they want to become something greater, something beyond the limitations of our realm. And if they succeed..." His voice trailed off, leaving a silence filled with unspoken horrors.

"We can't let that happen," I said, my voice firm. The weight of our mission intensified, every heartbeat echoing the urgency of our situation. "We need to stop them."

"Agreed," Vincent said, his resolve solidifying. "But how do we infiltrate their ranks? We need to be smart about this."

Alaric straightened, a flicker of admiration passing through his eyes. "I might know a way in. But it won't be easy, and you'll have to trust me completely."

Trust. The word hung heavily in the air, a precarious balance of hope and trepidation. I glanced at Vincent, his jaw set with determination, and I felt my own resolve harden. If we were going to face the Breed and their nefarious plans, we would need every ally we could muster—even one as unpredictable as Alaric.

The stakes had never been higher, and with every moment ticking by, the storm drew nearer, threatening to consume everything in its path. The flickering candles cast long shadows around the room, and I realized we stood on the precipice of a decision that could alter the course of our lives forever.

"Let's do it," I said, my heart racing. "Let's take the fight to them."

As we began to discuss our next steps, the door swung open once more, and a chilling laugh echoed through the café, freezing us in our tracks. A figure stepped inside, dark and imposing, the very embodiment of the chaos we sought to prevent. It was one of the Breed's leaders, and they had found us first.

Chapter 22: Beneath Broken Skies

The rain drummed relentlessly against the pavement, a chaotic symphony that drowned out our footsteps as we navigated through the labyrinth of forgotten machinery and crumbling brick. Each droplet seemed to carry with it a whisper of the lives once vibrant in this forsaken place—a factory where ambition and sweat had mingled, only to be silenced by time and neglect. Rusting girders loomed above us like skeletal fingers reaching for a sky that felt as heavy and foreboding as our own fate.

Vincent walked slightly ahead, his silhouette cutting through the gloom. He was a force of nature, a storm unto himself, yet there was a tightness in his posture that betrayed a turmoil beneath the surface. I watched him, drawn to the way his strong shoulders tensed with every gust of wind, as if they bore not only his own burdens but also mine. The muddy ground squelched beneath my feet, a constant reminder that we were stepping deeper into the unknown, both literally and metaphorically. "Do you think they'll come?" I asked, my voice barely above a murmur, the fear palpable in the air.

"Does it matter?" Vincent replied, glancing back at me, his eyes flickering with a mix of apprehension and resolve. "We can't turn back now. Not when we've come this far." The weight of his words pressed down on me like the humidity in the air, thick and suffocating. I nodded, though I wasn't sure whether it was courage or foolishness that propelled us forward. A part of me wished for the sanctuary of familiarity, for the safe confines of my apartment with its cluttered comforts. But the ritual was a necessary risk, a gamble with our very lives, and I knew I had to trust Vincent—trust him to shield me from the lurking shadows that threatened to engulf us.

As we approached the heart of the complex, a flicker of movement caught my eye. My breath caught in my throat. Shadows danced along the periphery, twisting and blending with the dark as if they were alive, taunting us with their silent waltz. "Vincent," I whispered, urgency tinging my voice, "we're not alone." He stiffened, turning sharply, scanning the area with hawk-like precision. The tension between us thickened, electric and charged, as the threat of the Breed loomed larger with every passing moment.

Suddenly, a figure emerged from the shadows, a stark silhouette against the backdrop of rain-slicked debris. My heart raced, a wild drum echoing in my ears, as the figure stepped into the dim light. It was a woman, her features obscured beneath a hooded cloak, but there was something in the way she carried herself that set alarm bells ringing. Confidence and danger intertwined in her posture, and I instinctively stepped closer to Vincent, seeking the protection he embodied.

"I've been waiting for you," she said, her voice smooth and inviting, yet edged with a chilling finality. "The ritual is about to begin, and you two have a crucial role to play." Her words hung in the air, thick with unspoken threats. Vincent's muscles tensed beside me, his protective instincts flaring as he moved in front of me, a shield against whatever dark intentions she harbored.

"What do you want?" he demanded, his tone firm, though I could hear the undercurrents of uncertainty that tinged his bravado.

She laughed, a sound that danced along the rain-soaked air like a haunting melody. "What do I want? Oh, darling, it's not about what I want. It's about what you're willing to sacrifice." Her eyes glinted with a knowing darkness, and I felt a chill race down my spine. It was the kind of fear that nestled itself deep, stirring old memories of threats and shadows that had plagued my past. I clenched my fists at my sides, ready to fight, but something in the woman's demeanor suggested that this battle was of a different nature.

"Lynn," Vincent said, turning slightly, his gaze locking onto mine with an intensity that sent a shiver of understanding through me. "Whatever happens, don't lose sight of who you are." The sincerity in his voice broke through my mounting anxiety, anchoring me even as the world around us threatened to spiral into chaos.

The woman stepped closer, her voice a silken whisper, "You both think you have control. You believe you can steer this ship through the storm. But the tides are changing, and you're just two pawns in a much larger game." With a swift movement, she gestured to the wreckage surrounding us, and I could almost hear the echoes of the factory's past mingling with her words—a cacophony of ambition and despair.

"Listen to her," Vincent said, his jaw clenched, a ripple of anger coursing through him. "Don't let her manipulate you." But her words had already carved a path through my thoughts, laying bare my insecurities. Was I just a pawn? A fragile piece on a chessboard that I didn't fully understand?

Before I could respond, the ground trembled beneath us, a low rumble that sent a shockwave through the air. The woman smirked, her satisfaction evident, and I realized with horror that her presence was a harbinger of something much darker. The shadows that had lingered at the edges began to writhe, coiling around us like serpents ready to strike. I clutched Vincent's arm, the warmth of his skin a grounding presence amid the rising tide of dread.

"Time's up," she said, her voice laced with a sinister edge, as the rain continued to pour, blurring the line between the real and the unreal. "Let the games begin." In that moment, as the storm raged both outside and within me, I knew we were teetering on the brink of a perilous descent into a darkness that threatened to consume everything we held dear. And the only way out was through the chaos that awaited us.

The shadows shifted around us, swirling like dark secrets unfurling in the rain-soaked air. The woman's laughter faded into an unsettling silence, leaving only the patter of rain against metal and stone as the world began to close in. My heart raced, echoing the thudding rhythm of impending doom, while Vincent stood like a stalwart lighthouse, the steady beam of his presence offering a glimmer of hope amidst the encroaching darkness.

"Can we just skip the part where we play mind games and get to the part where we kick your ass?" I shot back, channeling every ounce of bravado I could muster. She raised an eyebrow, an amused smile playing at the corners of her mouth, as if my challenge amused her rather than frightened her. It only fueled my resolve. "Because I'm really not in the mood for cryptic riddles."

"Oh, darling," she said, her voice dripping with mock sympathy. "It's not about what you want. It's about what you need." With a flourish of her cloak, she gestured toward the ruins around us, and the air thickened, charged with an energy that was palpable. My instincts screamed that we were caught in a web, and each word from her lips was a thread tightening around us.

Vincent's hand tightened around my wrist, a silent reminder that we were in this together. "What do you know about the ritual?" he demanded, a fierce edge to his voice. "Why are you so eager to involve us?"

"Because you're key players in a game far older than you can imagine," she replied, her tone slipping from playful to dangerously serious. "This ritual will determine the fate of many. You think it's just about you two? How quaint."

I felt a shiver race down my spine at her words. "What do you mean by 'the fate of many'?" My voice wavered slightly, the weight of her implication heavy in the air.

The woman took a step forward, her eyes gleaming with a predatory light. "The Breed seeks to regain their power, to reignite the ancient fires of control. You're just the spark they need. A bit of chaos, a dash of passion, and voilà—a perfect recipe for destruction." Her smirk was triumphant, as if she reveled in our uncertainty.

"Sounds like a great party," I quipped, forcing a laugh that barely masked my rising fear. "Too bad I'm on the guest list by mistake."

Vincent glanced at me, a flicker of appreciation dancing in his eyes, though the tension in his jaw remained. "We're not playing your games," he said firmly, though uncertainty lingered in his tone.

"Ah, but you already are." She tilted her head, the shadows playing tricks on her features. "The ritual is set, and your presence is a requirement, whether you like it or not. You can resist, but in the end, the storm will come for you both. You can either fight it or let it sweep you away."

With a sudden flourish, she spun around, her cloak trailing like a wisp of smoke as she walked away, her laughter fading into the distance. I could feel the ground shift beneath me, the uncertainty gnawing at my insides as I turned to Vincent. "What do we do now?"

"We prepare," he said, determination blazing in his eyes. "We gather information, find allies, and we don't give in to fear. There's always a way to fight back." His words ignited a flicker of hope within me, but as I looked around the dilapidated complex, a cold reality seeped in.

"This place is a graveyard for lost dreams," I murmured, feeling the weight of the memories embedded in the crumbling walls. "How do we find our way out of here?"

"By not losing sight of who we are," Vincent reiterated, his gaze steady on mine. "We'll carve our own path, no matter how twisted it may become."

With that resolve solidifying between us, we moved deeper into the heart of the complex, our footsteps echoing against the damp concrete. The air was thick with decay and secrets, each corner we turned revealing the remnants of a world that had once thrived—machines lay scattered like discarded hopes, their purpose long forgotten. The dim light cast an eerie glow, and I could almost hear the whispers of the past beckoning us forward.

A sudden rumble of thunder crashed overhead, rattling the windows and sending a shiver through the air. I jumped slightly, glancing at Vincent, who merely raised an eyebrow in silent acknowledgment of my startled reaction. "You've seen worse," he said with a half-smile, trying to lighten the mood. "And I've heard your shrieks over far more terrifying creatures than thunder."

"True," I admitted, rolling my eyes at his teasing. "But thunder doesn't usually mean impending doom."

Just as we reached the center of the complex, a flicker of movement caught my eye. A figure stepped out from behind a rusting machine, startling me. My heart raced, but I quickly steeled myself. It was another woman, with wild hair framing her face, dirt smudged across her cheeks, and eyes that gleamed with an intensity that matched my own desperation.

"Are you lost?" she asked, her tone casual but edged with urgency. "Or just foolish enough to wander into a lion's den?"

"Depends on who's asking," Vincent replied, his protective stance returning. "And who you are."

"Names are unnecessary." She waved a hand dismissively, but her posture shifted to one of alertness. "You're here for the ritual, aren't you? You must know what it entails."

"Not exactly," I admitted, sensing the gravity of her presence. "We were just told we were part of some larger scheme."

"Then you have much to learn." She stepped closer, her eyes narrowing. "And little time to do so. The Breed is powerful, and their games are treacherous. You'll need allies—those who know the ins and outs of this world."

"Do you know where we can find them?" I asked, feeling the urgency spike within me.

"Follow me," she replied, glancing over her shoulder. "But be warned—the path is fraught with danger, and there are eyes everywhere."

Vincent exchanged a glance with me, and though uncertainty lingered, I saw the flicker of hope in his expression. We had to trust, to embrace the chaos swirling around us.

With a deep breath, I nodded, stepping into the unknown, knowing that the darkness would only deepen from here on out. But together, with Vincent by my side and this new ally leading the way, I felt a spark of determination igniting within me—a fierce reminder that even amidst the shadows, there was always a chance to rise, to reclaim the light, and to carve our own fate.

The woman led us deeper into the industrial labyrinth, her movements fluid and confident, as if she were born of the shadows themselves. Each step we took echoed against the cold concrete, the sound reverberating like a warning through the abandoned space. My senses heightened, I couldn't shake the feeling that we were being watched, that unseen eyes tracked our every move, lurking just beyond the fringes of light.

"You're not afraid, are you?" the woman asked, glancing back at me with a wry smile. Her confidence was infectious, but it only amplified the tremor of apprehension within me.

"Of the shadows? Please." I shot back, my bravado louder than my heart, which was currently attempting to leap out of my chest. "I'm more worried about whatever's hiding in them."

Vincent remained steadfast, his presence a comforting anchor. "What's your name?" he inquired, his voice steady as we maneuvered through the maze of rusting machinery and broken windows.

"Call me Nessa." She replied without hesitation. "And you're going to need to remember that names carry weight in this world. The wrong ones can lead you straight into a trap."

"Like the one we're currently in?" I quipped, shooting a glance at Vincent.

"Touché," Nessa replied, her laughter a welcome distraction from the heavy atmosphere. "But trust me, this is nothing compared to what's ahead."

We paused at the entrance to a wide room, its ceiling so high it felt like the sky itself could spill in, were it not for the debris littering the ground. A few flickering overhead lights cast a sickly glow over the chaos—dilapidated crates, shattered glass, and tangled wires lay strewn about like discarded dreams. In the center, there was a makeshift table draped with grimy cloth, various objects scattered atop it, each radiating an air of significance.

"This is where we gather," Nessa said, her tone shifting to something more serious. "We plan, we plot, and we protect ourselves from the Breed. This is our hub, though it may not look like much."

"I was expecting a throne room," I replied, surveying the haphazard collection of artifacts. "Or at least some candles and incense for ambiance."

"Very few people would willingly venture into a place like this, which is why it works," she explained, stepping closer to the table. "We keep our plans close to our chests, and we use this space to build alliances."

"Speaking of which, how many allies are we talking about?" Vincent asked, the edge of caution returning to his voice.

"Enough," Nessa replied cryptically, as she rifled through a box. "But they'll want to see proof of your worth. The world out there doesn't tolerate weakness, especially not now. You need to demonstrate that you're not just players in this game, but pivotal pieces."

"Great. I was hoping for a nice, easy initiation," I said, crossing my arms. "How about a game of charades instead?"

Nessa shot me an amused glance, but Vincent stepped forward, his expression serious. "What do you need from us?"

She paused, weighing her words. “Information. The Breed is gearing up for something big, and we need to know what they’re planning. If you can infiltrate their ranks, discover their intentions, you’ll earn your place among us.”

Infiltration. The word sent a jolt of dread through me. It sounded both thrilling and terrifying, like standing at the edge of a cliff, teetering over the unknown. “And what if we get caught?” I asked, unable to hide the tremor in my voice.

Nessa leaned closer, her gaze intense. “You won’t be alone. We’ll be watching, and we’ll provide support. But you must be willing to take the risk. The Breed will stop at nothing to protect their secrets.”

Vincent nodded, his resolve palpable. “We’re in. Whatever it takes.”

I felt my heart leap at his words, a rush of adrenaline surging through me. If he was all in, then so was I. “Count me in, too,” I said, forcing a confidence I didn’t entirely feel.

Nessa smiled, a flicker of approval lighting her features. “Good. But first, you must understand the nature of your opponents. The Breed isn’t just a group; they’re a network, and their reach extends far beyond what you can see. They have eyes everywhere, and they won’t hesitate to eliminate threats.”

“Great, so it’s a fun little game of hide and seek,” I remarked dryly. “Where the stakes are life and death.”

Vincent caught my eye, a hint of amusement in his expression despite the gravity of the situation. “You have a way of making everything sound so charming.”

“It’s a gift,” I replied with a playful smirk, but beneath the banter lay a thread of fear. I could sense the enormity of what we were about to undertake, and the thrill of adventure was now laced with a sobering reality.

Nessa turned back to the table, rifling through a stack of papers. “If you’re going to take this step, you’ll need to be equipped with the right information." She pulled out a folded map, its edges frayed and stained, and laid it out before us. "This is the territory the Breed patrols. It outlines their strongholds, their routes, and potential weak points. Familiarize yourselves with it."

I leaned over the map, tracing the ink lines with my finger. Each mark was a reminder of the risks we would face, the encounters we would have to navigate. "So this is our treasure map, huh?" I mused, half-joking.

"Only if you consider danger a treasure," Nessa replied, her tone grave.

Vincent studied the map intently, his brow furrowed in concentration. "We'll need to devise a strategy. We can't just rush in blindly."

"Rushing in has been my specialty," I joked, though my stomach twisted at the thought of our upcoming mission.

Nessa gave me a sharp look. "That may work in some situations, but the Breed is not forgiving. They'll expect boldness, but they'll also be ready for it. We'll need a plan, and we need to move quickly."

A sudden crack of thunder shook the room, the lights flickering ominously, and for a moment, the shadows seemed to pulse around us. A chill crawled up my spine, and I turned to Vincent, who was watching the entrance with an intensity that suggested he sensed something was amiss.

"What's wrong?" I asked, feeling the tension thicken in the air.

"Something's off," he murmured, his voice low and steady.

Before I could respond, a loud crash reverberated through the building, a shuddering roar that rattled the very foundations. Dust fell from the ceiling as Nessa grabbed the edge of the table for support. "What was that?" she exclaimed, eyes wide.

"An ambush?" Vincent suggested, already moving toward the door. "We need to get out of here."

Without a second thought, we rushed toward the exit, but the moment we stepped outside, chaos erupted. Figures cloaked in darkness poured from the shadows, their faces hidden, their intentions clear. The Breed had come for us, and as the rain poured down in torrents, mingling with the adrenaline coursing through my veins, I realized with a sinking dread that our gamble was about to cost us everything.

"Run!" Vincent shouted, his hand finding mine as we sprinted toward the relative safety of a nearby corridor, but the darkness was closing in, and I could feel the weight of the world pressing down on me. Just as we turned the corner, I heard a voice call out, slicing through the rain-soaked air like a knife.

"Stop! You can't escape your fate!"

I glanced back, my heart racing as the figures surged closer, the air thick with the promise of chaos. A split second later, the ground beneath us erupted in a deafening roar, and I barely had time to scream before everything went black.

Chapter 23: The Blood Moon

The air vibrated with an unsettling energy, a rhythm that seemed to resonate with the very fabric of the night. Each heartbeat of the ancient stone pulsed through the cavernous chamber, drawing me closer, yet urging me to step back into the shadows. I could feel Vincent's presence beside me, a solid anchor in this swirling tempest of dread and expectation. He exhaled softly, a whisper of tension that curled into the air, mingling with the metallic tang of rust and the earthy decay that lingered in the corners like forgotten memories.

The Breed leaders stood in a tight formation, their dark cloaks billowing like storm clouds around them. Faces obscured, they seemed to summon shadows from the very walls, their voices weaving a tapestry of sound that curled around me. I shivered, half from the chill that permeated the room, half from the primal fear that clawed at my insides. The words they chanted were foreign, dripping with an ancient weight that felt alive, slithering over my skin like a cold serpent. I couldn't understand them, but the tone was unmistakably sinister, a call to something deep and unfathomable.

As I gazed into the center of the circle, my heart raced. There it lay, the blood-red crystal—its surface slick and glimmering, as if it were alive. It pulsed in time with my heartbeat, an echo that made my entire being tremble. The room was suffused with a malevolent light that flickered from the crystal, casting twisted shadows that danced against the stone walls. This was no ordinary ritual; it was a summoning, and I was the unwitting audience to a spectacle of dark ambition.

"Are we too late?" I whispered, the words barely escaping my lips, laced with panic. Vincent tightened his grip on my arm, a silent vow that he wouldn't let me slip away into this nightmarish dream.

"Not yet," he replied, his voice low and steady, a calm in the eye of the storm. "We wait until we see what they unleash. Then we strike."

The tension crackled in the air, thick as smoke, as the leaders reached a fever pitch. Their voices escalated, harmonizing into an almost hypnotic chant that pulled at the edges of my consciousness. I felt the ground beneath my feet tremble as if the very earth resented their presence. The crystal responded, shuddering violently, its cracks spreading like a spider's web, glowing brighter with each moment. I held my breath, unable to tear my gaze away from the unfolding chaos.

Then, in an instant, the crystal erupted with a blinding light. It shot upward like a fiery fountain, illuminating the cavern and casting harsh shadows that contorted and twisted in wild abandon. I shielded my eyes, heart racing as I sensed the very air shift, a tangible pulse that thrummed in sync with the crystal's frantic energy. The leaders staggered, their chants turning into cries of alarm, but it was too late; whatever ancient power had been summoned was breaking free, and it was hungry.

"Now!" Vincent barked, and instinct took over. We surged forward from the shadows, weaving through the chaos. My heart pounded in my chest, a frantic drumbeat urging me onward as the crystal splintered into a thousand shards of brilliance. Each piece seemed to whisper secrets of the ages, a cacophony of voices that clawed at my mind, pleading, demanding.

As we dashed toward the circle, I felt a surge of adrenaline mixed with an intoxicating rush of fear. What awaited us in the heart of this darkness? My breath came in shallow gasps, yet I felt exhilarated, the thrill of the unknown wrapping around me like a lover's embrace. I had always been the one who held back, the one who hid in the safety of the shadows, but tonight was different. Tonight, I was ready to confront the chaos head-on.

Suddenly, a tendril of light shot out from the heart of the crystal, wrapping around one of the leaders, who screamed in terror as it drew him toward the fractured stone. I watched, horrified yet entranced, as the light enveloped him, his figure twisting and contorting until he was nothing more than a silhouette against the blinding brilliance. The other leaders faltered, their chant faltering into a chorus of panic, glancing at each other with wide, fearful eyes.

"Focus!" one of them shouted, but their authority was slipping as the energy surged wildly, crackling through the air.

Vincent and I exchanged a glance, and in that instant, we understood. It was now or never. We lunged forward, adrenaline fueling our every movement as we dashed toward the chaos. I could feel the energy swirling around me, a maelstrom of power that threatened to pull me under.

As we closed in, I reached out instinctively, my fingers brushing against the cool surface of the crystal's remnants. The moment I touched it, a shockwave coursed through my body, a violent jolt that sent me staggering back. Visions flashed before my eyes—glimpses of ancient worlds, of shadows and light colliding in an endless dance of creation and destruction. I gasped, overwhelmed by the rush of sensations that clawed at my senses, but somewhere within that chaos, a thread of clarity emerged.

"Together!" I shouted, grabbing Vincent's hand. In that moment, as the world spiraled into a cacophony of light and shadow, I felt the weight of destiny settle on my shoulders, an invitation to step into the fray and reclaim what was ours. The darkness could not hold me. With a fierce determination igniting within, I prepared to fight for our future, to wrest control from the ancient powers that had dared to awaken.

The moment my fingertips grazed the surface of the crystal, the world twisted, a kaleidoscope of light and sensation that threatened to swallow me whole. Time itself seemed to stretch, each heartbeat reverberating through the chamber like the tolling of a distant bell. I could feel Vincent's presence beside me, his warmth a reassuring balm against the chaos erupting around us. We were not merely spectators anymore; we had crossed the threshold into a battle that defied the boundaries of our understanding.

"Keep your wits about you!" Vincent shouted, his voice cutting through the cacophony like a lifeline. I nodded, though my mind was still reeling from the visions that flashed before my eyes. In that instant, the gravity of our mission settled heavily upon my shoulders. We were here to confront the Breed and whatever dark forces they had summoned, yet the power now thrumming in the air felt like a tempest, unchained and volatile.

The leaders of the Breed had begun to break apart, their formation faltering as the crystal emitted waves of energy that rippled through the room. One of them, a tall figure with a commanding presence, staggered backward, his hands raised in a futile gesture of control. "This isn't what we planned!" he screamed, his voice laced with panic. "Regain your focus!"

A wry smile tugged at my lips, despite the peril we faced. Their bravado had unraveled in the face of the very power they sought to command. I could almost taste their desperation, mingled with the metallic scent of the air. This was the moment we had waited for, the chink in their armor that promised a chance to disrupt their dark ambitions.

"Now!" I urged, dragging Vincent toward the heart of the fray. He followed, determination etched across his features, and together we charged into the whirlwind of chaos. I could feel the energy swirling, thrumming against my skin, a potent reminder of the force we were up against. But I also felt something else—a flicker of hope igniting within me. The darkness could be challenged, could be driven back.

As we reached the remnants of the crystal, I caught sight of the tendrils of light swirling like serpents in the air, snaking their way toward the leaders who now stood rooted in place, their faces drawn with fear. The blinding brightness pulsed, each beat of the crystal sending shockwaves through the chamber, as if it were alive, angry at being disturbed. I could hear the whispers again, sweet and sinister, beckoning me to join them in the depths of the unknown.

"Don't let it in!" Vincent's voice was a fierce command, breaking through the fog of temptation that threatened to pull me under. I gritted my teeth, forcing my mind to focus. The crystal was a beacon, an anchor of power, but we had to turn that power against the Breed. I reached for Vincent's hand, squeezing it tightly as I steadied my resolve.

"Let's break their hold," I said, my voice a fierce whisper, determined to drown out the siren call of the crystal. Together, we moved to the center, where the leaders had begun to regain their composure. They were gathering their strength, rallying against the light that threatened to consume them. But they had underestimated us, just as they had underestimated the ancient force they had dared to awaken.

"Don't let them through!" the commanding leader bellowed, rallying the others. They raised their hands, channeling their energy toward us, and I could feel the pressure building, a wave of darkness surging in our direction.

"On three!" I shouted to Vincent, adrenaline surging through my veins. "One... two..."

The air crackled with tension, and as the third count echoed in my mind, I summoned everything I had—the strength of my convictions, the resolve that had brought me this far—and thrust my hands forward. The light responded, a blinding flash that erupted from the remnants of the crystal, surging toward the Breed leaders with a ferocity that took even me by surprise.

It struck them like a tidal wave, the force sweeping them off their feet, their cries mingling with the blaring energy that filled the chamber. I felt a rush of triumph as the tendrils of light intertwined with the shadows they had conjured, battling against their malevolence. The leaders struggled, grappling with their own unleashed power, their attempts to regain control slipping away like sand through fingers.

In the chaos, I locked eyes with Vincent, a spark of understanding passing between us. We were the anomaly in their carefully orchestrated symphony of darkness, and we were not about to let it end here. "Together," I breathed, and he nodded, a fierce determination igniting in his gaze.

We surged forward, fueled by a shared purpose, each step bringing us closer to the heart of the chaos. The room pulsed with an energy that felt almost tangible, the light battling against the shadows, illuminating the faces of the leaders as they twisted in desperation. The sight was almost poetic, a reminder that even the strongest forces could falter when confronted by something greater.

Just as we reached the core of the tumult, a blinding flash erupted from the crystal, momentarily stealing my breath. I stumbled, the world spinning around me, and for a moment, I feared we had lost control. But then I saw it—a fissure opening in the crystal's remnants, a dark void swirling with a hypnotic allure, threatening to swallow everything whole.

"Do you see that?" I shouted to Vincent, fear and awe mingling in my voice. "We have to close it!"

He nodded, his jaw set in determination. "Then let's end this."

With a fierce resolve, we pressed forward, the chaos swirling around us like a tempest, but we were no longer afraid. We were warriors in our own right, determined to banish the shadows and reclaim the light. As we reached the center, a fierce heat radiated from the dark void, a pulse of ancient energy that begged for release.

I could feel it in my bones, the promise of power, but I knew we couldn't give in.

"On three!" I called out, and Vincent clasped my hand tighter. We counted together, a rallying cry against the encroaching darkness. "One... two... three!"

We thrust our combined energy toward the void, our determination igniting into a blazing light that surged forth, a brilliant force pushing back against the shadows. In that moment, the air was electric, alive with the power of our resolve. As the light clashed against the darkness, I felt a surge of exhilaration, a knowing that we were about to change the course of this night forever.

The brilliance of our combined energy surged like a tidal wave, crashing against the dark void. As the light engulfed the room, I could feel the very air around us vibrate with intensity, a palpable force that both terrified and exhilarated me. Shadows flickered and writhed, caught in a desperate battle between light and dark. The leaders of the Breed, once so confident in their power, now appeared as marionettes, strings frayed and tangled, struggling against the will of something far greater than themselves.

Vincent's hand felt warm and steady in mine, a reminder that we were not alone in this fight. "We can't let it escape!" he shouted over the tumult, his voice fierce and resolute. I nodded, the weight of the moment heavy on my heart. Each pulse of light we generated was a heartbeat of hope, pushing back against the encroaching shadows that sought to envelop us whole.

The void roared in defiance, the sound a low growl that reverberated through the stone walls, making the ground tremble beneath our feet. The air grew thick with the scent of ozone, charged with energy that made my hair stand on end. I focused, channeling every ounce of strength I had into our light, trying to drown out the whispers that clawed at the edges of my mind, promises of power and secrets that felt almost too tempting to resist.

"Hold on!" I called to Vincent, feeling the pull of the darkness like a siren's song, trying to lure me into its depths. "We can do this!" The flicker of uncertainty in my own voice fueled my determination. If we failed, the consequences would ripple far beyond this moment, potentially awakening an ancient force that should never see the light of day.

The crystal remnants began to crackle and sputter, sending out sparks that felt like fire against my skin. I caught a glimpse of the Breed leaders, their faces twisted with rage and fear. They were scrambling, their attempts to regroup futile against the sheer force we had unleashed. The commanding figure, who had once exuded authority, now looked like a cornered animal, desperate and wild-eyed.

"Stop them!" he bellowed, rallying what remained of his cohorts. But it was too late; their chants were now lost in the roar of the energy surging around us.

With one last heave, I pushed harder against the darkness, and it shuddered in response. The void began to retract, sucked back into the remnants of the crystal as if our light was a vacuum, devouring its very essence. I could see the shadows receding, their grasp on the leaders loosening. But just as I began to feel a surge of triumph, a sharp pain shot through my body, a searing heat that spread from my fingertips to my core.

"Ah!" I gasped, staggering back as the tendrils of darkness lashed out, wrapping around my ankles, pulling me down into its depths. "Vincent!" My voice cracked with desperation, panic clawing at my throat.

He didn't hesitate. "I'm here!" he shouted, rushing to my side, his own light pulsing fiercely as he fought against the dark forces that threatened to claim me. He grasped my arm, trying to pull me free, but the shadows were relentless, coiling around me like a vice.

"Fight it!" he urged, his eyes fierce with determination. "You're stronger than this!"

I closed my eyes, summoning every ounce of my will. I could feel the darkness whispering sweetly in my ear, promising strength, power, control. It was tempting, so tempting. But I remembered the faces of the Breed leaders, their arrogance, their greed, and how they sought to harness this darkness for their own twisted desires. No, I could not give in.

With a guttural scream, I pushed against the shadows, channeling all my frustration, fear, and anger into a singular point of light. "You will not have me!" I roared, the words spilling forth like a mantra. The energy surged, and with it came a shockwave that rippled through the chamber, throwing Vincent and me backward.

I landed hard, the breath knocked out of me. For a moment, the world blurred, and I gasped for air, struggling to regain my senses. When my vision cleared, I looked up to see the void collapsing in on itself, the shadows retreating with a hiss, but not without leaving a parting gift. From the center of the fading darkness, a figure emerged—a silhouette woven from shadows and light, standing defiantly as if birthed from the very chaos we sought to control.

"Foolish children," it said, its voice smooth as silk yet crackling with an underlying menace. "You think you can banish me? I am eternal." The figure stepped closer, and the air thickened, an oppressive weight settling over us. I could feel the remnants of power radiating from it, an ancient force that seemed to hum with the energy of ages long past.

Vincent pulled me close, his body shielding me from the dark presence that loomed before us. "What do we do now?" he whispered, the tension palpable in the air.

I shook my head, searching for an answer that eluded me. "I don't know. We can't let it get any stronger."

The figure chuckled, a sound like glass shattering. "Oh, you've awakened something far greater than yourselves. You cannot hope to contain what has been released."

I felt the edges of fear nibbling at my resolve. "Then we'll find a way to stop you!" I shouted, my voice steadier than I felt.

"Such spirit," it replied, its eyes gleaming with an otherworldly light. "But it is misplaced. You cannot hope to fight against the blood moon's wrath."

Suddenly, the chamber shook violently, and a blinding light erupted from the center of the crystal. I shielded my eyes, the brilliance threatening to consume everything. "Vincent!" I cried, reaching for him, but the ground split beneath us, a chasm opening wide, swallowing the light and the darkness alike.

As I fell, the last thing I saw was the figure's mocking smile, a promise of chaos yet to come. "You cannot escape your fate," it echoed in my mind as the world around me dissolved into nothingness.

Chapter 24: The Rift

The air crackles with tension, thick like a summer storm about to break, as the chaos around us spirals into a frenzy of shouting and confusion. The leaders of the Breed scramble like ants disturbed from their nest, their faces a mosaic of disbelief and rage. Shards of the crystal, once a symbol of their power, now lay scattered across the floor, glinting ominously in the flickering light. I can feel the remnants of its energy thrumming beneath my skin, an unsettling mix of dread and allure. It's as if the darkness wants me to embrace it, to surrender to its intoxicating embrace, and for a fleeting moment, the idea feels tantalizing.

But Vincent. He's the anchor in this storm. His eyes, usually filled with that confident spark, are now wide with concern as he reaches for me, his hand stretching across the wreckage. I can almost taste the fear in the air, sharp and metallic, as he yells my name, each syllable a desperate plea. The sound slices through the chaos like a beacon of light, guiding me back from the brink.

"Stay with me, Luna!" His voice is a lifeline, pulling me back from the precipice of darkness that threatens to engulf me. I can see him fighting against the energy, his body taut with effort, as if he can wrestle the very shadows that threaten to claim me. I blink against the encroaching dark, each flicker of the room's light illuminating fleeting images of despair, doubt, and swirling shadows.

The moment feels eternal, suspended in the tension between light and dark. I can feel the darkness trying to weave its way into my mind, whispering seductive promises of power and freedom, but then there's Vincent's warmth—his presence pushing back against the void. My heart thuds in rhythm with the chaos, a war drum calling me to choose. I reach for him, fingers trembling as I grasp his hand, our connection igniting something fierce within me.

"Let's get out of here," I manage to say, my voice a mix of determination and vulnerability. The energy roils around us, but now, it's not just chaos; it's a battle of wills. As I pull Vincent closer, a surge of courage floods my veins, igniting a flicker of resistance against the darkness. "Together."

With a sharp inhale, I push against the weight of the energy surrounding us. The dark tendrils snap back as I forcefully take a step forward, pulling Vincent with me. He looks at me, uncertainty etched in his features, but his grip tightens around mine, a silent promise that we will face this together.

We weave through the chaos, dodging the panicked figures of the Breed leaders, their voices drowned out by the rushing tide of shadows. I can sense the desperation in the air, their carefully orchestrated plans crumbling like dust in the wind. As we reach the doorway, I glance back, the tumultuous scene unfolding behind us—a sea of confusion, ambition turned to chaos. The sight sends a shiver down my spine, the realization that this is just the beginning sinking in like a stone.

"Luna, we need to move faster!" Vincent's voice is urgent, snapping me back to the present. I nod, my resolve hardening. We burst through the door into the coolness of the night air, the fresh breeze a stark contrast to the turmoil we've just escaped. I can feel the pulse of energy still clinging to me, but it's weaker now, fading as we put distance between ourselves and the madness.

The moon hangs low in the sky, casting a silver glow over the landscape. I take a moment to breathe, the air filling my lungs, and I turn to Vincent, my heart pounding not just from fear but from exhilaration. "What the hell was that?" I ask, trying to catch my breath.

"Something we weren't prepared for," he replies, shaking his head as if trying to dispel the chaos from his thoughts. "But we need to regroup. If the Breed can harness that power—"

"They won't." The words slip out before I can think. A fire ignites in my chest as the memories of the shadows swirl in my mind. "They can't control it. It's too volatile, too unpredictable."

Vincent studies me, the flickering light from the moon highlighting the determination in my eyes. "You felt it, didn't you?"

I nod, the memory still fresh. "It was like... it was calling to me, Vincent. I could feel its power, but it wasn't something I wanted to embrace."

"What if it's not just about the darkness? What if it's about who we are when we confront it?"

His words linger in the air, weaving through my thoughts like the shadows we just escaped. Could confronting the darkness give us clarity? Could it forge a new path for us—one that we control, not the chaos?

"Then we have to figure out how to use it," I declare, feeling the weight of my resolve settle around me like a cloak. "Not for them, but for us. We have to find a way to turn this chaos into something we can wield."

Vincent's expression shifts, a mix of admiration and caution flickering across his features. "You're suggesting we dive back in?"

"I'm suggesting we don't let it consume us," I say, confidence surging through me. "We can't be afraid of the darkness. We have to confront it, to challenge it, or it will define us."

A smirk curls on his lips, and for a moment, the shadows of the night seem less daunting. "You really know how to get a guy to reconsider his life choices, don't you?"

I chuckle, the sound breaking the tension. "It's a gift. Now, let's figure out where to start."

As we stand there, the weight of the night pressing down around us, I can't shake the feeling that this is only the beginning. A rift has opened, not just in the world we know but within ourselves, and the journey ahead will demand every ounce of courage we have.

The night air is cool against my flushed skin, grounding me in a reality that feels almost surreal after our brush with chaos. As the adrenaline begins to ebb, the weight of the moment settles around us like a thick fog. Vincent stands beside me, eyes narrowed, scanning the shadows as if expecting the remnants of the darkness to leap out and consume us once more. I take a moment to breathe deeply, inhaling the crisp scent of pine and damp earth that surrounds us. Each breath is a reminder that we are alive, that the darkness may have tried to claim me, but it failed.

"What's our next move?" Vincent asks, breaking the silence with a voice low and steady. There's a tension in the air, a current of unspoken fears swirling around us like the leaves caught in the night breeze.

I can see the flicker of doubt in his eyes, but more than that, I sense a deep-seated determination. It's contagious. "We need to figure out what that energy was and how to harness it," I reply, my mind racing with possibilities. "It's not just some random outburst; it's part of something larger, something the Breed can't control."

Vincent nods, his brow furrowing in concentration. "You really believe we can control it? After what just happened?"

"Not control," I clarify, feeling the words take root in my mind. "Channel. We need to channel it. If we understand its nature, we can protect ourselves and maybe even use it against them."

His lips curl into a wry smile. "You've always been the optimistic one."

"Optimism is just realism dressed up in a pretty dress," I quip back, unable to suppress a grin. "Besides, I'm not about to let some supernatural force dictate my fate."

"Fair enough." He leans back against a nearby tree, crossing his arms as he considers my words. "So, where do we start? With a dark energy extraction manual?"

"We could always consult the local library of horrors," I say, my tone light even as I feel the shadows lurking at the edge of my thoughts. "Or we could start with the one person who might have answers—Rhea."

"Rhea?" His brow arches, skepticism written all over his handsome face. "You mean the same Rhea who leads the opposition against the Breed? The one who might just see us as collateral damage in her little war?"

I shrug, brushing off his concerns with a wave of my hand. "Desperate times call for desperate measures. If anyone knows about the dark energy, it's her. She's been battling the Breed for longer than we've been alive; she's bound to have some insights."

Vincent considers this, his fingers tapping rhythmically against his arm. "And if she doesn't? If she decides to turn us in to the Breed for even thinking about talking to her?"

"Then we improvise." I feel a flicker of excitement at the prospect of the unknown, the thrill of stepping into a situation rife with danger and intrigue. "We're good at improvisation, remember?"

He shakes his head, chuckling softly. "You're incorrigible."

"Thank you, I do my best." I give him a mock bow, reveling in the lightness that comes from bantering with him, even amidst the impending darkness.

The decision made, we set off through the dense underbrush, the world around us transforming from chaos to the eerie stillness of the woods at night. The path ahead is winding and fraught with shadows that dance at the corners of my vision, but my heart beats steadily in my chest, a reminder that fear can't rule us. Not now.

As we tread deeper into the woods, the air shifts, and an unsettling quiet envelops us. It's as if the forest holds its breath, anticipating our next move. I can't shake the feeling that we are being watched, a chill creeping down my spine as I glance over my shoulder. The trees loom like ancient sentinels, their gnarled branches reaching out like skeletal hands.

"Did you hear that?" Vincent's voice is barely above a whisper, and I stop, straining to listen.

At first, it's nothing but the rustling of leaves, but then I catch it—a low hum, resonating in the air, a sound that sends shivers down my spine. It's coming from deeper within the woods, a rhythmic pulsing that seems to echo my own heartbeat.

"Luna," Vincent says, his expression now serious. "I don't think we're alone."

"Yeah, I gathered that," I reply, my voice steady despite the flutter of nerves in my stomach. "But I think we need to investigate."

With a nod, we move cautiously toward the source of the sound, the underbrush crackling beneath our feet. Each step feels like a risk, the forest closing in around us as the hum grows louder, vibrating through my bones. The shadows shift and swirl, and I can't shake the feeling that something ancient lurks just beyond our sight.

Suddenly, the trees part to reveal a clearing bathed in a silvery glow. In the center stands a figure cloaked in darkness, their features obscured, but the aura surrounding them pulses with the same energy that erupted from the crystal. My heart races as I realize this is no mere coincidence.

"Who goes there?" Vincent calls, his voice firm despite the tension in the air.

The figure turns slowly, and for a heartbeat, I can see their face—a woman with wild, dark hair framing sharp features, her eyes glowing like embers in the night. "You seek the darkness, do you not?" Her voice is low, seductive, and it wraps around me like a silk scarf.

"Who are you?" I ask, feeling the weight of her gaze settle on me.

"I am the keeper of the shadows," she replies, a small smile playing on her lips. "And I know why you're here."

I exchange a glance with Vincent, uncertainty hanging in the air like the fog around us. "What do you know?"

"Enough to understand that you are not afraid of what lies ahead." She steps closer, the shadows swirling around her like a living entity. "But fear can be a powerful ally—or a deadly foe."

"Great, more riddles," I mutter, trying to mask my unease with humor. "Can you just tell us what we need to know?"

The woman tilts her head, amusement dancing in her fiery eyes. "Straightforwardness is refreshing, but the path you tread is fraught with peril. If you wish to harness the energy, you must first embrace the darkness within you."

A chill runs through me at her words. "Embrace it? You mean we have to accept it?"

"Yes." She moves closer, and I can feel the pull of her energy, a strange and intoxicating allure that tugs at the corners of my mind. "But understand this—once you embrace it, there is no turning back."

Vincent steps in front of me, his posture protective. "What do you gain from this? What's your angle?"

She laughs, a sound like tinkling glass, and it sends a shiver of uncertainty through the clearing. "I seek only to guide those willing to walk the line between light and dark. But be warned, not all who tread this path survive."

My heart races as I look between Vincent and the enigmatic woman. The weight of her words hangs in the air, a heavy shroud that wraps around us, and I know this is just the beginning of a journey that will challenge everything we believe. The shadows pulse with anticipation, and somewhere deep inside me, I can feel the darkness stir, waiting for its moment to rise.

The woman's presence is electric, her dark energy radiating around her like a shroud. I can almost taste the power swirling in the air, a bittersweet tang that ignites something primal within me. It's intoxicating, yet I feel the hairs on the back of my neck prickle in warning. I exchange another glance with Vincent, who stands firm beside me, his brow furrowed as he assesses our surroundings.

"Embracing the darkness?" I repeat, attempting to mask the tremor in my voice with an air of bravado. "Is that your idea of a good time?"

The woman smiles, her teeth gleaming white against the shadow of her cloak. "Only if you seek true power, dear." Her eyes flicker, hinting at an ancient wisdom that sends a ripple of uncertainty through my heart. "What you face is far beyond the trivial squabbles of the Breed. This is about survival, about claiming your destiny."

"Sounds a bit dramatic, don't you think?" I retort, crossing my arms defiantly. "I'd rather not sign up for a horror story just yet."

"Ah, but life is a horror story in its own right, isn't it?" she counters smoothly. "You've already tasted its darkness tonight. You felt its call, and it didn't frighten you. You're here for a reason."

Vincent shifts beside me, his energy a steady reassurance. "We need answers, not riddles," he says, his tone firm. "If you know something, speak plainly."

The woman chuckles, the sound oddly melodic. "Very well. You seek to harness the dark energy, but understand that it is not merely a tool. It is alive, a force that will challenge you as much as it will empower you. To control it, you must first accept what it reveals about yourself."

"Sounds like therapy with a side of existential crisis," I mutter, rolling my eyes.

"Such a quaint view." Her smile is sharp, amusement dancing in her eyes. "But the reality is far more complex. The shadows whisper secrets, and those who listen may uncover truths about their desires—fears they hide even from themselves."

"Is that supposed to scare us?" I ask, my voice steady despite the brewing tension.

"It should," she replies, her tone suddenly serious. "For some, the darkness reveals their deepest longings, their most potent regrets. Embrace it, and you may find your heart's desire. Resist it, and it could very well be your undoing."

"Now you're just trying to make it sound dramatic," I say, trying to keep my tone light, but I can feel the weight of her words pressing against me.

"And yet, you linger," she replies, tilting her head in an almost predatory fashion. "You're drawn to the unknown, are you not? You crave the thrill of discovery, even if it terrifies you."

"Who doesn't love a little danger?" I shoot back, the words coming out more confidently than I feel. "But I'm not diving headfirst into a shadowy abyss without knowing what I'm getting into."

The woman nods, as if pleased by my resolve. "Wise choice. But knowledge comes at a price. What will you sacrifice for the truth?"

Vincent steps closer, the tension between us palpable. "We're not interested in sacrifices. Just answers."

"Ah, but everything has a cost. You seek to manipulate forces beyond your understanding, yet you want to pay nothing?" Her voice takes on an almost mocking lilt, and I feel my patience fraying.

"Why do you care?" I snap, the heat of irritation rising within me. "What's in it for you?"

"Perhaps I simply enjoy watching mortals grapple with their destiny," she replies, her smile enigmatic. "Or perhaps I want to see if you have the strength to endure what is to come. You may need it more than you realize."

Before I can respond, a low rumble shakes the ground beneath us, a deep sound reverberating through the trees. The woman's expression shifts, her eyes widening with a mix of intrigue and concern. "The energy stirs; it senses your presence. You must decide quickly."

Vincent's grip tightens on my arm, and I can feel the electric charge in the air rise, the shadows pulsing around us like a living thing. "Luna, we need to get out of here," he urges, his voice urgent.

"No." I shake my head, resisting the impulse to flee. "Not yet. I need to know what she means."

"Very well," the woman says, her voice low and almost sultry, as if inviting us to dance on the edge of danger. "But know this: the more you learn, the more you will be tested. What you discover may shatter your understanding of who you are."

With a quick glance back at Vincent, I nod, feeling a rush of determination. "Let's do this."

The shadows swirl around us, and the ground trembles again as the air thickens with energy. The woman steps closer, her aura enveloping us both in an otherworldly embrace. "Look into the darkness, and you may find what you seek."

I swallow hard, my heart pounding against my ribs. "What do I do?"

"Close your eyes," she instructs, her voice a soothing balm amidst the rising chaos. "Trust in the shadows; let them reveal your truth."

Taking a deep breath, I shut my eyes and feel the energy wrap around me, a cool caress that sends chills through my body. The world fades away, and I am left in a void, floating between reality and something deeper. Shadows dance at the edges of my consciousness, whispering secrets I can't quite decipher.

Suddenly, a vision bursts into view—a swirling maelstrom of light and dark, flashing images of my past. I see my childhood home, the warmth of laughter echoing in the halls, the scents of baking cookies and blooming flowers. Then, darkness encroaches, memories twisted by fear and doubt. My heart races as I see flashes of faces I loved and lost, moments filled with regret and pain, feelings I had buried deep within myself.

A voice, low and familiar, cuts through the chaos. "Luna." It's Vincent, his tone urgent and filled with concern. "Open your eyes. We're running out of time!"

I force my eyes open, the vision fading as I'm thrust back into the clearing. The woman watches me with a knowing gaze, her expression unreadable. "You've seen a glimpse of your truth," she murmurs, her voice echoing with weight. "Now you must decide if you're ready to confront it."

Before I can respond, the rumbling intensifies, the ground shaking violently beneath our feet. The shadows around us grow thicker, swirling into tendrils that grasp at my ankles, pulling me toward the darkness. I feel the energy surge, a raw force that fills the air with electricity, and panic bubbles to the surface.

"Luna!" Vincent's voice slices through the chaos, but the shadows are relentless, their grip tightening.

"Hold on!" I cry out, reaching for him, but the energy swirls between us, a churning vortex threatening to swallow us both whole.

"Fight it!" he shouts, desperation etched on his face. "You have to fight!"

But the darkness closes in, and I can feel it whispering to me, promising power and understanding if I just let go. My mind spins, the conflict raging within me—fear or power, light or shadow.

With a final burst of determination, I push against the pull of the darkness, my heart screaming to fight, to hold onto the light. But just as I feel myself break free, a blinding flash erupts from the center of the clearing, illuminating everything in white-hot brilliance.

And then, just as quickly, the light is snuffed out, leaving nothing but an oppressive silence and the echoes of Vincent's terrified voice fading into the void.

"Luna!"

Everything goes dark.

Chapter 25: Heart of the Fire

Every flicker of torchlight along the stone walls seemed to breathe life into the shadows, dancing with a sinister grace that whispered of danger lurking just beyond reach. The air felt electric, crackling with the tension of our hurried breaths and the promise of what lay ahead. I could feel the pulse of the ancient complex thrumming beneath my feet, a heartbeat resonating with the urgency of our mission. As Vincent and I pressed deeper into the labyrinth, the weight of our choices hung heavy in the air, a thick fog that threatened to suffocate the flicker of hope I clung to.

Vincent moved with a practiced ease, a fluidity that reminded me of the wolves prowling the forest outside our town, a predator confident in its domain. His presence was a steady anchor amidst the chaos that threatened to consume us. The scent of him—earthy, warm, and undeniably comforting—wrapped around me like a blanket, shielding me from the encroaching fear. I found solace in the way his fingers brushed against my skin, igniting a fire that burned brighter than the darkness surrounding us.

"Are you sure about this?" I whispered, my voice barely more than a breath, the weight of uncertainty hanging between us like a taut string ready to snap.

He turned to me, his deep-set eyes gleaming with a fierce determination that sent a thrill down my spine. "We don't have a choice. If we turn back now, we're as good as dead."

"Then dead it is," I replied, managing a wry smile, though my heart raced with apprehension. It was a bold attempt to mask my fear, to convince myself that bravery was an option. But the truth was, the further we ventured, the more I felt the gnawing edge of dread. The Breed was out there, their anger palpable, and we were a mere step away from the abyss.

Navigating the narrow corridors, we maneuvered past heavy wooden doors, each more foreboding than the last. They loomed like sentinels, guarding the secrets held within. As we paused to listen, the echoes of our surroundings grew louder, the distant murmur of voices carrying through the halls like a ghostly serenade. The Breed was gathering, their numbers swelling with every passing moment, fueled by the fire of vengeance ignited by our interference.

The walls around us began to close in, a palpable tension that made the very stones feel alive, pulsing with an energy that seemed to draw the breath from my lungs. The flickering lights painted jagged shadows, twisting the space into something surreal. My mind raced, grasping at thoughts like lifelines thrown into a churning sea. What if we were too late? What if our journey had been in vain?

"Vincent," I breathed, my heart pounding with a sudden surge of anxiety. "What if they're waiting for us? What if this is all a trap?"

He paused, his expression sharpening with intensity. "Then we'll face them together." His confidence steadied me, yet the echo of his words trembled with an unspoken fear. Together. It was a promise wrapped in a challenge, a bond that transcended the chaos around us.

We pressed forward, the weight of our shared resolve a comforting shield against the uncertainty. The air thickened with anticipation, a tangible force that urged us onward. With every step, I felt the thrill of impending confrontation coursing through my veins, mingling with the fierce love that had ignited my spirit.

Suddenly, we rounded a corner, and the corridor opened into a vast chamber, its grandeur both awe-inspiring and terrifying. High above, the ceiling arched like the wings of a giant bird, adorned with intricate carvings that whispered tales of old—stories of battles fought, of victories won and lost. And in the center of the chamber, beneath the ghostly glow of an ethereal light, the Breed gathered in a tight circle, their silhouettes dark against the shimmering backdrop.

I felt a chill race down my spine as I recognized the leader among them, a figure cloaked in shadow, eyes glinting with malice. The air thrummed with tension, and I knew instinctively that they had sensed our presence. "Vincent," I whispered, gripping his arm as the gravity of our situation sank in.

"We need to find a way to get closer," he murmured, his gaze locked onto the gathering. "If we can disrupt their ritual—"

Before he could finish, a voice cut through the air like a knife, sharp and commanding. "So, the little lovebirds have come to play." The leader stepped forward, a smirk curling his lips, reveling in the chaos he had sown. "I wondered when you'd finally find your way here."

"Back off," I shot back, a fire igniting within me. My hands balled into fists at my sides, defiance surging in my veins. "You're not getting away with this."

He laughed, a low, menacing sound that echoed through the chamber, filling the air with a chill. "You think your bravery can save you? This is where it all ends."

Vincent stepped in front of me, his body a shield against the darkness. "Not if we have anything to say about it."

And just like that, the chamber ignited into chaos, a storm of fury and determination, as the Breed lunged toward us, their eyes glowing with hatred. I felt the ground shake beneath me, but I stood my ground, the fire of our love fueling every heartbeat as we prepared to fight for our lives and the future we dared to dream of.

The chaos erupted like a tempest unleashed, the echo of our defiance bouncing off the cold stone walls as the Breed surged toward us. The chamber transformed into a battleground, a swirling maelstrom of shadows and flashes of fury. Vincent's grip tightened around my waist, pulling me close as we navigated the onslaught. Adrenaline coursed through my veins, igniting every nerve ending, sharpening my focus amidst the swirling confusion.

"Do you always have to pick a fight with the entire room?" I shouted over the din, trying to inject a bit of levity into the moment, even as I ducked under the outstretched arm of a snarling figure.

Vincent flashed me a quick grin, a brief reminder of the man I loved beneath the warrior facade. "What can I say? I thrive on the unexpected." He launched himself forward, a force of nature, and I followed, our movements synchronized as if we'd practiced this dance a thousand times.

In the midst of the chaos, I caught a glimpse of the leader, still smirking, as if our struggle were an elaborate game. He raised his hands, calling forth a wave of energy that shimmered with dark intent. I felt the pull of it, like a tide trying to draw me under, and instinctively I stepped closer to Vincent, drawing strength from his unwavering presence.

"Stay close," he warned, his voice low and fierce, a protective growl that made my heart race for more reasons than one. I nodded, determination surging within me, a fire of my own that threatened to ignite as we faced the gathering storm together.

Suddenly, a figure darted past me, dark hair streaming behind like a comet's tail. It was one of the Breed, eyes glinting with malice. I barely had time to react before Vincent was there, intercepting the blow aimed at my side. The impact reverberated through me, a jolt that snapped my focus back to the present.

"Got your back," he said, breathless but unyielding, as he shoved the attacker aside. I could see the feral determination etched across his face, an expression that made my heart swell with a fierce pride.

"I appreciate it. You know I can handle myself," I shot back, even as I threw a punch at another assailant approaching from my left. It connected, a satisfying thud that sent the figure staggering back. I couldn't let fear dictate my actions—not now, not when everything was at stake.

But the room was alive with chaos, the Breed attacking like wild animals, drawn to us like moths to flame. They moved as one, a dark tide threatening to drown our spark. I could hear their snarls and shouts, but one voice rang out above the rest—the leader's, commanding and cold.

"Enough!" he bellowed, and the world seemed to still. The chaos halted as if the very stones had paused to listen. "You think you can defy us? You think love can shield you from the darkness that binds us?"

"I think you underestimate the power of love," I retorted, my voice ringing clear, fueled by a sudden surge of courage. "You're wrong if you think you can extinguish what you don't understand."

His eyes narrowed, and I could feel the ripple of fury that coursed through the assembled Breed. I knew that taunting him was dangerous, but there was something intoxicating about standing my ground, defiance surging within me like a roaring flame.

"Love?" he sneered, advancing toward us. "Love is a weakness. It makes you vulnerable, exposes your heart to ruin."

"Maybe," I shot back, clenching my fists, "but it also makes us stronger. And you've got it all wrong if you think it makes us afraid."

Vincent stepped forward, mirroring my defiance. "You don't get to dictate our fate. We will fight for what we believe in, for each other."

The leader's smirk faltered, his confidence wavering as he regarded us with a newfound intensity. Perhaps, in our defiance, we had managed to plant a seed of doubt in his twisted ideology. For a fleeting moment, I could see a crack in his armor—a glimpse of uncertainty that only made me bolder.

But then, without warning, he lunged. The world erupted into chaos once more as we braced for impact, dodging and weaving through the onslaught of the Breed. I fought with everything I had, every punch and kick fueled by the fire of our shared love and the desire to protect what mattered most.

Just as I was starting to feel the weight of exhaustion tugging at my limbs, I caught sight of Vincent, his figure a whirlwind of motion. He was magnificent, a force to be reckoned with, and I couldn't help but admire the way he fought—like a lion defending its pride.

Then, in an unexpected twist, the leader fell back, his dark energy crackling like lightning in the air. "You think this is over?" he spat, his voice a low growl. "You are merely delaying the inevitable."

With a sweeping gesture, he summoned the shadows, dark tendrils reaching out like hands grasping for something just out of reach. I felt a chill race down my spine, a primal instinct urging me to run. But I stood firm, refusing to back down.

"Maybe you should take your own advice," I said, my voice steady despite the tremor of fear. "You're the one who doesn't understand what you're dealing with."

The shadows recoiled momentarily, as if my words had struck a chord. It was a flicker of vulnerability that I hadn't expected, and I seized the moment. "You think you're strong, but you're just a coward hiding in the dark. Strength comes from unity, from love, not fear."

Vincent was at my side, his presence grounding me. "And we're not alone. We fight for our people, for our home."

The leader's expression twisted into a snarl, the confidence he had exuded fading into something darker, more desperate. The shadows pulsed, flickering as if they were unsure whether to respond to his command or retreat.

In that moment, I felt the air shift—a glimmer of hope piercing the darkness. Our combined light was a beacon, challenging the encroaching shadows. And as the Breed faltered, I knew that love had indeed ignited a fire within us, one that would not be extinguished easily.

With a sudden surge, the room erupted again, but this time it was not just chaos; it was a fight for our very souls, a clash of ideals where hope battled despair, and I would not stand down.

The air thickened with the weight of uncertainty, shadows swirling like an ominous fog as the clash of bodies filled the chamber. With every punch, every dodge, and every breath I took, I felt the bond between Vincent and me tighten, a fierce tether that defied the chaos around us. The leader of the Breed stood at the center, a malevolent storm, his face twisted in rage, and I could sense the dark energy radiating from him like heat from a forge.

"Is this really the best you can do?" I shouted over the din, hoping to provoke him further. "I've seen more coordination in a drunken ballet!"

His expression darkened, and I could almost see the gears turning in his mind, assessing the shift in power. The shadows he had summoned swirled restlessly, flickering with his rising anger. "You think your bravado can save you? You're outnumbered, outmatched, and, frankly, out of your league," he spat, the venom in his voice sharp enough to cut.

"I'd argue that being outnumbered is just an opportunity for a better story," I replied, channeling every ounce of sarcasm I could muster. "But you wouldn't understand that, would you? Your idea of a good time is trying to terrify a bunch of innocents."

"Enough!" he roared, raising a hand that crackled with dark energy. I felt the air grow heavier, the very room vibrating with the intensity of his power. "I will not let your insolence go unpunished."

Vincent and I exchanged a quick glance, a silent understanding passing between us. Together, we launched into action, dodging another surge of shadows that threatened to ensnare us. I could see others from the Breed trying to regroup, moving in a calculated way to flank us. Their eyes glowed with malevolence, and for a moment, fear crept in, gnawing at the edges of my resolve.

"Vincent!" I shouted, barely avoiding a blow that would have knocked me off my feet. "We need to split them up! Is there anything in here we can use?"

He glanced around the chamber, his sharp gaze assessing the environment, then locked onto a series of ancient pillars, ornate but crumbling, their surfaces etched with runes that pulsed with a faint light. "Those pillars—they might be our best shot! If we can lure them into the right position, we could collapse one of them and create a barrier."

I nodded, adrenaline surging as we moved with purpose. "On three?"

"One, two—"

Before we could finish the count, the leader struck, unleashing a bolt of dark energy that shot toward us with blinding speed. I barely managed to pull Vincent out of the way, the force of it narrowly missing us, splintering a nearby pillar into a shower of stone. The dust filled the air, momentarily obscuring our view, but as it settled, I could see the Breed recovering, their focus sharpening on us again.

"Your little games are futile!" the leader called out, frustration seeping into his voice. "You can't hide behind those pillars forever."

"Then let's not hide," I replied, finding my footing in the chaos. "Let's give them something to chase."

With a fierce battle cry, we darted toward the far side of the chamber, weaving through the thick haze of combatants. The dark energy pulsed behind us, the leader's rage propelling his followers forward, and I could almost hear the echo of their snarls and the crash of fists against flesh.

"Just keep running!" Vincent urged, his breath warm against my ear as we narrowly dodged another attack. "We'll draw them to the pillars, and then—"

I didn't need to hear the rest. I could feel the plan forming in my mind, a strategy born of desperation. We sprinted toward the nearest pillar, weaving past our pursuers, who were now fully focused on us, intent on taking us down. I could hear the pounding of footsteps behind us, the primal growls of the Breed pushing us onward, the thrill of danger intertwining with the exhilaration of the chase.

As we reached the pillars, I felt the air thrum with anticipation, a tension that thrived in the space between us and our enemies. "Now!" I shouted, turning to face the oncoming tide.

We were ready, adrenaline and fear mixing into a potent cocktail as we launched ourselves back into the fray. Vincent and I worked in tandem, our movements synchronized, a dance of chaos and strength. With swift, calculated strikes, we pushed back against the Breed, trying to create a rift between them and the pillars.

"Over here, you miserable wretches!" I taunted, baiting them closer. "I thought you were supposed to be fierce! Where's the bite?"

The leader's face contorted in rage as his followers began to react, charging toward us, their focus sharp and singular. "Get them!" he yelled, and with that, they surged forward, a wave of dark energy closing in.

"Now!" Vincent shouted again, and with a powerful kick, he struck the base of the nearest pillar. It trembled under the impact, the runes flaring momentarily before beginning to crack, the sound echoing like a thunderclap through the chamber.

The Breed faltered, confusion flickering in their eyes, but it was too late. The pillar began to give way, stones cascading down, the ancient structure crumbling as the leader's eyes widened in horror.

"Retreat!" he roared, but it was a cry that would never reach his followers. The collapse sent a shockwave through the room, and I felt the ground shudder beneath me as I grabbed Vincent's arm, yanking him back just in time.

The dust settled as the pillar crashed down, creating a barrier that split the chamber in two, severing the advancing Breed from us. For a brief moment, a silence fell over the chaos, punctuated only by the creaking of the remaining pillars and the distant echoes of the scuffle still ongoing in the shadows.

But that silence was short-lived. From the darkness, the leader's voice rose once more, cold and chilling. "You think you can stop me with rubble? You're only delaying the inevitable. I will have what is mine!"

The tension in the air thickened, a palpable force that wrapped around us like a noose. I could feel Vincent's pulse quickening, his body tense beside me, and I knew we were running out of time. The leader, fueled by rage and desperation, would find a way to breach our makeshift barrier.

And just as I turned to Vincent, the ground trembled beneath our feet—a warning tremor before a greater disaster. I looked down, panic rising in my chest as fissures snaked across the floor, threatening to swallow us whole.

"Vincent, we need to—"

But before I could finish, the floor cracked wide open, a chasm yawning beneath us, and we were falling, the darkness reaching out to engulf us as we plunged into the unknown. The last thing I saw was Vincent's determined face, his hand reaching for mine, before the abyss swallowed us whole, the chaos above fading into silence.

Chapter 26: The Last Stand

The air was thick with tension, a palpable force that twisted and churned in the confines of our hiding place. It was a dilapidated barn, its once bright red paint now dulled and peeling, a relic of a simpler time. The smell of hay and aged wood enveloped us, a faint comfort against the impending storm. Outside, the sounds of the Breed's forces echoed like thunderclaps in the distance, their boots pounding the earth with a menacing rhythm that set my heart racing. I squeezed Vincent's hand tighter, seeking solace in his steady presence. His gaze met mine, fierce and unyielding, as if he could read the flicker of doubt that dared to surface within me.

"We can't back down now," he murmured, his voice low and urgent. I could see the shadows dancing across his jaw, accentuating the lines of determination etched into his face. I had never seen him like this—raw, passionate, and utterly committed. It stirred something deep within me, igniting a flame of resolve that I had thought long extinguished.

"I know," I replied, forcing a bravado I didn't entirely feel. "But look at us. Just two against an army. What can we possibly do?" My voice quivered, betraying the trepidation that coursed through me.

Vincent's fingers brushed against my cheek, gentle yet firm, grounding me in that moment. "We fight. Together."

I nodded, though uncertainty gnawed at my insides. Memories of past skirmishes flashed through my mind, moments filled with panic and chaos. Yet amidst the fear, there had been glimmers of hope, shards of victory that reminded me we were not without allies. We had each other, and for now, that had to be enough.

Outside, the cacophony grew louder, a testament to the Breed's relentless pursuit. I could hear their voices, guttural and commanding, issuing orders that crackled through the air like static. Adrenaline surged through my veins, each heartbeat a reminder of what we were up against. It wasn't just the threat of physical confrontation—it was the very essence of what we stood for, a battle for survival and the future we envisioned, one untainted by the darkness they represented.

"We need a plan," I said, my mind racing as I scanned our surroundings. The barn was a maze of shadows, but there were tools scattered about, relics of a past life: old pitchforks, rusty chains, and a forgotten wagon wheel.

Vincent followed my gaze, and I could see the wheels turning in his mind. "The roof," he said suddenly. "If we can get up there, we might have the advantage."

A flicker of hope ignited within me, and I motioned toward a stack of hay bales piled high in one corner. "Let's climb. We can see their movements and maybe even create a diversion."

Together, we scaled the bales, the rough texture scraping against my palms. I steadied myself, glancing down to find Vincent's steadying hand always at the ready. As I reached the top, I peered over the edge of the barn's roof, my breath hitching at the sight before me.

The Breed's forces were assembling, a dark tide flowing across the field, their uniforms stark against the vibrant autumn hues of the landscape. A chill crept down my spine as I recognized faces I had once thought were allies—betrayers now, willing to sell their souls for power. I gritted my teeth, fury mixing with fear, a volatile cocktail that demanded release.

"They think they're invincible," I whispered, my voice laced with a newfound defiance. "They don't know what we're capable of."

Vincent's presence beside me was a comfort, a reminder that I was not alone in this fight. "They underestimate us," he replied, his tone a mix of confidence and challenge. "Let's show them just how wrong they are."

I took a deep breath, letting the cool air fill my lungs. It was time to act. We gathered what we could—a few small stones, a loose board from the roof—and prepared ourselves for the confrontation ahead.

As I hurled the first stone into the gathering throng below, a sense of exhilaration rushed through me. The stone struck true, drawing startled glances as chaos erupted. I joined in Vincent's laughter, the sound ringing out like a battle cry amidst the chaos, igniting the fire within.

The moment felt electric, an infusion of power surging through me. With each stone we tossed, with each shout of defiance, we broke through the fog of despair that had threatened to swallow us whole. We were not just two against an army; we were a force to be reckoned with.

Yet, in the midst of our uprising, a figure emerged from the ranks of the Breed. Tall and imposing, he radiated authority, his eyes scanning the area with an unsettling calm. I felt the air shift, tension coiling around us like a noose. Vincent stiffened beside me, the laughter fading from his lips.

"Who is that?" I whispered, a cold dread settling in my stomach.

"Ronan," Vincent breathed, his voice barely a whisper. "The one who orchestrated it all."

The name echoed like a death knell, a chilling reminder of our past encounters. The very air around us seemed to thrum with danger, and I knew in that moment, this was more than just a battle; it was a reckoning. With the Breed's forces rallying and Ronan advancing, we were on the precipice of something monumental.

"Together," Vincent said, gripping my hand with renewed fervor. I nodded, my resolve hardening. We would not back down. We had come too far, and I refused to let fear dictate our fate.

In that instant, I understood the stakes. This was not just about survival; it was about reclaiming our narrative, rewriting the ending that Ronan had penned with malice. And with Vincent by my side,

I felt ready to face whatever storm awaited us, even if it meant standing against the very embodiment of our darkest fears.

The tension in the air was thick enough to cut with a knife, and I could almost taste the metallic tang of impending conflict on my tongue. Vincent stood resolute beside me, his jaw set, determination radiating off him like heat waves on a summer's day. I mirrored his stance, heart racing as the chaotic orchestra of battle played out below. The Breed's forces had begun to advance, their synchronized movements a chilling display of unity and ruthlessness.

"We can't let them reach us," I breathed, my voice steadying as I focused on the task at hand. Each breath felt like a drumbeat urging us forward into the fray.

"Then we'll give them something to think about," Vincent replied, a hint of mischief glimmering in his eyes. "If they want to dance, let's make it a waltz."

I couldn't help but smile, despite the grave circumstances. "Is that your grand plan? A fancy footwork lesson?"

"Hey, you know I've got two left feet," he shot back, the corners of his mouth twitching upwards. "But I can throw a punch."

As if summoned by our banter, the first wave of the Breed surged forward, their shouts mingling with the wind, a cacophony of threats and taunts that sent shivers down my spine. I crouched low, my heart pounding in rhythm with the adrenaline surging through my veins.

We launched into action, the stones we had gathered becoming our first line of defense. I hurled one with all my might, watching as it struck the shoulder of a soldier, causing him to stagger. A satisfied grin broke out on my face, and for a fleeting moment, I felt invincible.

"Nice shot!" Vincent shouted, following suit, his aim deadly accurate.

As we rained down our makeshift artillery, a sudden roar erupted from the throng below. Ronan, the imposing figure who seemed to loom larger than life, had finally caught sight of us. His dark eyes narrowed, and an ominous smile curled his lips, revealing a confidence that sent a chill skittering down my spine.

"Ronan's here," I muttered, barely able to keep the tremor from my voice. "We need to move."

"Not yet," Vincent replied, a fire igniting in his gaze. "We need to keep them distracted. If we can hold them here for a few minutes longer, we might just turn the tide."

The wisdom of his words sank in, and I nodded, biting my lip as I gauged the enemy's movements. Each face was a mask of resolve, but beneath that hard exterior lay uncertainty. Perhaps they were as nervous as I was. With that thought came a flicker of courage, and I called out to them, my voice ringing clear.

"Hey! You think you can scare us? You've got another thing coming!"

A few heads turned, and my heart raced at the sight of their surprise. I seized the moment, my confidence bolstered by their hesitation.

"Come on, is that all you've got? You're just a bunch of wannabe tough guys with bad haircuts!"

Laughter erupted from my lips, and I could feel Vincent's gaze on me, filled with admiration and incredulity. His smirk widened, and he joined in the taunting. "At least we didn't have to rent our outfits from a discount store!"

A ripple of amusement spread among the soldiers, but it was short-lived. Ronan raised a hand, silencing them with an icy glare that could freeze fire. I felt a shiver run through me as he turned his attention fully toward us, his expression darkening.

"Enough of this nonsense!" he bellowed, his voice echoing like a thunderclap. "You think your little games will save you? You're outnumbered and outmatched. Surrender now, and I might just let you walk away."

Vincent scoffed, and I couldn't help but admire his bravery. "Walk away? Why would we want to do that? We're having too much fun!"

Ronan's face twisted in irritation, and a sense of unease crept back into my chest. He didn't strike me as the type to take mockery lightly.

"Foolish children," he hissed, and with a flick of his wrist, he signaled to his men. "Make them regret their arrogance."

With a surge of dread, I felt the ground tremble beneath me as the first wave of soldiers advanced, charging toward our position. Panic clawed at my throat, and I could almost hear the echo of my heart as it raced against time.

"Vincent, we can't hold them off forever!" I shouted, my voice barely rising above the din.

"Then we'll create a distraction!" he yelled back, his eyes gleaming with a wild, reckless determination that was infectious.

I watched in astonishment as he leaped from our vantage point, landing with a determined thud, startling the nearest soldier. Without a second thought, I followed him, adrenaline propelling me into the fray.

The chaos enveloped us like a storm, and I felt the thrill of battle ignite my senses. I ducked and dodged, landing punches that connected with flesh and bone, feeling the rush of power surge through me. I was not just fighting for survival; I was fighting for every breath, every moment, every dream that had been threatened by Ronan's relentless grip.

As we pushed our way through the throng, Vincent and I moved in tandem, our movements instinctual, honed by the countless battles we had faced together. We were a whirlwind of energy, defiance sparking like fireworks around us.

Then, amidst the chaos, I caught a glimpse of Ronan, his imposing figure slicing through the crowd with terrifying ease. He was a predator, and I felt the instinctive urge to flee. But I couldn't back down now.

"Vincent!" I shouted, desperation creeping into my voice. "He's coming for us!"

"I know!" he replied, determination flashing in his eyes. "We need to find a way to draw him away."

I nodded, the wheels in my mind turning as I scanned our surroundings. We were near the barn's entrance, and beyond lay a field, ripe with the promise of an escape route. But we had to buy ourselves time—time to regroup, time to fight back.

"Follow my lead," I said, my heart hammering with the weight of the decision. I had a reckless idea, one that could either save us or seal our fate.

As Ronan closed in, I turned on my heel and sprinted toward the field, my feet pounding against the earth. "Hey, Ronan! Catch me if you can!"

The sound of his enraged roar filled the air, a primal echo that urged me to run faster. Behind me, Vincent fell into step, his breath even, the two of us weaving through the chaos, the world blurring at the edges.

We raced toward the open expanse, my heart pounding not just from exertion but from the sheer exhilaration of freedom. The Breed's forces stumbled behind us, confusion reigning as they tried to comprehend our sudden maneuver.

"Let's give them a show," Vincent called, his eyes sparkling with mischief.

I glanced back just in time to see Ronan tearing through the crowd, fury blazing in his eyes, and a wild laugh escaped my lips. "Let's dance!"

Together, we surged forward, daring the storm to chase us, armed not just with stones and fury, but with a heart full of hope that refused to dim, no matter how dark the path ahead seemed.

The world around us dissolved into chaos, and for a moment, time seemed to stretch, allowing the rush of adrenaline to surge through my veins like wildfire. Vincent and I, entwined in our frenzied dance of defiance, forged a path through the throng, every strike and sidestep a testament to our determination. I could hear the clamor of boots pounding the ground, mingling with the shouts of commands that rang out like a war drum.

"Did you see that?" I yelled over my shoulder, exhilaration bubbling within me as I narrowly dodged a soldier's swing. "I think I might have a future in competitive stone-throwing!"

Vincent chuckled, his voice rich with warmth even amidst the turmoil. "Forget the stones; you're a natural with your fists! If this whole saving-the-world thing doesn't work out, I think you'd make an excellent professional boxer."

Just then, a sharp jolt of pain shot through my side as a soldier lunged, catching me off guard. The air whooshed from my lungs as I staggered back, only to find Vincent right there, his presence a steadfast anchor against the tide of chaos.

"Stay focused!" he urged, his expression a mix of concern and fierce resolve. "We need to keep moving!"

I shook off the pain, feeling the fire of determination flare even brighter within me. "Let's create some distance! I have a plan!"

We pushed our way toward the barn's entrance, the scent of dust and hay swirling around us as I caught a glimpse of our surroundings. The field beyond lay open, a canvas of golden grass swaying in the wind, the perfect stage for a final showdown.

"On three!" I called out, raising my voice to cut through the din. "One... two... three!"

With a burst of synchronized energy, we sprinted forward, our feet pounding against the earth, a battle cry erupting from our throats. As we crossed the threshold into the sunlight, I felt the warmth envelop us, a stark contrast to the chill of fear that lingered in my bones.

"Now what?" Vincent asked, scanning the area as we skidded to a halt. The Breed's soldiers hesitated, momentarily disoriented by our sudden dash.

"Now we make a stand," I replied, drawing in a deep breath, the air fresh and invigorating. "We need to draw them out. There's no way Ronan will let us slip through his fingers."

Vincent nodded, understanding flickering in his eyes. "I'll create a distraction. You find a way to lure him in."

Before I could respond, he sprinted off to the left, his movements fluid and agile. I watched as he darted around a stack of crates, picking up anything he could find—old tools, rusty nails—and tossing them into the air like confetti.

"Hey! Over here!" he shouted, laughter tinged with madness. "Is this the best you've got? I expected more from you lot!"

The soldiers turned, their attention momentarily drawn to Vincent's antics, confusion flashing across their faces. In that instant, I seized the opportunity. I crouched low, heart hammering as I slipped behind a cluster of bales, my breath steadying as I prepared for my part in this precarious dance.

"Ronan!" I yelled, my voice echoing across the field, a bold challenge against the chaos. "You're hiding behind your lackeys! Come face me yourself!"

The soldiers hesitated, looking back at their leader for guidance. The tension thickened like a heavy fog, and for a heartbeat, I thought I might actually pull this off. But then, the moment of hope shattered as Ronan's voice sliced through the air like a whip.

"Foolish girl!" he roared, his voice rumbling like thunder. "You think you can provoke me into the open? You're nothing but a pawn in this game."

My heart sank, but I pressed on, digging deep into the well of courage that had carried me this far. "And you're a coward, hiding behind your minions! If you have any spine, step forward and show us what you're made of!"

A menacing chuckle rolled across the field, and then, like a shadow cast by the setting sun, Ronan stepped forward, his eyes glinting with malicious intent. "You'll regret this, little one. I will savor every moment of your defeat."

I swallowed hard, adrenaline coursing through me as I caught a glimpse of Vincent in my periphery, still keeping the soldiers distracted with his antics. There was a brief moment when Ronan's attention shifted, and I knew I had to act quickly.

"Vincent!" I called out, urgency lacing my voice. "Get ready to retreat!"

He glanced my way, eyes narrowing in understanding. I gestured toward a group of barrels at the edge of the field, each one filled with hay and a little kerosene—an improvised incendiary device waiting to be ignited. "We're going to create a diversion!"

Vincent nodded, the mischief lighting up his eyes once more. "A little fire to spice things up? I like it!"

As I darted toward the barrels, I could see Ronan's soldiers regrouping, their formation tightening as they prepared to charge. I reached the barrels and grabbed a nearby match from the remnants of an old toolbox, my hands shaking with anticipation.

"On my mark!" I yelled to Vincent, my heart pounding in sync with the soldiers' footfalls.

But just as I struck the match, a piercing scream cut through the air—a soldier, having noticed my intent, surged forward, eyes wild with panic. "Stop her!" he shouted, pointing straight at me.

In that instant, the world slowed, and I felt the weight of impending doom settling over me like a cloak. Ronan's expression darkened, and I knew I had to act, had to push through the fear that threatened to consume me.

I flicked the match against the side of the barrel, the tiny flame igniting with a hungry hiss. "Now!" I screamed at Vincent, hurling the match toward the kerosene-soaked hay.

The fire roared to life, a blaze that crackled and leapt, sending sparks soaring into the air like fireflies. The soldiers froze, fear spreading through their ranks as the inferno erupted, illuminating the field in an orange glow.

"Run!" Vincent shouted, his voice cutting through the chaos. We took off together, adrenaline propelling us forward, dodging the scattering soldiers who suddenly found themselves caught in the fiery spectacle.

But as we raced toward the treeline, the flames casting eerie shadows around us, Ronan's furious voice boomed over the chaos, cutting through the night like a knife. "You think this is over? You're making a grave mistake!"

Just as we reached the edge of the forest, a sharp crack pierced the air, and I felt a sudden jolt of pain explode in my shoulder. I staggered, vision blurring, and in that moment, I turned to see Ronan standing there, gun raised, fury etched across his face.

"Vincent!" I gasped, clutching my shoulder, feeling the warmth of blood seep through my fingers. The world tilted on its axis as darkness encroached around the edges of my vision.

"Hold on!" Vincent shouted, his voice filled with desperation as he rushed toward me, his face a mask of concern. But in that split second, I felt the ground beneath me slip away, and as I crumpled to the ground, the fire still roaring behind us, I realized that our battle was far from over.

Ronan stepped closer, a predator relishing the moment before the final strike. "You'll pay for this, little girl," he sneered, his voice dripping with menace.

And as the world faded to black, I couldn't shake the feeling that this was only the beginning of our reckoning.

Chapter 27: The Turning Tide

The air crackled with tension, a palpable energy that coursed through the streets like a live wire. It was as if the very ground beneath us trembled in anticipation of what was to come. I could feel the vibrations in my bones, resonating with every hurried heartbeat, each one echoing the fear and resolve that warred within me. We stood on the precipice of change, the remnants of our makeshift barricades towering around us like stubborn monuments to our defiance. Each splintered piece of wood, every jagged stone, was a testament to our struggle, a silent witness to the fight we had waged against the relentless tide of the Breed.

Vincent stood beside me, his expression a storm of emotions—determination, worry, and a flicker of something that ignited my own courage. His dark hair whipped in the wind, framing his face as he surveyed our beleaguered forces. I could see the fire burning in his eyes, a fierce glimmer that seemed to whisper promises of victory. It was contagious, stirring something deep within me, something I had thought long extinguished by the weight of despair.

"Are you ready?" he asked, his voice low but steady, cutting through the chaos that swirled around us.

I nodded, the answer spilling from my lips with surprising conviction. "I've never been more ready." My heart raced, and as I spoke, I felt a surge of power radiate through me. This wasn't just a fight for survival; it was a fight for the future we envisioned—a future free from the suffocating shadows of oppression.

With a swift motion, I raised my fist, rallying our ragtag band of rebels. The soldiers who had once cowered under the Breed's iron grip now stood resolute, their faces a mosaic of defiance and hope. The faint glow of dawn peeked through the clouds, casting a golden hue over our battlefield—a sign, perhaps, that the tide was indeed turning.

"Listen to me!" I shouted, my voice rising above the din of clashing metal and anguished cries. "They thrive on our fear, on our despair. But we are not their puppets, nor will we ever be again! We have something they don't—hope! Together, we are stronger than their darkness!"

My words hung in the air, pregnant with meaning, and in that moment, I could see the flicker of resolve igniting within the eyes of my comrades. It was as if a spell had been cast, binding us in a collective resolve. One by one, they stepped forward, fists raised, ready to fight not just for themselves, but for each other, for the freedom we so desperately craved.

The Breed advanced, their soldiers clad in dark, imposing armor that gleamed ominously in the dim light. They were a wall of shadows, an intimidating force that had once instilled terror in the hearts of even the bravest among us. But as they moved forward, I felt something shift. Fear gave way to courage, and for the first time, I dared to believe in our victory.

As the first clash of steel rang out, echoing like a clarion call, I found myself side by side with Vincent, our movements synchronized as we parried and thrust against our foes. His eyes sparkled with a fierce intensity, a reminder that I was not alone in this fight. The world around us blurred into a cacophony of sound, our surroundings reduced to a haze of movement and instinct. Each swing of my sword felt imbued with purpose, with a resolve that flowed not just from within, but from the collective strength of those fighting beside me.

We surged forward, pressing into the ranks of the Breed, our cries rising above the clamor. Vincent's laughter mingled with battle cries, a sound that seemed both absurd and glorious amidst the chaos. "Is this what you call a walk in the park?" he shouted, ducking under a wild swing and retaliating with a swift jab that sent one of the Breed crashing to the ground.

I laughed despite the seriousness of our situation, my heart racing as adrenaline surged through my veins. “Next time, I’ll pack a picnic!” I retorted, dodging a blow and striking back with a fierce determination.

As we fought, I could see the tide turning, the Breed soldiers faltering as our defiance washed over them like a wave. With every enemy that fell, the morale of our group soared. They were no longer just faces in a crowd; they were my friends, my family, united by the hope that had once seemed so distant.

And then it happened—an unexpected twist that sent a shiver of disbelief through me. From the corner of my eye, I spotted a familiar figure, cloaked in the shadows of the battle. It was Eloise, a former member of our circle, who had once betrayed us, her allegiance bought by the Breed. But now, she stood at the edge of the fray, her expression unreadable.

What was she doing here? My heart pounded in my chest, confusion mingling with the adrenaline as I fought. Had she come to finish what she started, or had the weight of her choices finally crushed her into seeking redemption?

As if sensing my gaze, she turned, her eyes meeting mine across the chaos. There was something in her stance, a vulnerability that had not been there before, and in that moment, I realized she was not just a traitor but a person caught in a web of her own making.

Before I could dwell on the implications, a surge of soldiers pushed toward us, forcing my attention back to the fight. The ground shook beneath our feet, the air thick with the scent of sweat and smoke, and I knew that victory was within our grasp. We just had to keep pushing forward.

Together, Vincent and I pressed on, an unstoppable force fueled by the strength of our shared hope. And as the sun began to rise, spilling its golden light over the battlefield, I knew that the darkness of the Breed was beginning to crumble. We were not just surviving;

we were reclaiming our lives, our freedom, and with every blow we struck, the tide turned further in our favor.

The battlefield transformed into a chaotic tapestry, the sounds of clashing steel interwoven with the shouts and gasps of the fallen. As we pressed forward, an electric energy coursed through our group, a tangible force that seemed to lift us above the fray. Each swing of my sword felt like a declaration, a promise that we would not falter. The air thickened with the scent of earth and sweat, punctuated by the acrid smoke curling up from burning debris, but amid the chaos, hope flickered brighter than ever.

Vincent and I fought side by side, our movements fluid and instinctual, as if the world around us had faded, leaving only the rhythm of battle. With every enemy that fell, I felt a surge of power. It was intoxicating, propelling us into a fierce dance of survival. "You know," I shouted over the clamor, "I always imagined my first real fight would involve a dragon or at least some flashy armor!"

He grinned, ducking a blow and retaliating with a swift kick. "Dragons might be more fun, but this has its charms—like the lovely aroma of charred leather!"

A loud crash nearby jolted my attention, and I turned just in time to see one of our comrades—a stocky man with a fierce heart—being overwhelmed by two of the Breed. Panic surged within me, a sharp stab of fear, but I couldn't let it paralyze me. I was part of this fight; we were all part of something greater than ourselves. With a battle cry, I lunged forward, determination fueling my every step.

The skirmish morphed around me, a swirling tempest of movement and sound, yet I focused solely on that moment, on the figure of our fallen friend, pushing aside the chaos to hone in on purpose. "Hey! Over here!" I yelled, my voice slicing through the din as I closed the distance.

The Breed soldiers turned, momentarily distracted, and I seized the opportunity. I brought my blade down with all my strength, catching one soldier off-guard. He staggered back, eyes wide with surprise, and I felt a rush of exhilaration surge through me as I caught my breath. "Your mistake, darling," I taunted, the thrill of the moment making me bold. "You should really pay attention!"

As I fought, I caught glimpses of Vincent, his fierce movements mesmerizing. He seemed to glide through the chaos, a force of nature in his own right, disarming foes with a finesse that had me marveling even in the midst of battle. Every punch he threw and every slice of his sword echoed with an almost poetic rhythm. I realized, then, that we were not just fighting for survival; we were creating a story, a narrative of our defiance that would linger long after this day was over.

But amid the adrenaline and excitement, a flicker of doubt crept in. Eloise. What was she doing here? The thought nagged at the back of my mind as I exchanged blows with a particularly brutish soldier. I glimpsed her again, standing at the edge of the battle, her eyes wide, caught between the past and the choices that had led her here. It was a moment that drew my attention away from the immediate threat, and I could see a shadow of regret flitting across her face.

"Focus!" Vincent's voice broke through, and I snapped back to the fray just in time to block an incoming strike. I nodded, shoving the thought aside. There would be time to ponder her intentions later—right now, I had to concentrate on the battle at hand.

As we fought, it became clear that our numbers were dwindling, yet the fire in our hearts blazed bright. We pushed forward, an unstoppable force against the dark tide of the Breed, the adrenaline binding us in a fragile unity. Just when it seemed like we might gain a foothold, a massive figure emerged from the swirling chaos. A general of the Breed—tall, armored, and exuding an aura of intimidation that chilled the air.

He surveyed the battlefield, eyes narrowing as they landed on me and Vincent, his lips curling into a sneer. "You think you can challenge us?" he bellowed, his voice a rumble that echoed through the tumult. "You're merely insects beneath my boot."

I felt a shiver dance down my spine, but with it came a spark of defiance. "Insects, perhaps," I shot back, mustering all the bravado I could, "but we sting, and believe me, we bite back!"

With that, I charged, my sword raised high, but he was faster, lunging forward with a menacing speed. I sidestepped just in time, the air crackling with the energy of our duel. Each clash of our weapons sent vibrations up my arms, a sharp reminder of the stakes at hand. I could feel the tension shifting in the air, the balance of power teetering precariously as the general's frustration grew.

Vincent circled around, creating a pincer move, and together, we pressed the attack, our minds weaving in tandem as we fought. The adrenaline coursed through my veins, sharper than any blade, and I felt invincible as we turned the tide against this formidable foe.

The battlefield shifted; our cries of defiance mixed with the sounds of the Breed soldiers faltering, their confidence shaken. It was a moment that would be etched in my memory forever, the swell of hope mingling with the bitter taste of revenge. Just as I thought we were gaining ground, a sudden shout pierced the air.

"Eloise!" It was Vincent, and I turned to see her rushing forward, her face set in grim determination. I didn't know whether to cheer or curse, my heart racing at the sudden shift in the dynamic. Had she come to rejoin us, or was this yet another twist in the tale?

"Get back!" I shouted instinctively, fearing she might be caught in the crossfire.

But she was already there, in the thick of it, her sword raised as she charged at the general with a fierce cry. A mix of shock and admiration coursed through me. In that instant, as she struck, the air crackled with possibility. Maybe this was her redemption arc; perhaps she had truly come to fight for us.

The general turned his fury towards her, a growl escaping his lips. "You dare betray us again?"

"I dare to choose," she replied, her voice steady, holding her ground. "And I choose this—freedom!"

In that moment, I knew we weren't just fighting for survival; we were fighting for each other, for the choices that defined us, and for the hope that shone brightly even in the darkest hours. I could feel the tide shifting once more, our unity becoming an unbreakable force. As the sun broke through the clouds, bathing us in a warm glow, I felt the weight of our struggle begin to lift. Together, we could face anything.

The dust settled slowly, like a thick fog reluctantly retreating from the light. Breathing heavily, I scanned the battlefield, my heart pounding with an exhilaration I had never known. The remnants of the Breed's forces were scattered like autumn leaves, their resolve crumbling under the weight of our united front. Yet, amid this strange calm, I could feel the pulse of uncertainty. Victory was tantalizingly close, but it felt precariously fragile, as though it could slip away with the next breath.

Eloise stood a few paces away, her sword still raised, an enigmatic silhouette against the morning sun. The earlier intensity in her eyes had transformed, reflecting a mix of fierce determination and something softer—regret, perhaps. I couldn't help but wonder if she was truly here for us now or if her heart still danced on the edges of betrayal.

"Are we supposed to hug now, or should I prepare for another surprise attack?" I quipped, crossing my arms and raising an eyebrow at her.

Vincent chuckled beside me, though I could see the tension coiling in his muscles. "I'd prefer the former, but I'm ready for the latter."

Eloise rolled her eyes, the corner of her mouth twitching upward. “No hugs just yet. I’m not that soft.” She stepped forward, her gaze intense. “You have to understand, I was trapped. The Breed—” she paused, her voice catching. “They know everything. I had no choice.”

“Spare us the excuses,” I shot back, though my voice lacked the venom I intended. “What you chose to do was unforgivable.”

“It was survival!” she shot back, her eyes flashing. “I did what I thought I had to. But now? Now I’m choosing to fight with you.”

Before I could respond, a loud rumble echoed across the field, drawing our attention. It was a sound unlike any other, a deep, resonant growl that reverberated through the air and sent a chill down my spine. The ground trembled beneath our feet, and I instinctively glanced at Vincent. His expression mirrored my concern, confusion knitting his brow as he scanned the horizon.

“What is that?” I whispered, fear creeping into my voice.

Eloise stiffened, her posture rigid. “The general... he was just the beginning. There’s something far worse coming.”

Before we could process her words, a massive shadow loomed over the battlefield, blotting out the sun. I squinted into the distance, my breath hitching in my throat as I tried to comprehend the sight before us. Emerging from the smoke and debris was a monstrous creature, a fusion of steel and sinew, glinting ominously in the morning light. It towered over us, its hulking form a grotesque imitation of life, with gears whirring and metal grinding against metal in a dissonant symphony of menace.

“What in the name of all that is holy is that?” Vincent’s voice was a mix of awe and terror.

“The Enforcer,” Eloise replied, her voice trembling. “It’s a war machine—the Breed’s ultimate weapon. They’ll stop at nothing to crush us.”

A rush of adrenaline propelled me into action. "Then we can't let it reach us!" I shouted, turning to rally our remaining forces. "We need to—"

But my words were drowned out by the deafening roar of the Enforcer as it lumbered forward, a cacophony of destruction. Its eyes blazed a fierce red, locking onto us with an unsettling intelligence. I felt a primal instinct rising within me—a fight-or-flight response that urged me to run, but I refused to back down now. We had come too far, sacrificed too much to let fear dictate our actions.

"Vincent, get the others!" I yelled, my heart racing. "We have to fight it!"

He nodded, his determination hardening as he took off toward our remaining fighters. Eloise and I shared a look, the weight of what lay ahead pressing heavily upon us. "Are you ready for this?" I asked, my voice steadier than I felt.

"Ready? No. But we don't have a choice," she replied, gripping her sword tightly. "We can't let it intimidate us."

As the Enforcer approached, the ground shook with every step, its massive limbs creating a shockwave that threatened to topple us. The air smelled of oil and burnt metal, a nauseating blend that sent my instincts screaming for safety. "What's the plan?" I shouted, adrenaline coursing through my veins.

"We have to find its weak spot!" Eloise shouted back, her eyes narrowing as she observed the hulking machine. "Look for anything that isn't reinforced!"

I nodded, scanning the beast's armored shell, its surface gleaming menacingly in the sunlight. As we darted forward, the Enforcer unleashed a deafening roar, sending a shockwave that knocked us off our feet. The sound reverberated in my chest, and for a moment, I was dazed, blinking up at the chaos unfolding around me.

Vincent's voice rang out, rallying our comrades. "Get up! We're not done yet!" He was a beacon of strength amid the chaos, his presence grounding me.

Eloise grabbed my hand, yanking me back to my feet. "We need to flank it!"

Together, we moved in sync, dodging debris and the erratic movements of the Enforcer as it swung its massive fists in our direction. I felt the adrenaline heighten my senses, every instinct honed in on survival.

"On three!" Vincent shouted, positioning himself at the front with a determined look. "One... two... three!"

We charged forward, hearts pounding, swords raised high. The creature whirled, its eye-beams scanning for targets. It let out a furious growl as it focused on us, the lights in its mechanical eyes narrowing dangerously. My stomach dropped as I realized the creature was targeting us directly.

"Move!" I screamed, diving to the side as it swung its massive arm, the force of its movement stirring the air violently.

The ground erupted around us as the fist struck the earth, sending shards of rock and dirt into the air like projectiles. I heard shouts and cries from our group as we scrambled to avoid the chaos.

But amidst the tumult, my gaze locked onto something glinting on the Enforcer's side—a panel, slightly ajar, that seemed less fortified than the rest of its armored shell. My heart raced as I realized that this could be our chance.

"Eloise! There!" I pointed, my voice hoarse with urgency. "We can hit that panel! It might be its weak spot!"

She nodded, determination flaring in her eyes. "Let's do it!"

We dashed towards the beast, dodging the flailing limbs as the ground trembled beneath us. With every step, my heart pounded louder, urging me forward. I could see Vincent fighting off a couple of the Breed soldiers, his movements powerful and precise, and I felt a surge of pride. We were fighting not just for survival but for each other, for a world beyond this horror.

But just as we closed the distance to the Enforcer, a blinding light erupted from its core. The energy surged outward like a shockwave, pushing us back and sending us sprawling to the ground.

My world spun as I fought to regain my footing, the air thick with dust and the acrid smell of burnt metal. I could see Vincent, barely ten feet away, wrestling with a massive soldier, and my heart raced at the sight. The Enforcer reared back, its massive eye-beams targeting our group.

"Get clear!" I yelled, panic clawing at my chest.

The last thing I saw before the world erupted into chaos was the terrible gleam of the Enforcer's eyes as they locked onto me, the unmistakable promise of destruction brewing within. My heart raced, and for a split second, I thought of what lay ahead—of everything we had fought for, and everything that could be lost.

Then, in a deafening explosion, the light consumed everything.

Chapter 28: A World Reborn

The sun hung low in the sky, spilling golden light across the city, igniting the cobblestones with warmth and a hint of vibrancy that had long been buried under shadows. The aftermath of the battle felt like the gentle unfurling of a flower after a storm—fragile yet undeniably alive. Vincent's hand clasped mine tightly as we walked through the bustling streets, our fingers entwined like the branches of a new tree. The air buzzed with laughter, chatter, and the unmistakable sound of life reasserting itself. Children darted past, their faces painted with bright colors, remnants of the festivities that erupted from the ashes of despair.

I paused for a moment to drink it all in—the scent of freshly baked bread wafting from a nearby bakery, the sweet tang of fruit from market stalls overflowing with autumn's bounty, and the lively strains of music that floated through the air like a call to joy. It was a symphony of recovery, and it wrapped around us, buoying our spirits higher with each step we took. Vincent glanced down at me, his lips curling into that half-smile that always sent my heart racing. "We did it," he said, his voice low and filled with wonder, as if he couldn't quite believe it himself.

"Yes, we did," I replied, a grin breaking across my face. "And look at this! Look at everyone." I gestured towards a group of friends gathered around a fountain, splashing each other playfully. Their laughter rang out, mingling with the gurgle of water spilling from the fountain's stone mouth, each note a reminder of what we had fought for.

Vincent's expression turned serious as he looked beyond the crowd to the horizon, where the remnants of our past still loomed—a jagged outline of dark clouds hanging stubbornly in the distance. "We still have work to do," he said, his brow furrowing.

I squeezed his hand, drawing his gaze back to me. "Of course we do, but let's take a moment to breathe. We deserve this." The way his eyes softened made my heart flutter. I knew the road ahead wouldn't be easy, but standing there, surrounded by the glimmers of hope rising from the city, I felt invincible.

We strolled further, weaving through the throng of jubilant citizens, where every face seemed to tell a story of survival and newfound resolve. I recognized the baker from our neighborhood, flour dusting his apron, beaming as he handed out loaves of bread to anyone who approached. A couple embraced nearby, their expressions a beautiful blend of disbelief and elation. It felt surreal, this transformation from the darkness that had gripped our lives for so long.

As we reached the edge of the square, Vincent suddenly stopped. He tugged me gently toward a narrow alley, half-hidden by colorful awnings. "There's something I want to show you," he said, a spark of mischief lighting his eyes.

Curiosity piqued, I followed him, heart racing with anticipation. The alley opened up into a small courtyard, vibrant with blooming flowers spilling from pots and planters. At the center stood a statue, newly erected, depicting a warrior with outstretched arms and a defiant expression—an embodiment of resilience. I felt a swell of pride as I traced the lines of the statue with my eyes, its presence a testament to the struggles we had overcome.

"Who did this?" I asked, my voice barely a whisper as I marveled at the craftsmanship.

Vincent grinned, a twinkle in his eye. "The people came together to create it. They wanted to commemorate not just the battle, but the hope we've ignited."

My heart swelled at his words, a warmth spreading through me as I imagined the late nights and hard work that had gone into this monument. “It’s beautiful,” I said, tears threatening to spill over. “It truly is.”

Just then, a group of children ran past, giggling and chasing each other, their carefree spirits infectious. One little girl, her hair a wild halo of curls, skidded to a halt in front of us, staring wide-eyed at the statue. “Who’s that?” she asked, pointing a tiny finger at the warrior.

I knelt down to her level, a smile brightening my face. “That’s a hero,” I replied. “Someone who fought for everyone to be happy and free.”

The girl nodded seriously, her eyes widening with understanding. “I want to be a hero too!”

“Then you will be,” Vincent interjected, crouching beside me. “You just have to be brave and kind. That’s what being a hero is all about.”

Her face lit up, a smile bursting forth that could rival the sun itself. “I can do that!” she declared, before scampering off to join her friends.

Vincent and I shared a look, both of us laughing softly at her exuberance. It was the first time I felt a genuine lightness since the battle, the weight of uncertainty beginning to lift. Yet, as we stood in that courtyard, surrounded by the living echoes of our victory, I couldn’t shake the feeling that our true test was yet to come.

As twilight deepened into a gentle dusk, the city transformed, lanterns glowing to life, flickering like stars against the velvet sky. Vincent pulled me close, our bodies brushing, and for a moment, I lost myself in the rhythm of his heartbeat against mine. The world around us was alight with the promise of tomorrow, and as I gazed up at the stars beginning to pierce the night, I made a silent vow to cherish this newfound peace, to embrace whatever lay ahead, together.

The evening sky deepened into a velvety indigo, studded with twinkling stars that shimmered like distant promises. Vincent and

I ambled through the heart of the city, where laughter and music spilled out from doorways and open windows, each sound a celebration of life reclaimed. We followed the melody of a lively fiddle, its notes dancing in the air, pulling us toward a small square that had transformed into an impromptu gathering place.

The square was alive with movement, people swaying and twirling, their faces glowing under strings of lanterns that cast a warm, golden light. I spotted an elderly couple in the center, lost in their own world as they spun each other around, their laughter infectious. It was a reminder of the beauty that could flourish even after the harshest storms. I turned to Vincent, who was watching the scene with a soft smile. "Shall we?" I asked, tilting my head toward the dancers.

He raised an eyebrow, the corners of his mouth twitching into a playful smirk. "You think we can keep up with them?"

"Only one way to find out!" I laughed, pulling him into the throng. The rhythm was infectious, wrapping around us like a blanket, and soon we found ourselves caught up in the whirl of bodies, moving to the spirited tunes that filled the night air. The music seemed to pulse through the ground, and with each step, I could feel the worries of the past week melting away, replaced by a heady sense of freedom.

Vincent's hands found my waist, guiding me as we stumbled through the dance, laughter bubbling between us. "You have two left feet," he teased, spinning me around, and I gasped as I nearly lost my balance, clutching onto him to steady myself.

"Only when I'm dancing with you!" I shot back, mock indignation spilling over my words.

We twirled until the world blurred, the faces of friends and strangers merging into one jubilant kaleidoscope of color. I could feel the pulse of the city around us—the heartbeat of its people, their resilience, and joy. It was intoxicating, a mixture of hope and newfound strength that lifted us both higher.

As the song came to a close, we stepped back, breathless and grinning like fools. Vincent brushed a damp strand of hair from my forehead, his fingers lingering a moment longer than necessary. "You really are remarkable," he said, his gaze warm. "I never would have imagined we'd be here, dancing in the streets after everything."

I shrugged, a wave of shyness washing over me, though I couldn't suppress the warmth that blossomed in my chest. "I think it's a testament to our excellent taste in music."

He laughed, a sound that seemed to melt away any remaining shadows. "Well, in that case, let's see how many more songs we can dance to."

But just as I was about to agree, the lively atmosphere shifted. A sudden hush fell over the crowd, rippling outward like a pebble dropped into still water. I followed the gazes of those around us, my heart plummeting as I noticed a group of newcomers entering the square. They were cloaked in dark fabrics, their faces obscured, a stark contrast to the vibrant energy of the celebration.

My instinct was to step closer to Vincent, my fingers tightening around his. He sensed my unease immediately, his body tensing beside me. "Stay close," he murmured, eyes scanning the newcomers with cautious intent.

The atmosphere shifted, electricity crackling in the air as whispers swept through the crowd. Some people backed away, concern etched on their faces, while others stood defiantly, unwilling to let fear disrupt their newfound joy. The leader of the newcomers stepped forward, pulling down their hood to reveal a face I recognized—a figure from the past, a remnant of the chaos we had just escaped.

"People of the city," the figure called out, their voice smooth yet chilling. "You celebrate too soon. The battle may be won, but the war is far from over."

A murmur of discontent rippled through the crowd. "What do you want?" someone shouted, anger and defiance bubbling to the surface.

I looked up at Vincent, whose expression had hardened. "We should leave," I whispered urgently, my heart racing.

He shook his head, his resolve stronger than mine. "No, we can't let them intimidate us. Not now."

The cloaked figure continued, their gaze sweeping over the crowd. "You are celebrating a fleeting victory, yet shadows linger. We have not forgotten the power we hold. We are here to remind you that you cannot escape the darkness."

The air was thick with tension, the flickering lanterns casting eerie shadows as the crowd began to react. I could see fear mingling with anger, and I felt a swell of bravery rise within me. "If you think we'll let you control us with fear, you're wrong," I shouted, my voice strong despite the quaking of my knees. "We fought for our freedom, and we will not surrender it so easily."

Vincent's gaze met mine, a mixture of pride and surprise reflected in his eyes. I felt emboldened by the energy around me, my heart pounding with determination. The crowd began to rally, voices rising in agreement, a chorus of defiance against the darkness that threatened to encroach once more.

"Leave us be!" someone shouted, and the sentiment echoed, a rallying cry that rang through the square. The atmosphere shifted again, from fear to resolve, and I could see the uncertainty in the faces of the newcomers.

The leader faltered, their confidence waning as the spirit of the people surged forward. "This isn't over!" they shouted before retreating, dragging the rest of their group with them, cloaked figures melting back into the shadows from whence they came.

The crowd erupted into cheers, the vibrant energy of the celebration reigniting, laughter and music spilling back into the night. I turned to Vincent, our eyes wide with shared disbelief and exhilaration. "Did we just do that?" I asked, breathless with excitement.

He grinned, pulling me close again. "You did that. You were incredible."

A warm glow enveloped me, the sense of accomplishment washing over like the tide, reminding me that even in the face of darkness, we could stand united. The music started again, a joyous tune that felt like a victory anthem, and as I danced back into the embrace of the crowd, I knew one thing for certain: we were ready to fight for this world reborn, together.

The atmosphere buzzed with an energy that felt electric, as if the very air were charged with the thrill of new beginnings. The dance had swept us up in a whirlwind of unity, but as the last notes of music faded into the night, an undercurrent of unease lingered. I could still feel the presence of the cloaked figures hanging over us like an ominous cloud, a stark reminder that shadows were never far away, even in moments of triumph.

Vincent tightened his grip on my hand, his touch reassuring yet firm, as we moved away from the center of the square and found a quieter corner. The glow of lanterns illuminated our faces, casting a warm light over the contours of his expression, revealing both the strength and vulnerability that lay within him. "We can't let this happen again," he said, his voice low and steady. "They'll regroup, and next time, they might not back down so easily."

I nodded, the reality settling in like a weight on my chest. "You're right. We need to be prepared."

A sense of urgency coursed through me as I recalled the stories of the battle we had fought, the alliances we had formed. "What if we could reach out to the other towns? We could unite against them, share our resources and knowledge. There's power in numbers."

Vincent's eyes lit up with a glimmer of hope, but it was quickly tempered by a frown. "That's a noble idea, but convincing everyone will be difficult. Many are still reeling from what just happened. They might not be ready to fight again so soon."

"Then we give them something to fight for." My words hung in the air, and for a moment, it felt like a spark igniting in the darkness. The people of our city had shown resilience; perhaps other towns had that same fire burning within them. "If we share our story—how we stood together, how we fought back—we can inspire them."

"Do you really think so?" His skepticism was palpable, but I could see the flicker of belief growing in his eyes.

"Absolutely." I took a deep breath, channeling all my conviction. "We need to show them that this is just the beginning. That our hope can't be extinguished by a few dark figures lurking in the shadows."

Just then, a sudden commotion erupted nearby, the sound of hurried footsteps and raised voices slicing through our conversation. We exchanged glances, and without another word, we moved toward the source of the disturbance. The square was rapidly filling with people again, their expressions shifting from celebration to concern.

As we pushed through the crowd, I caught sight of a group gathered around a young man, who was waving his arms in animated panic. "They're coming! I saw them in the woods!" he shouted, his voice cracking with urgency. "A whole army! They'll be here by dawn!"

A hush fell over the crowd, disbelief mingling with fear. My heart raced as I exchanged a look with Vincent. "This is exactly what we were afraid of," I whispered, my stomach knotting with dread.

Vincent's expression hardened, determination etching itself onto his features. "We have to act now. We can't let them catch us off guard."

The crowd began to murmur, the tension palpable as uncertainty settled like a fog. I stepped forward, heart pounding in my chest. "Listen!" I called out, my voice strong. "We've faced dark days before, but together we've risen above them. We have a choice to make right now—will we stand united or let fear scatter us?"

A few people nodded, their faces shifting from panic to resolve, and I felt a flicker of hope igniting within me. But before I could continue, a voice cut through the noise. "And what exactly do you propose we do?"

A woman emerged from the back of the crowd, her expression sharp, skepticism radiating from her like an electric field. "We're just supposed to believe some half-baked idea will save us?"

"It's not half-baked!" I retorted, surprised at the fire in my own words. "If we act together, we can defend our home. We've already shown we're stronger than they think."

"Strength in numbers, yes," she replied, crossing her arms. "But what if it's not enough? What if we fight and still lose everything?"

Her challenge hung heavy in the air, and a sense of despair threatened to take root. Just as I was about to respond, Vincent stepped forward, his presence grounding and strong. "We can't afford to let fear paralyze us. If we prepare, if we stand together, we increase our chances of survival. That's the only option we have."

As he spoke, the crowd began to murmur, their energy shifting. I could see the glimmers of resolve breaking through the fear, but the woman remained skeptical. "And if we fail?"

"Then we go down fighting," I said fiercely, my voice ringing out over the crowd. "But I refuse to let fear dictate our fate. We've fought for our freedom before, and I believe we can do it again."

The woman's gaze bore into mine, and for a moment, I felt the weight of her doubts. But as I looked around at the faces of the people gathered—some wary, some eager, all weary—I saw the flicker of hope mirrored in their eyes. "We need to organize," I continued, my heart racing with adrenaline. "We can scout the woods, fortify our defenses. We can prepare for whatever is coming. And if we need to fight, let's make sure we're ready."

A ripple of agreement began to spread through the crowd, a heartbeat of resolve forming amidst the uncertainty. Just as hope began to take hold, a shadow moved at the edge of the square, drawing my attention. My breath hitched as I spotted a figure watching from the periphery, their eyes glinting with a familiar malice.

"Who is that?" I murmured to Vincent, my voice barely above a whisper.

Before he could respond, the figure stepped into the light. It was one of the cloaked figures from earlier, the same one who had declared our celebration a fleeting victory. A cruel smile twisted their lips as they surveyed the crowd, and I felt the chill of fear creep down my spine.

"Is this your rallying cry?" they called out, their voice dripping with mockery. "A handful of defiant souls, thinking they can resist the inevitable? You are deluding yourselves."

The crowd bristled, anger flaring at their audacity. "You have no power here!" someone shouted, but the cloaked figure only chuckled, their laughter echoing in the stillness that followed.

With a flourish, they raised their arm, and from the shadows behind them, figures began to emerge, dark shapes gathering like clouds rolling in before a storm. My heart raced as the realization sank in—this was no empty threat. They had returned, and they were not alone.

As the crowd began to panic, I locked eyes with Vincent, fear and determination swirling together. "We need to warn everyone," I said, urgency lacing my words.

But before we could make a move, the cloaked figure grinned wickedly, their voice slicing through the chaos. "Oh, but this is just the beginning."

And in that moment, with shadows encroaching, the air thick with uncertainty, I knew that our fight was far from over.

Chapter 29: Bound by Fire and Light

The scent of fresh earth and the faint whisper of wildflowers greeted us as we stepped into the clearing, a small oasis tucked away from the chaos that once dominated our lives. The sun filtered through the leaves overhead, dappling the ground with patches of golden light, creating a sanctuary that felt like a secret whispered just for us. Vincent paused beside me, his hand brushing against mine, sending a familiar spark coursing through my veins.

"Isn't it beautiful?" I said, taking a deep breath as the breeze tousled my hair, carrying with it the remnants of spring's sweet perfume. The air seemed to hum with possibility, a tune only we could hear, weaving around us as we stood on the threshold of something new.

He glanced sideways at me, a playful smirk dancing on his lips. "Beautiful? More like a scene from a romantic movie, minus the overacting and questionable plot twists." His eyes sparkled with mischief, and I felt the corners of my mouth curve up involuntarily.

"Hey, I'll have you know that romance often thrives in lush settings. It's practically a rule," I retorted, nudging him playfully with my shoulder. There was something intoxicating about the ease between us, a rhythm we had forged through trials that threatened to tear us apart. Each teasing exchange was a stitch in the fabric of our relationship, binding us closer together.

Vincent chuckled, shaking his head as if dismissing my logic. "If that's the case, then where's the danger? The fiery conflict that makes every story worth telling?"

His words lingered in the air, a reminder of the battles we had fought, both external and internal. There was a depth to the tension in his voice that struck a chord within me, reverberating through the stillness of the clearing. My heart tightened at the thought of the sacrifices we had made, the friends we had lost, and the shadows that clung to us like unwanted memories.

"We've had enough danger to last a lifetime, don't you think?" I murmured, the lightness of our banter giving way to the weight of reality. The shadows of the past still flickered at the edges of my mind—those harrowing moments when survival had been our only focus. But now, with the sun warming my skin and Vincent's presence steady beside me, I felt the burdens begin to shift.

"I don't know," he replied, a thoughtful furrow appearing on his brow. "Danger has a way of keeping life interesting." His gaze drifted toward the horizon, where the mountains stood sentinel, their peaks kissed by clouds. The grandeur of the landscape mirrored the tumultuous journey we had traversed together, each trial molding us into something fierce and unyielding.

"Interesting?" I raised an eyebrow, crossing my arms. "Is that what we're calling nearly losing our heads in the last fight? 'Interesting' sounds like an invitation to a dinner party, not a life-threatening adventure."

Vincent turned to me, his expression a mixture of amusement and admiration. "I appreciate your flair for the dramatic, but sometimes a little chaos is what keeps the flame alive. Otherwise, we become too comfortable, too predictable."

"Predictable?" I feigned shock, clutching my heart as if he'd insulted my very character. "I'm anything but predictable. You should know that by now!"

"True," he conceded, his voice softening. "But you have to admit, we've grown from the chaos. From everything we've faced, we've become stronger."

I considered his words, letting them settle into the crevices of my mind. He was right; through every fire we had weathered, we had emerged anew. Yet the thought of inviting more chaos into our lives left a knot in my stomach. I didn't want to lose the peace we had fought so hard to achieve.

"Maybe we can find a middle ground," I suggested, my voice steady. "A little adventure, yes, but without the life-or-death stakes. Just... fun."

"Fun?" He grinned, and the warmth of his laughter filled the air. "So, what's your idea of fun? Skydiving? Cliff diving? Spontaneous dance parties in the rain?"

I rolled my eyes, the image of us tripping over ourselves in a downpour sending a ripple of laughter through me. "Okay, maybe not that extreme. But how about a hike? Just us, some snacks, and the beauty of nature?"

Vincent considered it, his brow furrowing in mock concentration. "A hike? I can work with that. But I want some sort of challenge. Something that gets the adrenaline pumping."

"Adrenaline?" I shot him a pointed look. "This isn't a reality TV show, you know. Let's keep it simple. No bear wrestling, no climbing sheer cliffs."

"Fine, fine. Just know that I'm mentally preparing myself for whatever mischief we stumble upon," he replied, the glint in his eyes suggesting he was ready for anything.

As we began to walk deeper into the woods, the soft crunch of leaves underfoot became a soundtrack to our newfound plans, each step resonating with promise. The sun peeked through the branches, casting playful shadows that danced at our feet. With every passing moment, I felt the remnants of our past struggles begin to fade, like mist evaporating under the warmth of a new dawn.

"Just so you know," I said, glancing at Vincent, "if we run into any wildlife, I'm hiding behind you."

He laughed, the sound echoing through the trees, and in that laughter, I found a flicker of hope. We were bound by fire and light, shaped by every trial, and ready to embrace whatever the future held—together.

The path ahead wound deeper into the forest, each turn revealing a new facet of the vibrant landscape. Sunlight poured through the canopy, creating a mosaic of light and shadow that flickered like a playful spirit eager to guide us. The air was thick with the scent of pine and damp earth, a heady mix that invigorated my senses. I let out a breath I hadn't realized I was holding, a release that felt almost sacred in the embrace of nature.

Vincent kept pace beside me, his long strides carrying him effortlessly over the uneven terrain. "You know," he began, breaking the comfortable silence, "I've always believed that every adventure needs a good backstory. Something like, 'In a land far away, two brave souls set forth to discover the legendary—'"

"Legendary what?" I prompted, curious to see where his imagination would lead.

"Legendary snacks!" He grinned, pulling a crinkled map from his backpack. "A mystical journey to uncover the rarest treats in the universe. Rumor has it there's a hidden treasure trove of granola bars somewhere around here."

"Granola bars? How thrilling," I deadpanned, trying to stifle a laugh. "Should I prepare my 'excited explorer' face?"

He stopped and turned, putting on a mock-serious expression, eyebrows raised high. "You absolutely should. It's vital for maintaining the illusion of our adventurous spirit. Otherwise, we risk being mistaken for mere mortals."

"Right, can't have that," I replied, mimicking his serious tone, which only made him chuckle. There was an ease to our banter that felt like a warm blanket, wrapping around the remnants of anxiety that occasionally flickered to life in my chest.

As we continued, the trees began to thin, revealing a breathtaking vista of rolling hills that stretched out like a patchwork quilt beneath the sky. A river meandered through the valley, glistening under the sun's golden touch, and the sound of water cascading over rocks reached my ears like a soothing lullaby.

"Now this," Vincent breathed, taking in the scene with an awestruck grin, "this is a worthy backdrop for our legendary snack quest." He gestured grandly, as if presenting an award-winning film.

I stepped closer to the edge, the wind tugging at my hair, and let out a contented sigh. "I could get used to this. Nature has a way of reminding us how small we really are in the grand scheme of things, doesn't it?"

He joined me, leaning against a sturdy tree, his expression thoughtful. "Yeah, it does. But sometimes being small isn't such a bad thing. It puts things into perspective. Makes you appreciate the little moments, like this."

A comfortable silence enveloped us, and I could feel the weight of his gaze. In that moment, I realized just how much I had missed this connection, the way he could ground me without even trying.

"Okay, so what's next?" I asked, eager to keep the momentum going. "Legendary snacks aside, I could go for a little exploration."

Vincent smirked, his eyes sparkling with mischief. "How about we follow the river? I've heard rumors of a hidden waterfall up ahead. The kind that might just be a perfect spot for a spontaneous adventure—or a daring leap into the unknown."

"A daring leap into the unknown?" I repeated, arching an eyebrow. "Sounds like an invitation for disaster."

"Or an opportunity for fun," he countered, nudging my shoulder playfully. "Don't worry, I'll make sure you don't die of excitement before we find the snacks."

"Charming," I replied, rolling my eyes while trying to suppress a smile. "Lead the way, then, oh fearless adventurer."

As we made our way down the path, the sound of rushing water grew louder, filling the air with an energetic hum. I followed closely, feeling the anticipation bubble within me. Each step felt lighter, as if the burdens I had carried were shedding themselves in the embrace of the wild.

After a few minutes, we rounded a bend, and there it was—the waterfall, cascading with magnificent force into a shimmering pool below. The sunlight hit the water just right, casting rainbows that danced across the surface like fairy lights.

"Wow," I breathed, mesmerized by the sight. The beauty of it was overwhelming, and for a moment, I could only stand there in awe, feeling as though I had stumbled into a dream.

Vincent, sensing my reverence, stepped closer to the water's edge. "You know what they say about hidden waterfalls—this one must be magical."

"Magical?" I asked, laughing softly. "What do you mean?"

He grinned, the sparkle in his eyes unmistakable. "It's said that if you make a wish while standing in the mist, it will come true. But beware of the magic; it has a way of twisting wishes into something unexpected."

"Oh great, now I'm afraid to wish for anything," I joked, glancing at him sideways. "What if I accidentally summon a dragon or something?"

"Hey, I'd totally help you slay a dragon if it meant securing your dream snack collection," he replied, mock-heroic, hand on his heart.

"Such loyalty!" I feigned dramatic surprise. "A knight in shining armor, ready to take on the forces of nature for a granola bar."

With laughter bubbling up inside me, I moved closer to the waterfall, feeling the cool mist against my skin. "Okay, I'm going to wish," I declared, closing my eyes and lifting my face to the sun. The sound of rushing water was all-consuming, a powerful heartbeat that pulsed with life.

"What will you wish for?" Vincent asked, his voice barely rising above the roar of the falls.

"Something simple," I said, opening my eyes and peering over at him. "Maybe just a moment of peace, something that reminds me to cherish what we have. After everything, that feels like a good wish."

He looked at me, a soft smile breaking across his face, and for a heartbeat, the world around us faded away. In that instant, I realized that amidst all the chaos, we had built something beautiful—something worth wishing for.

"Then let's do it together," he said, stepping closer, his presence radiating warmth. "On three."

I nodded, excitement fluttering in my chest. "Okay. One... two... three!"

We both closed our eyes, casting our wishes into the spray, and for that fleeting moment, the world felt perfect. The rush of water and the laughter we shared seemed to blend into something magical, promising adventures yet to come, all while reminding us of the strength we had found in each other.

The mist from the waterfall enveloped us, a refreshing veil that danced around our legs as we ventured closer to the water's edge. The sound of rushing water harmonized with the chirps of distant birds, creating an enchanting melody that seemed to celebrate our moment of peace. I felt alive, every nerve ending tingling with exhilaration, the beauty of nature reminding me of the vibrancy of life itself.

Vincent knelt at the water's edge, his fingers trailing through the surface, sending ripples cascading outward like laughter. "This is better than any snack I could imagine," he said, glancing up at me with that boyish grin that always managed to melt my heart. "Though I still wouldn't mind a granola bar or two after all this excitement."

I laughed, shaking my head. "You know, it's hard to believe we almost let the world's chaos drown out this kind of moment. Here we are, wishing for peace while you're plotting snack conquests."

"Every great adventure needs sustenance, my dear explorer. And snacks are a vital part of our continued success," he replied with mock seriousness. "Without them, we risk becoming fainting damsels in distress."

"Fainting damsels, huh? I'll keep that in mind when the next quest for snacks arises," I shot back, crossing my arms playfully. "Just remember, I'm not fainting anywhere near a dragon."

"Fair enough. Only granola bars for the faint of heart," he retorted, rising to his feet. The playful banter was comforting, yet a small part of me remained aware of the shadows lingering from our past. The battle we had fought might be behind us, but it was impossible to ignore the scars left in its wake.

As we wandered closer to the waterfall, the sunlight caught the droplets in the air, transforming them into tiny prisms that danced like fairies around us. I felt an urge to dip my toes into the cool water, and I moved forward without hesitation. The moment my foot touched the surface, I gasped at the chill that surged up my leg.

"Careful!" Vincent laughed, watching me teeter as I adjusted to the temperature. "Don't let the waterfall sweep you away. I can't swim like a fish."

I shot him a look, half-serious. "I think we should add 'advanced swimming lessons' to our list of things to do, just in case."

"Right next to 'learn to wrestle dragons,'" he quipped.

The sound of laughter echoed around us, but it was soon joined by another sound—a rustling in the nearby bushes, sharp enough to catch our attention. I froze, a shiver racing down my spine as I glanced in the direction of the noise.

"What was that?" I whispered, my earlier amusement replaced by a prickling unease.

Vincent's teasing demeanor shifted instantly. "I don't know, but it sounded big." He moved cautiously toward the source of the sound, his protective instinct kicking in. "Stay behind me."

I nodded, though my heart raced with curiosity and apprehension. The underbrush parted, revealing a figure emerging from the shadows—a tall silhouette with broad shoulders and an air of familiarity that sent a jolt of recognition through me.

"Wait, is that...?" I squinted, trying to make sense of the scene unfolding before us.

As the figure stepped into the light, I gasped. It was Leo, a friend from our past, the last person I had expected to see here, in the middle of nowhere. His face was gaunt, shadowed by a grim expression that made my heart sink.

"Leo!" I exclaimed, rushing forward, but something in his eyes made me pause. They were wild, darting as if he were not fully present, and that familiar warmth from our friendship felt distant, overshadowed by an urgency I couldn't quite grasp.

"Get back!" he shouted, his voice hoarse, filled with an edge of panic that cut through the air like a knife. "You shouldn't be here!"

"Leo, what's going on?" I asked, alarm creeping into my tone. "We thought you were—"

"I know what you thought," he interrupted, glancing over his shoulder as if expecting someone—or something—to follow him. "But it's not safe. They're coming."

"Who's coming?" Vincent demanded, stepping protectively in front of me. "What do you mean it's not safe?"

Before Leo could respond, a growl echoed through the trees, low and menacing. My heart raced as dread pooled in my stomach. It was a sound that felt too primal, too close to our past struggles.

"Get to higher ground," Leo urged, urgency propelling his words. "Now!"

"What are you talking about? What's happening?" I pleaded, my voice barely above a whisper.

"They're hunting, and you need to get out of here!" Leo's eyes flickered with a desperate intensity. "If they find you—"

The ground trembled beneath our feet as the growl grew louder, a sound that resonated deep within my bones. I felt a shift in the air, as if the very atmosphere had thickened, charged with an electric tension.

Vincent reached for my hand, his grip firm, grounding me against the rising tide of fear. "We're not leaving you, Leo. Whatever it is, we'll face it together."

"I don't have time to explain!" Leo shouted, panic edging his voice. "Just run! Trust me!"

In that moment, the underbrush parted violently, revealing a massive creature emerging from the shadows, its eyes gleaming with hunger. It was unlike anything I had ever seen—part animal, part nightmare, and all too real.

"Run!" Leo screamed, and instinct kicked in as I felt Vincent pull me away from the chaos. We stumbled back, hearts racing, the terror in Leo's eyes imprinting itself on my mind as the creature lunged forward, its growl echoing through the woods.

We turned and ran, the world blurring around us, adrenaline surging as the sound of pursuit echoed behind us. Whatever had come for us, it wasn't just hunting; it was chaos unleashed, and we were caught in its merciless grip.

"Faster!" Vincent urged, his voice slicing through the panic. And as we sprinted into the unknown, I couldn't shake the feeling that the battle was far from over.

Milton Keynes UK
Ingram Content Group UK Ltd.
UKHW030855151124
451262UK00001B/137